LAWBREAKER

LAWBREAKER

Raised on the streets, **Shay Morgan** yearns for a real family, where love is unconditionally offered—even when trust doesn't come easy. Before that day arrives, she trespasses and steals in order to provide for the few people who've gone out of their way to protect her.

Born to privilege, **Ben Bishop** loathes his family for the despicable things they've done, and not done. He vows to be different, play by the rules, do the right thing. Building a thriving nightclub with those who share his values dominates his world.

One explosive night at his bar, Loading Zone, changes everything. For both of them. Forever.

A dance of opponents commences as they thwart with suspicion, start to trust, then sidestep to protect themselves from a fatal blow. Until they soon wonder if they've been fighting for the same side all along.

As they begin to open their hearts, they up the stakes with a one-week pact. She shows him the power in breaking the law. He demonstrates the virtue of following it.

Then a far-reaching crime is suddenly exposed—that his family committed. And for one chance moment, Shay and Ben hold the key to right the wrong, correct the injustice. *But at what cost?*

Will they be able to return from the other side together? Or will their differences tear them apart?

Flirting with danger...has never been so tempting.

LAWBREAKER

Kat Bastion
with Stone Bastion

Lawbreaker

COPYRIGHT © 2018 Kat Bastion with Stone Bastion. All rights reserved. Except by a book reviewer, who may quote brief passages for the specific purpose of reviewing this book, no part of this book may be reproduced, copied, stored, scanned, transmitted or distributed in any form or by any means, including but not limited to mechanical, printed, or electronic form, without prior written permission of the authors. Please do not participate in or encourage piracy of copyrighted materials in violation of the author's rights. To reach the authors, please visit either their blog at www.talktotheshoe.com or their website at www.katbastion.com and complete the contact form on Kat & Stone's Connections page.

Cover Design by ©Sarah Hansen, Okay Creations
Image provided by Love N. Books
Photographer: Rick Day
Model: Stuart Reardon
Interior Book Design by:

emtippettsbookdesigns.com

First Printing, September 2018
ISBN-13: 978-0998232928
ISBN-10: 0998232920

Praise for
HEARTBREAKER

"This book has definitely earned its five stars and I am just floored right now. The passion is explosive, the story itself is beautiful, and the emotions are so real my heart is ready to burst. Beautiful book. Absolutely breathtaking."

~ *One Page at a Time*

"Heartrending, passionate, and captivating! *Heartbreaker* is a riveting page-turner that will leave you breathless with raw emotions, and the need to hold tight to the ones you love!"

~ *Beneath the Covers Blog*

"This book is all about flawless writing, exemplary storytelling, f*#king insane character development. The right dose of sexy hotness..."

~ *Love N. Books*

"The Bastions are at it again with this beautiful and heartbreaking story. You will absolutely fall in love with Kiki and Darren's love."

~ *Under the Covers Book Blog*

"*Heartbreaker* is a phenomenal story."

~ That's What I'm Talking About

"I loved it...wonderfully compelling, a story that touched my heart in so many ways and characters I will remember for a long time to come."

~ Girl Who Reads

Praise for the
NO WEDDINGS
SERIES

"One of the best romantic comedies of the year!"

~ *Agents of Romance*

"The No Weddings series is one of the best I have read that follows one couple. Cade and Hannah are both lovable characters, the storyline is real and entertaining, and the banter is fun and witty."

~ *Lives & Breathes Book Blog*

"I loved it, and I mean REALLY loved it!"

~ *Orchard Book Club*

"This is an exceptional series...You find yourself fully engrossed in their world and can't put the book down."

~ *Books -n- Kisses*

"The No Weddings series has a group of such amazing characters; you can't help but relate to them and feel the emotion in every situation they encounter. It has been a long time since a story has made me feel that way let alone an entire series!"

~ *Under the Covers Book Blog*

"The story of Cade & Hannah's relationship is realistic, heart-warming, and filled with real-world connections that shook me in a way that few titles I've read this year have managed...I have loved every minute of the No Weddings series."

~ *That's What I'm Talking About*

OTHER BOOKS BY
Kat Bastion
with Stone Bastion

Standalone Novel
The Espionage Effect

Unbreakable Series
Heartbreaker
Rule Breaker
Lawbreaker

No Weddings Series
No Weddings
One Funeral
Two Bar Mitzvahs
Three Christmases
For Valentine's
(a steamy nightcap novella)

BOOKS BY
Kat Bastion

Highland Legends Series

Forged in Dreams and Magick

Bound by Wish and Mistletoe

Born of Mist and Legend
(future release)

Found in Flame and Moonlight
(future release)

Romantic Poetry for Charity

Utterly Loved

Foreword by Sylvain Reynard

To our beloved Helen…

We think of you often.
"What would Grams do?"

1
BOMBS AWAY

Shay…

I t's real. What I mentally repeated for the millionth time. What I'd been trying to convince my doubting self for days. Because awesome things—good and pure and decent things—didn't happen to people like me. Only—it had.

Finally. I'd done it.

No more scraping and clawing *and wanting.*

No more lying, cheating, conning…stealing.

Even so, I flicked another glance at the nightclub's front door, waiting for the inevitable to happen, expecting someone to turn my world upside down. Again. Distrust had become habit.

No. I rejected the gnawing doubt. I had to believe. *You earned* this. *You worked so hard for this chance.*

"It's real." The slow whisper fell from my lips, finally spoken aloud. "I've made it." From my coveted position

1

behind the bar, I coasted trembling fingertips over the cool metal of a brushed stainless steel bar top. Clean. *Sanitized* clean.

The only rust in sight came not from decay and neglect; it had been placed with great care and intention. Ancient brick lined the walls behind worn leather booths at the far end of the room, but the aged patina and rough edges lent the joint a vibe all the customers drinking and laughing and dancing within it wanted.

Loading Zone? A world away from a dingy back alley.

Yet...*not so far at all.*

We'd both come a long way: I'd seen the decrepit old warehouse in her former state for years. Had drifted by almost every night, loitering as I stared up at her ghostly form, wondering if someday she'd shine again. For her to no longer have broken windows, rotting wood, dirty brick... derelict—forgotten.

And then to be a part of what breathed new life into her?

For her to be an essential part of me in the same way?

Kicked. Ass.

The industrial vibe continued into other areas too, like in the employee "lounge", where roughed concrete spanned the floors, reclaimed wood beams served as changing benches, and lockers bore the perfect amount of dented and slightly rusted. Six galvanized metal stools perched under a hammered zinc worktable that served as our own bar. Cold drinks came from a vintage Coca-Cola cooler. The two generous private shower stalls had repurposed tiles and roughhewn gliding doors that had been salvaged from a barn.

Then there was the boss's office. Yeah, the "off-limits" one. As if that'd ever stopped me. I'd been told the revered-by-one-and-all Benjamin Bishop was away on emergency. I'd found the door that guarded the forbidden space to be locked. *All the more tempting. And perfect to get to know the absent mystery man in control of my fate—my way, on my terms. Covertly.*

What had I discovered?

Blown-up pictures of challenging golf course holes hung at eye level. All had breathtaking scenery. Two captured ocean waves as they'd crashed against black rocks behind vibrant manicured greens in the foreground. Most had the same handsome dark-haired guy with a golf club in hand and a wide grin on his face. Some featured him alone. One had been posed with a few other guys, arms slung around each other's shoulders.

A massive polished ebony desk spanned the larger sidewall. On it, a square paperclip holder had been positioned exactly two inches from each side of its back-left corner. Two exposed vintage Edison bulbs stuck straight up from a funky galvanized steel light which stood perfectly centered along its back edge.

One wide-barreled pen, made of wood that had light-and-dark stripes running lengthwise, rested off to the side, parallel to the desk edge. But it laid within reach of a man who would sit in the sage-green ergonomic work chair parked under the desk, dead-center in the middle.

Ordered.

Perfect.

So damn perfect, my fingers had itched to knock its owner off-balance.

I'd left my mark before leaving: nudged the pen a little to the left, rotated the lamp a few degrees off-center. Had done both with the side of my thumb, not a fingerprint left behind—not my first time breaking and entering.

I smiled, remembering how, as a final parting, I'd bumped the chair's arm with my hip, swiveling it from its neatly tucked position.

"Racked, Shay?" A solid smack echoed out. Five frosty pink manicured nails drummed once, pinky to thumb, on the shiny stainless steel of the servers' station to my right.

I blinked back into the here-and-now, then moved, my hands blurring as glasses clinked, liquids poured, and drinks loaded onto her tray beside the order screen: dirty martini, beer, scotch, three screaming-orgasm shots.

After a quick once-over, I gave a firm nod. "Locked and loaded." Staring at the mash-up of drinks, I flung my bar towel over my shoulder, then met Jillian's impressed gaze to hazard my usual expected guess. "First date?" Yep. Smartass, through and through.

"Nope." She half-rolled her eyes, then kept her gaze stuck at the ceiling for a prayerful beat. "Bachelorette party."

"Ah. My condolences." Our nightly joking came as easy ritualistic banter for me. What I'd learned from observing the privileged for years. How I'd gotten skilled at fitting in, climbing up, staking my claim in a world that didn't hand out anything to anyone who didn't fight hard for it.

She winked long black lashes at me. "Piece o' cake." A

veteran server. No doubt she had the challenging group in the palm of her hands.

I knew the feeling–had learned my craft well. How to read people, play their weakness, manipulate a situation just enough to get what you want without their realizing they'd been played. How I'd survived. How I'd made it.

To get here...

Unexpected tears sprung to my eyes. Ugh. Annoying. Doing my damnedest to be normal, to blend in, I blinked the irritating moisture back and sucked in a strengthening breath. Then I soaked in the fleeting moment; I knew how rare and precious the good ones were.

What we're lucky to get in our sucky world. Scraps of joy between all the suffering. Words echoed from ages ago on a bitter cold night, stomach clenched in ravenous hunger.

But all that suffering and despair had changed, little by little. And the pinnacle to my arduous climb? Only a few short days ago, when I'd stepped foot on the hallowed ground beneath my feet...*when I'd vowed to go legit.*

I'd used the last few dollars I'd squirreled away for myself to buy vintage jeans that hugged my hips under the tight T-shirt provided by Loading Zone, their bartenders' uniform. My shoes had been worn only once on a one-night con job: black distressed-leather mules with a three-inch heel, comfortable and stylish.

The new getup? All for a standard paycheck. The kind with acronyms like FICA, where the government apparently dipped invisible hands into what I'd toiled for. Long hours in exchange for far less pay than what I'd pinched with little sweat in the past. But working aboveboard was safe, one step closer to real…normal. And the renowned bar that I stood in wrapped itself around me like the pseudo-family it had long been rumored to be.

"You workin' or daydreamin'?" The loud crack of a bar-towel corner snapped a scant inch from my chin.

"Workin'."

Definitely workin'.

Worth it.

Dropping my gaze with steady focus, I busied myself behind the bar, filling orders from customers packed two rows deep at the barstools. But I shot a quick glance at my towel-snapper and fellow bartender for the night.

Cade. Good guy. Wicked smart. Master fighter and manipulator, but with a different moral code. He wouldn't break the law. *I would.*

"*Stop,*" I growled to myself under my breath, pissed at my runaway thoughts. Ingrained, my brain had randomly locked on to Cade, analyzed, filtered, and spat out gut instincts. Like I'd done with every mark. Only Cade wasn't a mark. None of the new family surrounding me were.

I berated myself with another needed self-correction. *I* had *broken the law. Had.* Past tense. *Often.* But that was before. "You're done now." I sharpened the harsh whisper with finality.

My thoughts zeroed back in on the here-and-now. *Family.* Such a strange concept. Mine—the ragtag few who truly cared about me—protected me, had been pieced together from chance encounters, earned through selfless actions, trusted only to a point: all I'd ever allowed, with anyone.

"Bomber," Cade called out from the other end of our shared territory, his voice clear to me over the pumping music and shouted conversations.

"Trick question." They always were, the nightly pop quizzes he'd been drilling me with since day one. Not because Cade doubted my abilities, but because, as he'd explained on my first shift, he wanted to see me succeed, thrive. I wanted that too. "If you mean, the B-52 Bomber..."

I glanced his way for clarification.

He folded his arms, expression blanked.

No clues. Because custom drink orders might not have any either. We had to decipher them. No server wanted to hump back to a customer through a dense and thirsty crowd for clarification.

Yep. The B-52. But I didn't need to take the easy way with my answer. Anyone could rattle off three ingredients. And he'd stumped me on at least one drink puzzle every night since I'd been tending. So, he wanted to test my abilities? Fine.

"I know you don't mean a Cherry Bomb, which is *cachaça*, Brazil's premium liquor distilled from sugarcane." Yep. He asked? I provided the mountain of information I'd been studying. "Plus an ounce of kirsch also known as *kirschwasser*, a German cherry brandy, a splash of fresh lime juice, and topped with club soda."

I paused for effect, then raised my brows as I continued on with my explanation while still filling drink orders. "You might've tried to con me into thinking an Irish Car Bomb, also known as an Irish Bomb, but I doubt it. We don't have it on our menu; it's insulting to the Irish." And some bars got into trouble with it. Got nothing to do with the Irish. It's an American-invented drink, with the only thing Irish about it its ingredients. "But if a customer wanted one, I'd layer the shot glass with Jameson Irish Whiskey poured over Baileys Irish Cream, all to be 'bombed' in front of the customer into a glass of Guinness Stout." The resulting eruption of foam? Guaranteed crowd-pleaser.

I tilted my head. "Incidentally, if we had ice cream—"

His brows hiked a fraction. "We don't have ice cream."

"If we *did*...I make a mean Irish Bomb *Float*. A long pour of Jameson into a pint glass, add two scoops of Ben & Jerry's Dublin Mudslide, topped off with twelve ounces of Guinness Stout." Deadly calories. Maximum yum.

"But you said 'bomb*er*', so I'm thinkin' you want the *B-52* Bomber, which, according to my education" —and he had no idea said education was my own brand of bartending self-training— "is a layered shooter supposedly invented by a bartender-fan of The B-52's band."

Cade's eyes sparked with amusement.

Knew it. "Kahlúa." For the dark coffee liqueur support at the bottom. "Baileys." The creamy pillow in the middle. "And Grand Marnier." The decadent aged orange liqueur capped on top. "In that order."

He gave me a brief nod. All the praise I'd get. But I caught a glimpse of pride in his eyes.

Not that I needed a gold star. Hadn't gotten approval

from anyone in a long time. *Years.*

Yet a little bit of unsolicited recognition at a job well done? Felt...nice.

Cade's challenges and praise made me want to stick with it because each night proved an opportunity to grow, to better myself. The company itself did that too, which was rare. It's what made the place family. We didn't only belong to the bar. The bar was ours too: To work at Loading Zone meant we got a piece of the action, a percentage of the profits. If we loved what we did, and took care of the customers so they had an amazing experience, the company coffers didn't just get fatter, our own wallets did too.

And I liked that.

People taking care of their own.

What I'd done most of my life.

Without another word or glance, Cade turned and disappeared to his section of the bar, before *rackin' and packin' 'em.*

"School's out for the night," I murmured, okay with my relative independence. Probably wouldn't talk to one another for hours, if Friday nights were like I'd heard.

Back to the grind. Drink orders flew over the bar's electronic system. Music blared. Bodies danced. Our third bartender came on shift with a chin-up greeting to Cade and me before he took responsibility for the far end.

And in between nonstop mixing drinks for servers or fielding orders from the anxious throng at the bar, I still flicked the occasional glance at the door.

Waiting.

Wondering.

Then doubt trickled in. Because I'd been there before, that warm fuzzy place where good things happened. Calm comfort sank into my chest to the point where happiness lulled me into feeling safe, complacent.

That fairy-tale illusion had put me at risk long ago.

Never again.

And so, distrust had become second nature.

I'd probably go decades into a decent and good life, and I'd still be watching the door, waiting for something bad to happen—expecting someone to snatch it all away.

Recognizing the deep-rooted fear, miniscule but real all the same, helped me cope. But with a solid grip on my survival instincts, I tucked the steady awareness into the back of my mind and dove into the present.

By muscle memory, I served up drinks, one after another. Margaritas. Manhattans. Whiskey neat. Bourbon sour.

At some point over the course of the busy next hour, my restless mind drifted from drinks back out into the place around me, then toward Cade at my left. The rundown of his *good* makeup flashed again, that damned analysis-mode kicking in, no matter how I tried to mute it.

But instead of fighting the impulse, I rolled with it, reprogramming the data streaming in. "Cade: *not* a mark. *No one* here is. No one *anywhere*." I exhaled in relief at my small mental progress. *Old habits die hard?* A phrase coined by the weak-minded. *Make* new *habits.*

The next time I glanced toward the door, I imagined the boss coming through it, Cade's ex-partner. The one I hadn't met yet but knew by everyone's reverence for him. The one who apparently surpassed Cade in his *good*ness. And according to Cade, the guy was razor-sharp, genius in both reading people and running his business.

But rumors painted the now-sole owner of Loading Zone as darker, edgier. Especially in the last month. Before he'd taken the most recent couple of weeks off—unheard of in the almost two years since they'd been open, according to Jillian.

"Ben!" Some overly excited female across the room shouted the name at the exact moment it settled into my mind.

An instant wave of energy crackled through the nightclub, hotter and more alive than anything the music or dance floor pulsed out. Slight movement rippled through the vast space of the reclaimed warehouse—toward the same metal roll-up entrance door that had been haunting me all night—as heads craned to see, breasts pushed out a little farther, and bodies pressed closer, like a powerful magnet pulled them uncontrollably forward.

Even I couldn't look away.

After the initial crowd crush, I could see his occasional nod, a brief smile. He angled deeper into the club and scanned an assessing look across the bar, starting at Cade's section. Seconds later, his sights landed on me—and stayed there, fierce gaze locked on to mine.

My breath caught at the intensity radiating from halfway across the room.

Ben. His simple name echoed larger than life in my head.

The crowd parted as he strode through the room. He stood a good head taller than other men he passed. Broad shoulders strained his black T-shirt with every slight rolling turn as he moved. Dark hair, cut closer on the sides, curled down over one side of his forehead. Shadowy stubble covered a defined jawline as it clenched. Thick brows drew together over eyes that narrowed as he stared hard at me. He stepped through the now three-deep crush at the bar, then planted flat palms on the edge of the metal bar top in front of me.

"What are you doing back there?" he snarled, tone low, heavy with accusation.

Cade braced his arms on the bar beside me, mirroring him. "She's a new hire."

Ben never looked away from me. "I asked her."

Holding his unwavering gaze, I straightened my shoulders, undaunted. "*Her* name is Shay. And she's behind your bar...working. Hard."

Dark eyes narrowed a fraction more, boring into mine. "How old are you?"

Great.

Here we go.

"Old enough." All he needed to know.

A muscle in that clenched jaw tightened. "Not what I asked."

"You sure about that?" Because yeah, I looked young, no matter how old I really was. But his heat-seeking-missile aggression? Totally unwarranted.

"ID." He kept at the groundless demand.

"I'm not some underage club-bunny at the door. I'm an

employee. I've already been hired."

"I don't give a shit. I'm the boss. And I want to see your ID."

"No." *Not gonna happen.* I couldn't risk it.

He gave a slight nod, smug satisfaction in his eyes. "So, you're *not* eighteen."

"I didn't say that." Yet somehow, I sensed our verbal tug-of-war had dragged me across lost ground.

"Are you or aren't you?"

"I am," I gritted out, angry that I'd been foolish enough to want something so bad.

"Then no big deal." He rose back to his impressive height, crossing his arms, confidence plastered on his face. "Prove it."

Damn. My first weekend night, not even a full one, and already the life I'd earned, had fought and bled for, had begun to slip through my fingers.

Disappointment seeped heavy into my chest. What naïve people got for having hope.

The inborn fight in me remained. Pride too. With every tightening breath, fury burned my lungs, for being judged without cause.

"No. You either believe me…or you don't. I filled out my application. Gave my ID then. Got interviewed. Got hired. And I've *proved* myself over the last few days, tonight. Ask anyone here."

"Doesn't matter."

But it did. My actions mattered to me. They were all my life had been based on. Everything I'd ever accomplished had been from what I had done—not who I was, what anyone thought, or what society believed.

I crossed my arms too, refusing to bend, by principle, if not more.

His expression hardened.

Commotion grew around us, two immovable blocks of granite, as thirsty patrons called out for drinks. Cade steadfastly remained beside me. While the poor lone fresh-shift guy hustled ass to fill orders.

The atmosphere grew charged between Ben and me. The sounds of the club faded to background noise as my heart thumped harder against my ribs, my pulse drummed louder in my ears.

Ben planted his hands on the bar again, staring me down as he leaned forward inch by inch. His eyes bored deep into mine, penetrating. Any other girl might've thought *intimidating*.

I didn't twitch a muscle.

He towered over the bar, head lowered, a ferocious wolf who'd cornered an unknown threat. That shaggy dark hair spiked over darker piercing eyes. Unshorn scruff peppered an unforgiving jaw. An unhidden snarl curled his lip, baring white teeth.

No resemblance to the wholesome happy guy I'd spied on in the pictures hanging on his office wall.

Oddly, more attractive.

Most women would've gone weak in the knees. Some would've put on a layer of flirt, feigning vulnerability or exposing true fear, hoping to snag the obvious alpha in spite of the glaring warning signs. Maybe because of them.

I'd never been a bleating sheep in my life, wasn't about to pretend with fluffy false clothing.

Wolf, too, buddy. I leaned forward, matching him inch for inch. My trim nails clicked on the bar top as I dug in, holding my ground.

Alpha all the way.

But then my breaths quickened, some ancient response forged from tens of thousands of years of saber-toothed tiger versus spear-wielding hunter. I knew it was coming. Had been on the powerless side enough to know when the ground was about to spin under my feet. I skimmed my hands back and gripped the edge of the bar, bracing for the inevitable as I swallowed hard past a thickening throat.

Honed survival instincts kept me on my toes as I widened my stance, pulled in a deep breath, and tightened my thigh muscles. Ready or not, I'd fought too hard for solid ground to flinch now.

Not that it made a difference. The rug was about to be yanked out from under me anyway. And the asinine quick-to-judge man staring hard at me, but not seeing a thing, held the carefully knotted corners in his tightened fists.

"*You're fired.*"

The soft-spoken words punched through me with punishing force.

Moisture stung my eyes and my chest burned, but I drew in a slow, deep breath and held his unwavering gaze. I refused to give him the satisfaction of knowing that I had ever cared one bit about his stupid job. "Fine by me."

What didn't escape me was the steady way he breathed in and out. Like he worked to control his breaths too.

Good. Let the jerk suffer for the mistake he'd just made. Because I was done with the place. Done with him. Done with hope and that naïve vow.

Only little girls believed in fairy tales.

I tossed the bar towel between us.

"Obviously, you're not the man I'd heard you were."

2
OFF THE RAILS

Ben...

"**F**uck."

Shay's cutting judgment shot straight to my gut and churned there.

Because she'd shrewdly pointed out that I'd become no better than a man I'd grown to hate.

I huffed out a regretful breath, disgusted with the cold realization of what I'd done—shredded someone without pausing to think, bothering to care.

With her head held high in spite of the misery I'd caused, she casually turned her back on me. Then she sidestepped Cade and soon vanished into the thick crowd on the dance floor. I stared off at the dark ceiling of the hallway she'd been aiming toward, where the locker rooms were.

Why do I now *give a damn?*

The walking contradiction? Young, yet somehow hardened?

Maybe it was her rare fire and grit. Stubborn beyond reason, she'd stood her ground.

And I'd been a barreling train wreck and exploded right through her.

"What just happened?" Uncertainty fogged my brain.

Cade eased closer until he stood where she'd been, across the bar from me. He planted his palms on the space between us and leaned forward as he pegged me with an unforgiving look.

"You just kick-punted a great employee."

"Was I wrong?" Couldn't tell anymore.

He glanced at the still-visible wake she'd left on the dance floor. "You tell me."

"You hired her?"

His face contorted into a brief scowl. "No. You know better than that. I'm filling in for a couple of weeks. As help, not management. I'm not here to confuse your crew."

Right.

Don't be an idiot. Cade's your best friend. Get your head screwed on straight.

We'd created Loading Zone back when I'd first graduated college and Cade had begun earning his masters. But even though he'd sold his share to me last year to chase other ventures, Cade's help, dedication, and a big piece of his heart still remained.

For his unshakable loyalty, to the club, to me, I remained eternally grateful.

Especially after the last weeks from hell.

I gave him an apologetic nod.

He chuckled, then shook his head. "Dude. You were a heat-seeking missile. Most people introduce themselves, offer a hand to shake. You? *Boom!* Carved a right hook" —his fist arced through the air then jarred to a stop halfway across the bar top— "outta nowhere."

I winced at his take of the unprovoked damage I'd done.

His gaze held mine a beat, then scanned my jawline. "You look rough. Lose your razor?"

"No." I scrubbed a hand along the short beard I'd developed. "Just the give-a-fuck to use it."

"That bad." His words flattened into a statement. My best friend knew without explanation: no rose-colored glasses would fix that clusterfuck.

"Yeah, that bad."

He gave a curt nod but said nothing further. Not the time or place.

Instead, he spun around and gripped the neck of my favorite scotch. Amber liquid filled a tumbler two fingers tall before he pulled back. I didn't object. As I stared at the alcohol, I accepted what it was: temporary salvation and permanent curse.

Even with the stinging reminder, I knocked back my medicine.

Just to take the edge off.

But I left a quarter inch behind. Always. A reminder. My control test.

Cade stared at the symbolic portion I'd left, fully aware

of my challenge, then capped the bottle. "Not rock-bottom bad, then."

"Nope."

Not yet.

But not far.

I'd just walloped abuse on an undeserving girl. Asinine. *Reckless.*

With a resigned sigh, I faced what had to be done. I had to fix my fuck-up before it was too late—before my random carnage proved I was no better...*than him.*

Actions. Thoughts and intentions didn't mean shit. Reality got better by doing not thinking. "What do you know about Shay?"

"Besides a girl working her ass off that has a great personality?" He shrugged. "Gabe hired her. Rafe vouched for her, knows her personally."

Rafe. Our head of security. Someone we'd hired without much checking. His reputation had been *that* good.

My thoughts drifted back to that young, beautiful landmine of attitude: strong jaw, squared shoulders, and glinting eyes...full of fire. Damn, her determination and fight had been something. But for a split second at the end—when she'd let that granite control of hers slip—a flash of hurt had sparked in her eyes. And the wound seemed deep, old.

Not that it'd mattered.

Nothing could've stopped the avalanche of anger and frustration I'd needed to blow.

And the defiant lawbreaker behind the bar?

Had dared me from across the room like a shining fucking test.

After weeks of bottled frustration, hands tied to be able to save someone else, to suddenly see a giant red bullseye target? One I had the power to do something about?

No brainer.

Literally, no brain cells had been involved.

My harsh judgment had been pure reaction. Yet it had felt justified. Cathartic, even.

But after her inadvertent flash of hurt then rapid exit—dark brunette head held high in spite of the devastation she'd been dealt—I felt like shit.

I *was* a motherfucking shit.

The fogging mental haze cleared enough for me to focus back on Cade's grinning mug.

"What?" The uncontrolled word had growled out. Great. *Caveman.* I let out a weary sigh.

Mirth glittered in Cade's eyes before they widened. "You're going after her."

He knew me well.

His approving expression gave me the mental shove I needed to fully commit.

I straightened from the bar with a nod. "You bet your ass I am. Any idea where to find her?"

"Nope." The smartass laughed. "But have fun figuring it out."

I got the sense he meant more than simply discovering her whereabouts.

No surprise there. I'd been lost without a compass when it came to understanding women. And *lost* felt stamped across my forehead lately in every corner of my life.

I scrubbed a hand over closed eyes and concentrated on

the task at hand. *Rafe.* Cade had said Rafe had vouched for the girl personally. *Vouched for* Shay. *Use her name, Cretin.* My anger kept flaring, itched under my skin like a rash: a side effect of stifling true feelings for too many days on end, grinding teeth on bitter words that I'd badly needed to use, but hadn't.

Stuffing down my unresolved issues, I searched out our head of security toward the entrance where I'd earlier caught a glimpse of him through the thick crowd on the way in.

Rafe caught sight of me seconds before I approached and gave me a chin-up greeting. "Hey, Boss."

I popped a chin-up back at the hulking guy overseeing our door flow. "How's it going?"

"You want it for real or for Fire Marshall?"

I blinked.

He suppressed a smile. "Just kiddin'. Busier than the last watering hole in the Sahara." With a clipped wave of his fingers, he beckoned his second to relieve him.

"Good to have you back." He folded his arms while he scanned the crowd.

Not everyone shared his opinion. "Rumor has it you know where to find Shay."

His gaze cut to the bar. "Rumors tend to be wrong more than right."

"I pissed her off. And she left." The nuts and bolts of it. "Know where to find her?"

"Maybe."

"How close to a yes is that?"

"With Shay?" He huffed out a short laugh. "As close as anyone's ever gonna get."

3
FOUND GIRL, LOST BOY

Shay...

The industrial back door slammed shut behind me as I slung my backpack over my shoulder. I hoofed it out of the back alley, rounded the corner, and stepped into the far shadows of the side street before the drops of moisture leaked from my eyes. With a frustrated headshake and a slow, deep breath, I blinked the stupid tears away and set myself straight again.

You're made of tougher stuff than this.

And I'd already begun to chameleon back to my old self: those newer distressed-leather mules, their open tops now tucked between curved fingers, had been exchanged for well-worn Converse; Loading Zone's T-shirt had been tossed on the end of a bench in the locker room in favor of my standard threadbare basic black. By the time I walked the length of the building to its front, I'd downshifted my attitude to its core: wary, controlled, and indifferent.

Ahead to the right, a thick line of hopeful bar-goers buzzed with energy, cordoned off by black velvet ropes. When the end of the line blocked the entire cobblestone sidewalk, I hopped over the gutter and veered toward the centerline until side street met Main Street.

A gust of wind smacked me in the face as a glossy black Hummer barreled by. Its driver's head was bent down, oblivious face illuminated.

"Slow down!" I chased after the idiot for a few steps, itching to throw a rock through his disappearing back window. But all I had was a pair of leather shoes I had other plans for. "And stop texting," I grumbled, realizing what that bright bluish glow had been.

Furious at the parade of ignorant people with no regard for how their selfish actions affected others, I continued across the street, out of the exhaust-wake belched from Mr. Entitled Hummer. Once on the far corner—a respectable distance from both of my offenders—I shifted my glare from dimming taillights up toward the building I'd just left, to the flickering glow behind windows that arched two stories above the line of bar customers waiting outside. Then my heart softened as I took in the entire grand structure. There she stood in all her restored splendor, my ghostly factory building, vibrating with new life. Far different than the shell she'd been: broken windows framed for years by sooty bricks now gleamed, whole once again.

Back then, I'd hoped to see her shine one day.

"You do," I whispered, grateful that if I couldn't be a part of it, at least I'd been able to witness her becoming something better than her former self, beautiful in her unique way. And she'd do so with a loving family of people dedicated to her welfare. "Sorry that it also couldn't be me."

Anger fired hot in my belly again at the reason. *Ben.*

For the second time in my life a selfish man had tried to take something from me, stomping on my naïve dreams with a crushing boot. The first time? I hadn't seen coming. Eight years later, a little older and plenty wiser, I had dared to hope I could have something more, had trusted that I had more control this time, could prove my worth.

"That's what you get for trusting again." Burned.

I spent a handful of slow breaths memorizing the scene beyond my reach, erasing every good thing that I'd experienced inside, replacing fluffy dreams with my harsh reality. Like every other night that had come to mean anything to me, I stood on the outside. But I stood far out on that edge stronger for it, making a bigger difference where it mattered most.

Then I struck out in the opposite direction. "Got better things to do tonight anyway."

And thanks to Ben, not much time to do them.

September's late-night air kissed coolness over my skin, but I welcomed the splash of reality. Ben had done me a favor, actually. No point in getting too comfortable in a world that had never made any sense. Better to stay on my own, take care of myself. Safer that way.

After a dozen blocks at a brisk pace, the familiar sprawling park that had become home base for me over the years opened up. I eased my pace, then stopped and spun in a slow circle, getting my bearings again as I inhaled a deep breath.

The crisp air smelled of freedom spiced with a hint of salt, the ocean saying hello with the help of an onshore breeze from the Atlantic a few blocks over my left shoulder. Farther behind me, Loading Zone pulsed some unheard beat, out of sight.

Out of mind.

Dead ahead, across dozens of neighborhoods and hundreds of lives, lay where I'd come from so many years ago: the past, and yet my present, the very thing that made me who I'd become.

Farther north and stretching inland? Philadelphia, glimmering with equal parts beauty and danger, steeped in history. She wore triumphs proudly and scars deeply. Both could be seen at once to someone able to see, someone who knew.

I turned my back on the bright glare of the city, like I'd done long ago when I'd been unwilling to get sucked down into the gutter like forgotten trash, and jogged to the bench in the center of the park. I dropped the shoes on the grass, and as I'd done on a million other nights, I leapt up, planted a foot on the wood-slatted seat, a second at the bend of its wrought iron handrail, and launched onto the leading edge of the massive boulder that guarded the base of an ancient rock outcropping. Then I scrabbled up familiar gritty surfaces, fingers into a crevice here, toes into weathered footholds there, until I reached the top.

Pools of light from streetlamps at the perimeter of the park fringed my vision, but I stared off into the distant north where the Appalachian Trail bordered. Old-growth forest waited there, protective and life-giving. I'd spent many long days there over the years, pretending I was one of Peter's Lost Boys. Not Tinkerbell. *Never* Wendy. I didn't have magic. Or a family. And after everything I'd ever believed in had been shattered, I didn't want either. I needed real. The truth as *I* determined it to be. That's all I'd wanted then.

"All I want now," I whispered. "True. Real."

I held out my arms to the darkness of the night sky, rotating to take in the small town of Glenhaven, *my* haven, and reminded myself who I was, what I'd been shaped into. With knowing eyes, I scanned over my streets, watched a throng of rich drunk tourists stumble by, imagined urbanites tucked into warm beds, the new generation gentrifying old neighborhoods.

What had first been jealousy, as I peered out at the entitled world from my leafy forest hideout, had soon turned into curiosity. Until the possibilities of what someone invisible to the world could do slowly transformed into an obsession, much like a religion. Before long, hiding in the shadows, and what I'd learned to do when I darted out of them, had become second nature...as easy and right to me as breathing.

Because I hadn't just imagined myself a Lost Boy in those woods. As I'd grown hungry, when desperation had hit—and thankfully luck had shined down on me with a few well-placed guardian angels—I'd dreamed of more...and then made it happen.

Destiny had met determination.

A gust of wind rustled through the leaves of the nearest tree, dipping a young branch shaped like a perfectly curved bow into my sightline. I laughed and nodded up and out at Mother Nature. "I remember." Back then, I hadn't actually fashioned a bow and arrow, but I had pretended. And I had stolen, for real.

"First for myself, then for others," I murmured the mantra, my code, as I worked my way down the outcropping, the boulder, the park bench, picked up my shoes, then started off across the grass.

People were waiting on me; I had connections to make. Would've been after my shift and with my own money from the tip-out for the night. But shit happened—*tonight* Ben *happened*—and I got over it and moved on. After years of the repeated lesson, I'd gotten used to the first and perfected the rest.

Two turns down adjoining alleys brought me to the back of a closed bookstore. Under the protection of a weathered awning—beside an empty bistro set where bookshop employees took their breaks and a rectangular planter filled with flowers whose petals had closed for the night—a pile of dingy jackets topped by a wide-brimmed hat leaned against a brick wall.

I scuffed the soles of my sneakers on the gravelly pavement, claimed an open spot a respectable couple of feet from the jacket-pile, then planted my butt against the wall and slid downward until dry jeans pockets hit damp ground. The layer of grime and soot I'd just painted my backside with didn't faze me. Matched my tarnished soul.

"Cold tonight." I rubbed my hands together, ignoring the familiar stench of uncleanliness.

The jacket-pile stirred to life, its hat brim lifting a bare inch. "Same as evah." The deep timbre of her voice croaked out from parched lips.

"Lookin' warm, Charlene." Not Charlie, or any other nickname. When someone gave me their name, it was sacred. And nothing gave me or anyone else the right to twist it into something different. That right belonged to its owner, no one else. "Plenty of jackets." Four, if I'd counted correctly. Every last one needed for the scrawny frame I knew hid somewhere beneath them.

"Hand-me-down," she explained. One of them, a thicker blue fleece whose cuff extended beyond her fingertips, she'd graciously received from me. The tattered others she'd collected from free piles at thrift stores. The hat brim dipped an inch lower, hiding any traces of a face behind a sliver of shadow. "What we lucky ta git in ah sucky world."

A weary smile tugged my lips at her common phrase. And as was our habit in these last few years, I finished her statement—one I'd been reminded of not more than an hour ago. But with Charlene, I devolved into our local street-talk, her language, the only way she'd listen to me. "Scraps o' joy 'tween all da sufferin.'"

And that's what my visits had become for her and for me. A gift of hidden joy, of solace in a human connection.

Balancing what I'd brought farther onto the pads of each fingertip, I stretched my arm far in front of me before drifting the leather mules closer to her, slow and deliberate. "Brough' ya somet'n." I settled the shoes onto the empty pavement between us, a little closer to her than to me, but still in the neutral zone, safe. "Got no use for 'em anymo'." The truth, but she needed to hear it. Pride prevented her from accepting a hand-me-down any other way.

Time ticked by without further words. The mountain of jackets remained motionless. I waited. Distant traffic sounds rumbled a couple of times, marked by an engine accelerating, its bass tones growing in decibels as it neared, then fading away once again.

After the third passing car's exhaust disappeared, so did the shoes. I'd been looking away at the time. How our exchanges had always been. And what Charlene needed? I respected.

No thanks came, but she didn't have to. We took care of each other, her, me, and dozens of others hidden in the shadows of our city-forest. The gratitude was understood, humbled us—made us strong.

The shoes would never be worn by her, whether or not they were a good fit. They were worth their weight in gold for a barter of her choosing, maybe for something she needed immediately, or a trade for another link in the barter-chain for some unknown thing she'll need in the future.

"Don't got none mo'." Nothing more than shoes. *Asshole* Ben had seen to that. "Not yet."

"I be a'ight. Fret none on me."

I did anyway. She was one of mine. And we took care of our own.

"Hit Tony's, latuh. I give'm da drop, if I can." Hadn't missed one. No lost bartending job would make me start now. Later bought me a couple of hours. And I would do everything I could to provide for the only family I could handle, the one who never asked a thing of me—never took. A situation I controlled. Because I was the one that provided.

I waited another full minute, just in case Charlene had another pearl of wisdom, or request. None came.

The hat brim settled back down onto the peak of jackets piled over bent knees. A low raspy grunt sounded. I'd been acknowledged and dismissed.

With a nod, I flexed my thighs, planted my hands low on the cold bricks behind me, and pushed up from the ground while shouldering my backpack once again. Then I headed off farther down the alley toward the next interconnected street on my habitual route.

A short side street, another turn, then an informal alley created by two hedges between houses dumped me out onto the beginning of the street that edged my beloved park, only four blocks beyond where I'd begun.

On the sidewalk ahead, stood a guy about my age, unofficially guarding a storefront whose wide plate glass windows had gone dark for the night to hide a vintage music store that boasted the largest collection of vinyl on the eastern seaboard. The guardian watched over more than the neighborhood's cultural relic, so permanent a fixture in that same place, in his same bent position, I often imagined him made of stone, immovable unless he wanted to be.

And he wanted to be, coming to life by straightening his

lanky frame the moment he spotted me. Because we were the same, the keepers of our streets. He jerked his chin up the slightest fraction at me. "Lookin' good, Shay."

Anyone else would've thought it was a pickup line. Which was fine, we liked our camouflage.

His eyes darted down the street behind me, then shifted to a squint as he turned his head and scanned the path he knew I'd yet to take.

"Same as, Lando." Landon served as eyes and ears for our network. Informal security for the record store, for me, and for anyone else from our crew who went out of their way to cross his path for his nightly report.

My gaze drifted across the street toward a lamppost on the corner, frequently occupied but vacant at the moment. "Chrissy okay?"

"As evah." He shrugged.

Not much we could do for her. She'd fallen beyond our reach. Had gotten snatched up a couple of years back by a pimp that governed her. She didn't pick up johns on our street; the territory this close to the park didn't belong to her or her pimp, it belonged to us. And we kept it a prostitute-free zone. Always had been, at least for the time I'd made it my home. And as long as I pulled breath in my lungs, it always would be. We'd become a safe haven for the lost, a defended place where forgotten souls could heal and flourish the way we chose to, as best as we were able to.

But even though she'd left the safety of our territory, she religiously visited the pool of light under that streetlamp at least once every night, in full view of Lando. As if to say to her former world *See me. I'm here. I'm still alive.*

We couldn't say anything back. She didn't belong to us anymore, by her choice. No parting letter, no explanation. I'd guessed at what'd happened, as way of explanation to myself when nothing else made sense, that Chrissy had needed more than our invisible existence. Flying under the radar, right under the noses of a society that didn't have room for us, that overlooked us, hadn't been enough for her. She'd needed attention, someone's affection—even if it wasn't real, even though her body had been bought, even if her soul paid the higher price. *Too high a price.*

Any care I'd had for Chrissy had been severed at the why of it. Because nothing would ever make me surrender control of my body. No one would ever again get the chance pull me under. *I'd rather die first.*

"Tony's?"

I blinked at the question that brought me back from the mental whirlpool. Lando shoved his hands into the pockets of his jacket, his penetrating gaze on me. The question he asked of me wasn't for him, even though he benefited from the answer just like the rest of us; the information allowed him to play telegraph with every other soul who'd yet to wander by.

"Latuh." I gave him a sharp nod, determined.

Then I turned and continued on with my nightly patrol path.

But different than any other night, an unusual urgency began to buzz through my veins, a sudden need to touch base with my roots drowning out all else.

My mentor waited.

"I'm coming," I whispered the promise to myself, resigned to my fate.

On my streets. Where I belonged. *No place* for people like Ben.

4
TEMPTING TROUBLE

Ben...

We rolled out of the back lot in Rafe's truck thirty minutes later. Earlier, when he'd nodded a group of four ladies into the club, he had assured me later would be better with Shay.

"Thanks for hangin," he said as he hooked a right and gunned the engine.

"No problem." I hated waiting. But I'd become a saint at it lately. And with nothing else to go by, I believed him.

I'd spent the idle time checking the club. It had taken only a couple of minutes to realize Loading Zone remained in capable hands. The place probably ran smoother than clockwork because I *hadn't* been there micromanaging things.

"Why you goin' after her?" Rafe glanced my way.

Honor. Duty. "I fired her." Simpler.

"My point." He shot me a heavy *no shit* look, one that clearly questioned my sanity.

Right. Because why would you fire someone, then hunt them down? Indecision was a foreign concept to me. And Rafe knew it.

Nothing about the warmth in my chest felt like indecision, though.

It burned more like…recognition.

Of what? Anger? Bitterness? No. More like quiet suffering. And strength in spite of it. Only Shay harbored something even greater. An unshakable defiance. Maybe even resilience from the depths of heartache.

Or maybe all that bullshit was simply me projecting.

So, in fact, I had no clue about the reason for my whole back-pedaling chase-down.

But I didn't need a rational explanation. No point.

What I'd done back at the bar had been a knee-jerk reaction. After a shitty couple of weeks, I'd sought out the one place that made me feel good about myself, then lashed out at the first thing I could find to piss me off.

What I'd done had nothing to do with Shay.

"I'm thinking I made a mistake."

He snorted. "You did."

"How do you know?"

His gaze shot back to the road ahead, eyes narrowing. His broad shoulders tensed, hunching up and inward, as if in protection. Of what? Shay? Surely not the enormous doorman himself. His lips tightened, battening down that hatch of information.

"Just do." His clipped tone cut with absolute certainty. He held Shay in high esteem. Respected her. Believed in her. To the extent that it made me want to understand what fueled such unwavering faith.

He strangled the steering wheel until his knuckles flashed white, then released his grip on a forced inhale. And I got the unspoken message: Shay and Rafe had intense history.

After a right on Gibson, he turned down a narrow side street. We'd left behind the last of our town's small shops marked by colorful awnings and flowered window planters. Damp aged brick pressed in on both sides of the truck and stretched up toward a sliver of starry sky.

"What do you know about her?" *What are you so tight-lipped about?*

He sighed, not happy about the rock and the hard place. "Only what she lets *anyone* know."

But apparently more than he was willing to share. "Her past?"

He jerked a headshake. "Not a thing."

"Cade said you vouched for her." *You have to know something.*

"From what little she's let me see? Shay's worth ten of anyone I know."

Wow. High praise coming from you. "Her character." Which meant more than any past.

Rafe shot me a hard look. "Solid."

After slowing a block in, he stopped at the entrance of an adjoining alley, engine idling. He nodded toward the right, "She's down there."

I stared down into oppressive darkness and listened through the open truck window. From the intersection behind us, the distant hum of car engines rose and fell, but no sound came from the alley. "You sure?"

He gave a short nod. "As sure as it gets." He thrust the shifter into park. "But I can get out and check for you."

A part of me wanted to grill him on *how* he knew. But I refused to cross the unspoken line between boss and coworker.

"Nah." I opened the door and climbed out. "Thanks, man. I got it from here."

Maybe.

Hopefully.

Didn't have any clue what I'd be walking into, but I could go anywhere she could. Kinda owed it to her, since I was the coldhearted bastard who'd chased her there.

When I shut the truck door, its clang echoed through the urban slot canyon. The rumble of Rafe's engine revved up, then faded away as he left the mouth of the alley.

On a night that had earlier been cool, a sudden warmer humidity cloyed at my skin. I passed through stagnant air trapped between the steel backside of a dry cleaner's shop on my right and a taller brick apartment building on my left.

I cocked my head and listened for signs of life as I took wary steps into the darkness. I'd walked through unknown alleys before, but never by choice, not at night. And I couldn't imagine anyone going to an alley as a destination itself. Not Shay. Not even Rafe.

Every outside light fixture had empty sockets, but faint

glow from several windows above lit my way. With every step, pebbles crunched, the slight sound megaphoned into the glaring silence.

I tucked my thumbs into the front pockets of my jeans and blew out a calming breath. Then I pulled my shoulders back with confidence. No gleaming blade could possibly stab me tonight. *I've got things to do tomorrow.*

But the farther I walked, the deeper doubt crept in. Not the reason, that was noble.

It was the sanity in my method of finding her. Alone. In unfamiliar territory.

Maybe I should've taken Rafe's help after all.

Somewhere in the near distance, cat screams screeched out. The muffled sounds of TVs behind closed windows droned eerie competitive hums.

A rusty dumpster, most of its surface colored in graffiti, edged into view to my left. It overflowed with loose trash. A wall of flattened boxes leaned against its back corner. At its far end, a blanket-filled shopping cart parked in front narrowed the alley ahead down to a few feet.

Nearby, a hollow metallic clang sounded, and I jumped.

"Go away, Ben." A low familiar voice vibrated with steely anger.

Right place after all.

I sighed as guilt pierced my gut; I'd caused that anger. "Just came to talk."

"You already talked. *Listening.* That's your problem."

One of many. "I came to listen, then."

Shay stepped out from behind the dumpster, arms

crossed over her short-sleeved T-shirt. Light flickered from one of the overhead TV-apartment windows casting her in a faint glow. Dark-brown hair fell down around her shoulders. Black lashes fringed darkened eyes before they narrowed at me. "I'm done talking."

"You sure about that?" I'd tossed her words from the bar back at her.

She glared at me. "You're not welcome here."

"In this particular alley?"

"In my space."

Which space? I wanted to ask. The words burned on the tip of my tongue. Her mental space? Her world in general?

She'd fled to the dank alley we stood in. Her safe haven?

Her home? I hoped not. Somehow, I'd convinced myself she wasn't homeless. The idea, for her, didn't compute with me.

Which meant I couldn't leave. Because the more questions I had, the more I needed to know about the intriguing creature standing so defiantly in front of me. "To eat, then."

A single brow rose. "Try again. No five-star restaurant here."

Undaunted, I pressed on. "Pretty good one nearby."

"Not interested."

What would you be interested in? "Even for a job offer?"

"Not buyin' it."

Yeah, me either. Honor or not, I had a business to run, and a safe world for me and my crew didn't include undocumented underage bartenders. But it did include compassion, a virtue on short supply with me lately. Which I needed to correct with her. She hadn't deserved the brunt of my frustration. "Look, I was a total asshole back there."

"Total. And complete."

Was that amusement in her tone? Probably just mocking. Didn't matter. Progress either way. "Give me another chance?"

"Why should I?"

Too many reasons to list. A few for me. My gut told me a couple for her too.

But before I had a chance to answer, a hulking shadow spread up and out from behind the dumpster, inches from Shay. Easily seven-foot, a good two-eighty, the hulking form had long fuzzy dreadlocks and dark skin. A wiry mass of black hair hid the lower half of his face.

Shay didn't flinch or cower when he eased close enough for his arm to brush her shoulder. Instead, her shoulders squared, her chest rose, and her chin lifted a fraction in easy confidence.

The creature's head cocked a little to the side, the way a puppy tries to figure out a curiosity. "Come close, Ben." The guy's deep voice purred out slow and soft, tones a gentle friend would use to invite another to come play. Only his words were totally at odds with the death glare he blasted at me from hooded eyes.

"Yeah, I'm good here." Safe. From Bigfoot.

I almost laughed that a slight girl stood between us. As if she protected me, from him.

With a healthy dose of caution, I stared over her shoulder, sizing up the guy.

And how do you wash that gnarly head of hair anyway?

Shay gave a slow headshake. "You're not *good* anywhere." Mocking humor edged her tone. "And you're not safe here."

Her voice softened at that last. Into concern? For my well-being?

"One drink." There. I'd gone out on a ledge. A peace offering over the very thing that had started the whole fucking bonfire.

"Don't drink." Automatic comeback.

My mind blanked as the dual ironies of that tidbit crashed in my brain.

Questionably aged bartender? Meet the bar owner who has drinking issues.

"Coffee, then." Yep. I kept at it.

"Too late."

"Food."

"Not hungry."

Yet someone's stomach growled loud enough to be heard; wasn't mine.

No one moved.

"I am. And..."

"And...what?" Her head dropped as her eyes narrowed. The tough girl I'd chased down wasn't giving an inch.

"And, I need to apologize. Grovel. Explain my actions. Ask for your understanding. Beg forgiveness."

The corners of her lips twitched a little. No mistake. Definite amusement.

She lifted her shoulders slightly and inhaled a patient breath while her gaze rolled up toward the apartments above us, as if she considered coming with me...and couldn't believe her idiocy. Then she turned her body enough to no longer appear squared-off with me and took a step closer. Away from the menacing mountain behind her.

The mountain matched her step—a baby-step for him—then boomed low, "*Blink.*"

His growled command made me do exactly that. Blink. Heavily.

"S'okay, Bear." Shay paused and looked over her shoulder. "You know I can take care of myself."

Bear. As in ferocious wild grizzly. One animal she'd apparently tamed.

"Go." Bear rested his giant paw on the slender curve of her shoulder. Instinct made my thigh muscles twitch, as if to lunge for her, protect her. But again, she didn't flinch at his touch. His gravelly voice fell lower, softer as he angled his face down toward her. "Eat some. For me."

She turned toward me for a beat, then glanced back up conspiratorially at him. "Guess it'd be cool to hear him grovel. Maybe show the dickhead what *active listening* sounds like."

Dickhead? Yeah, guess I deserved that. Probably more.

"Still not eating," she muttered as she brushed past me in the alley.

Bear chuckled behind us. Like he knew her well. As if they held vast secrets between them.

Unsettled by their comfort at camping out in an alley behind a dumpster, I followed her, then jogged to catch up as the distance between us grew.

Long legs on a lean athletic frame took her all the way to

the sidewalk. She'd rounded the corner by the time I reached the spot where I'd gotten out of Rafe's truck.

A block in, she whirled around under the glare of a streetlamp. "What do you really want from me?"

"Everything I said back there."

"Bullshit." Tough as nails. "No one does something out of the goodness of their heart anymore."

"Maybe more should."

Hard lines of anger twitched into a dubious expression. Then, in her wide stance two feet away and full of every bit of the fire she'd flared back at the bar, she searched my eyes as if seeking the truth while at the same time looking as if she wouldn't believe it even if she found it.

And as she took her doubt-filled time looking, so did I. I took a fresh look at the girl I'd judged in one instant faraway glance—and had gotten wrong.

Idiot. But then, I knew that. Why I'd come to rectify the grave mistake.

But so much more unfolded in the seconds we stood in the now-cooler air in the middle of the night along the side of the road. I stared at a complete stranger, who seemed oddly familiar. Both of us remained motionless longer than needed. Her eyes widened a fraction, as did mine, but neither of us moved, neither said a word. It was as if two wounded animals stumbled out of the forest and faced off, uncertain what they actually confronted, hesitant to trust the other: *friend or foe?*

The unusual moment felt unique and beautiful. Just like her.

And I got the sense we weren't strangers at all. Even though we hid our scars well, we shared damage—deep-wounding and soul-altering. The kind that made a person rip and shred first, then question, having been on the receiving end one too many times. The kind that made girls tougher than they needed to be, because they'd been hurt bone-deep and didn't know if they could recover from another blow.

Her gaze softened. Whether out of pity for what she saw in me or remorse for giving me the spiked end of her protective shield, I hadn't a clue. But I'd take it.

I stepped closer. "Ready to hear me grovel?"

Her arms splayed wide as she glanced at the cobblestone sidewalk on either side of her. "Right here works for me."

"Ah, but 'right here' doesn't have coffee."

Those slender arms crossed, head lowering as it tilted a fraction. "Not necessary for groveling."

"Not all I had in mind."

Her eyes narrowed.

I held up my hands in surrender and blew out a heavy breath. "I give. I fucked up. One horrendous day after the grueling last two weeks, then seeing you behind the bar? Dropped the cherry on top of my toxic sundae."

Her brows raised. "Gee, thanks."

Not doing well with the groveling. "I'm sorry."

Expression deadening into disinterest, her attention dropped as she lowered her hand, rotated a relaxed fist, then began inspecting her nails.

"Look." *Just be honest.* I sighed, remembering every excruciating detail, letting my real pain bleed out. "I've had a *monumentally* shitty day."

She took a deep breath, then her gaze crept up, interest sparking there as it met mine.

Now or never. Take it all the way. "No excuse to rail on you. But I saw you and…well, I wasn't thinking straight."

Her brows raised slightly again, the hint of a smile tugged at the corners of her lips. "Too young." She stabbed me with a hard look. "You were so damn sure."

I nodded, willing to admit I'd jumped to conclusions. "Smart mouth, too." My gaze dropped to it. "Made me crazy." *Makes me crazy now.* Those full soft lips had slung words that had shredded me. What would they be like if she decided to be tender, soothing…

Food.

Job.

Don't get distracted.

"C'mon. I know a place not far from here." I stepped to the side and nodded back the way we'd come, but *well beyond* the alley she seemed so comfortable in. "And I grovel better when I'm not starving."

As I opened the diner door for Shay, a small bell tinkled above our heads, but she paused before her foot hit the white tile floor. Then her shoulders squared, her head raised taller, and she continued through, walking into the tiny reception area.

Warm air pumped out from a shiny black radiator to the right of the door, but it was the smell of fresh coffee and baked goods that engulfed me. My stomach took its turn at a loud growl. *When had I last eaten? Not dinner. Lunch had been a joke. Rarely touched breakfast. So yeah, fuel. Now.*

While I stood beside the *Please Wait To Be Seated* sign, Shay ignored it, drawn as if in a trance to the train memorabilia in the back.

Large black-and-white photographs of gleaming steam locomotives filled the wall and continued on through the restaurant. According to a placard in the middle, they chronicled the executive transcontinental tours of the late 1800's. Grand station masters proudly wore their pressed uniforms beside wealthy passengers: men in three-piece suits or tuxes with top hats, women in dresses draped in jewels, some with furs wrapped around their shoulders. Bygone days when celebrating to get from here to there faster was novel, held prestige, and had been only available to those with money to burn.

But Shay's actions captured my full attention. With measured steps and an indiscernible expression, she approached the only collector's item outside a large display case along the wall: a shining brass train whistle. Nearly three-feet tall, it had been mounted high on a wall where it'd been designed to look like the actual engine it might've been on.

When she lifted her hand, trembling fingers hovered over the unmarred surface. Her expression became reverent a split second before she fully faced the relic with her back toward me.

But I still saw the evidence of her distress: head lowering, breaths quickening.

"Table for two?" A cheery woman with short silver hair broke into the silence.

Shay blew out a heavy breath as her shoulders fell. When she turned, relief washed over her face. She darted a glance at me, as if to check if she'd been caught.

I gave nothing away, nodded to our server.

After our menus were slapped down onto the table of one of the window booths in the middle of a deserted section, we sat opposite one another. She crossed her arms, defiance written all over her face.

Her eyes narrowed. "You said something about a job offer."

"I did." But I hadn't yet worked out the kinks of that idea.

"I won't waitress. Not gonna squeeze into one of those bustier things." She swept her fingers up in front of her breasts, then cupped her hands out a fraction while scrunching her face.

"Don't like 'em?" Yeah, I couldn't help myself. She'd baited me.

"My boobs?" She glanced down.

I followed her gaze. "I happen to think they're spectacular, in case you were wondering."

"But…" Her eyes widened, then her brows furrowed and she gave a quick headshake. "No. *Nooo.* The bustier. It's ridiculous."

I flipped open my menu, pretending not to notice how flustered she'd gotten. For a split second, her vulnerability had been adorable. But stark panic had flashed an instant later. And my goal had been to put her at ease, have her let me in—not shut me out.

"So, what'll it be?" I nodded toward the closed laminated menu in front of her.

But she didn't move. She stared straight at me.

Maybe because the question was loaded, with more than food options on a menu…

That I'd chased her down.

That she'd agreed to come.

Whether or not she'd consider a job offer.

Annnd…why we both were inexplicably attracted to our clear polar opposite.

5
INTO THE WOODS

Shay...

What'll it be? *From* him? "Nothing."

I didn't want food or anything slick businessman Benjamin Bishop offered.

The weight of his stare landed on me. Assessing. Like if those dark penetrating eyes lasered deep enough into my brain, he'd expose all my secrets.

He laid down his menu, leaned back, and crossed his arms. "You don't ever need anything." An accusation. A challenge. And it fell heavy between us, like a judgment to some falsehood he'd discovered.

I shrugged. *Air. Water. Food.* My gaze dropped to the menu's laminated picture of a melty cheeseburger.

Then I pegged him with a hard stare back. "We all need things."

"Just not tonight."

Nothing to do with need. Want, maybe. Curiosity made me follow him out of the safety of my alley, nothing else. But time ticked by as the night's deadline loomed. People were counting on me. And I counted on myself. No one else. Never again. "Not from you."

My stomach grumbled for the second time in angry protest, but I ignored it, even as my mouth watered with each slow inhale of tempting fried food.

The pang of my heart? I refused to listen to that too.

I didn't feel comfortable eating in front of him. *Especially* in the place we sat in.

And I did my best *not* to think of the imposing man who sat in front of me all relaxed and casual, as if he hadn't chased me down—the first time anyone had ever cared enough to want to make things right with me. And I got the sense it had more to do with him than me. Which made me feel a little better, a little safer, and a whole lot more curious about the what and why of it.

Fidgeting on the booth's burgundy vinyl seat, I forced myself to look around, take in the late-night version of the old railcar diner, overwrite idyllic memories that haunted me with their shallow lies.

A familiar elderly man sat at the end of the bar, his overflowing army duffel carrying what I'd often suspected were his only possessions. The ends of his thin silvery hair brushed the countertop. Leathered fingers gripped the edge of a white dinner plate heaped with fluffy eggs, blackened sausage links, and toast shellacked with butter that glistened under the harsh lights. His pale gray eyes darted toward the exit every few seconds, making him look as uncomfortable as I felt.

But Jim, the owner, who probably still ran the kitchen himself, had always had a strict homeless policy: no begging at the back door like a dog. "You sit at the counter, like a human being." Jim's clear voice, overheard by a wide-eyed little girl over the chattering hum of a busy breakfast crowd, echoed into my head a dozen years later. But I'd never forgotten him. Jim stood out as the best kind people in my book.

The brief memory disappeared as more powerful images exploded in: sunny booths jam-packed with families fresh from Sunday service, a line out the door and around the corner, laughter and giggles from kids in colorful clothes and shiny shoes. Not just from other booths, from mine too.

"You okay?"

I blinked. Moisture flicked down onto my cheek. I sighed and brushed it away with my hand, irritated at the weakness. "Yeah, why?"

"You started to smile. Thought maybe the world had ended."

"Ha. Ha." And maybe the world as I'd known it pre-Ben had. Because when I'd been busy fighting against believing him, daring to hope again, he'd distracted me into one of the places I'd sworn never to return to.

"*Sooo...*" —he dipped a nod at my untouched menu— "not eating."

"Nope." No point in throwing the whole thing up from the nerves that churned in my gut.

"Coffee, then." He held up his white mug to the server as she approached again.

After she filled both of our mugs with her pot, he sipped his, black. "So, what's your story?"

Right. *Do I look like an open book?* "None of your business."

"True." He settled the mug onto the table. "Would be if I wanted to hire you."

With the tips of my fingernails, I pushed the base of my steaming mug to the center of the table, parking it to be even with the bottom edge of my rejected menu. "You just fired me. Make up your mind."

"Not helping."

"Not trying."

"Okay." He kept that relentless stare on me. "So...no ID you want to share. No story. How do you expect to get hired anywhere?"

"Don't."

"What if I *did* want to hire you? You obviously have Rafe on your side. What does Rafe know that I don't?"

Way more than I want anyone to know about me. But Rafe was built like me. Bear too. We did what we had to— had done whatever we'd needed to—in order to survive.

I planted my hands on the table edge and pushed up from the booth. "Let's blow this place." Done with facing my demons, I listened to my deadline-clock, every next tick echoing louder in my head.

Ben peered at me over the rim of his mug, taking a slow last pull of his coffee. Then he stood, reached into his pocket, and fanned a handful of singles out before tucking them under a saltshaker.

"That's too much," I scoffed. "Your coffee was a buck twenty-five."

"We still took up her time."

Furrowing my brow, I counted the green dog-eared corners. "Not five-hundred percent of her time." Without guilt, and determined to fight for my share of control every step of the way, I swiped three of the bills.

Ben said nothing, simply watched me with interest as I walked over to the old man at the counter.

"Hey, Joey," I murmured. Everyone from my world knew him. The man often talked to himself, anyone willing to listen, or no one in particular who just happened to be walking by. When he turned weary eyes my way, I put a gentle hand over his, then curled the few dollars under his palm. "Somet'n fo' latuh."

"What was that?" Ben frowned and stared back at the meek homeless man. Joey had already returned to his late-night dinner plate, chewing another bite with slow precision, like it might be his last. The hearty meal was probably the first food Joey had eaten all day.

"Redistribution." The way the system should work. Instantly. Where it mattered.

"Of my money."

"Consider it a *non*-tax-free donation." Yep. No qualms about twisting the language of the rich. Went right along with warping their "justified" self-benefiting laws.

I stepped back out into the crisp night air, and the bell

above the door tinkled again.

"Where you going?" Ben called out, suddenly farther away from me, but still inside.

I glanced over my shoulder to see him back at the booth we'd abandoned. He peeled and dropped down a few more dollars for the waitress. Then he jogged back but paused behind Joey to slip out what appeared to be a crisp twenty from his wallet and slid it beside Joey's plate. Ben then handed him something else, smaller, a slip of paper or a card...maybe a hotline number?

Interesting.

But not enough to wait around.

I bounded out into the street, took a deep inhale of mineral-rich air, then stared up at a dark sky where a thin layer of glowing clouds obstructed all but a sliver of moon ghosting through.

"What'd you hand Joey?" I asked as he walked out the door. I contemplated the possibilities. That I'd been wrong about Ben. That he wasn't one-dimensional. That he hid something deeper—a strong moral compass. Why else would he have hunted me down? And maybe he was hiding more than simple morality—the extra bills to the server and to Joey, handed over without a second thought; the monumental "shitty day" he'd had. Maybe he protected secrets...like me.

"*Where* are you going?" The soles of his shoes clicked louder as he gained ground.

"Better food," I replied, eyeing my ultimate destination at the far edge of the park.

"A business card," he finally answered. What he'd handed Joey.

"Hiring the homeless now?" Shocked at the lengths Ben Bishop seemed willing to take, I stopped at the curb and crossed my arms, reassessing yet again the man who'd ruined my night, a man I couldn't seem to shake.

"No. Cade owns a restaurant with his wife, Hannah. Gave him one of their cards. If Joey comes here at night, maybe he'd go to their restaurant in Fairmount Park during the day."

Ah. Okay. Great idea. Ben continued to redeem himself, bit by bit. I made a mental note to check out the place, make sure it was good enough for Joey, maybe tell the rest of my crew.

A horn honked as I stepped off the curb, tearing me back into the real world. The one where my stomach growled as mouthwatering scents of cooked salt and fat teased through my nostrils, luring me on.

But I couldn't eat yet. Not until I'd earned it.

I scanned the pedestrians, searching each for possibility, even with Ben right on my heels.

When I darted across the street, I picked up the pace. But Ben jogged to catch up again, his footfalls scuffing the asphalt in my wake.

"Better food." Doubt laced his tone. "Out here?"

"Yep." Hearty food. Made by real people. Not industrialized. Not commercialized. No overhead, no employees, no parking spaces to hold overpriced cars—or vintage train booths haunted with memories.

"The Station Diner is Zagat rated."

The moment the words left his mouth, my attention landed on a weathered park bench. Not just any park bench. *My* park bench. At the base of a boulder outcropping, in sight of a massive forest, a place of protection, where a lost little girl had come to dream...learned to hunt.

Forcing my thoughts from the past—grounded by my place, in my home—I glanced up at him. "Not everything worthwhile is acknowledged by snobs." Not even close.

His gaze locked with mine, searching, wanting to understand.

Refusing to give him even the slightest hint, I hardened my expression.

Amusement lit his eyes. "Defiant much?"

"Any other way to be?" If there was, I hadn't figured it out yet. Anti-authority had gained me my freedom. Anti-establishment had given me purpose. Anti-culture had offered me a home, the only true protective family I'd ever known.

Freaking out a little from the unexpected self-analysis, I glared at him. Then I turned and charged up the street at a brisk pace. Taking the scenic route with purpose, I veered along a pristine tree-lined sidewalk, then angled toward the corner of Grammercy Park and Fifth; executives from our growing financial district streamed by from there. Late on a Friday? Guaranteed pickings.

Suddenly, I spotted the perfect mark: camel hair trench with a scarf draped under the lapels, three-piece suit, crisp white shirt, impeccably knotted ice-blue tie. Black leather wingtips reflected a soft shine from the lamplight that the mid-forties man passed under.

Too tempting to ignore, I resolved one final time to break that naïve *go-legit* vow and keep my deadline. Ben had put me right back where I belonged, after all. Why bother fighting the forces of the universe?

Done.

With a sudden rush of adrenaline, I spun around, thrust my hands up toward the night sky, then beamed my best fake smile toward Ben. "Isn't it amazing?"

The edge of my sneaker caught on a sidewalk crack. Weight thrown from my twirling momentum, I collided with Mr. Impeccably Dressed right as he strode onto my sidewalk square.

We grabbed one another for balance, eyes wide with surprise: his genuine, mine flawless.

"Oh, my God!" he exclaimed.

"So sorr…didn't s…see," I stuttered out.

The stranger patted me down, innocently, of course, to make sure I remained unharmed. I patted him in a similar way, under his coat where my hands had landed, naturally, not at all innocently, to relieve him of the unnecessary weight burning a hole in his left inside coat pocket.

"Are you okay?" The man's eyes searched mine.

With a convincing nod, I smiled a little. "Good. Thanks." For righting me, plus a handful of others who needed righting too.

It all happened in a flash. The stumble, the righting. Four seconds, tops. The slip? *In a blink.*

Not turning to look at Ben, whose presence I sensed

close in on my other side, I continued with quick steps that led me to the edge of the sidewalk and up a grassy berm.

"What was with...the sudden excitement?" His tone weighed heavy. I took it as doubt.

Good. Men off-balance? The best kind to take advantage of.

Finally, the stainless steel food cart I'd spotted ten minutes ago, and had been smelling for a block and a half, came into view. "No excitement. Just randomness."

"No. I don't think so." His voice softened as gentle pressure gripped my upper arm.

When I paused, turning and glancing up to face him, my breath caught at the compassion in his dark eyes as they searched mine. He reached up, caressed my cheek with his fingertips. "You don't always need to be tough, you know. I'm not going to hurt you."

My pulse quickened, his words burning into my heart. I forgot for the tiniest moment what it was to be me: alone, fighting for everything, strong all the time. Letting out a slow exhale, my eyes drifted shut, and I leaned into his touch, pretending for precious seconds that the world wasn't out to hurt me, that maybe one guy might actually be one of the fabled good guys. *Maybe Ben.*

Had he caught what I'd done? I'd intentionally blocked his view, or I thought I had.

If Ben found out, would he agree? Would law-abiding Ben let my criminal act slide, open his ever-flowing wallet and add to the cause?

A bicycle bell rang from the sidewalk, and I blinked back to reality.

No.

And no knight in shining armor existed. Only in the fairy tales I'd read so long ago with…

"Right," I muttered and gave Ben a nod before taking quick steps toward my destination and increasing the distance between us. "You won't hurt me." The words were spoken into the crisp air, directed not just toward Ben, but to everyone out there in the world. "Because I'm not going to let you."

Distant laughter and the scents of grilled meats and spun sugar wafted from a block to our west. The Arts District's inaugural First Friday had been going on for hours, the road supposedly blocked off at either end with the art galleries and boutiques open till midnight.

Colorful fliers had been posted in coffeehouses and other neighborhood stores for weeks. To someone like me, the opportunity would've been a gold mine of temptation. But I'd refrained from even going there in my mind the last week, new job and all. Which I no longer had. *Hmmm…*

But I had a more important errand to run.

"How far do we have to hoof it to get this great food, New York?" Ben's teasing voice came from a few paces back, but I could hear those pavement-scuffing shoes getting louder. He'd never make a decent pickpocket. Might as well wear a bell around his neck.

I slowed with a growing smile. *Not about Ben.* In fact, we'd arrived. Plenty more important things to focus on. A few yards ahead, at the end of the sidewalk, where the park ended and a row of charming brownstones began, stood my destination. My deadline.

Tony's Hot Dog Cart. "Antonio!"

"*Ciao bella!*" Hello, beautiful!

The Italian greeting had been our thing from the moment I'd met Tony eight years ago. Made funnier, because he served nothing from his homeland from the cart, and I'd teased him about it the first time he'd ever served me my first taste of heaven in a bun—on the house, he'd insisted. Tony had carved a sweet little niche for himself capturing those dedicated executives, typically stock traders who'd skipped dinner to work late finishing West Coast business but detoured by his cart on the way home for the best dogs served in town.

Only available from 7:00 p.m. till midnight, Monday through Friday.

Tony had a pizza joint to run during the day.

And a wife counting on him to feed their eight hungry mouths, with a ninth on the way.

But he also served as a stopping point for our greater family, those in need who couldn't provide for themselves. Tony was passionate about helping others—like a starving girl who'd believed herself to be a Lost Boy. And I'd returned the favor, helping Tony and his growing family stay off the streets when they'd once struggled to make ends meet.

"Two, please. Both of 'em with the works." I nodded back toward Ben. "I've got company."

Blocking Ben's view with my body for a moment, I pulled a wide-mouthed tip jar from its high perch on the upper corner of Tony's cart and lowered it to the edge of his prep area. Then I dropped the entire wad of cash I'd stolen.

LAWBREAKER

The rest of the wallet? Dropped into the trash can at my feet.

Tony's eyes widened an instant before they began to glisten with moisture.

I shot him a stern glare, lowered my brows, and gave him a nearly imperceptible headshake, trying desperately to wave him off.

He took a deep breath, eyes still watering in gratitude and disbelief.

I forgave him instantly.

Even though we took care of one another, me and Tony, and—with the help of our street network—our extended family, it still got to each of us that *anyone* cared enough to help, tugged hard at our hearts to know that humanity showed its colors brighter down where we lived, ground level.

"Seriously?" Ben eyed a mustard tube, then surveyed the steaming trays lined with foil, seemingly oblivious. "You dragged me all the way down here for a hot dog?"

No. We had guardian-angel work to do.

"Yes." My renewed glare held Tony's gaze for another brief beat, then shifted toward Ben. A zipped-lip Tony handed him a steaming dog that had already been loaded with mustard, white onions, and crisp pickle slices.

"Not just *any* hot dog," Tony defended with pride.

From not just any vendor. Our work for the night was done. Tony had what he needed to make his rent and food without worry, plus enough to share with Charlene, Lando, and anyone else who needed food or a few bucks to tide them over.

Ben had his food, something to distract him from being on my back about the job. And I could relax for a few minutes.

When Ben turned toward the far corner of the cart and grabbed a fistful of napkins, Tony handed me my dog with a last look of gratitude, eyes welling again with moisture, behind Ben's back.

I winked at Tony, trying to end his misty-eyed emotions.

Tony held up two beers, brows raised.

With a headshake, I politely declined and grabbed two waters from his cooler instead.

A groan sounded from Ben's direction, and he turned back toward me, mouth filled with a third of his dog as he chewed. "*Mmm…*" All he could manage before his eyes rolled toward the back of his head.

"Told you." I inhaled the scent of heaven, then took a more manageable bite.

"Best dog ever," Ben urged around a mouthful of food.

I nodded, in complete agreement. "Something to do with his spices. I figure Tony laces 'em with something special. Like some ancient Italian family recipe hides under the casing. But he passes it off as ordinary street food while he addicts us all with his secret drug."

Ben eyed me, but said nothing.

I handed him a bottle of water, then walked along and ate my dog, following a line of lampposts, one yellow glowing pool after another, toward the increasing sound of laughter and music.

"What's with all the revelry?" The warmth of Ben's shoulder brushed my arm.

I gasped at the shock of our unexpected contact. But when I glanced up, Ben seemed unaffected, unaware even, as he chomped down the last quarter of his meal. He wadded up the paper wrapper, then arced the foil ball into a wrought-iron-caged trash can to his left.

Forget the jolt of his touch that still sizzled across your skin in the best kind of way. Focus on his question. Which hadn't been about us at all.

He'd meant the live folk band streaming an electric violin solo, the buzzing of dozens of conversations, the clinking of glasses. A street party in full swing. "First Friday."

"Right. Heard about that."

Me too. Unable to stop ingrained habit, my gaze flicked across the crowd, identified brand names, gleaming precious metal, bulging pockets weighed down with excess money.

"So, about that job." Ben remained beside me, shoulder to shoulder, close, but no longer touching.

Still impacting me, though—down to my bones.

What is it about you that makes me want to risk...touch?

On a frustrated sigh, I dove into the middle of a foursome of wealthy girls who stumbled by. They were ridiculously easy marks with their designer bags dangling, forgotten, while glazed eyes tried to focus on the red wine that sloshed in the mason jar each girl held steady with great care—their liquid valuables seemingly more precious than any other at the moment.

Child's play.

A whole lot easier than a boring, feet-aching, eight-hour bartending shift. "*No* job."

"Yes, job."

"Why?" I whirled around and planted my hands on my hips, abandoning the treasure trove of unsuspecting donators. The girls weren't going anywhere fast, but Ben sure as hell needed to be.

As in gone. Off my back.

Because I couldn't handle new and different. I couldn't handle Ben—not with everything I'd been through. And I definitely didn't want to find out why he affected me to such a great degree.

"Because." He pegged me with that penetrating-stare thing again. "You need me."

I snorted. "You're high."

He took a step closer, spoke lower, slower. "You *want* what I have to offer."

Ouch.

I did want it. Or had *wanted it.*

The job. *You naïve fool.* Not *him.*

Yep. I'd wanted *that bartending job.*

But that'd been before he'd yanked the rug out from under me. Before I'd gone out on a limb and trusted in something new, an ideal I'd thought I'd wanted. Not gonna happen again.

"Not buyin'."

"Not selling."

"Sounds like you're sellin' it pretty hard to me."

"How would you know? You won't even listen." He raked a hand through his dark hair, ruffling it until several locks tumbled in a wild mess over his forehead. "*Please.* Hear me out."

His voice had softened. Frustration pulled down his brows, but then he raised them a fraction, wrinkling his forehead. Big dark-gray puppy-dog eyes pleaded with me.

"Fine," I grumbled.

I'm gonna regret this on so many levels.

But I couldn't turn away someone in need. Hadn't ever been able to. Had been there once. *Very, very* in need. And in my darkest hours, when I'd really needed the smallest act of kindness to keep up hope, I'd gotten it. Since then, I'd made it my life's mission to help those who asked—and those who didn't.

Ben hadn't outright asked for help. But he definitely needed it. His pain rode between the lines in his expression, shimmered in his eyes.

"I can't have you work behind my bar."

I waited. That listening part? Apparently involved a huge amount of patience. "Established. But I'm not bussing tables. Not waitressing."

"Not yet, anyway."

"*Uh...*I'm never waitressing." *In a boob-puffing bustier?* No way. "My only interest is in bartending. I can't work behind your bar? Stalemate."

He gave a subtle headshake. "I meant not yet *behind the bar at Loading Zone.*"

"Intriguing." *Congratulations. Interest piqued.* "Go on. Wherever am I going to tend bar *not* at your bar."

"At a charity event."

Amazed he had any other business besides Loading Zone, my mind blanked for an instant. Then it rebooted at the appealing idea. Helping others. Legitimately. Only there had to be a catch. Why would Loading Zone's bar be off-limits, but no problem with me working a charity? Maybe the money sucked. Or the event.

"What *kind* of charity event?" I took a couple of slow steps back, placing Ben squarely between me and the tempting street party.

I'd learned about crazy charity events, through bits of eavesdropped gossip at expensive restaurants while I'd been doing *my own form* of charity. The last one I'd overheard, auctioning off hot eligible bachelors for a date—while they strutted down a catwalk in nothing but their underwear—popped into my brain.

Drawing in a shaky breath, my gaze drifted down Ben's body as I imagined him in nothing but his underwear: black briefs hugging lean hips, clinging to muscular thighs.

My skin heated as I stared at some imaginary line under the denim he now wore, where the bottom of those black briefs would end. And what hung, heavy in my mind, above that imaginary line.

"Golf," he said.

Annnd done. Mind *totally* blanked.

6
SCRAMBLED

Ben…

Shay's thick dark lashes fell in a slow blink. Then her widened eyes locked on to mine. "Golf."

I gave a half-shrug, as if I hadn't noticed her checking me out seconds before.

But her skittishness?

Made me want to divert all her attention away from the chemistry sparking between us.

I watched her back away from me, but I only let her get so far. We walked down the street in tandem, while I took one larger step closer for her every three in retreat.

The chaotic music and laughter of the street party faded behind us. Calmer sounds of a city neighborhood nearing midnight edged in: rumbles of distant car engines, the hums of nearby air conditioners.

Approaching the next lamppost, she slowed. I closed the distance between us.

But I still respected her invisible armor, saw the need to tread lightly: all business.

No big deal. Only a charity event. Only golf. "A scramble, actually."

"Scramble."

Her expression turned priceless, full of doubt and suspicion: brows lowered, eyes narrowed, head turned the slightest degree to the left.

I fought a smile. "What's with the sudden word repetition?"

"Better than stunned speechlessness." Her confident resolve had visibly shaken. And the unsteadiness looked good on her, showed vulnerability under all that spiky armor.

Gotcha. I'd worn her down, then left-fielded her. *I need to keep you on your toes more often.* "Got a problem with golf?"

"No. Never given golf enough thought to have a problem with it. It's so…sedate."

"Golf can be exciting." To those competing, maybe. Or betting. But I'd bet every last cent I had that golf with Shay would be *anything* but sedate.

Amusement sparked in her eyes. "Oh, really? Enlighten me."

Something drew me toward her, lured me in, tempted me to work harder to unearth all the emotions she kept an airtight lid on. Complexity churned under that calm surface she tried valiantly to maintain. Earlier at the bar, I'd been in too much of a blind rage to see it. But now, with all the usual racket in my head silenced, with just the two of us sparring together and the pressures of the world blurred out, I saw her depth…felt it.

"Depends on who you're playing with and what's at stake."

In golf.

In everything.

"So, why is bartending at a charity event—"

"*Golf* charity event," I interrupted.

Yeah, I went there. Found a weak spot? Gonna exploit it, soften those sharp spikes.

Her steady gaze held mine. She drew in a slow breath. I could almost hear the leash on her control snap taut as she reined in her fiery temper. "—*better* than at Loading Zone," she finished.

"We really goin' there again?" Couldn't seem to avoid it. That line we'd toed at the bar kept appearing between us, threatening, daring.

"Apparently." She folded her arms. Determined. Stubborn.

Be honest. I didn't have to tell her the truth, but my gut told me she needed to hear the real reason. Even if I didn't share the *hows* and *whys*, I could give her the basic truth. "I can't risk the bar. It's all I've got."

A frown tugged down the corners of her mouth. "But you can risk the charity?"

I didn't like that frown...that I'd caused it. "No. I'm not the boss at the charity event. The charity is Cade's mom's baby, The Unity Foundation; it helps at-risk kids. I'm a subcontractor for Invitation Only, an event-planning company that Cade and his sisters own."

"Oh, I get it. It's okay for *them* to risk me, but not *you*."

"Never said that. It's still my ass on the line for my bar at the event. But my two businesses are legally separate. If shit hits the fan on one, I'm not risking the other."

"*Shit*" —her brows raised slightly— "being me."

"No. Stop putting words into my mouth."

"Just trying to clarify all the vagueness spewing out of it."

Right. Honesty. But only so far. "My shit day? My shit couple of weeks? Have nothing to do with you. That's the 'shit.'"

Give her more.

My gut screamed at me that Shay was important. She was the shrewdest, feistiest woman I'd ever encountered. Yet some urgent need not to let her get away boiled down to a few seconds—how much I shared, what I chose to reveal.

Make it about her.

Hell, maybe the purest truth existed there anyway.

"*You* are the exact opposite. I'm not here because you're trouble. I'm here because you shine. Cade and Rafe vouched for it, for you. I don't know you well, but I can…sense it. Have mercy on a guy that's had nothing but a shit life lately. Bring a little goodness into it."

Her face began to brighten with a slow smile. "You think I'm good."

I downed a long swallow of water, amazed by her sudden change. I'd apparently hit pay dirt. "Am I wrong?"

"Depends on your definition."

"Enlighten me." Yep, I lobbed her same sarcastic words right back at her.

Those expressive eyes flared a little wider. Then her chin

raised an inch. "My intentions are moral."

"And your actions?"

Her gaze hardened, eyes narrowing a fraction, as if thinking, assessing.

I stared calmly at her. *Trust cuts both ways.* No doubt she wondered how safe I was. And how much she needed to reveal to get what she wanted. *Back at ya, babe.*

She pursed her lips and gave a slight nod, decision made. "My actions behind your bar—no matter where it's at—*were* and *will be* moral, legal, ethical, and every other thing you need to keep your business safe."

Truth rang in her words.

Yet deception also lay somewhere under there.

I'd been around subterfuge enough to identify it like a hardwired lie detector. But I didn't want to push her. Not when she seemed ready to come onboard and protect what I'd created in the process.

Still, her about-face threw me.

"Why?" Why so cooperative? Why the sudden profession of loyalty?

"It's important to me." Her voice quieted, tone lowering. "The job. And…the charity."

A car passed, its headlights shining a flash across her eyes—that sparkled with moisture.

Tears? You definitely *have layers goin' on.*

"You're hired." Better lock that down while she remained agreeable, vulnerable.

"Not so fast. I'm not applying yet." Her expression hardened again.

"Of course, you aren't. Gotta put me through the wringer, I bet."

"Yep." She gave a clipped nod. "What's the pay?"

"Working every event that we've got scheduled for the next two months? About the same as your weekly take as Loading Zone."

"How many nights a week?"

"Two, on average. This week? Only the charity."

Her eyes widened. "*Damn.*"

"Invitation Only pays well. Their clients are some of the wealthiest on the East Coast."

Her gaze lowered to the sidewalk between us, flicking back and forth a little as if she furiously calculated. Calculating what? The pay? The odds?

Me and my motives?

Which are...what, exactly?

A fine mist began to swirl on a breeze. It coated her hair with infinitesimal droplets that sparkled in the pale moonlight.

While distracted, when not trying to battle the world, she looked gorgeous. Young, for sure. But maybe not as young as I'd first thought. The more we talked, the more convinced I became that the bravado and shrewdness of the girl who'd acted so tough behind my bar covered a sweet innocence, a great vulnerability she didn't want anyone to see.

Only she wasn't just a girl.

Everything about Shay demanded that she be recognized as an equal—and as a woman. Yet while she wielded her power, she seemed completely unaware of what lay beneath, of her rare beauty.

Which made her all the more attractive.

Yeah. Better ditch the vague *between us right now.*

"Things between us would be strictly professional." There. I'd laid down the law.

For both of us. For some reason, around her, I needed the reminder.

She glanced up in surprise before a hint of a smile returned. "Where's the fun in that?"

Was she serious? Flirting? Teasing? Or giving me a dose of my own medicine, trying to knock *me* off-balance. I went the safer route, assumed the latter. "You bustin' my balls?"

She paused, expressionless, then gave a slow nod. "Expect plenty of it."

"You sayin' we have a deal?"

"Yeah…" Her voice softened, as if amazed by her own agreement. "We have a deal." Then she shrugged. "No big. I'll tend bar at your charity event."

"*Events.*" One wouldn't be enough.

"One at a time." She crossed her arms, narrowed her eyes, defiance back in full force.

One, then. All she was willing to give? All I needed. For now. "Good. What's your cell phone? I'll text you the details."

"Don't have a cell phone."

"How can you *not* have a phone?"

"Easy." She spun around, sat on the edge of a brick planter, then lifted her feet up. She clicked the white heels of her faded black Converse together. "Need to protect my feet? Got shoes." She lifted her half-full water bottle and shook it, scattering droplets of condensation onto her jeans. "Thirst?

Water. Basic need. Got it."

She stretched her left hand over the sidewalk, her small empty palm facing up. She glanced at it with a nod. "Electronic leash? Nope. No got."

I scowled. "What if someone needs to get a hold of you?"

"They don't."

"Yeah, that's not gonna work for me."

She fisted that open palm. "Tough."

Yep. Tough. You *in a nutshell.*

I'd been so sure I had our situation under control. Problem? Solution. No phone? Get one.

But her smug expression? Meant no. And dared me to push the issue.

"Address..." *Where do you live?* I worried about the alley again, the dumpster with that cardboard stacked on its corner.

Her expression fell as uncertainty washed over her features. We'd stumbled back into her familiar skittish territory again.

Don't go there. Don't push her.

I stared up into the falling mist, wondering if all the trouble with Shay would be worth it. Would the warning signs she'd posted all along lead to a horrendous wreck...or a glorious ride?

Strictly professional. My words. Loading Zone's rules. The way it needed to be.

"Where and when?" Her sudden words broke into my distracted brain.

My gaze dropped to meet hers and I blinked. "What?"

"The *who* is me." She pointed to her chest and stood. "Think we got the *why* covered." Confidence hardened her expression again as she inched up her chin. "Got a great memory." She tapped her temple as she passed by me, heading back toward the park. "Tell me where and when we need to meet. I'll remember."

Nice sidestep to the whole "address" thing. But then, her particulars hadn't been my problem before tonight. And I got the message loud and clear they weren't any of my business now.

I followed her down the street again, then rounded a corner where she'd disappeared.

She'd already hopped up onto a curb, across the street.

"We need to do some training first," I called out as I jogged to catch up. "Monday, 3:00 p.m. On the corner of Lexington and Riverside: Urban Stroke."

She turned on a dime, nose scrunching in the most adorable way. "That a bar?"

I dug in my heels to avoid colliding right into her.

We stood bare inches apart. A light floral fragrance drifted up between us.

My voice softened, crackling a little. "No. A driving range."

"Ah." The stunned-speechless expression returned. A split second later, she spun around and skipped away from me again.

"Where you going?" I didn't want her to leave, wasn't ready for our sparring session to end.

She lifted her hands toward the misting sky and made

a lazy twirl into the center of the glistening street, like she rejoiced in the night, owned the city around us.

"To bed," she called out, her back toward me. The words barely hit my ears before she vanished through the trees at the edge of the park, into the darkness.

I stared at the empty space she'd just occupied.

Her direction? Angling toward where I'd found her—the alley, with cardboard lean-tos and overflowing dumpsters.

My gut clenched at the thought of her returning there to sleep for the night.

To bed. Her exact words echoed in my head. Not *to sleep.*

I prayed that *to bed* for Shay meant somewhere safe, her beautiful body and bright soul nestled down in clean sheets and on soft pillows.

Then...I wished I hadn't imagined her so vividly in bed.

7
TARGET PRACTICE

Shay…

"Golf."

Three days later, and I still couldn't get over it.

Ben and…*golf.* The two had failed to mesh well in my brain.

Because even after that office break-in last week, when I'd spied on the minimalist perfection of his desk and giant photographs of him at faraway places—including an exotic green perched on a cliff with its ocean backdrop—I still struggled to picture the Ben I knew actually *on* a golf green.

From the couple of hours I'd spent with him Friday night? *Nope.*

The man had been too rugged, rough around the edges. Dark-brown hair had tumbled in wild pieces over his forehead. A firm jawline had rebelled with its dense scruff of beard. Black brows had slashed over penetrating charcoal eyes. Faded blue jeans? The broken-in kind, threadbare from years of abuse but still holding strong. His black T-shirt? An unusual short V-neck that'd hinted at a smattering of chest hair; its thin material had stretched over sizeable biceps and hiked-up long sleeves had revealed a thick tribal tattoo that encircled his right forearm.

And his behavior at the club? Those barely restrained emotions?

Had been far from civilized. Primal, even.

Not remotely close to...*golf.*

But he'd reined it all in, Businessman Ben. He'd sought to right his wrong: had chased me down, groveled even (as far as a man like him could.)

And when he'd scoffed at my not having a phone? Had dismissed the issue in a heartbeat with his *Yeah, that's not gonna work for me* attitude? He'd seemed so sure of himself; his expression had broadcasted *problem solved.*

The expression that I'd fired back had said *too bad, not my problem,* and *you sure about that?* all with my easy smile.

His confidence had faltered.

Good. Because that man bulldozing over me? Never gonna happen again.

But then...*golf.*

Three days later, we strolled side by side down a walkway along a curving row of stalls. Each numbered area housed a gleaming metal machine, a polished wood bench, and had been carpeted in bright-green fake turf. Five stories high the structure went, creating a coliseum of golf-obsessed insanity. Nearly every slot held a golfer who swung away onto a field littered with balls, each oblivious with how ridiculous they all looked, how comical the whole scene was.

"Yep." Ben swung up the single club he carried to rest on his shoulder, mimicking me. "Golf."

I stared at him, trying to make sense of what he wore now: lime-green collared shirt with tiny indentations in the fabric, lime-green-and-black plaid shorts, black-and-white wing tip golf shoes.

Plus…the hat. "Does it have to be *so* white?"

"What?" He glanced down at me, expression innocent, clueless.

"Your hat. It's hurting my eyes." I held up a hand to block the glare.

"Wear sunglasses." He took off his tortoiseshell pair, then held them out to me.

I narrowed my eyes, refusing to take them.

"Or don't look." His mouth twitched into a slight smirk.

Smug bastard; he had to know how good he looked. Black suited him better, no doubt. But the white set off the subtle tan he had, softened his dark features. The visual contrast mimicked the man. Like from the outside in, he'd become a mysterious contradiction.

Which made some crazy part of me want to solve him.

I sighed at what the man did to me by just existing, grabbed his damn sunglasses, and slid them on. Better than him seeing my eyes. The way he searched them when we squared off, like *I'd* become the mystery he wanted to solve, unnerved me.

And the one thing I hated more than anything else? Feeling out of control.

"What?" He'd caught me staring again.

"Sorry. The sunglasses aren't helping." I handed them back. "Your clothes don't fit who you are."

With raised brows, he glanced down at the lime catastrophe he wore as he clipped the sunglasses onto the collar of his shirt. "Who am I?"

I stared at his tribal tattoo. The dark cuff that'd peeked out from under his long-sleeved tee a few days ago now spread over a chiseled forearm, wove around insane biceps, then disappeared under a pastel layer of deception. "Wolfish."

He glanced back up at me, tilting his head a bit. "And what am I dressed like? A sheep?"

"More like Bo Peep."

His stare held mine. That whole *reading-me* thing lasered between us again, only I scorched back at him a *reading you too*.

Then his smoldering gaze upped the contest: *I'm picturing you in a sunny wildflower meadow, wearing low-cut pastel ruffles.*

But I lost the battle with a sharp inhale, eyes widening, as my body reacted to all the heat he blazed my way. I wondered if he read me true: *All I see is hungry wolf.*

He had the decency to fight a smile before he continued walking. He also hadn't taken any jabs at the clothes I wore, the same ones I'd had on the other night, basic tee, old jeans, battered Converse. While staring at his back as he passed the next stall then another, I took two deep breaths to slow my racing heart, then jogged after him to catch up.

"Number twenty-nine. This is us." He planted the black

duffel bag he'd been carrying onto a bench, then zipped it open. "You right-handed or left?"

Back to business. As if we hadn't just caused a near meltdown seconds ago.

"Right."

He fished around inside the bag, then pulled out a white leather glove, still in its packaging, in my size: *Women's Small.*

"Just happened to have a glove for me layin' around?"

"Borrowed." With a loud crackle, he broke open the hard plastic, then held the pristine glove out.

"Ah." I didn't take it. Instead, I stared at him, mystery hunting. "Lots of country-club friends?"

"Yeah…" He dropped the lonely glove onto my side of the bench, hesitation in his tone unmistakable. "You could say that."

I didn't pry. No point shining a light on his secrets. I had plenty of my own I wanted left in the dark.

"So, if I've gotta be out here, with you wearing that" —I gestured my hand up and down at his bright-white-and-green get-up— "let's do this and get it over with." I dropped my backpack onto the bench.

Then I pulled the seven-iron loaner the check-in desk had given me off my shoulder, pointed the end straight toward an enormous green field speckled with white balls, then drew back and swung forward at chest height, pretending the thing was a baseball bat.

On my second bat swing, at the end of my arc, he stepped in front of me, grabbed the clubhead with his large hand, and stared hard at me. "*Serious*, Shay. I need you serious. You goof around and someone's gonna get hurt."

"Says the guy standing in my crosshairs."

His jaw clenched. "You here to learn or talk shit?"

"Learn," I grumbled. "Gee. You had your coffee today?" The man needed to chill. "And why exactly am I learning to golf?" I planted the club and leaned on it. "Thought I was tending bar."

"You're serving drinks to golfers. Helps if you know their world."

You mean your *world.*

He pulled his club off the bench. "Now focus. This is a typical grip on the shaft."

Grip. Shaft. My thoughts instantly guttered, and I swallowed hard.

Focus. His directive held great wisdom. *Get* out *of your head.*

"This *V* between your thumb and index finger aims down the shaft." His gloved right hand hugged the black leather grip. "Your other hand wraps around it, not too tight, but nice and snug."

Seriously? Do you hear how it all sounds? The amusement echoed in my head, but I said nothing. No chance in hell would I open that Pandora's Box with him out loud. Subject off-limits.

Strictly professional. More Ben wisdom-words echoed in my head.

"Now, put your glove on and you try." He nodded to my club.

"The grip or the swing?"

"Both."

I put my club down and swiped up the glove.

"Goes on your left hand."

Opposite of his. "I know. I've got eyes." Apparently, the glove protected the non-dominant hand. I slid my fingers into the soft leather glove. The fit was snug across the back of my hand, but the material stretched with ease as I fastened the Velcro to cinch it up.

His brow furrowed when he realized what I'd admitted. "You know I'm left-handed?"

I shrugged, brushing my observation off. "I know a lot of things about you, Ben Bishop."

"Yeah?" The corners of his lips twitched, and he crossed his arms. "Like what?"

Do not *notice the sexy cuts of his biceps.* Focus *on that ridiculous lime-green shirt.*

"You think you have everything together in life. But you don't. In fact..." I took a hard look at him, thought about every little thing I'd noticed, his neat-freak office, the way he'd fired me with such reckless fury, then how quickly he'd hunted me down to apologize. Guilt ran deep in him. All that perfection? A ruse—overcompensation for something very imperfect in his life. "Your life is fucked up, same as mine." Our similarities resonated with me deeply: the same plight of frustration, fiercer determination because of it. I tilted my head, longshotting a sudden suspicion as I watched his hands start to fist. I began to smile. *The mystery of Ben, unraveling.* "Maybe even more fucked up than mine. If I had to guess, I've hit *real* close to home. Literally. Because all the worst mind-fuckery begins there."

He sucked in a sharp breath at my last words, as if in surprise that I'd read him so well. His expression darkened, brows lowering in protection, even as his eyes softened then searched mine, trying to do more of his reading-me thing.

"Stop." I narrowed my eyes, blocking the unwanted return analysis as I pointed my seven iron at him. "I'm not yours to be dissected. If you're making me be out here with all these pansies swinging away at tiny little balls, then let's get this thing over with."

"I'm not making you do anything." Challenge edged his tone.

I stared at him a long beat, then sighed. "Fine. But for the record, if anyone asks, I came to see you in that outfit. Whacking the hell out of tiny balls? Pure bonus."

He said nothing. Just stared at me.

Good. You knock me off-balance? I send you reeling.

"Okay." *Focus.* I tried to place my hands on the club like he had. Left gloved hand, *V* between finger and thumb pointing down. Right hand covering the first. "How's this?"

"Good. Only move your other hand like" —the heat of his body suddenly wrapped around me from behind— "this."

I flinched at the unexpected contact, the heat of his chest curving against my back. But I took a deep breath, forcing myself to banish knee-jerk panic, as his broad shoulders bracketed mine. Logic told me he believed directing by touch was the best way to teach.

Maybe. Couldn't he direct me verbally? From five feet away?

But another thought crowded in as his muscular biceps, forearms, and hands all made gentle contact, his incredible warmth seeping into my skin as he showed me where he wanted my hand. Maybe he'd *wanted* to touch me, even though it hadn't been necessary. Seconds ticked by, neither of us saying a word.

He kept our close contact.

I adjusted my grip.

And while he cocooned me, innocent or not, the heat from our connection spread: a slow advance, lower—deeper.

"Perfect." His word whispered over the shell of my ear.

A shiver rippled down my spine as I wondered if he spoke the truth. Each from very different imperfect worlds, we'd been battered. Did the two of us together make us whole?

Are we *perfect? Are you the one I've been waiting all this time for?*

8
SWEET SPOT

Ben...

Don't move.
    Shay? Me?
    Both.

I closed my eyes. Some bone-headed instinct had me wrap myself around her. And I didn't want to let go.

The prickly woman got under my skin.

What shocked the hell out of me? I liked her there.

I tightened my hands over hers, pressed my chest to her back, and tried to act like my moves were all about golf. Not sure who I'd fooled. Not me. And by the way she had tensed for that split second? Not her either.

I tried to figure out the next move, but my head fogged as her subtle fragrance hit me. Something floral, maybe.

Then all of a sudden, she shook me off. "Give me room. The grip *and* the swing," she reminded, back on task.

Decision made. By her.

One of us sure as hell needed to keep us on track. *Strictly professional.*

Her gaze traveled down the sweeping inside curve of the driving range, to the other golfers swinging away. "Not even gonna show me how it's done?"

"Nope." I took a couple of steps back and folded my arms over my chest, watching carefully. "No point in teaching something that comes naturally. Some are born with it. Let's see what you've got."

"Okay." She lined up sideways, then wiggled her ass.

A sexy little ass, hugged by soft-looking denim.

Eye on the ball. *Watch her swing.*

After a glance out toward the horizon, gaze dropped again down over the ball, then a single deep breath, she arced the club back, then swung forward—with spectacular timing and a flawless follow through.

I narrowed my eyes. "You golfed before?"

She remained frozen in position for a long moment, club still high on her opposite shoulder, body twisted, facing out toward wide blue sky where her ball had soared before disappearing. Then, with a short laugh, she untwisted to look at me. She planted her club on the turf and leaned on it. "Why would you think that?"

"*That* was a great swing."

She shrugged. "Guess I'm a natural."

Didn't answer my question. And her closed expression? The shrug? Reminded me of how she'd acted back behind my bar that first night. Warning bells went off in my head. She had deception written all over her.

But I ignored the warnings. *Who gives a shit?* It's golf.

"Perfect cadence." Like a seasoned pro.

"Cadence?"

"Sure." I grabbed the seven iron I'd brought, like hers, to demonstrate. "An ideal swing carries a cadence with it, great timing delivers the maximum amount of power from your shoulder torque, through the swing, and into the clubhead on impact."

"Uh-huh." The blank look on her face almost made me laugh.

"Watch." When I stepped closer, she gave me a wide berth—wider than necessary. I blew out a calming breath, relieved to know I wasn't the only one still affected by that hands-on-instruction stunt I'd pulled without thinking.

She watched me from the far back corner, clear self-preservation instincts in play now.

Better for both of us. Keep it all business.

"The perfect swing rhythm has a three-to-one ratio in its tempo." After a slight in-and-out quiver of my clubhead in front of the teed-up ball, I arced the club back and slow-counted aloud to demonstrate. "*One...two...three*" —the windup stretched through my body as I twisted the club up over my left shoulder— "*one,*" I called on the exhale as I powered through the down stroke. The clubhead hit the ball with a satisfying ping and launched the ball in a high classic arc to hit the turf at about two hundred and fifty yards.

"Wow." She put her hand over her brow, watching where the ball landed. "That swing was so slow. But look how far the ball went."

"Speed has nothing to do with it. The power is in the rhythm."

"And that tinny musical sound..."

I nodded. "The ping. Means I hit the sweet spot. What happens when what we aim for is struck pure and true."

For a long beat, she stared hard at me.

Then with a scooting wave of her hand, she signaled me out of her way. "My turn again. And I'll say out loud what I'm thinking during my swing."

Amused by her smartass tone, I happily complied and stepped back to the far corner, her designated safety zone.

The second time around, she followed her same pre-swing ritual. Same ass-wiggle. Same horizon-glance. Same ball-gaze. All at the same speed. But when she moved the club, she spoke aloud her three-to-one ratio. "*Yeaaah...two... three...whatever.*"

"As in, you're not taking this seriously?"

"Ping." She pointed out with a nod toward the sky where her soaring ball had disappeared, again. "*Annd*...as in, if I don't get invested, I don't get disappointed."

Touché. "Would you take it *somewhat* seriously?"

Her golf swing? Knocked it out of the park.

If only I could get her attitude there, get her to believe just a little. "I promise not to let you down." The very least I could do. If she gave working for me her all, I'd back her all the way.

Her steady gaze held mine for long seconds. Like even though she'd heard my words, she searched my soul for hidden subtext.

Apparently satisfied with her mental pat-down, she gave me a slight nod. "Yeah, I could do that. *Somewhat* seriously."

"Not *substantially* seriously."

"Nope." She gave me a headshake before stepping up to the ball again. After another little ass-wiggle, she lined up her club then fired off another one of her textbook shots. "That's your problem." She held her follow-through position, watching another ball soar.

"My problem?" *This oughta be good.*

She unwound, then pegged me with a hard stare. "You're too serious."

"Too serious?"

"Yep. Could be fatal." Her stomach growled. Then she scanned the grounds, tracking back toward the entrance. "Speaking of, they got any grub at this place? I'm starving."

"Up top." I pointed my club up toward the range's cantilevered restaurant. "Casual pub. New York-style pizza, Texas-sized burgers, Chicago dogs."

"Works for me."

While she still stared up toward the restaurant, I quickly dropped something I'd brought for her into her backpack.

But when I glanced up, her gaze landed right on me.

Busted.

Yet her expression remained neutral.

Maybe I was fast enough. I went with that thought. Casual. *Nothing happened.*

I picked up right where she'd left off as I grabbed my club and bag, then stepped out of the stall and onto the sidewalk. "*Fatally* serious?"

"Sure." She appeared beside me, backpack slung on one shoulder, club perched on her other. Just like before. Maybe not busted after all. She gave a cool shrug. "Heart attack. Stroke. Aneurysm."

We walked at an easy pace, talking about medical devastation as if it was a weather forecast. "Sounds dire."

She punched the elevator button with her thumb and the doors immediately opened. "It is," she continued as we stepped in. "Death by self-inflicted wounds." The numbers illuminated as we ascended. "That's the problem with grown-ups. They forget how to live. Become fatalistic."

The elevator doors reopened as her words sank in.

Shay left me behind, stepping up to a hostess at the pub's front podium.

I caught up and followed them to an empty four-top by the window.

"Enjoy your meal." The hostess left our menus on the polished wooden table.

As if anything could be appetizing while talking about death-by-seriousness.

"You talk about grown-ups like they're a separate class. Sure you don't want to confess? Still in high school, acting like a 'grown-up'?"

"*Not* in high school. Nothing to confess. And I hope I *never* act like a grown-up."

Fair enough. And don't we all. Yet apparently, I'd been failing miserably. Seriously. *Fatally.*

What I wouldn't give to be able to let go. Not give a damn, even if it was only some of the time. *Can you show me the way?*

"Am I incurable?"

"Remains to be seen."

Our server showed up. Shay never even glanced at the menu. "I'll have a slice, a burger, a dog, and a Coke."

"Death-by-seriousness is no match for cardiac-on-a-plate."

Shay grinned, unapologetic.

I handed both of our menus to the server. "Same."

"Ha! I'm converting you."

Maybe. "Hardly."

"Today, food." She shot me a pointed look, brows raised, then gave a slight nod. "Tomorrow? Lighthearted. Happy-go-lucky. Not a care in the world."

I folded my arms, leaning back in the booth, liking the fearless confidence in her.

"I could save you." She drummed trim fingernails once on the table.

Bet you could. "What would your prescription be?"

"*Lighten up* all that seriousness. Live a little. If you're gonna die anyway—

"—and all of us are at one point or another," I interjected as I grabbed my Coke the second our server planted it in front of me.

"—might as well have some fun in between," she finished with a nod, then took several long pulls of Coke through her straw.

We sat silent for a few moments as we both stared out the window at the dramatic view. The glistening blue of the Schuylkill River snaked through belts of green as it flowed toward a nest of shining metal skyscrapers in the distance.

But Shay didn't seem interested in the river or where it led. She stared with great focus at a large swath of forest to the north, lost in thought, expression stone-cold...serious.

"Serious can't be fun?"

She shot me a deadpan look. "Not usually."

I made no comment that she'd gone there herself.

"Well, since you made the prognosis, what are the details of that prescription?"

"You tell me. Let's start with why you fired me."

Whoa. *And the barbs fly.* But I realized why she'd flung that one. The underlying reason of my rage that night—which she had no clue about—had been very serious. That damn clusterfuck had consumed two wasted weeks. The root cause of which had shadowed my entire life. But I'd become successful in spite of it. *Way* too serious for a discussion over lunch.

Evade and deflect: toss it back at her. "You know why." The reason I'd given the other night would have to be enough.

Our food came, three plates apiece. Grease glistened across a giant pepperoni slice. A browned pretzel-bun capped a mountain of fresh toppings that teetered on a thick burger, all of which had been surrounded by crispy thin fries. And buried under chopped pickles and onions, a fat hot dog drizzled with mustard stretched off both ends of a toasted bun.

The server, Janice by her nametag, gawked at the enormous buffet. "If you finish all that food, the fudge brownie's on me."

Shay dug in, apparently up for the challenge.

Once she swallowed her first gargantuan bite of dog, she stared hard at me, then veered back toward the conversation: why I'd fired her. "Because you're an ass?"

"Hey, I apologized for that." Not a proud moment.

"Doesn't change the fact."

I gave her a nod. I *had* been an ass.

"But what's the real reason?"

Well, fuck. I sighed. *Guess you're not gonna let it go.*

With no roadmap to rely on, I scoured my brain to find a detour.

More evasion, a shitload more deflection. "No way you could have been old enough."

"Wrong." Not even a glance my way with the accusation. Simply folded her double-sized slice and stuffed an impressive amount of it into her mouth.

I didn't bother to keep up with the food shoveling. After I polished off my burger, I let the rest sit, more interested in our banter, in learning more about what made her tick.

"So you keep saying. Without proof." *Oh, yeah. I went there.* Better to shine a giant spotlight on her than have it glare on me.

"Not my point." Her pizza had vanished. She smashed the big burger down, then lifted. "Your stupid assumption wasn't the cause. It was the symptom."

Damn. She knew how to dance. Maybe better than me. I folded my arms, sweating under the heat of that spotlight she'd spun around and blasted my way.

She ignored my closed-off posture—or got spurred on

by it—and dialed it up a notch. "What does me being old enough, or not, have to do with *your* actions?"

But I didn't take the bait. No underlying cause was getting revealed. Face value, as far as I was willing to go. Her age, the topic.

"If I've got someone underage behind the bar, then I'm breaking the law."

"Bingo."

I blinked, totally lost. "What?"

"Too serious."

Ah, full circle.

And a whole lot safer than where we'd been headed.

"What? Because I want to be careful with Loading Zone? Because I want to stay open for business? Well, if that makes me too serious, then I guess I am."

"Haven't you ever broken the law before?"

I stared out beyond her, toward those distant skyscrapers, searching my brain. In case I'd forgotten some small thing, a repressed memory, as if I'd find a different answer than the one we both knew to be true. But not even a stolen pack of gum came to mind.

I landed a confident gaze squarely back on her. "No."

"Not even a traffic ticket, no speeding, no improper parking?"

I tipped my head down, angling a little closer to her as I lowered my voice, "Don't have a jaywalking wrap, either."

She didn't seem surprised. But her expression darkened.

You're disappointed?

And why did that suddenly deflate me?

The uncompromising guy that had fired her? Lived and breathed right over wrong. Laws were to be followed, without question. I'd found comfort over the years in that rigidity. Being on the right side meant I stayed safe. Bad things happened when laws were broken: prison time, lives destroyed.

I'd suspected she lived on the streets. Maybe her code followed a different set of rules.

And with the sleight of hand she'd pulled the other night, the "accidental" bump into the wealthy businessman—yeah, I'd seen Tony's once-empty tip jar magically flush with cash—I had no doubt she'd broken plenty of laws.

Big difference between her and me. *Maybe too big.*

She popped one of her last remaining fries into her mouth. "Like I said, fatal. Life is meant to be lived. You should step out of your black-and-white box to enjoy it once in a while."

"What about you?"

"I'm not stuck in a suffocating world of laws made by people who stand to benefit the most from them." Conviction flashed in her eyes. "It's easier to know the truth, be real and free. But you have to open your eyes and see the beauty in the gray."

Not an admission. But while she was baring her soul, I bet I'd get one.

"I meant your law question, back atcha."

I jabbed a crispy fry into my mouth right as Janice glided by. With wide eyes, she took in the demolition on Shay's three plates, then panned to the one empty space on mine.

She wisely said nothing, just slipped us our check and took my American Express card.

"I don't own a car."

Smartass. Not what I meant. And by the spark in her eye, I knew she knew that.

Still, there were argument grounds along that thread. "Don't need to own one to drive one." Every lie-detector sense I had screamed that she was hiding something. *Grand theft auto?*

Her eyes searched mine, assessing, calculating. "No traffic tickets of any kind."

So...a *careful* thief.

One who took my measure and found me lacking.

But I wanted to know her truth, ugly or not. And I wanted Shay to feel safe in telling me. After the bad way I'd handled the situation when I'd fired her, I owed her that much. She needed to know I wouldn't judge. She could confess, no repercussions.

I took a deep breath. *Here goes nothing.*

"Have you ever broken the law?"

Her steady gaze held mine. Nothing was said as her eyes hardened in defiance, then softened, as if impressed. "Define law."

"*Any* law." Let's start there.

"Yes."

"More than once?"

"Yes." No twitch. No hesitation.

"Big laws, small laws?"

She cocked her head in thought. "Define big."

Tricky. Big to me might be no big deal to her. "Misdemeanor?"

"Yes."

"Felony?"

She stared hard at me. "Maybe..."

Okay. So many places to go with that. But her tone? Bold warning sign I'd just stepped onto thin ice. "Stealing?" Safer. What I already thought I knew. Which she probably knew too.

"Yes." She dipped a nod my way.

Suspected and confirmed.

"Breaking and entering?"

"Yes."

Interesting. Cat burglar? "Often?"

"Define often."

"Daily?"

Her eyes softened further, the corners of her lips twitched in an almost smile. "Sometimes."

Whatever thought I'd just triggered brought her joy... peace, maybe.

Then a stab of worry hit me. I didn't know her well. And that *define* thing went both ways. Had she ever been armed? Knives? Guns? "Have you ever hurt anyone?"

"Never."

Janice interrupted our rapid-fire Q-and-A session with our receipt. I tipped her heavily, scrawled my signature, then handed it right back to her.

With Shay talking so honestly for the first time, I wanted to finish what we'd started.

But she'd folded her cloth napkin over her plates, expression closed again, already done.

She stood and offered me her borrowed seven iron that had been balanced against the wall. "I'd love to stay for twenty questions, but ten's my limit." Her mood had shifted on a dime from lighthearted teasing to wary, guarded.

I took the club, noting the resignation in her voice. "We're not done here."

"Aren't we?"

"Not by a long shot."

"So, all of that" —she gestured a wild circling hand over the table as if the confessed words still hung there in the air— "didn't scare you off?"

"Nope." Scary, yeah. But not scared off.

Curious, more than anything.

What would it have taken for her to go to those lengths? I had so many questions. Did she live on the streets? How long had she been breaking the law? All alone? Would she stop if given the opportunity? Could a job make her give it up?

"Okay," she said.

That one word held a mountain of hesitation. And in the handful of seconds since she'd handed me the club, her eyes had flicked toward the exit door. Twice.

Maybe I'd pushed her too far.

Maybe she'd decided to be done with me.

I plowed ahead before she bolted from me. Again. "The golf scramble's at Glenhaven Country Club. Wednesday, 9:00 a.m." With a quick scan of her same-as-before T-shirt, jeans, and battered Converse, I frowned. My worried stare got stuck on those faded shoes. "Do you have anything else to wear?"

That sounded bad. Like I thought those were her only clothes. But hell, what did I know?

"Yeah." Amusement sparked in her eyes. She gave me a once-over and her nose wrinkled. "But nothing as *Bo Peep* as you."

Ha! There *you are.*

Fling those sharp barbs, tease me mercilessly.

I preferred the fierce girl who gave me shit than the wary thief looking for an escape hatch.

"Got it. No light green or bright white in your closet." If she even had an actual closet. But my gaze fell to her no-collar threadbare T-shirt: a V-neck that hinted at very nice cleavage—which I'd valiantly ignored all through lunch. Definitely not standard golf-course attire. She'd get booted off our club's course for sure.

While she lifted her backpack from the corner of her chair, she lightly bounced it once on her fingertips, as if weighing it. The top zipper gaped open a few inches, and she stared hard into its dark void. Then her eyes scanned lower, as if she had X-ray vision.

Distract her! Piss her off if you have to. "Still, I'd like you to show up a few minutes early. Stop at the pro shop, and I'll make sure they've got clothes and shoes there for you." I punched the words with plenty of command.

She pulled in a deep breath as the backpack-stare continued. "I don't need your handouts."

"Not a handout."

Her jaw clenched. "My clothes aren't good enough?" Her gaze raked my way, a single brow arched in silent outrage.

Good. Be mad at me now. Get backpack-*mad later.*

"Didn't say they weren't." Not a damn thing wrong with her comfortable clothes. They fit her body like they'd been custom made for her: worn fibers that softened her hidden sharp edges. "But country clubs and golf courses are strict. Collars. No denim. Proper shoes."

Her breaths grew more rapid with my every word.

I had no idea what had ratcheted up her freak-out: my voice, golf clothes, or the country-club world itself. But I got the sense we'd blown way past her glancing at the exit and teetered a split second away from her sprinting toward it.

"Consider it a work uniform," I blurted. A last-ditch attempt to sweeten the olive branch. "Part severance pay, part investment from me into your bartending future."

She said nothing. Just glared at me one more beat. Then she turned and walked away. Head held high. Cool attitude.

I stared at her retreating back for the second time inside a week.

Had I played it right? Or wrong...again?

"So, I'll see you Wednesday?" Didn't bother to hide the tone of doubt, or hope.

Her lazy gait slowed, then she paused and half-glanced over her shoulder. "We'll see."

9
SAFE PLAY

Shay...

Dusk intensified the shadows surrounding the homes in the affluent neighborhood.

Each passing second made it darker.

Every slow breath brought me closer.

Most times, I made a game out of it. How long could I make out fine details like sidewalk cracks or address numbers?

My backpack shifted off of my shoulder. I thumbed the slim strap and hiked it back into place. Jaw clenched, I forced myself to ignore its half pound of added weight. And the implications of that.

Ben thought he'd been covert at the driving range. Never mind that I'd turned to see his hand pulling away from my bag. Or that his widened eyes, flushed cheeks, and held breath had plastered guilt all over him.

LAWBREAKER

Lights inside the luxury home went dark. I stared with spiked alertness from the bushes. The massive front door opened, then was closed, locked from the outside, and double-checked.

I waited for the sensible blue Outback to drive away.

Until the coast was clear.

Like I'd done a thousand nights before.

Only the thousand-and-first time felt different somehow. Nervous energy hummed through me instead of my routine composure.

Random thoughts kept flashing back to Ben, the heat of his touch, the danger there. Not just from the raw sexuality I'd long ago convinced myself never to want, but also the security there, the promise of safety, like he was both the raging storm and the soothing calm.

Too many contradictions.

A smart girl would run away from temptation like that.

Only...*I don't want to.*

Different from any man I'd encountered, something deep inside of him called to me on an elemental level. Shoving the realization out of my brain did no good. Denial? An idiot's game. Because lying to myself only hurt me in the end.

We were the same in ways I didn't fully understand: I felt it to my bones.

And it pissed me off.

I blew out a head-clearing breath, then checked my internal clock. About four minutes had passed, plenty of time for my way to be clear.

Flushing myself out from my hiding spot, I casually

strolled over the grassy landscape to the meandering sidewalk, owning the territory like I belonged there. Dim blue glows from solar lights lit my way. Any nosy neighbor would think the Outback driver had returned; we had the same dark shoulder-length hair (no accident). Plus, a manicured hedge obscured most of the driveway.

The front door was shrouded in darkness: Last week I'd unscrewed the porchlight just past the point of going dark. By feel and instinct, I knelt in front of the lock, inserted my two favorite metal pins, and picked the mechanism with cool efficiency.

Piece o' cake.

Hadn't always been. The first months had been grueling trial and error. But what had been the premise of *Outliers*? (Yes, I read. From the Underrated Library of Nightstand Finds.) *If a person performs a task more than ten thousand times, they master it.* Eight years of nightly lockpicking, plus multiple times a day for jobs and practice…and challenge to cut through the boredom? I'd more than earned my mastery.

Besides, there were other challenges to consider.

As I opened the door, a natural security system bounded into the marble-tiled entry. But instead of baring teeth, a tail wagged. Clipped nails clicked repeatedly on the floor.

"Bruno!" I dropped my backpack on the entry table, squatted down, and wrapped my arms around his big brown-and-white furry neck. "Who's a good boy?" Not for his watchdog stealth, for sure. But definitely for watching over me.

For the last six consecutive nights, the loveable St. Bernard had kept me company. Starting this coming Wednesday, Phyllis Dover's green-eyed Abyssinian, Chesterfield, would stalk a nocturnal feline watch, guarding his usual territory plus me. When I needed a serious chill, and scheduling permitted, I chose the saltwater reef occupants in the modern estate on Third Street.

No, I didn't pet-sit or house-sit. Not on any official basis.

I "borrowed" spaces: watched over others' little ones on a voluntary basis. My fee? A hot shower, soft towels, warm bed, and two square meals a day. No, I didn't barbecue up steak or raid the caviar. Whole eggs have a complete protein profile. Salad greens wouldn't have lasted the week anyway. And any self-respecting official house sitter should watch over all aspects of the house. *I call dibs on the refrigerator.* With a smile, I collected a few additional ingredients in quantities too small to miss or raise an owner's eyebrow.

Mouthwatering aromas soon filled the kitchen as I sautéed shallots with chopped garlic before pouring in two scrambled eggs as I whipped up an omelet: a handful of Thai basil leaves snipped from a windowsill herb, three paper-thin slices of fragrant Parmigiano Reggiano, a quick flip of one half with a fork. Then I slid my dinner masterpiece onto a flat bone-china dinner plate.

"C'mon, Bruno." I switched off the overhead stove light, dousing the dimly lit kitchen into complete darkness, then padded barefoot across cold tile to looped carpet. The hundred-fifty-pound dog happily followed, knowing he'd get a choice bite of our dinner.

My laptop already glowed its floating screensaver from

the center of the master's king-sized bed. The screen's Night Shift cast an amber hue onto the pristine white duvet. With practiced care, I settled in front it, making certain not to leave even one droplet of olive oil as evidence anyone had been there.

Bruno rested his chin on my thigh. He directed a raised eyebrow my way after every slow bite. He waited, knowing that I savored them. And he'd been well fed only an hour ago by his paid patron. That's what I loved about Bruno. He was patient, loyal, and protective, making sure I got fed too.

That's what I loved about all of my animal friends in their hijacked lodgings. They knew I wasn't supposed to be in their domain. But they accepted me as if I belonged, just the same. Quietly. And with loving appreciation.

I rubbed behind Bruno's velvety ear as I scrolled through the pet-watcher's schedule—hacked into years ago by *Outlier*-me (thanks for the skills, Rafe).

Phyllis Dover had confirmed for Chesterfield, giving me a place to lay my head and a trusted companion for the next handful of days. How I rolled: in the moment, one step at a time.

Hope-filled bubbles didn't get burst that way. Hard to be disappointed when you didn't count on much.

Pinching off the last corner of the cheesy-egg dinner, I moved off the bed. Bruno obediently followed, watchful gaze on his prize hovering over the plate. He sat in front of the kitchen sink until I held it out in front of him. The lovable beast gently snarfed the bite-sized treat, moistening my hand with his soft muzzle.

"Good boy, Bruno." My heart warmed as I gave him a full head rub.

Sometimes the best love is the simplest. Minimal expectation. Maximum gratitude.

After washing, drying, and stowing the dish by my dependable stove light, I switched the light off again. Then I did a routine visual and audible sweep to verify that all remained dark and uneventful, including neighboring houses visible through the windows.

Satisfied I was safe and alone, I headed to go shower before bed.

By the time I toweled my hair dry, my thoughts spiraled again to the newest additions to my tightly controlled world.

Ben *and* what he'd added into my backpack.

Bruno had taken up his sentry post at the threshold of the bedroom, already peacefully hunkered down for the night.

From my larger duffel that I'd hidden under the bed on my first night, I tugged out a clean black T-shirt and pair of boy-short underwear and got dressed. Then I stowed my laptop away in the bag and shoved it all back under the bed, out of sight.

I sat on the bed and tucked my legs under the sheet and blanket.

My small backpack sat innocently on the nightstand.

As if it felt the weight of my stare, an electronic sound *bleedled* out from inside.

I ignored the sound, remained motionless.

Ben thought he'd been sneaky. He'd been wrong.

Some "guy" directive programed into his DNA made him think he could exert control.

Wrong there too.

I decided what governed me. If I wanted some damn phone, I'd have gotten one.

The other items in my backpack were special to me. Sacred. They'd come from my past. They'd become talismans as I'd wandered on my journey, protecting me.

The newer item bulged out a portion of the bottom left corner, anchoring the bag with its weight. When I reached for the bag, I continued to ignore it.

Instead, one at a time, I identified each of my most prized possessions. When my fingertips glided over silky fabric, I pulled out a white satin elbow-length glove, then arranged it along the front edge of the nightstand, smoothing out its wrinkles. With a metallic click, the antique silver coin, weathered with a dark patina, took its station near the open palm of the glove. My turn with an ancient tin of lip gloss came next: eyes closed, lid opened, deep inhale...*strawberries and cream.*

Another *bleedle* sounded from the bag.

But I'd already wrapped my fingers around the fourth and last item, the most important, the one that had come exactly one year after the others. Then, it'd been both a first anniversary and a twelfth birthday present, from and to myself. Stolen from the same place. Earned as my reward for all the hardship I'd endured. Coveted, then taken. Revenge and payment.

And protection.

LAWBREAKER

With a flick of my thumb on its centered stud, I opened the well-balanced AL MAR, a superior tactical knife that had been made in Japan in a thousand-year-old sword-making factory. The blade made a satisfying click and gleamed under the lamplight. Its black stamped-rubber grip balanced on my palm. The solid weight felt right in my hand.

Supposedly, the folding blade had been made in the early 1990's; my entitled family member had been vague. He'd forbidden me to touch it, hidden it away when all I'd wanted to do was to look at it. "It was *his*," he'd said.

Oh, yeah?

Mine now.

Only thing I'd ever stolen out of vengeance. Only thing I ever would.

Not that I planned to use the weapon. Plenty of other ways to incapacitate a person without the mess of blood. The human body had vital airways to obstruct, sensitive nerve centers to exploit.

Grow up on the streets? Learn fast how to defend yourself.

Rafe had taught me well. Bear had seen to it.

My backpack *bleedled* a third time; the newcomer fought to be recognized.

Fine.

Taking care with the knife, I depressed its release latch and secured its razor edge, breathing nice and steady. By nightly ritual, I positioned the knife between me and the silken glove, the antique coin, and the gloss tin, lining it up with the near edge of the table, folded blade tucked away, but at the ready.

I didn't plan to use it. But that didn't mean I wouldn't.

Anyone dumb enough to square off with Bruno would have me to answer to.

A fourth *bleedle* sounded as I reached inside.

"Really?" And Ben had seemed shocked that I wanted nothing to do with a phone.

My fingers wrapped around a rectangular object. Its surface felt...studded?

When I pulled it out, I blinked. Heavily.

Then I scowled.

The thing was sparkly. And pink. *Bright* pink.

Its illuminated screen went dark.

When I clicked the center button, it flashed on again, a screen of icons appearing.

I switched off the bedside lamp and settled under the covers, examining the device. I'd seen people using them before, just hadn't ever held one myself. Never saw the point in becoming a slave to technology.

A green box with a white convo bubble had a red *4* in its upper corner.

I touched the *Messages* icon with my fingertip.

A stream of gray message bubbles appeared. I read them top to bottom, oldest to newest.

So...
Welcome to your phone.

Not my *phone.*
Yes.

No.

Yes. (I can hear you saying no while you read this.)

"Can you see me too?" I hefted the weight of the phone in my hand, gauging how far I could make it fly.

The phone vibrated as I held it. Guess it only *bleedled* when being ignored. Another bubble flashed up.

Wait! Before you throw it at the wall...

I waited—doing my damnedest not to be amused.

I promise not to bug you.

Another gray bubble appeared with three scrolling dots, then came through.

Too much.

I started to smile.

You're grinning now, aren't you?

My lips firmed. *How do you suddenly know me so well?*

So, anyway. Consider it an employee perk.

Like the clothes I was to pick up at the pro shop. A way for him to give me stuff.

"Doesn't mean I have to accept it," I grumbled.

And thought you'd like the pink, Blink.

A sudden rage fired up from my belly at the nickname, one I hadn't realized he'd picked up on from Bear in the alley—that Ben had *no* right to use.

My fist tightened around Ben's pink, sparkly attempt at a leash.

Then I launched the damn thing across the room. It deflected off the doorjamb and ricocheted into the bathroom. A satisfying clatter echoed. Ceramic tile floor? Meet Ben's phone.

From the doorway threshold, Bruno lifted his head, alerting.

With a relieved sigh, I settled into the clean bedding, under the covers.

And as I nestled down into my comforting darkness, so did Bruno on his patch of the floor from where he guarded the room. With the all-quiet, things had once again become right in his world.

As I closed my eyes, sleep tugging me down, my last thoughts drifted over my talismans that guarded me: the silken glove, the patinaed coin, the scented tin, my sharpened knife.

A last *bleedle* carried to my ears, barely heard, its effect on me weakened from whatever abuse it'd suffered and from the vast distance it had to cover from where it'd been outcast.

Banished.

I smiled as I drifted into dreamland, images floating through my mind of me tucked in, safe and sound. And Ben relegated to where he belonged: locked out.

Everything's exactly as it should be in my world too.

10

WHAT'S YOUR HANDICAP?

Ben...

"**R**eally?" Low and soft, a familiar voice purred from behind me. "Those hideous shorts? Again?"

Shay.

Relief flashed through me that she'd showed—after nothing but deafening silence since she'd walked away a day and a half ago.

I fought a grin. *Hell yes,* again. *All the easier to rile you with.*

Then I glanced at my watch, for the third time in ten minutes, and fronted my best scowl. "You're late."

When I turned, I caught her half-shrug. But damn, she looked incredible.

Her dark hair had been scraped back into a thick ponytail except for layered bangs that framed her face. For the first time, I realized her hair wasn't simply dark-brown; the morning sun glinted a deep mahogany off the top strands. And her eyes weren't always stormy emerald. In the light of day, they sparkled like pale sea glass.

Dark lashes slow-blinked over those startling green eyes. "Sorry. Had to catch a ride."

"A ride? With who?" Since Miss Independent seemed to get around fine on her own, it never occurred to me that she'd need a lift. "You should've let me know." *You should've called.*

"The   *GreaterPhiladelphiaTransportationDepartment,*" she blurted out in one long word.

I gave her a blank look while I decoded what she'd said.

"The bus," she translated. "And I 'should-*not*-'ve' anything. Better get on board with that right now."

No rules. No restrictions. Loud and clear.

Electronic leash? She'd practically said *Not a fat chance in hell.*

And yet, I'd already taken that thousand-degree chance anyway. "You get the phone?"

"It's pink." Her voice flattened in judgment.

"Don't like pink?"

"Not even a little bit."

"You know, it's customary to reply to texts." The last one I'd fired off to her Monday night? Had said *Sweet dreams, Shay.*

"I'm not customary."

No kidding. "Yeah, I got that."

"You got a problem with that?"

"Not even a little bit." Yeah, I'd tossed her words back

at her. But mine held more punch. Meant more to me than rebelling at color. Sounded a lot like I'd taken a stance on a vital issue.

Her hard stare held mine.

My next words? Softer tone, even heavier impact. "It's what I like best about you."

Her next breath sucked in quicker. Then her gaze flicked up to my same blinding-white hat. Her eyes squinted as she held out an open palm.

I bit back a laugh, then handed her my sunglasses. "Good choice on outfits."

She'd chosen the darkest of the three the pro-shop guy had recommended. The slim collar of a gray sleeveless top hugged the back of her neck and partway around the sides, but plunged at her throat, revealing flawless tanned skin that disappeared under the shadow of its deep *V*. Short black skirt-shorts—embroidered with a silver dandelion whose tiny umbrella seeds floated above the hem as it ruffled in the breeze—highlighted toned legs. Gray-edged socks peeked out from the tops of black-and-gray saddle shoes.

With a slight chin lift, she stabbed my sunglasses onto her face. "Good thing I don't have a sense of humor."

She meant the fourth outfit.

The one I'd tossed into the mix: a bright white hat, light-green shirt, black-and-green Bermuda shorts.

What I'd worn Monday. What I wore now.

"You're funnier than you think. The best kind. Dry humor. With plenty of smartass."

She arched her slender brows, pinched a corner of my

sunglasses, then lowered the frames down her nose to reveal those beautiful eyes. "What would the country-club set have thought if I'd taken you up on it?"

Doesn't matter. I *would've loved it.*

The hilarity alone would've been worth it. "Work uniform?"

She shot me an exacerbated look over the tortoiseshell rims, then shoved them back, hiding her eyes. "More like *clubbie twinsies* of the *most* hideous kind." She plucked the corner of her narrow shirt collar. "This is more my speed."

Yeah, it was. Nothing flashy. Understated, yet edgy. Just like her.

Not one thing pink about it. Which reminded me... "Where *is* your phone?" Didn't see her small backpack. And if that tiny skirt she wore had pockets, no phone could've possibly been hidden in there.

"I don't have a phone."

"Fine. *My* phone that I left with you."

"Away."

Not in her backpack, or she would've said so. Not in some apartment I hoped to God she lived in rather than slumming on the streets. An image flashed of her tossing the "electronic leash" into a garbage can on some random street corner.

I stared hard at her, words unable to form. The woman frustrated me. And the more I tried to figure her out, the less I understood.

Her brows raised a fraction. "A locker, okay? Apparently, you wander into this club and you become royalty. A personal concierge offered me cucumber water, custom-sized shower shoes, and a fluffy lavender-scented robe. And a locker. With a security code. To stash valuables in."

She shot me a *duh* expression as her eyebrows arched ever higher. "Hope you don't expect me to carry that thing with me everywhere."

"Nope. Don't expect a thing." Just glad she hadn't destroyed it.

"Good." She gave a short nod. "That's usually best with me."

Don't I know it. But I'd begun to learn the unexpected was part of the fun with her. A surprise always waited around the next corner.

"Did it sustain much damage?" My random question had a purpose.

She'd physically distanced herself as we talked, had wandered toward the back corner of our cart. And curiosity had drawn her attention rearward, toward the procession of other golfers and their carts.

I also searched the line of parked golf carts, and anxiety spiked in my gut about who I'd *rather not* see today. Foursomes gathered, loading bags onto the back racks of their carts. In one group, two women hugged while their other halves laughed at some joke. On down the line, new introductions shook hands, reunited friends clapped a hand onto a shoulder.

But no unfriendlies spotted. *Yet.*

However, we still had about twenty minutes in the meet-and-greet hot zone before tee time, and I wanted to keep the both of us distracted.

"What?" She turned back toward me with an adorable sunglass-covered blank stare.

"The phone? Or the wall?" At the time, I'd been joking about her throwing the phone, yet my gut told me it'd happened anyway.

The corners of her mouth twitched, like she fought a smile. "Doorjamb's got a nice dent in it. Phone glass has a crack in the corner." She leaned a shoulder on the black tubing of the cart's roll cage, folding her arms. "Tile floor doesn't have a scratch on it."

Doorjamb. Tile floor. As in, an actual apartment or a house. Not the cement, cobblestone, or curb of a street.

She shrugged. "No big. Hope you've got good insurance on that thing." She held out her palm then bobbed it up and down a few inches. "It's got a nice heft to it. Might get another urge to practice my pitching."

Fair enough. Her abuse hadn't ended yet. Not even close.

I looked forward to every minute of it.

"Lookin' good, kids." Cade suddenly appeared through a mingling crowd of people.

He clapped me on the shoulder and gave Shay a respectful head-nod.

"*See.*" Shay pushed off from her back-o'-the-cart safety zone, then stepped closer. She pointed at Cade's shorts, accusation in her tone. "At least he's got on a *solid* color."

"Gray." Cade glanced down, then shrugged. "Safe."

Shay stared a couple of beats longer at his conservative golf shorts, then dropped her gaze toward my loud Bermudas. "*World* of difference."

Good. I didn't want her to lump Cade and me together. Different? Fine by me.

"Who's our fourth?" Yesterday, I'd asked Cade to slot us as close to the front as possible. He'd somehow gotten us positioned as first to play.

"Wait." Shay gaped at me. "We're *playing*?"

"Yep. Why do you think we went to the driving range?"

Brows arching high, she folded her arms. "Uhhh...*to gain an understanding of the clients we're serving.* Not become one."

"What better way to understand them?" I hefted a half-set of borrowed ladies' clubs onto the back of the cart beside my bag, then strapped both in.

"Sounds wise to me." Cade hoisted his bag onto the back of his cart, which had been parked in front of ours. "And our fourth is *Whoosh*, dude."

"Whoosh!" Our voices dropped an octave as we barked out our friend's name.

Confusion wrinkled Shay's forehead. "Whoosh?"

I gave her a nod. "Whoosh. *J.J. Whoosh.* Otherwise known to the world at large as Jefferson Jamison Washington. But never—"

"—ever—" Cade shot a pointed look at Shay.

"—call him that," I finished.

Cade clasped his hands together into a golf grip, gazed out toward the first fairway, then executed a smooth club-less golf swing. "The legend sinks eagles from the middle of fairways like a silent basketball whooshing through a hoop: nuttin' but air."

"Our ringer." No point in playing without winning.

"We need a ringer?" Shay stepped up onto the passenger side of our cart, gripped the metal framework, then swung around and dropped onto the seat.

From the cart's back storage area, I retrieved one of the two black goodie bags that a volunteer had given me at check-in, then handed Shay hers. "Gotta have some kind of decent showing with three lesser players."

Cade dropped me a deadpan look. "Two lesser and one greater."

I brushed off his comment with a shrug. "Not one as good as Whoosh."

"Did someone call my name?" The nearby crowd parted when a tall blond man spread his arms up and wide, as if for his adoring fans.

Shay gave Whoosh a mere cursory glance, then busied herself with checking out the multiple outer zipper pockets of her goodie bag.

Gratitude filled my chest. Why? Because Shay hadn't succumbed to what every other female within a twenty-foot radius of Whoosh always had: model handsomeness, Olympian physique, and an air of confidence that said *life always worked out perfectly*—because it always did...for him.

The rest of us mortals had to work hard, leverage risk, and hope we didn't fuck things up.

I clasped forearms with Whoosh, and we tugged into a rough shoulder-hug. Whoosh and Cade did the same before the crowd split again and another childhood buddy pulled them away for a brief reunion.

When deeper anxiety spiked again, I swept another check down the line of waiting golf carts. And I spotted what I'd been dreading. The who-I'd-rather-not-see? Had shown.

Great. I'd probably get stalked. Maybe verbally assaulted. Most definitely guilted.

Thank fuck *Shay's here.* I needed to focus on her raw goodness; she lightened all the badness that had weighed down my life lately.

"My name's on this?" Childlike wonder filled Shay's soft-spoken words.

I stepped closer, fully alerted to one of those rare moments when she'd let her guard drop.

She hovered fingertips over an engraved brass tag that had been riveted into the rigid canvas bag's front. Then she unzipped its main circular top and flipped it open. Out puffed swag provided by the event's sponsors, most of which boasted our country club's name.

"Yep. All participants receive one; it's part of the entrance fee."

"Entrance fee," she murmured. "Which is…"

Thousand bucks a pop.

She pulled out a burled walnut case, opened it, then angled its shining contents toward me with an arched-brows *What the hell are these?* expression.

I answered her vocalized question. "Covered." Steep. But members got a discount. The rest of the exorbitant cost? A business write-off for the sake of more training.

Or so I told myself. Somehow the lines of justification began to blur with Shay. Being around her whatever the dollar cost? Worth it.

I finally nodded at the two colorful enameled disks in the case she held. "Ball markers." When her brows furrowed further, I added. "For the green."

"Of course." She snapped the lid shut, her bored mask back in a flash.

A deep male voice suddenly interrupted, "And who's this lovely nubile novice?"

Whoosh swept between us. His hands gripped the top edge of the cart, face hovering low over Shay's bag as he shamelessly stared into her eyes through her sunglasses.

"My employee, Whoosh." I clamped a hand on his shoulder and yanked him backward. "Off-limits." To him.

And me...due to the whole employee thing. That principle mattered. Another easy self-lie.

I kept piling the denial on. Because it worked hand in hand with irrational behavior: Somehow, I'd become territorial about her. Which was unacceptable.

Dating staff had been forbidden from the start. How Cade and I had set things up to protect Loading Zone's work ethic and morale. And I'd stuck to that code without exception. Because I'd learned over the years that I failed at relationships. *So why shit where you eat?* Besides, through college—and especially over the past six months of being single again—plenty of willing women had proven casual sex worked better. Bedsport was less complicated, more fun. And no workout on earth beat sex-gym for stress relief.

To clear my head of everything not appropriate during a golf tournament, I stared at Shay's goodie bag as she continued to rifle through it.

I spotted a black baseball cap and snatched it out. Then I tucked it onto her head.

She scowled, tore the hat off, and yanked my sunglasses off her face to glare at me. "*I* decide who I'm off-limits to." To emphasize her point, she cast an appraising glance at Whoosh.

But I watched her carefully. No fire lit in her eyes. No deep breath revealed any kind of gasp. Whoosh only received a cool assessment from her, like she sized up an opponent.

"I'm Shay." She pointed at her bag's name tag, fierce gaze locked on said opponent. "New bartender at the event. Novice *only* to the game of golf. *Nubile to no one.*"

She stared at Whoosh with an unforgiving expression until he relented with a short nod. Then she glanced at Cade before landing a hard look at me. "I'm one of the guys. Just another golfer. I expect to be treated like one."

Right. One of the guys. Even though I stared at a woman like no other I'd ever met: soft curves yet hard edged, vulnerable under a fearless façade, giant heart with no mercy when it came to betrayal, *moral compass a little off when it came to abiding by laws...*

An announcement blared through the speaker system. "Welcome, welcome one and all to our Thirty-Seventh Annual Unity Foundation Event."

Shay calmly slid my sunglasses back on her face. Then she snugged the baseball cap back on and looped her long hair through its adjustable back opening. The echoing directive continued, "...in groups One through Four, please proceed to your carts. First foursome tees off in ten."

"Okay, boys and girls, time for a last-minute warmup," Cade said. He and Whoosh grabbed a wedge and putter each before crossing to the far side of the practice green.

"C'mon, *Blink*. Let's see what your short game looks like." I slid our putters from our bags.

Shay gripped the side rail of the cart and froze halfway into the process of standing. She lowered her brows at me. "Don't call me that."

Ahhh, there's *your fire again.* A fire that burned hotter when it flashed out toward me.

"*Bear* gets to. But *I* don't?"

With a burst of movement, she launched from the cart, then swiped the putter from my hand. "Exactly."

I fought a grin, glad I'd pissed her off. Every time I pushed her buttons, I learned more about the woman under the layers of her bulletproof armor: The big guy from the alley was more than a casual acquaintance. Bear had been protective of her the other night. I wondered just how close they were if he rated nickname-status with her.

Shay stopped on our side of the practice green, out of earshot from Cade and Whoosh, and pointed the head of her putter at me. "*Not* nubile, *not* novice," she repeated. Whoosh had hit a sensitive spot earlier. "Not *Blink*." She stopped a few feet from the nearest hole and stared at me another few seconds while I followed her. Then she sighed and her shoulders relaxed. "Shay." Her voice softened as I approached. "I'm just Shay, okay?"

You're not just *anything.*

The more time I spent with her, the more I discovered

a tangle of contradictions under her skin. Raging fire and hard ice. Heroic bravery masked an innocent vulnerability. Wildness vibrated deep within her—even though she did her damnedest to hold on to some level of tame.

"Okay," I yielded to respect the complex beautiful woman by giving her the space she needed. "Shay."

Relief washed over her face and she nodded.

"Is Shay short for anything?"

Her entire demeanor tensed with frustration again. "*No.*" She planted the head of her putter on the turf. "Speaking of…what's my 'short game'?"

Message received: Personal inquiries? Off the table. Golf? Safe zone.

We had only a few minutes left, alone. I decided to spend them wisely. On neutral ground. "At the driving range, we practiced the long game."

"Whacking the hell out of balls." The corners of her mouth twitched again. Neutral suited her. It brought out that brand of dry smartass humor she wore so well. And mildly amused? Looked amazing on her.

A memory flashed into my brain: her smartass *Yeaaah… two…three…whatever* swing-mantra followed by her *whacking the hell* out of the ball. "Those were drives and fairway shots. Once you're within striking distance of the green, your short game takes over: pitches, chips, and eventually putts. A specialty club is used for each, with the heaviest club in a golfer's bag being a carbon-steel sand wedge. Well struck, our sand wedge will get us out of the deadliest bunker."

"Sounds like a lot for a few minutes." Her attention

drifted farther out, toward where Cade and Whoosh practiced. Cade tapped a gentle three-footer into his cup. Whoosh stood downhill of a deceiving rise and cracked a gnarly pitch that shot his ball curving along the inside slope before it sank straight into the hole.

"We only have time for a handful of practice putts. When you need to pitch or chip, I'll teach as we play."

She wasted no time, not waiting for me to guide her. Like Cade had done, she placed a ball a few feet from the hole on even ground, held her putter in the same manner, then tapped the ball.

Nice. Her first try sank the ball with an echoing clunk.

"Did you hear that?" Pride radiated on her face as she plucked the ball back out.

"Yeah, I heard it." Not the clunk, the ping.

The sweet spot. A perfect connection.

If only the rest of life were so simple.

My gaze traveled back along the waiting line of players, across other club members, toward my past—and a not-to-distant future I didn't want to face.

"Why do they call it a scramble?" Shay angled fully toward me.

Her knee nudged mine as I swerved the cart to avoid a nasty bump on the left side of the path. I hadn't planned the bodily collision. *Much.*

But totally unexpected? Our continued contact.

She didn't readjust; her leg still touched mine.

The four of us had already played through Hole One, and Shay and I were back in our cart on the way to Hole Two. "Not sure why. Maybe because the other three players scramble to reposition their balls?"

She gazed at the path ahead, my sunglasses and that black tournament baseball cap still shielding her eyes. "So, on every hole, all four of us tee off in whichever order, but after that, we all play our own balls from the same position as the one closest to the hole?"

At the rise, I slowed to make a tight right turn. "Almost. We decide as a team each shot we like best out of the four we made, which isn't necessarily the closest one to the hole. Then we all move our balls to be even, within a club's length, with that 'best' shot to take our next shot."

"Makes the *stuffy* game of golf a lot more exciting."

"Exactly. The club does scrambles for charity and fundraising events to make the tournament fun for everyone. Not all members are great golfers. A scramble evens-up the playing field between teams. Novice or occasional golfers are matched up with at least one player who has a low handicap."

Whoosh parked at the next hole. He and Cade hopped out to retrieve their drivers from their bags strapped to the back.

I slowed our cart. Didn't want the remaining private time I had with her to pass any faster.

After a couple of silent seconds, her knee nudged mine. "What's a handicap?"

Oh, damn. I'd walked right into that hornet's nest. *Maybe I can dance around it.*

Act dumb. *Or deaf.* "Handicap?"

"You just said a 'low handicap.' And I heard a guy talking about it earlier, when I walked by the registration table."

Shay missed nothing. Listened to everything.

"It's what a golfer uses to record their skill compared to par on a course."

"What's par?"

"The number of strokes an expert golfer should take to complete a hole. That first hole we played? Was a par-5; but we did it in four strokes, or one under par. All eighteen holes, with each requiring anywhere from four to five strokes— three on a couple of short holes—makes our course a par-72. A handicap is gauged by what a golfer's average typical score is on a course, or in a tournament. So, if a course is par-72, and a player usually scores a 75, then he's considered a 3-handicap golfer."

"Or *she* is."

I parked at the tee box for the second hole. If I'd driven any slower, the cart would've been at a standstill. She'd talked about golf the entire sixty-seconds. I'd thought about her knee.

"What's your handicap?" she asked. Her knee? Still up against mine.

You are. "I don't have one."

She turned toward me, rested her hand on her own knee. The slight pressure of her fingertips touched my leg. But her expression? Innocent. "Because you don't compete?"

"Something like that." *Had the sun fired up ten degrees?* On that note, I broke that amazing but perplexing knee contact and got out of the cart. *Strictly business.*

When I rounded the back corner of our cart to get my driver, Cade's smug mug stared straight at me, inches away.

I cut him a warning glare. But maybe he hadn't overheard.

He grinned. "Don't be humble, Ben." He handed me my driver, then glanced at Shay as he pulled hers free. "Our boy here is a scratch golfer."

Yeah, he'd heard.

"Scratch?" She glanced over her shoulder at me as Cade led her up to the elevated tee box.

He leaned his head toward her, conspiratorially. "No handicap. Because he golfs at par."

By the time I caught up and heard the bastard confess for me, Whoosh joined the fray. "*Below* par, more often than not." Whoosh deadpanned me, then glanced at her. "He should've gone pro. He'd win next Saturday's annual tournament, if he bothered to play."

"*He*" —I teed up my ball and lined up my driver since they only seemed interested in talking— "is *golfing* right here. And has no interest in any other game." I took a smooth swing and launched the ball to land a couple hundred yards down the fairway.

With a short fuse on their golf-harassment, I left the others in my wake for them to chat up my forgone golf prospects. Years ago, I hadn't been interested in some leisure sport loaded with pressure. Working hard as a bar owner to help the masses forget the insanity of their lives? More on par with my life than any course could've ever been.

We played through the next several holes. The banter between the four of us stayed light. And Shay had reestablished her safe distance with me: no more knee-touching.

But she did something even more incredible.

With every shot she made, with each joke and teasing insult us guys lobbed back and forth, Shay had begun to slowly unfold like a wildflower exposed to its first rays of the sun.

"Birdie, baby!" Her arms shot up into the air, delight brightening her face, about the shot Whoosh had made for our team, as if she'd sunk the fifteen-foot uphill putt herself.

My chest burned a bit as I took in her sudden transformation. When she finally relaxed, actually let go, it was an incredible sight. And I felt lucky to get a glimpse of it.

But a greedy part of my heart surfaced through that ache; I didn't want just a glimpse.

I want it all.

Which made no sense.

Women and me? Had never worked.

Business and personal? Bad combination.

Doesn't matter. I want you anyway.

Shay defied all logic. She'd become the exception.

Then, on Hole Eleven she really let go. And took my heart with her.

She lobbed her club at the green. "A fox just stole my ball!" The club hurtled end over end until it chunked up a sizable divot at the edge of the rough.

None of us guys had been paying attention.

"A fox." Whoosh's tone held disbelief as he looked off into the woods.

"I swear. The damn thing trotted onto the green from those bushes, scooped up the ball like it'd found an egg, then bounded behind those trees." She pointed in the direction of where her club had landed.

Then she ripped off her sunglasses and charged up to me, fierceness in her gaze as she stared into my eyes. Then she shot a pointed look back toward the forest, like I'd invited her here, she'd been clearly wronged, and she expected me to do something about it.

But all I wanted to do was wrap my arms around her.

Instead, I teased her. Much safer in mixed company. "Uh-huh. Sure, it did."

Whoosh leaned his face in between us, then winked at her. "You've been out*foxed*."

But a few holes later at the tee box, all hell almost broke loose. *On Whoosh.*

"Seriously?" Shay gripped two edges of a laminated folding map in front of her face, my sunglasses folded in her hand, arms spread wide. "This thing's a big circle?"

I glanced over after launching my drive, the last of the four of us in our rotation. "The course?"

She peeked up over the top edge. "Yeah."

"A figure eight, to be precise," Cade righted the map for her.

"A good walk spoiled." Whoosh gazed at a cloud-dusted sky, channeling literary wisdom.

Shay shot him an indignant look, then folded and

dropped the map into our cart. "If you're going to mock, the line forms here."

"I'm not mocking. I'm quoting Mark Twain."

She glanced at me for confirmation, not trusting Whoosh.

Atta girl. I arched my brows but shook my head. "*Not* Mark Twain. The quote first appeared in *The Saturday Evening Post* in 1948 and they misattributed it to Twain. Twain died in 1910. Harry Leon Wilson said..."

Cade held his clubhead up to his mouth like a microphone. "Golf has 'too much walking for a good game and just enough game to spoil a good walk.'"

Shay grinned. "Good ol' Harry and I would've gotten along."

"Yeah, well, Mark Twain's more romantic." Whoosh appeared undaunted as he strolled closer to her, one lazy step after another. He held his club off to the side, the head grazing the tops of fresh-cut blades. "Seduction, Shay. The way to win the heart of the course is by smooth strokes and a gentle touch." His explanation slowed, his voice growing lower and softer with every word.

My thigh muscles tensed. My hand fisted at my side.

Some crazed protective part of me wanted to lunge between them.

And after my clear warning to him before we'd started play, I should've decked the guy.

I didn't have to.

The instant Whoosh stepped within swinging distance, Shay planted the fat titanium clubhead of her driver square into his sternum so hard he coughed.

The slick-talking womanizer blinked in surprise.

His shocked gaze lowered in comedic slow motion to the shining black impediment blocking his way. Wet clippings of grass smudged the white fabric of his shirt.

Shay's eyes narrowed. "The *only* seduction happening here is *you* with *your course.*"

He held his hands up in surrender, as if the club were a submachine gun that'd been dug into his chest. He gave a nod. "Only the course."

She lowered her weapon. "Good."

You're both damn right *good.*

Cade clapped Whoosh on the shoulder, then leaned close, as if about to impart secret advice. "She's sprawled out and waiting for you. But will you bring game enough to tame her? Eighteen holes. Any man's dream." They turned and began to walk onto the fairway.

The tension faded from the moment.

And I didn't have to kill my old friend.

But Shay didn't move when the guys played on.

Concerned, I closed the distanced between us.

Her gaze remained unfocused, fixed on some random section of clipped turf a few yards from her feet.

I took a risk and stepped into her line of sight, within club-stabbing distance.

But she didn't step back.

She didn't slam a block of titanium against my chest either.

I took her hesitation as permission. *Hell, it isn't a no.*

Her breaths grew faster, shallower. Eyes dilated, they began to widen. She slid my sunglasses back on and swallowed hard.

No need for her to slam a golf club between us. Every subtle sign screamed that she was a microsecond from bolting.

Not that it mattered; I couldn't stop myself. Some urgent need drove me, pushed me on.

I took another step closer, tested our new boundary.

She tested too: Trembling fingertips skated over my hands, up my arms. Her face tilted up.

Under her black baseball hat, my sunglasses obscured those expressive green eyes. A part of me wanted to rip them back off, read her true self, connect with the most vulnerable part of her. But her body language already spoke volumes: those full lips barely parted, her slight frame leaning against me.

I bent my head down, aching to kiss her.

Her warm breaths coasted over my chin, my lips.

We drifted together. But right before we made contact, her body tightened, then shifted.

A gentle weight pressed onto my chest.

I glanced down.

Her flattened palms rested between us. "You should play in next Saturday's tournament."

Bewildered by the change in direction, I blinked. "I should?"

She took a deep breath, then exhaled slowly, as if she'd found her balance, had gained solid footing again. "Are you good at it?"

"Golf? Or tournaments?" Thanks to the ever-helpful Cade, she already knew I was a scratch player. But maybe she wanted to hear what I thought.

"Both." Her voice was quiet, tone resolute. She'd latched onto that kernel of info and wasn't letting go.

She also hadn't pulled away. The woman who'd distanced herself for days had rocketed from touching knees in a golf cart to a full-body press on the course.

And I didn't want her to move. But she'd only stepped out on the ledge because I dangled out there too. My turn to answer her questions, give her a reason to stay there.

Honesty. "I hold my own." I went further, wrapped my arms around her.

"Do you like it?"

I like you. "Golf's okay. The game's gotten a whole lot better with you in it."

She tilted her head a little, as if my candor barely brushed the surface. Then her expression brightened a little, brows raising. "Could you win?"

I sighed, admitting defeat to a better opponent; the focused woman in my arms seemed hell-bent on a mission. "Depends on who's playing."

"What would you win?"

"Gotta play to win. And I'm not playing."

A frown tugged at her lips. "But...suppose you *did* play, hypothetically. What would you win?"

Damn, I hated that frown. Even more than I hated where the conversation had detoured. "Hypothetically..." I caved a little, wanted to keep her in my arms a few seconds longer. I stared above her shoulder out toward the sky, thinking. "The tournament a week from Saturday is an annual club event. This year's purse is eight million. About a million and a half will go to the winner."

"*Holy shit.* That's an obscene amount of money."

"That I don't need."

"If you won, would you donate the money to Cade's mom's foundation? The one that helps at-risk kids?" Her voice softened. A quiet plea lay heavy in the undertones.

"Without doubt." Where I would've wanted the money to go even if Shay hadn't asked—if I played.

But there were plenty of sane reasons not to play in the club's tournament. I'd been there before. My tormenters had too. And I wanted to rehash that shit with them again like I wanted to take a sand wedge to the head.

"I'd like you to play."

We all have unrealistic wishes.

My hold tightened around her, then I cast my crazy wish. "I'd like you to go out with me."

Didn't need to see her eyes behind those dark lenses. Her dropped jaw telegraphed that I'd stunned her with my decision to be blunt.

"What happened to strictly business?"

"That was before..." *You in my arms. Your knee against mine. And so much longer ago than that.*

"Before..."

"You."

She leaned back a little, but didn't break my hold. Then she finally pulled my sunglasses off her face. Piercing green eyes stared up at me. "I thought that was a hard-and-fast rule."

"For you? They're all made to be broken."

She searched my eyes, then the corners of her mouth twitched up as she gave a slight headshake. "Well, look at you. Breaking the Laws of Ben."

Laws of Ben? She saw me as an outsider to her world, the place where laws were broken and the crisp lines of right and wrong were blurred—out of necessity. She'd thought I didn't bend, couldn't understand, wouldn't see her as worthy, as an equal to those in my world.

You're wrong. On all counts.

"*Only* for you."

She took a deep breath. Exhaled even slower. "So...will you play?"

Will you go out with me? The question burned on my tongue, but I didn't ask it.

Even though she'd relentlessly pursued her goal, I saw wisdom in pulling back with mine. Because her hesitation about me couldn't have been more evident. And I didn't want her to say yes just to get me to play in a golf tournament.

No strings attached, I wanted her to want me. And I needed her to know it came from her.

"Might be too late." Sure as hell hoped so. Then letting Shay down wouldn't be all my fault.

"Too late for what, lovebirds" —Cade strode by, arms gestured up in a *what the fuck* with a nine iron in his hand— "holding up play? *Way* too late. Whoosh and I already played through. Meet us at the next tee if you're still in the game."

He began to hike a shortcut toward the woods that led to the next hole.

"Too late for Ben to play in next Saturday's tournament?" Shay called out after him. She still stood in my arms, apparently unspooked by the intrusion or his label.

Cade turned with a shit-eating grin on his face. "Nope. Sign-ups till Friday. Two slots left."

She glanced back up at me with a hope-filled gaze and pressed her fingertips a little harder against my chest.

Done. Me—and any argument I might've had—done and gone.

"Yeah, I'll play." My defeated tone came on instinct. Because to give her what she wanted came at a high personal price.

But the wide smile on her face before she broke out of my arms? Made my heart soar.

When she turned and began to head back to our cart, I made one last play. Couldn't help myself. I needed a reward to motivate me through the obstacle course, one just for me. "But only if you go to the gala with me."

She spun around and planted her hands on her hips. But instead of being mad, her brows drew down in confusion. "Gala?"

Players from the foursome after us parked their two carts behind ours. They filed in front of Shay, each nodding or waving to us in turn as they went. Shay and I returned their polite greeting, tolerating the interruption we'd caused to happen.

Then I closed the distance between us, to a few feet, as

far as I dared. "Black-tie soirée after the tournament. Your star player will need a date."

Her face hardened as she shook her head. "I don't do black tie."

You do now.

Defiance flashed in her eyes, daring me.

I couldn't resist the bait. "I play, you play. Think of all the at-risk kids we'll help, together."

Bingo. Her expression brightened like an Edison bulb had flicked on: I'd hit her hot button. And whether or not she liked the deal, she sealed it with a silent decisive nod, then slid the sunglasses back on.

I followed her as she walked ahead to our cart. But the front pocket of my shorts vibrated as my phone jolted to life.

Cade. I punched the button.

"Yo, Mark Twain. You still documentin' the scenery? Or we hittin' balls?"

"Get off my ass. It's only been five minutes." I put the cart in gear and took off. "We needed to settle a debate."

Cade chuckled. "Who won?"

"Shay."

"And Ben!" she shouted, clearly hearing Cade over the slight electric whine of the cart.

We'd missed an entire hole-and-a-half of play, but caught up with the guys at the sixteenth.

On the eighteenth green, after Cade and I had putted, while Whoosh and Shay took their turns, Cade squared up next to me, shoulder to shoulder. "What the hell are you doing?"

141

We stared at Shay while she sank a perfect putt. "I have no fucking clue."

Her arms shot into the air as she turned our way, pure joy on her face.

Cade nodded. "Well, whatever you're doing, it's working."

I glanced at him, then back at Shay. "It is?"

Had he witnessed the change in her too?

"Not for her, Mark Twain. *For you.*"

11

WEALTHY OR NOT, HERE WE ARE

Shay...

What am I doing *here?*

Golfing. With three rich guys who I had issues stealing from.

One, edging closer to me than I'd ever let a man get before. *Too* close.

Ben, what have you dragged me into?

An entire tournament of outrageously wealthy club members was about to descend around me. A street-kid's dream target-rich environment. The needle on my analyzing-people meter vibrated at baseline, winding up to explode into redline.

"Here's all your top shelfs: whites, darks, exotics." Ben gestured at the lineup behind the bar, oblivious to my identity crisis. But I still watched with intent focus, listened to every word. "Tools are here." He tugged out a linen-lined wooden crate from under the center of the stainless steel counter, then tucked it back. "Barware, stemware." His brief nod directed the location of each item as he gave me the thirty-second rundown. "Everything'll be restocked by the club's busboys, as needed."

The busboys. From the country club itself. "There's no 'nineteenth hole' here?" I'd heard two older men mention that they planned to "hit it" for drinks after the tournament.

"For the next few hours? *You're* the nineteenth hole."

No big. I'd handled more customers on each of my slow first Wednesday and Thursday nights at Loading Zone. And thanks to Cade's intense training, I could handle anything those country-clubbers tried to toss at me.

But the fully stocked set-up they'd built on the grass beside the walkway surprised me. "Glass? Outside?" I picked up one of the lowballs, then twisted the short tumbler as I held it up.

Sunlight caught the deep etchings in the glass's pattern, refracting a prism of delicate rainbows onto the rough edges of his face.

"Crystal." His dark gaze landed on me. "Only the best with Invitation Only, even outside." When I made no comment, he stared hard at the dark lenses of his sunglasses. As if with some kind of X-ray vision he tried to see my eyes, read my thoughts. His eyes narrowed a fraction. "That mandate isn't just from Invitation Only; it's club policy. Traditionalists don't do paper and plastic."

Traditionalists. Interesting label the mega-rich slapped on themselves.

"Any questions?"

The sudden intensity of his gaze caught me off guard.

My brain flashed back to mere moments ago, when he'd held me in his arms, when I'd felt his strong heartbeat under my fingertips.

I sucked in a steadying breath. *A million questions.* But none I was brave enough to ask.

His gaze softened. Like he knew I struggled. And maybe he knew because he struggled too. With gentleness, he eased his sunglasses from my face. Then he slid them back over his beautiful charcoal eyes.

Silent on the matter, on every matter apparently, I gave him a headshake. "No. I got this." Everything got figured out eventually, one way or another.

Those dark sunglasses dipped down an inch. I could no longer see his assessing eyes, but I knew they watched me closely.

After another beat, he gave a short nod. "If you need anything, I'll be over there on the patio with the guys." He tipped his head toward where Cade and Whoosh sat at a round table at the back in the shade, nearest the clubhouse.

If I need *anything...*

What did I need? I couldn't tell anymore. *Want* had begun to battle need.

I watched as Ben left to join his friends and thought about all that he represented in my world.

Danger.

The second the reality hit me, I blew all the stupid remaining indecision out of my mind. Then I focused on

Ben's broken rule, reenacted it, and made it my own: *strictly business.*

Ben had already put his boss hat on anyway, had done so seconds after we'd finished the eighteenth hole. I'd felt the shift, recognized the heavy silence.

And he'd just taken a seat with his friends, ensconcing himself back into his world. Even though he still faced my way with intent focus—ever the watchful eye over me.

With every passing second, I grew grateful for the renewed physical distance between us. Gave me a chance to breathe. Find my rhythm again. Prove myself worthy in a world I'd abandoned long ago.

Carve my place in it.

How would I accomplish that? Do what I'd always done. Take stock of the general situation.

Identify everyone's strengths and weaknesses. *Exploit them.*

Discover what others were good at. *Be better.*

A sprinkling of single members sat here and there at a few of the other fifty tables decked out for the big event. Scalloped edges of white tablecloths rippled in the slight breeze. Centerpieces bursting with violet, fuchsia, and canary-colored blooms bobbed and swayed. Place settings stood at rigid attention, their silver flatware and crystal stemware shining and sparkling in invitation to a weary player to sit, rest, and dine.

In the opposite direction, from the rise that led down from the eighteenth hole, a caravan of golf carts had begun to appear in slow succession. Each pair of tournament players coasted down the meandering concrete path toward the golf valets. They were then directed to my bar station, situated just beyond.

But I remained calm, shoulders relaxed, breaths steady, ready for my impending customers.

And even though I didn't fit in with Ben's county-club world, I would blend. Had done it before.

And Ben does not *affect me.* What I tried to convince myself of. Because it didn't matter what I wore—my clothes or the ones he'd bought me, his glasses to shield my eyes or none at all—those assessing stares he kept blasting my way made me feel naked, fully exposed.

"You *do not* affect me," I clipped out right as my first thirsty foursome approached the bar. On a deep sigh, I smiled at them, grateful for the distraction.

Other players trickled in, men and women, two or four at a time, placing their drink orders. And I filled each at an easy pace. Whiskey. Bourbon. White wine. Dry martini.

Soon the floodgates opened, and I hustled, waiting on first-timers parched after their eighteen holes plus the repeaters wanting refills. But just as fast as the chaos had erupted, it soon died down. Players began taking their seats around the beautifully dressed tables and waitstaff took over their beverage needs.

At various points, before gourmet salads were brought out, then again before the aromas of grilled fish, roasted chicken, and charbroiled steaks filled the air, a lone male guest would wander over to fill his drink from my station, clearly flirting. Two were younger guys. One was old enough to be my grandfather.

Every time it happened, Ben stared my way.

Unable to help myself, I smiled and tipped my head toward Ben. *Tough, Bo Peep.* Part of the job. Then I turned away from him to focus on serving my fawning but misled customers.

About ninety minutes later, after the dining players had been served lunch and dessert and their plates had been cleared, announcements were made that the award ceremony was about to begin. A handful of guests hit the bar immediately, and I refreshed their drinks.

Then I planted my right butt cheek on a stool behind the bar and leaned my forearms on the bar top, alone again.

Until seconds later, I wasn't.

Ben appeared on my left, sans sunglasses. His forearms, heavily muscled under taut skin, came to rest on the bar top parallel to mine, with less than an inch between them. As I stared at that innocent gap, I remembered how those strong arms had wrapped around me and had to focus to keep my breaths steady. My pulsed kicked up a notch anyway, my body thrilling with its memory of his sensual heat, of the simultaneous danger and safety.

"How're you holding up?" He glanced my way.

I was fine *until you came along.*

I blew out a slow breath as I counted, trying to calm down. *One...two...three...* "Fine."

"Need a break?"

From you? Yes. "No. I'm good." I'd stood without a break for more hours that were left in the afternoon, countless times. No way I'd wimp out because I was suddenly on the clock—or at mortal risk of meltdown due to guy-proximity.

"Where'd you learn to bartend like that?"

Okay. Cool. Business talk. My blood pressure began to equalize.

"The library."

"Is that a bar?"

"No, it's a building downtown. It houses books." I paused, long enough to catch amusement spark in his eyes. "People borrow them."

"You learned to bartend from books?"

"Yep. *The Joy of Mixology* and *The Bar Book*. Those, and the Internet."

"They have the Internet at the library." His tone flattened in disbelief.

"Running water and telephones too."

He dropped me a deadpan look. "Just surprised me they have computers there and let anyone access the Internet."

"Afraid deviants might look at kiddie porn?"

He arched his brows, concern etched into his face. "Uh, yeah, a little."

"Think the library was too. It's been a while since I've used a computer there. Think you now have to log in with your library ID, so they can track the criminals."

He fought a smile. "Is that why you haven't used the computer there in a while?"

I clutched my chest, pretending to be offended. Then I resumed my prior position, forearm parallel to his, less than an inch between. I wanted to keep the distance he'd initiated, no more, no less. "Yep. Guess you can say I broke my criminal cherry on one of their computers."

"Cybercrime?"

"In a way." I glanced at him, wondering how much I should reveal, deciding how much I wanted him to know. For some reason, a little bit. Which surprised the hell out of me. "Hacking."

He choked out a laugh. "You learned how to hack on a library computer?"

"Yep."

"All by yourself?"

"Nope. Had a genius instructor." *Rafe.* The best.

"So you never had real-world bartending training?"

"Nope. Only the three days with Cade at Loading Zone." He winced.

At the reminder that you'd fired me?

"Baptism by fire."

Ah. Cade's ruthlessness. I nodded. "I'm a fast learner."

"Yeah, you are." Respect lay in his tone. "You're good."

"I know." No ego. Pure fact.

All of a sudden, his forearm moved. We touched, skin to skin. At the moment of contact, an electric current sparked into me. *No big.* What I told myself. And still, my breath quickened.

His arm kept moving, in slow motion, twisted enough for him to glide his large palm over my smaller hand. When he stretched to touch my fingertips, I sucked in a quiet gasp.

He drew in a slow breath. "Go out with me."

I stared at our connected hands, watched as his fingers curled between mine, tightening his hold on me.

What's wrong with you, Shay? Why aren't you pulling away from him? "No. You got me to agree to the tournament gala next Saturday. All you are gonna get. Strictly business."

His hand gently tightened once more, then released. "I want more. Take the risk. Make it personal."

I wanted more. Itched to take that risk. Ached to make it personal—with Ben.

"No," I whispered. Uncertainty weakened my tone. When I wondered if he picked up on that doubt, I yanked my hand away. But I didn't budge from my stool. Held my ground.

Ben didn't move either. He turned his head slowly, glancing at me. "*This* Saturday night."

I blinked in surprise. Of all the days in the year, this Saturday was special.

Was there a reason he'd weighted that word?

Why were those observant eyes staring at me so intently?

What do you know?

Didn't matter. This Saturday? Off-limits. "No. And I will keep shooting you down, no matter what day you choose." But my curiosity about why he'd singled out that day bulldozed right over my common sense. I did my best to sound indifferent about it. "Why'd you pick Saturday?" I also shook my head and scrunched my face, acting like his picking some arbitrary day made no sense to me.

That penetrating gaze held mine. His dark eyes narrowed, as if he'd caught me, had detected some weakness. Then he eased back from the bar and gave a slight shrug, matching my indifference to the whole topic of day-selection. "I'm free? It's a typical date night? And it's three days from now. Seemed like a decent cooling-off period."

Cooling off? He thought I needed time away from him. And damn if it didn't grind at me just how right he was about that. "No." I reasserted my stance. Firmly.

"Sunday, then."

Better. I sighed, relieved we'd moved on from Saturday. But no way would I give in now. Some female instinct made me dig my heels in. "No. Still gonna be no, any day of the week."

"Okay. Understood." He gave a single nod, then headed out from behind the bar. He glanced back over his shoulder. "Let me know when you need a break."

Thrown by his sudden one-eighty, I nearly fell off the stool as I watched him walk away. Then I stood and planted my feet, suspicion pinging to high alert. He'd given up too easily. And his last statement hit me with greater meaning than just as relief from my shift at the bar.

I'm not sure you do *understand.* Or maybe I didn't; I wanted him...but I didn't want to want him.

I'd also wanted to work at his bar. And he'd had the power to rip that away from me.

What would happen if I trusted someone again? Trusted Ben again? If I let myself want him—if I said yes and he gave himself willingly to me—would he eventually rip that away too?

"Could I have another?" A deep male voice interrupted my thoughts as an older man slid his empty crystal tumbler across the bar. A pair of female guests approached right behind him.

My gaze cut to Ben.

Do you *deserve another?*

Had Ben earned a second chance?

The bigger question was could *I* handle another? Would I survive it?

Without any comfortable answer, I shifted course and began filling drink orders.

Because when powerless, when control of any situation slipped out of my grasp, I immersed myself back into what I'd learned best: *ignore* what I wanted in order to help others in need.

A formidable presence materialized near me the instant the activity at my bar died, as the awards ceremony began.

"Don't mind me. I promise not to bother you." A pixie-like girl with dark shoulder-length hair and electric blue eyes settled at the end of the bar, leaning on her forearms, hands clasped loosely together. She stood a good couple of feet into the space behind the bar and about the same distance from me. As promised, she ignored me while she stared over a sea of tables of ten toward the podium.

"Sure. No big." But I eyed the valuable liquor within arm's reach, that I was responsible for—being legit, and all. "And you are?"

She glanced at me with a warm smile and held out her hand. "Cade's sister. I'm Kiki."

"Oh." *Boom.* "Shay." I shook her hand and suddenly saw the uncanny resemblance, same physical features and welcoming heart. Same stock didn't mean same essence; I'd found that out in my own heart-wrenching way. But in their case, I sensed their commonality ran deep. "I like Cade."

"Me too." Humor sparked in her eyes.

She stared at me a beat. Then she glanced in the direction of her brother's table. Cade and Whoosh were clapping and whooping it up with the crowd at something the announcer had said.

Ben? Stared our way, dead-serious expression on his face.

"He's a great guy, you know."

I blinked, confused. "Cade?"

"Ben."

Ah. She'd picked up on his intense vibe toward me. *Kinda hard to miss.*

I tore my gaze away from the subject of her statement.

Then I stared at the announcer. Maybe if I watched something else, listened to anything else, all things Ben would disappear. The announcer's words filtered into my brain: the punchline of a dirty golf joke.

The guy's joke had been weak. But I laughed anyway, for a dozen other thoughts I'd had over the last few days. "I knew I couldn't be the only one to think all this golf stuff is dirty."

Kiki nodded, then glanced at me. "Long stroke."

I thought back to phrases the guys had said while we'd played. "Sink it in the hole."

"*Hole.*" Her voice had dropped an octave.

We burst out laughing.

"Up and down," she added.

"Rigid shaft." My mind guttered every time I wrapped my hands... "Firm grip." One after another flooded in. "There could be a fortune made in T-shirts."

She pushed up away from the bar on a headshake. "No T-shirts allowed. Collars only."

"That's bullshit."

Her brows arched, but she gave me a nod. "Agreed. But golf has rules."

Rules. Laws. "Society could do with a shakeup, don't ya think?"

Kiki's eyes suddenly lit up. "You *could* make *golf* shirts. Civilized with a hint of raunchy."

"What kind of golf shirts?"

She turned fully toward me, leaning an elbow on the bar. "Like yours. Sleeveless. Embroider a small naughty saying on the collar."

"Or maybe even start on one side and finish on the other."

She nodded. "That only someone standing up close could read."

Excitement charged through me. A split second later, it fizzled right out. "I don't know the first thing about making shirts." Let alone selling them to the country-club crowd.

"Would you be interested in partnering with me?"

Taken aback by how she'd deferred to my judgment, gave me total control, all the say-so, I blinked, speechless for a moment. "You'd want to do that?"

"Sure. I'm partnered with Cade and my sisters in Invitation Only, helped create the business from the ground up. And this'll be even easier. Most of it'll be creative. And everything we need is on the Internet."

I stared at her, still shocked. That someone pure and wholesome would want to team up with me after we'd just met. After I'd hit the streets—because I'd had to—I didn't trust anyone. Why should anyone trust me?

However, instinct told me there'd be no safer bet than Kiki.

"Would it be okay if I thought about it?" Being around her felt right. But still, the world she and Cade and Ben had grown up in was mostly foreign to me. And business? Completely foreign. *Maybe I could ask Tony's opinion*...if selling pizza and hot dogs was anything like selling shirts.

"Of course." No hesitation or judgment in her voice.

"Thanks."

A greater thrill of excitement fired through me. Relief too. It seemed like I'd made a friend in Ben's world for no other reason than she liked my wit and trusted me on instinct. That not only felt good, it rang true with everything I'd learned on the streets. Well, the trust part? Only to a point.

Kiki stared at me a moment longer, blinked with a surprised expression, then grinned, eyes lighting up like she'd just been struck with a genius idea. "You should come to our barbecue on Friday."

"Yeah, you should go." Ben's deep voice vibrated right behind me.

Startled, I spun around.

He'd planted his forearms on the bar again. Only he stood on the other side, the bar top between us. Rogue locks of hair brushed over the top of those sunglasses that hid his eyes again, but his expression appeared neutral.

Interesting. Kiki and I had only been together for five minutes, but he'd decided that'd been enough. *Did you think we were talking about you?* "Are *you* going?"

"Depends."

I leaned on the bar top, my arms to the side of his, with plenty of safe space between them. "*Onnn...*"

"Whether or not *my going* affects *your going.*"

Ah. Interesting. I wielded power. Ben cared about my feelings. And I felt like taking a chance with Kiki and her family. Even with the risk of Ben being there. Maybe because of it. "I'll go. Whether or not."

"Good." Tone matter-of-fact, his expression remained cool.

I waited, watching him. When he volunteered no information, I arched a brow at him. "And?"

"And, what?"

"Are you going or not?"

Kiki waved her hands in front of her face at us. "*I'm* going" —she pointed across the packed luncheon tables toward Cade and Whoosh, who appeared deep in conversation as they stared our way— "over there. So we can *all* talk about you."

Yeah, good luck with figuring us out. I had a hard-enough time standing right in the middle of it. I glanced back at unreadable Ben.

But before Kiki walked between two waist-high planters that dripped with colorful blooms, she turned and walked backward. "The barbecue will be harmless," she called out. "It's at Cade and Hannah's. My sisters will be there. And you've *got* to meet Mase. He's a riot."

My heart clenched. *Family.* It all sounded like family. And Kiki wanted to include me.

She'd negotiated through a couple of tables, then spun around again. "And think about the other thing. We'll make a killing. And it'll be a blast." Then she turned and veered out of sight.

"What'll be a blast?"

"A business idea." I didn't offer Ben any other information. He didn't press for it.

Instead, he stared at me from behind those dark glasses. Then he gave me a slight nod. "Definitely."

"Going to the barbecue?" Something in his absolute tone made me laugh. "Were you always?"

"*Hell yes.*" He pulled back from the bar, standing tall. "That's Hannah's cooking we're talking about."

But I got the sense he was teasing. About a lot. Because I got the impression he would've bowed out if I'd had a problem with his going too.

A sudden thought hit me. I had no idea where Cade and Hannah lived. "You driving there?"

"Usually how I do it."

"Good." Problem solved. "You can pick me up, then."

He tilted his head a fraction. "Really?"

"Don't get all excited. It's not a date. And you're still not getting my address."

His expression morphed from offended to innocent, all in a heartbeat. "Wouldn't dream of it. So, am I picking you up at the end of an alley?"

I flashed him an unamused smile. "At the park."

"By the way" —his voice lowered as he pulled off his sunglasses and stared at me with those deep charcoal eyes— "I'm sorry about calling you 'Blink' without your permission."

An unexpected cramp hit my throat. I pinched my eyes shut to stop sudden moisture from springing into full-blown tears. *No big.* What I wanted to say, at first. But then the truth warmed my chest. His apology *was* big. Epic big. To me. Probably to him too.

I blew out a slow breath and glanced at him. "Thanks." I wanted to be just Shay with him, needed to be.

Cade rushed by, concern etched into his face as he nodded toward the sidewalk. "'Rents, two-o'clock."

"Rents?" I blinked, lost with their club lingo.

"Sure." Ben sighed, clanked the sunglasses onto the bar top, then turned and folded his arms over his chest. "Because every sunny-day golf tournament needs a dismal fucking downpour."

Cade stood shoulder to shoulder beside him and folded his arms too.

An attractive middle-aged couple walked along the sidewalk, a pair who hadn't yet come to the bar for drinks. The man, tall and broad-shouldered with dark hair that had silvered at the temples, gave a cursory glance our way before zeroing in on Ben with narrowed eyes. Glacial hatred suddenly frosted out toward Ben from the stranger. The woman with him, a willowy brunette with her hair sleeked back into a short ponytail, flicked a worried glance at her companion, then at Ben, before she looped her arm into the man's elbow and tugged him onward.

The whole time, Ben and Cade remained immovable.

The aggression from the bar outward? Unmistakable.

I almost kept my mouth shut. Then I decided it was a bartender's job to lighten her crowd. "What's with the stuffy power couple?"

Ben angled a bit toward me, keeping the couple in his sights. "Same shit. Different day."

"And we care what those people think because..."

"We don't." And yet, he continued to glare their way.

"*Sooo*...you're grumpy *becaaaauuuse*..."

"I'm not."

Uh-huh. "They're somehow important to you."

Cade clapped Ben on the shoulder without saying a word, then left us alone.

Ben finally broke eye contact with the couple, then turned toward me. After a slow breath, he gave a slight headshake. "They're not."

"Say it like you believe it."

He sighed. "Just because I'm older than you doesn't mean I have all my shit figured out."

"How much older?"

He choked out a laugh. "Really? We're discussing age now?"

"Nope. Got you to crack up, though. Mission accomplished."

His expression softened, like he was grateful. For the topic-detour? The humor?

All of a sudden, Cade's label for the couple defined itself in my head with a jarring echo.

'Rents.

As in par*ents.*

I blew out a heavy breath, heart aching for him.

Oh, Benjamin Bishop. We have more in common than I realized.

12
STRONGER THAN FLESH AND BLOOD

Ben...

Two days.

Forty-eight separate hours.

A segment of time that stretched the same no matter how you clocked it, in every time zone.

My last? Dragged for eternity.

Of course, first thing Friday, it'd been awesome. For about five minutes.

I'd texted her. Short and sweet.

Alley. 3:00 p.m.

She'd actually replied...instantly.

K

One letter. But I'd been the one who'd laughed. Because the world had shifted. I'd worn her down. She'd had two firsts in one day: She'd sent a text, and I'd picked her up.

We'd made progress. *Slow, but for damn sure.*

The slow part worried me a little. It'd been an uphill battle to convince her to work with me. And I'd sensed her internal struggle to agree to go to the barbecue. Every step of any direction that involved me had proven difficult for her.

Why? No other woman had ever been so hesitant. So... wary.

Who hurt you, Shay? Not a chance in hell I'd go searching for that landmine answer anytime soon. Because my interminable forty-eight-hour wait had finally ended.

Shay settled onto my truck's bench seat while I shut her door.

As I jogged around the front, excitement flashed through me, like I'd devolved into some anxious teenager on his first date.

I got in, blew out a fast breath, then shifted into gear.

When I pulled away from the curb, she glanced at me. "This isn't a date, you know."

"I know."

"Then why'd you open and close my door for me?"

To make sure you got in okay. "Door sticks."

She stared at me a moment, then faced forward as we turned left onto Sycamore Lane. "Speaking of...I thought you owned an Escalade."

"I did."

Her hands spread down her khaki shorts before resting

163

on her bare thighs. "But not anymore."

"Nope. Sold it. This fits me better."

She leaned forward, adjusting. Then she settled back again and crossed her arms. But she remained silent. For two straight blocks.

The vehicle change-up seemed somehow important to her. "Disappointed?"

"No. Just surprised, is all." She hovered her fingertips over an original Bakelite knob on the dash. "Why does this fit you better?"

"I've wanted an old farm truck since I was a kid. Been watching classic car sites, and this derelict resto-mod became available last week."

Her ankles crossed. "Does the door really stick?" She uncrossed them and planted petite feet in simple black sandals flat on the floorboard.

"Sometimes." I frowned, concerned with all her fidgeting that she might not feel well.

I was about to ask if she needed anything, but she fired off a question first.

"How far is Cade and Hannah's house from here?"

"About ten minutes. Hers backs to the waterway. Has a good-sized rear lawn that leads down to a boat dock."

"Hers?" Her brow furrowed. "I thought it was Cade and Hannah's house."

"It's theirs now that they're married. She inherited it from her grandmother."

We stopped at a red light. Shay quieted, but her restlessness continued.

I finally glanced at her and shifted the truck into neutral. We weren't driving any further with her in distress. "You okay?"

"Yeah." She drew in a deep breath, then let out a slow exhale. "Why?"

"You haven't sat still for more than three seconds straight since we took off. Are you nervous?"

"I am, a little."

"Why? There's no need to be. This isn't a date... remember?"

She glanced at me. "Oh, I remember. Clearly."

The light turned green. I shifted back into first, continuing on. "So, what's to be nervous about?"

She let out a heavy sigh. "You'll think it's stupid."

"I won't ever think anything you say is stupid."

"It's just...it's been a really long time since I've been in a house with people in it."

The way she said it, I got the impression she'd been in plenty of houses. Which sparked my curiosity. But I didn't pull on that thread. I wanted to make her more comfortable, not less.

"Not just people. Friends. Family."

"Maybe that's what I'm nervous about. I've never cared so much about people liking me before."

She slowly pressed a cupped hand over her mouth and closed her eyes, as if she couldn't believe she'd admitted that aloud.

I pulled over to the side of the road. "I feel exactly the same way."

"You do?"

"Hell yeah, I do. About you."

She stared at me and said nothing for several beats. But she'd stopped fidgeting altogether. "*I* like you."

"Well thank fuck for that."

She laughed and shook her head. "I guess you like me too."

"It's gone a hell of a lot past like."

Silence filled the truck cab. The two of us were finally alone with the heavy admission out in the open between us. But neither of us said a word.

Maybe because we didn't know how to take that next step.

I'd been raised in one world; she'd survived in another.

The rumble of the idling V8 engine vibrated through the truck.

Faint gasoline fumes wafted in through the cranked-down windows, then blew out just as fast on the crosswind.

But none of those distractions fazed Shay.

Her attention had fixed solely on me. "Why do you like me?"

"*More* than like you."

She didn't say anything to my clarification. Instead, those expressive green eyes searched mine. Her chest rose with a measured inhale, fell on a slower exhale.

Her slender brows twitched down for a split second. "But *why*?"

A million reasons came to mind.

But in that moment, one echoed with more force than the rest.

"You live loud...without saying a word. When you're around, you drown out all the noise. When I'm with you, there *is* nothing else."

Silence filled the cab.

We sat on opposite sides. Lap belts held us securely down.

But she flattened her small hand over the worn leather of the bench seat, into the space between us.

I bridged the remaining gap, spread my fingers wide, until my larger pinky touched hers, knuckle to tip.

Long seconds drifted by.

The engine rumbled.

The crosswind blew.

But we didn't move away from our fragile connection.

We stared at each other...and saw through every defense we'd built. As we inhaled and exhaled, breaths coming faster, shallower, I got the sense that we breathed common air for the very first time.

We'd come from different worlds, but we occupied the same space in that moment. In spite of our differences. Maybe because of them.

But on her next quick breath, her brow furrowed. Her hand twitched away.

Whatever she struggled with had broken through. That spiky armor clamped back around her.

Moment over.

And yet, she still stared at me. Gaze fierce. Jaw set. "When I'm with you, I become someone else. I forget who I am. And I can't let that happen. You make me believe I can trust again. And that terrifies me."

I stared back at her, undaunted. "I will never let you forget who you are. Become someone else *with me*, someone better. Get terrified; we'll only grow stronger."

After a long beat, she sucked in a deep breath. Then she pursed her lips and blew it out, nice and slow.

She remained silent. Committed to nothing.

But then I felt her pinky press against mine. Tentative, at first. Then firmer, solid.

She'd spoken, in her own way. And I'd heard loud and clear: *I'll become someone better, I'll get terrified...just as long as you don't let me down.*

I gusted out a relieved sigh. "Well, hell. No pressure there."

She didn't laugh. Her eyes narrowed.

I reached farther and slid my hand over hers. "I won't let you down."

Nothing in the world could make me blow this...even though the weight of our world rested on my shoulders.

Including lightening the mood. Now. *Before she changes her mind and bolts from your truck.*

"Kiki likes you." Divert back to topic, back to the barbecue. "So does Cade."

She gave me a weak smile. "I like them too."

"Well, that's three down. Almost half our crew. Their sisters, Kendall and Kristin, will instantly like you. Hannah will adore you. Mase? He'll probably give you shit. But that's his way of giving someone his giant stamp of approval."

The more I talked, the calmer Shay grew. Her shoulders,

once hiked up to her ears, had relaxed. The fidgeting? Vanished.

I arched my brows, tilted my head her way. "We good?"

"We're good." Her expression remained serious.

I stared at her a moment. When her lips finally started to curve into a genuine smile, I gave her a satisfied nod then drove off again.

"Kendall, Kristin, Kiki..." She ticked their names off as her fingertips tapped the bench seat between us. "All Cade's sisters?"

"Yup. Mase and I are Michaelson adoptees. Been friends since we were in kindergarten."

"That's a long time. Sounds nice..." Her voice wobbled a little.

I parked alongside the curb in front of their house and glanced at her. "Don't think you're any kind of outsider. You're going to their family barbecue. Unless they bodily throw you out, you're already in." I nodded toward the walkway that led to their backyard. "This is it."

She tried to open her truck door before I rounded the front end to open it for her. It stuck. But she gave it a powerful shoulder-shove and stumbled out as I caught her hand to steady her.

"Told you it sticks. It's a little temperamental."

She shrugged it off, winced, then rolled her right shoulder a second time.

When she reached up with her left hand and dug her fingers into the joint, I grew worried. "Sure you're okay?"

"Yeah," she sighed. "It's nothing. Shoulder's a little sore."

"Ah, new golfer." Battlefield sore. "That'll wear off soon. Need me to rub it?"

She blinked with a surprised expression, then took a step sideways, almost off the walkway. "Nah, I'm okay."

Back with the distance between us. Our own personal battle had become a tug-of-war.

"You look nice, by the way." She wore a simple black tank top and khaki linen cargo shorts.

"Thanks." When the walkway turned into a steppingstone pathway down the side yard, she paused and gave me a brief head-to-toe appraisal. "You've made a significant improvement."

"You think?" I took advantage of the pause, closed the distance to within arm's reach.

"Well, I *dunnooo...*" She ignored our closeness, didn't seem bothered by it. "That bright white and lime green had started to grow on me." She shrugged. "But this one's okay. I'll just have to deal with your boring ol' black tee, worn jeans, and comfy tennis shoes."

Her standard attire. What I typically wore. Our common comfort zone.

She smiled, then turned and skipped over the last couple of stepping stones, suddenly full of confidence.

We rounded the back corner of the house as a white slipcovered couch was being walked outside; Cade negotiated backward with the leading end, Mase brought up the rear.

"Hey, Shay." Cade was the first to notice us when he swung his end around. "Ben."

"Hey, guys." When Mase's end swung around, I nodded

at the scruffy blond dude. "Shay, this is Mase."

Mase gave her a chin-up and a lopsided smile. "Howzit."

Shay furrowed her brow and glanced at me for translation. "*How's it goin'*? Mase moved to Maui over the summer. Thinks he speaks Hawaiian slang now."

He slow-nodded, long hair swaying in front of his face. "Yo, we talkin' story. O' whut? I live fo' da surfin' and da hunnies. No mo' talkin' like Richie Rich."

She glanced at me, eyebrows raised, expression uncertain as hell.

I shook my head. "Ignore him."

Hannah and Cade's German shepherd barked and circled the couch as it paraded by. When the guys started lowering it, the dog jumped onto the teak coffee table then launched onto the center cushion of the couch.

Shay's face lit up as she stooped down with an offered hand to sniff. "*Awww*, who's this?"

"That's Ava." I crossed my arms, glad to see the gang naturally wrap around Shay.

Ava sniffed, then nose-nudged her with approval.

"Hey now, girl." Mase rounded the corner of the couch. "I turn my back for one second, and you're already cheating on me."

A kitchen window shoved open and a beloved brunette leaned her head out. "She's been cheating on you all summer, Mase. Better get used to it. She knows who feeds her." She spotted Shay and gave a friendly wave. "Welcome to the chaos, Shay. I'm Hannah. Grab a drink and make yourself at home."

"Shay!" Kiki burst out onto the patio, pushed Mase out of the way, ignored me, and wrapped her arms around Shay in a tight hug.

Shay froze, a stunned deer in headlights when faced with the hundred-mile-an-hour Kiki.

But I had to give Shay credit, she instantly relaxed in the warmth of Kiki's arms.

The Michaelsons had that absorptive effect on people. You didn't enter their sphere of influence without becoming one of them. I'd experienced the phenomenon firsthand—why I had every one of their backs, no exception.

Kiki eased back, taking hold of Shay's hands. "Did you give it more thought?"

"Yeah."

"Yeah, as in yes?"

"Yeah." Shay grinned. "Yes."

"Awesome. I've already done tons of research: checked for IP rights on phrases, priced out suppliers, and found potential shirts like the sleeveless one you wore Wednesday."

Shay blinked in surprise. "How sure were you that I'd say yes?"

"About being partners? Pretty sure. But if not, I'd have handed over all the goods. Your idea's too perfect not to at least give it a go."

"But...how will we sell them?"

"Oh, I've got all that figured out too." Kiki dropped her hands into the front pockets of her shorts and a distinct crinkling sounded out. Ava alerted upright on the couch. When Kiki pulled out her right hand, a few green treats rested on her palm. Ava bounded over, sat in front of Kiki, then waited. "Good girl," Kiki praised, then angled the treats toward Ava's black muzzle in reward. "We can always sell online, but it'd be *killer* if we could infiltrate the pro shops."

"Hi, I'm Kendall." The youngest Michaelson popped in out of nowhere and hooked an arm around Kiki's shoulder. "What's my sister roping you into?"

"And I'm Kristin." The oldest navigated out the kitchen door with a heaping platter of nachos. "Better not be anything we wouldn't do."

With growing amusement, Shay glanced at Kendall, then Kristin. "Edgy golf shirts."

"*Naughty* edgy golf shirts," Kiki corrected.

Cade returned outside with his beer bottle gripped in one hand and the necks of two fresh ones dangling between the fingers of his other.

I took one of the offered beers with a nod, then sat on the couch, out of the way. But curious about Shay and Kiki's unorthodox business venture, I glanced over at them. "How's *that* work?"

Kiki opened the drink cooler. "We're taking civilized golf shirts to a whole new level."

Shay rummaged through the ice, pulled out a grape soda, popped its top, then downed half the bottle with a few impressive gulps. "Yup. All those dirty golf thoughts? Embroidered right on the collar."

"Sex talk down the fairway." Kiki grabbed her own drink, then dropped the cooler top.

Shay angled her soda bottle at her. "Innuendo on the green."

Kiki fought a smile. "We're sneaking it in right under their noses."

"Around their necks."

A very pregnant Hannah waddled out from the back door with a loaded dinner plate. "What are we doing?"

Cade opened the grill and fired up the burners. "Scandalizing the country club."

"Forget hot under the collar—" Kiki glanced at Hannah.

"—we're putting hot right *on* the collar," Shay finished.

Kiki and Shay reached out and knuckle-bumped their shared thought.

Hannah balanced her heavy plate on one hand, planted the other on the back of the couch, then eased down into the corner beside me. "Oh, I'd pay to see that."

"Speaking of golf" —Cade pointed some kind of long-handled coiled steel brush at me— "you sign up for the tournament? Deadline's today."

Shay swallowed the last of her soda, then tossed the empty bottle into the recycle bin beside the barbecue. She glanced at me. "Yeah, did you sign up?"

My gaze locked with hers. I'd agreed to play for her. But she'd agreed to the gala with me. *Win-win.* "Yeah, I did."

Then I dropped a deadpan look at the meddling fucker. "And you know I did. You were standing right there."

"Oh, *that's right.*" Cade grinned. "Me chairing the player's committee, and all."

Mase then clapped his hands and rubbed them together as he eyed the nachos.

Kristen and Kendall disappeared back into the kitchen for more prep work.

Cade busied himself with oiling up the grill.

Ava chased Kiki down onto the lawn to play fetch.

And Shay smiled as she soaked up the unmistakable welcome from everyone.

In ten minutes flat, the Michaelsons had already proven Shay had nothing to worry about. But no shocker. Our motley crew? The best family experience I could offer Shay.

Far better than what I'd gotten from any of my flesh and blood.

13
LOST IN THE ROUGH

Shay...

They've accepted you. Without question of who you are. Without proof of where you come from. Just like Ben had promised. Piece o' cake.

So why had my hands begun to tremble?

Why had my breaths shallowed, my skin heated?

Ben. That's why.

He sat beside Hannah on the couch—watching me intently. *Where should I sit? By You?* No. Too close. But I scanned the other options: empty Adirondack chairs on the far corners of the deck, barstools at the barbecue, deep-cushioned chairs on either side of the coffee table.

"What've we got goin' on over here?" Mase grabbed a fork from the barbecue counter, then climbed onto the couch from behind, working his body between Ben and Hannah, shoving Ben over to the other end.

Ben shoulder-shoved him back. "Hey, I was here first."

"I *met* her first."

"*I* met her first," Cade growled from the kitchen. "And you two cretins *will* behave around my wife and unborn son. Be gentle or get kicked out."

"Yes, *Mom*," Mase grumbled. "Okay. Seriously." He surveyed Hannah's half-eaten food. "What *is* that?"

Ben's gaze returned to me.

I glanced at the nearest giant cushioned chair. Then at the one beside Hannah.

"No." Ben grabbed hold of my hand. "I'm not letting you sit off by yourself."

All of a sudden, he gave a hard tug.

I gasped and fell toward him, arms flailing. My heart jumped into my throat as I landed in a sideways-sprawling heap on his lap. But he'd leaned away from Mase and Hannah, softening my impact so they weren't affected.

Me? *Definitely affected.*

My cheeks flamed hot with the intimate hold. "Hey," I muttered. My muscles tensed as I arched away from his chest, fully intending to spring back up.

But gentle arms locked around me. "Stay," he whispered over my ear, his warm breath fogging over the sensitive skin of my neck.

"That's just...*wrong*." Kiki frowned, stopping in front of us with her hands on her hips. She gave a slight headshake, her expression growing dubious. But she wasn't talking about us; she stared at Hannah's plate.

"Looks damn good to me." Mase licked his lips, then

swallowed hard. "Smells good too."

"You guys get your own. This is *mine*." Hannah curved her shoulders around her plate.

Secured in Ben's hold, I leaned over to take a peek. It had thick yellow half-dried sauce smeared all over it, a handful of unidentified short translucent-white segments, and five dark-brown squares that resembled... *No. Couldn't be.* "What is it? That yellow stuff? The white?"

"Remnants of my over-easy eggs and onions." She picked up a brown square, dredged it through the egg, scooped up an onion, then popped the small morsel into her mouth.

"And...*chocolate*?" I blinked, astounded.

"Yep." Hannah groaned. "So damn good."

"Let me try," Mase begged.

"One." She pinched another chocolate piece, then used it to push a larger square toward him. "I should've known you'd be into weird food, Mr. Orange Juice and Grape Nuts."

The fun commotion between everyone else distracted me for a few seconds from my own disconcerting location—wrapped in Ben's arms. But the point of that began to sink in. Maybe intimate contact with someone didn't have to be frightening. Or dangerous.

No. Not someone. *Ben. This is safe with Ben.*

As startling as sitting on his lap was, I forced myself to stay there. Both as a test for me and as a challenge to his rigid code.

We'd both strayed beyond the safety of our comfort zones. And I still had no idea why he'd begun to break more of the rules that protected what he'd worked so hard for.

What about my issues? I took a steadying breath, thinking about it. So far, so good. No signs of panic: no further hand shaking, no breaking out in a cold sweat, no sudden urge to bolt.

"Damn, that's fuckin' awesome," Mase mumbled around his gifted chocolate-onion-egg piece, then glanced at the flaming barbecue. "Thought we're eating ribs and coleslaw."

"Coconut coleslaw, I hear?" Kendall leaned a hip on the opposite couch arm.

"Leilani's favorite." Mase nodded. "One of many secret food hand-me-downs from her mom. Leilani emailed Hannah the recipe when she knew she couldn't fly over this weekend."

"Sounds amazing." Kiki plopped into the nearest cushioned chair. "Where is the girlfriend?"

"Patagonia. A once-in-a-lifetime study opportunity; it's a Discovery Channel gig."

"Oh, wow." The untamed southern tip of South America. "*That* sounds amazing." For a girl who'd run wild in the Appalachian forest outside Philadelphia before hardening herself to survive on the streets of the city itself, the idea of adventuring through millions of acres of pristine wilderness blew my mind.

"Yep, we're having coconut coleslaw," Hannah continued. "And baby back ribs too. This is pre-lunch lunch. Baby-To-Be insisted. Cade's son waits for no one."

Kiki's face lit up with hilarity as she glanced over her shoulder at Cade, who'd gone back inside. "'Baby-To-Be'?"

Cade leaned out the kitchen window, raised his brows

slightly, and shrugged. "*Little Bean* is too yuppie. Hannah nixed *Bun-in-the-Oven*."

"Damn straight, I nixed that nonsense. I bake for a living. Buns in *my* oven have cinnamon, pecans, and sizzle with sugary butter. They're not made of Michaelson magic."

"And *Fetus—*" Cade had a wicked expression that flashed surprise before he ducked under the windowsill right as Hannah beamed a couch pillow at him. Deep chuckling sounded out before he walked the pillow back outside to his wife, then tucked it lovingly behind her back.

"Just..." Hannah scrunched her face at her husband, then shook her head. "No."

"Darren's not here today either?" Ben's tone flattened, as if he was a little disappointed. He glanced at me. "Kiki's boyfriend."

"Nope." Kiki gave a single headshake. "It's his monthly brother-sister day with Logan. And she'd been hounding him to help sow winter vegetable seeds in their garden."

"It's an original-gang day." Kristen sipped iced tea and sat on the big chair near the opposite end.

I tensed, straightening away from Ben as I sat up. "Plus one intruder."

Ben tugged me firmly back against his chest. "*Not* an intruder. *Never* that."

"What Ben said." Kiki glared at me, eyes narrowing. "Welcome guest. Got it?"

Everyone stared at me with unrelenting expectation: that I accept the kindness they offered. Relief flowed through my veins on a slow exhale, and I smiled a little. "Got it."

"Besides, there's preggers me. I'm not an original."

Cade wrapped his arms loosely around her neck and kissed her ear. "You got that right. You're an upgrade. A Michaelson 2.0. But you are definitely one-of-a-kind."

"You better like my originality. You're stuck with me."

"Nah. We're really holding you hostage. Only reason you're here is because you're on a nine-month courier mission to deliver our mascot."

She dislodged the pillow again and nailed him in the side of the head with it. "I'm the woman you love."

He lowered the pillow, then kissed her tenderly. "Lucky me."

My heart warmed at all the unchecked affection shared among the group.

Even though my head spun at how lucky I'd been too, to have stumbled into what I'd always dreamed about.

All through our late-afternoon barbecue, a carefree happiness filled the air. Relaxed conversations drifted along with ever-changing small groups.

And even though it felt amazing to be included for this snapshot in time, I found myself mentally drifting to the edge to take it all in. I'd grown comfortable being the outsider, the observer: safe.

My best thinking had been done from the sidelines as I'd figured out who I wanted to be—how I'd even fit in—in a mixed-up world that no longer had an automatic place for me.

Only I'd taken care of myself for so long, I'd failed to see how I could fit in to the bigger picture. The edges of my puzzle piece had been cut by my own hand and nothing seemed to match. I'd done that on purpose. I'd rejected the broken outside world and created my own, one I had a say in. And I'd gone it alone, every step of the way, year after year. That was the problem. No matter how badly I'd longed to have something resembling a family, the entire concept felt foreign.

Then again, how could I learn to get comfortable with it if I didn't put myself out there?

How do I even begin to trust again?

"Well? What do you think?" Toward the end of the day, Ben snuck up behind me as I stood alone inside, in front of the refrigerator.

My thoughts scattered. My gaze drifted from the group still gathered outside, then landed on a circular object sitting on Hannah's kitchen island.

"I think there's some serious wrong goin' on with that Jell-O mold."

"Hey!" Mase stepped inside the kitchen and pointed the mouth of his beer bottle at me. "I'll have you know I trained long and hard to make that masterpiece."

"Masterpiece?" Kiki sidled up on my far side, then tilted her head. "It's lopsided."

"And *orange*." The color oddity? Proof enough right there.

"It's *tangerine*." Mase took a swig of beer.

Kendall rounded the other side of the kitchen island. She poked the porcelain platter, making the roundish thing on it quiver. "Since when does Jell-O make a tangerine flavor?"

Cade leaned his forearms on the counter, concern etched into his forehead. "*Uhhh...* The bigger question here? When does a man admit to *anything* tangerine?"

"For your information, Jell-O doesn't make tangerine flavor, *I* did. From scratch. With fresh-squeezed tangerines. And since Hannah was the one who'd challenged me to do it, you better not be dissing on my dessert contribution."

"Damn straight." Hannah waddled into the fray and opened the fridge. "Made specifically with honey tangerines." She pulled out a squat orange fruit, then lobbed it at Cade who caught it midair. She slid out a glass bowl filled with whipped cream and placed it on the kitchen island. "It's a hybrid. Sweeter."

While Mase picked up a yellow silicone cake cutter, Kiki leaned closer. "What are the...*floaty* things?"

"The flat shavings are coconut."

I cocked my head. "And those pale blobs?"

"Duh." Mase stared at me like I'd never seen dessert before. "Mini marshmallows."

"*Oh.*"

At my quiet admission of cluelessness, Mase winked at me.

In a sudden whirlwind of assembly-line activity, jiggling wedges were plated, whipped cream dolloped, and spoons clinked before each dish was personally delivered by Mase with pride.

Second to last, my dessert appeared on the counter in front of me, then Ben's plate was placed beside mine. Without any further teasing, everyone else filed into the front sitting room.

"You know, I wasn't asking your opinion about sketchy gelatin. I meant...what you think about the Michaelsons, our gang? About letting people in, letting go—trusting someone besides yourself."

No idea. I gave a noncommittal shrug. "Seems okay for them."

"But not for you."

There it was. Called on my own weakness. "I don't know," I whispered. I wanted it to be okay. Damn, how many days and nights I'd wished for it.

"Go out with me."

"You're relentless. And you're breaking your own rules." I'd said it before, but it seemed important enough to repeat. Those strict rules had gotten me fired. Those rules had been clearly and wisely outlined in our verbal working agreement: *strictly business.*

"I can't help it. You do this to me. It's driving me crazy. *You* are." He stepped closer in from behind, our bodies almost touching, but not quite. His voice lowered. "I'm willing to take the risk. If you are."

My breaths shallowed. My fingers began to tremble again. I clenched them into fists.

He stepped around my shoulder, never once touching, but so close I could feel the heat from his skin. He stared down hard at me. "Don't think. Don't second guess it. Tomorrow night."

No. Not tomorrow night.

"Do it!" An unidentified female shout came from the front room.

I glanced over the half-wall between us to find the entire group staring at us. Kiki's loosely cupped hands formed a megaphone around her lips. "He's a good guy."

"And if he's *not*, if he so much as *thinks* of right-hooking you again" —Cade's serious gaze at me turned into a dagger-filled warning as he cut it toward Ben— "I will kick his ass."

"Me too. I second that." Mase gave a hard nod.

Everyone else thirded and fourthed and fifthed their oath to inflict dire harm on Ben if he stepped out of line.

"Shay." Ben's voice softened.

The muted sound barely filtered through the density in my head, like I'd sunk fifty feet into thick arctic depths. Hope and fear coalesced together, a raging tempest that I had no idea how to navigate, let alone survive.

"Shay." Ben's call grew louder, firmer. Then I realized he'd touched my arm and turned me to face him, slid his hands down into mine, and tangled our fingers together. He squeezed with solid pressure, becoming my anchor.

Finally, my gaze began to sharpen, gaining focus as it fixed on him. My breaths had quickened to such a degree, I felt lightheaded. Had my hands not been firmly secured by his, they'd have been shaking. As it was, I had to tense every muscle in my legs to keep my knees from wobbling.

"Don't listen to them. Hear me. I won't hurt you. I will never take anything from you again. I'm just hoping you like me enough to want to give me something, on your own... your choice."

"What do you want from me?" My voice fell to a rasped whisper.

His eyes softened, an unmistakable humble plea in their depths. "A chance."

In front of all of his friends as witnesses, pledging their wrath if he did me wrong, the freezing ice around my heart started to melt. I floated up, away from the depths of despair and confusion, toward the warmth and brightness of hope.

"I hear you," I murmured. And shock of all shocks, I believed him. Trust had never come easy for me, not since the betrayal that had shattered my world, not since I'd rebuilt my heart into an impenetrable fortress. But standing in Hannah and Cade's house, surrounded by family and friends with nothing but love for one another, I dared to take the risk—found the courage to trust again.

His gaze didn't waver when I paused. He stood there resolute, willing to wait, ready to give me whatever I needed.

"I need to think about the day, but" —I gave a single nod— "okay."

"Okay," he whispered with a nod of his own. A gentle smile began to curve his lips.

Whoops and hollers sounded over our shoulders.

I felt exhausted and elated, like together we'd just crossed the finish line after running a grueling marathon.

He'd promised not to take from me. He'd vowed not to hurt me.

But I knew my nature, understood where I felt comfortable and where I didn't. History had shaped me into who I'd become. And history had a bad reputation for repeating herself.

As I stared up into Ben's hope-filled eyes, my greatest concern echoed in my head.

What happens if I hurt you?

14
LIKE A TETANUS SHOT

Ben...

Let's get this over with.

Obligation had dragged my ass there.

Apparently, my sense of duty ran deep.

But that historically bottomless well? Had just run dry. I'd had enough.

Because of Shay? Maybe.

She definitely made all the bullshit more manageable.

"Time to shovel," I grumbled. "For the last time."

When I walked into the trendy French bistro in the depths of Manhattan, I didn't have to check with the hostess stand, didn't need to scan the dining room. Her favorite table sat outside on the far edge of the patio under an awning: the perfect place to see and be seen.

Not that *I* cared.

The sunny morning had already warmed the mid-

September air. Shoppers hustled along the sidewalk in front of stores that'd just opened for the day. Down the one-way street, freshly washed luxury cars gleamed as they coasted by, passed occasionally by yellow cabs.

Aromas of brewed coffee and baked pastries filled the air as I worked my way between tables for two. But one scent overpowered my sense of smell when a polished woman in her mid-fifties rose from the table to give me a hug; my next breath was laced with her signature perfume, something expensive and complex—mimicking her.

She pulled back with a smile, then kissed my cheek. "Ben." A slight frown tugged at the corners of her mouth. "You look tired." What she usually said.

"You look beautiful, as always." My standard reply.

The greeting had been our bit for years.

When the server came by with menus, she waved them off and placed our usual orders: a double espresso and croissant for me, a caffè latte and tart-of-the-day for her, which on that Saturday morning was caramel apple.

Once we were alone, she leaned back in her chair, crossing her legs. "Your father's moving us to the country." Her tone dripped with disgust. As if *the country* meant a musty hovel with mothballed furniture.

"Right to the point." I'd grown accustomed to it.

"You barely see me anymore. And I'm lucky if I get an hour with you."

What about you seeing *me at the golf scramble...and not saying a goddamn word because you were there with said father?* What I itched to remind her of.

Instead, I took my stance on a more important point. "You saw me for two weeks straight. Which, by the way, was a one-time deal." She'd begged me, guilted me, made me worry for her safety and well-being to such a degree, I'd felt I had no choice. "Don't expect it to happen again."

Kids should never *ever* go back home to sleep under their parents' roof. *That's what hotels are for. Sanity.*

Didn't matter anyway. No more rescuing. Well. Dry.

Her brows drew together, expression appearing hurt.

"Don't even. I'm on to your guilt trips. And I've become immune to them." *Thanks to Shay.* Somehow witnessing the determination of a girl who'd risen from the unforgiving streets into a woman fighting for her place in the world made me see clearly how fucked up mine was.

Her lower lip quivered. "What do you expect me to do?"

"About what?"

"About what your father's done to us."

"To *you*," I corrected.

That quivering lip firmed. "I'm being forced out of my own home."

"A sprawling penthouse on the Upper East Side." What a rough life.

She nodded as tears sprang to her eyes, my comment obviously mistaken as commiseration instead of blatant judgment.

I stared hard at her, baffled at how we shared the same DNA. "To 'the country', your renovated ten-thousand-square-foot colonial with two wings and a full staff of servants?" Yup. I layered on the sarcasm, still stunned we were even remotely related. We didn't just speak foreign languages. We came from different planets.

Bet I'm adopted.

"Yes!" she continued on with her misinterpretation.

The server lowered the caffè latte toward the table, but my mother grabbed the cup with two hands before its saucer ever touched the white tablecloth. She shot a glare my way, pursed her lips, then pinched the rest of her face as she took a sip, like some liquid caffeine would save her. "Haven't you been listening to me?"

Rhetorical question. "Yes. I have. If you want my advice—"

"I do."

"—which you never listen to anyway..." I took a sip of my espresso and paused for effect.

She had the good sense not to say anything. Hard to debate the truth.

"Do not tell a soul outside of this conversation you are 'having to move to the country.'"

"But...I don't know anyone there."

"Then make friends."

"What if" —she leaned forward and lowered her face toward the table— "they take both properties?" she finished on a whisper.

"Now you're complaining that you might have to move *away* from the country?"

I gulped down more espresso. *I need to wake the fuck up to handle this level of crazy.*

She leaned back and ignored my jibe. Then suddenly her

apple tart became the most fascinating thing. She searched the glazed surface of the pastry like it might foretell her future. Eventually she took a small bite.

"I'm not going to feel bad for you. Not when I've been telling you to leave him for years. And it's ridiculous to worry about which palatial home you might be relegated to or get kicked out of."

"He might be indicted soon."

"*When* soon?" Not that I cared much. Just wanted to be prepared for when shit hit the fan.

"His attorney said it's looking like Friday."

"Plenty of time."

She scoffed. "That's less than a week."

"You've both known for several weeks. And it seems *he's* known for decades."

Her breaths shortened, eyes widening as she leaned over our table again. "What if I become homeless?" she cut out under her breath.

I snorted. "I find it hard to believe the FBI has the authority to kick you out onto the street."

"But you don't know for sure."

"Were you complicit? Did you implicate yourself?"

She blinked, then gave me a vacant stare.

"Did you know anything about what he was doing? Because if you did, and they find out about it, then I definitely know you won't be homeless. Might be the smallest square footage you've ever occupied, though. And I've heard you have to put up with a roommate."

"Don't joke. This isn't funny."

"You should listen to everything you're saying from my side of the table. It's funny as hell to me." I took a bite out of my buttery croissant.

"What am I going to do without your father around?"

"I hope to hell you finally let him go. How ironic that it took his abuse of others—the federal government itself stepping in—to do what I've been trying to get *you* to do for years."

She sighed and picked at her pastry. "I wish I knew what's going to happen."

"Don't we all. This is what real life is like. No one knows how it's going to all shake out."

"I don't know if I'm going to be okay" —she lowered her voice— "*financially.*"

"Do you still have your trust fund from Nana?" When my grandmother died, I got a trust fund, as did Mom. Mine was a cool mill, most of which bankrolled my first car, four years of college, a two-month trip to Europe, and seed money to start up Loading Zone. Mom's had been substantially larger, a big fat zero shoving the decimal point over.

"Yes, I believe so."

"Dad never asked you to invest any of that money?"

"No."

Didn't surprise me. I'd been in kindergarten when Nana had died. And from what I'd heard, Dad had refused to take a penny of it for their personal use. He'd already pulled himself up from the lower middle class by the time he'd met my mother. And he'd still parked a giant chip on his shoulder with plenty to prove.

"Then you'll be fine."

"What if I run out of money?" She took another minuscule bite of apple tart.

"Meet with your accountant. Make yourself a budget. Welcome to the real world."

"I've never met our accountant. Your father always handled the money."

And look where that had gotten them. "I'll give you the number to mine."

Her expression turned morose. "I'm going to be all alone."

I slammed the rest of my double espresso. "Join a support group."

"A support group?"

Still with the language barrier. My parents' upper social echelon didn't get therapy. God forbid they ever mention it aloud.

"Recovering Wives of Convicted Felons?" Yeah, I couldn't help myself.

Her eyes widened. "That's a group?" she whispered.

"I'm joking." I lifted my cup high to signal our server for another double. The first one had barely kicked in.

Her expression shifted from shock to mild hope, as if it helped to think someone else might share her predicament.

"Look for one that supports grieving widows. It'd be a good place to start."

"Your father's not dead."

"You should get over him like he is. I have." *Even though he haunts me while still alive.* "This is your one chance to be free of him. Take it. After they haul him away on Friday, bury him and your horrible past with it."

Her eyes began to glisten with tears. "I can't do that, Benjamin. I can't abandon your father. Not when he finally needs me more than he needs anything else."

More than alcohol, you mean.

My replacement drink came, foamy crema on top, near-scalding liquid beneath. I drank it anyway as I glanced at my watch. Thirty minutes had passed. Almost over. *Like a tetanus shot.* How I convinced myself to go to Saturday breakfasts. The necessary evil jabbed with pain for a flash in time but benefited us in the long run.

"It's impossible for me to feel sorry for someone who has the knowledge and skills to help themselves, then chooses not to."

She glared at me, her lips firming into a tight line.

I sighed. We'd been there before. Nothing more to say.

My phone vibrated once. I pulled it out of my pocket to glance at the screen.

Shay.

I'd texted her right before I'd walked in:

Can I call you around 11:00 a.m.?

She'd just now texted back. No one-letter reply, either. Whole words. Sentences.

What makes you think I'm available at 11:00 a.m? Or even awake?

I put the phone down on the table, in the event it vibrated again.

"Do you need to take that?" She nodded at the phone. Too accustomed to her husband putting business—and everything to do with himself—first, she too easily gave up her right for attention.

Yes. "No. I've got a few more minutes." The least I could do. But Shay's text surged anticipation through me— amplified by four espresso shots.

"Will you be there on Friday?"

"No." *No way in hell.* I stared at the dregs in my empty cup, imagining how that scene would go down. "I don't think you should be either."

Her mouth fell open. "Why not?" She glanced around the patio as if concerned about how the general public would judge her. Then her panicked expression shifted into mortification, like the scandal had already headlined on every news outlet.

"How would you like to remember him? I'm guessing not in handcuffs."

Her expression relaxed, then turned thoughtful. "We could have a nice dinner party the night before."

"No. Just the two of you." Not sure how the Feds would take a swindler throwing his own going away party before they lock him away for twenty to life.

"You won't come?"

"No." Two weeks of two men nearly killing each other had been enough.

My phone buzzed on the table.

Shay again.

Do you realize how long it takes to type all these characters? No wonder I didn't want a phone.

I fired a quick text back.

After I hit send, I almost put the phone down. Then I sent one more character: a winking face.

I scraped my chair back and put my napkin on the table. "I gotta go." In the fifteen minutes I had remaining before the call, I needed a brisk walk to clear my head of all the negative.

Mom nodded, expecting the inevitable. But she made no move to get up. She'd probably stay a while longer, then shop with the last of the money she still had.

A final thought hit me, something I never would've considered sharing with her before. "I'm golfing Saturday."

She blinked with surprise. "In the tournament?"

"Yes. We'll have to skip next Saturday's breakfast. But it'd be cool for you to be there, at the tournament." Wouldn't be so bad to have her there, on her own terms. Support her son because she wanted to, not because my father expected her to. A great way to begin the first day of the rest of her new life.

A warm smile curved her lips. "I would love that."

A strange sigh of relief escaped me. That my mom might see the right path for herself and take it. Maybe I'd needed that hope for her more than I'd realized.

After a small kiss on her cheek, I left.

On my way down Fifth Avenue, as I passed people in thousand-dollar outfits, magnificent glass-fronted flagship stores, and historic granite buildings that'd housed generations of Mom's ancestors, I felt more disconnected than ever before to the shallow wealth all around me.

This isn't me. It never had been.

But the last week had taught me more about myself than any in the last twenty-five years. I'd discovered what I needed to do in order to find out who I wanted to be. Shay wasn't the only one about to take a chance. I had to step outside of my carefully constructed life in order to truly live it.

I rounded the next corner, then veered toward a side entrance of Central Park, one I'd rarely used. And as I merged onto a wide path with the late-morning crowd, filled with joggers and nannies, businessmen and bums, my steps grew quicker, my breaths sucked in a little faster.

Because I was about to make a very important call.

I needed to convince someone else to take a leap of faith.

15
ONE DAY OF THE YEAR

Shay...

Too many things are happening at once.

Good things, I hoped.

But still, I couldn't catch a solid breath. My heart raced like I'd sprinted an entire mile.

In twelve minutes, one new about-to-happen thing had been sprung on me: a call from Ben.

In seconds, the one I'd been waiting three hundred sixty-four days for would happen.

The house sitter's blue Outback reversed down the long driveway, swung a wide arc into the street, then puttered away.

I eased out from behind the wide tree trunk I'd been hiding behind. "There you are," I whispered, exhaling a held breath. From the shadows of the giant elm, I stayed motionless, watching, waiting. Hands clenched around the straps of my two bags—my small backpack slung from one shoulder, the double straps of my larger duffel tucked over the other—I began to loosen my grip.

Dead ahead, the modern Tuscan villa appeared gigantic across the wide asphalt street. To the casual observer, its heavy wood doors and shutters, stacked stone walls trimmed by stucco, and clay tile roof would seem out of place in a neighborhood dominated by Colonial Revivals and French Baroque's. Then again, the sleek cars parked in circular drives and under porte cocheres screamed new money, from the likes of Maserati, Bugatti, and even a matching pair of Teslas.

"Looks like home to me." At least for the next twenty-four hours, all I felt comfortable with. *All I need.*

Once all mechanical sounds in the neighborhood disappeared, car engines gone distant and garage openers silent, I stepped out into the warm morning sun in broad daylight and crossed the street. The new brazen move fired through me like a rite of passage. As if all of a sudden, on that one day, with that house, I no longer wanted to hide anymore.

"I blame you, Ben," I grumbled under my breath. But no anger powered the words, only a little humor. And maybe gratitude. After all, I'd been pushing Ben to test his limits. About time I did the same.

The salted cement driveway remained the same: spotless, not one tire scuff on it. I floated trembling fingers over a cape honeysuckle hedge that had been recently trimmed, its squared top softened by new-growth fluff and brightened by orange tubular flowers.

Around the corner, in the large arched entryway, two new sentries greeted me. Italian cypress spirals corkscrewed up from hefty stone planters and stretched far above my head.

But I didn't waste any more time on the sameness or differences as my heart raced faster. I wanted to be inside, the door closed behind me, to get past the anxiety I swallowed down.

Took me two tries to get the custom-made key to slide into its slot. No fumbling with lockpicks on the special houses; I'd made it a priority to get a set of keys made for our most important clients: Henrietta the house sitter's and mine.

But all my apprehension melted away when the deadbolt clicked open. I slipped inside, then locked up tight.

With giddy eagerness, I turned with a knowing smile, tugged even wider by who waited for me, possibly with more anxious excitement than I had.

A beautiful blue-point Himalayan sat at attention in the center of the entry hall, strong paws kneading against the tumbled travertine floor, creamy silver body vibrating, bright ice-blue eyes staring up at me with anticipation. Her deep bass purr echoed off the walls, broadcasting her joy.

Miss Princess Persephone. "Hello, little one." With care, I eased my bags to the floor, careful not to startle her. Then I lowered to my knees and held my hands out in greeting.

If she took an obligatory sniff, I'd missed it. Because her face skimmed along my fingers. She lifted her velvety chin, eyes closing, as I scratched under her jaw. Suddenly, she pounced forward onto my chest, and I fell back laughing as she began to knead those muscular paws against me.

"I'm happy to see you too, girl. I've missed you."

Tears stung my eyes as emotions flooded in. Eight years I'd been coming. Every year, same exact anniversary date, each just as special as the last. Because the borrowed house of Miss Princess Persephone's had been my first. We'd both been teenagers back then, her a downy half-grown kitten, me a scraggly mostly grown girl.

I rubbed through the silky fur over her shoulders, fingertips gently massaging the muscles underneath, remembering that gangly kitten that'd greeted me on my debut break-in. We'd had a lot in common back then: young, afraid, alone in a giant empty house for the first time in our lives.

Why I came back year after year. To celebrate both my independence and as a homecoming.

"*Awww*, that's right. You love to be rubbed there, don't you, Persie?" All her favorites flooded back to me, one after another, as I stroked the silken fur at the base of her ear, then stiffened the fingers of both hands as I massaged down along either side of her spine.

Both of us startled at the riotous sound of a ringtone coming from my backpack. And even though I'd been expecting the call, even though he'd texted me back with an *eighteen minutes* countdown text followed by a winky face, the intrusion felt bizarre. No one besides Persie and me had ever disturbed our private silence when I'd been there.

By the beginning of the third ring, I sat upright and

unzipped my backpack. The phone's screen lit brightly in the shadowy entry. One name appeared in bold block letters: **BEN.**

I clicked the button. "Couldn't go a whole day without me?" The barbecue had ended late yesterday afternoon, but the agreement I'd made with Ben over an unusual tangerine dessert—to have a date on some yet-to-be-determined day—had kept him on my mind ever since.

Apparently, Ben had missed me too, which made me smile a little.

"Nope. It's a special day today."

I frowned.

It is.

But how do you know that?

"For who?" Distant warning bells clanged in my mind, but I discounted the threat immediately. The whole world didn't revolve around me. *Of course. For him, he meant.*

"For you."

Oh. I closed my eyes, breath held while I said nothing. Maybe if I didn't acknowledge it aloud, Ben *knowing* wouldn't be true.

When the silence stretched, he cleared his throat. "Rafe told me."

I blew out a tense gust of air, relief washing through me. *Rafe.* A safe source. Because he would reveal only the bare minimum. Still, I didn't want a full-blown parade about it. "No big. No special day...just like any other day."

"It's your birthday. It *is* special. And I'm taking you out."

My heart started to thunder again. My breath reduced to short gasps. "I..."

Could I take the plunge? On today of all days? Never having put myself so far out there before, I hesitated. *But this is Ben.* And standing in a house that'd been my first break in—after surviving for years on my own, unafraid and daring to try anything—maybe I could.

Fear shot through me a split second later. Doubt flashed right after it.

No. This is Ben. Maybe if I reminded myself often enough, I'd believe Ben would be safe.

"I could pick you up at six..." His voice had softened, uncertainty in his tone.

We *both* wandered into the unknown, unsteady about what lay ahead, and that gave me a little courage. "No..." *Not here.* But where? "Could I meet you somewhere?" *Somewhere far away from here.*

Silence filled the seconds. Then a heavy exhale from his end. "Like where?" Frustration clipped his tone.

"Do you want to take me out, or not?" Because if Ben wanted tonight, it would be on my terms, at my comfort level, no matter how badly he wanted me to let him all the way in. I wasn't ready for more. *Not yet.*

A low chuckle came through. "Yeah, I do. But you won't make it easy on me, will you?"

"No way. Where would the fun in that be?"

He gave a light snort. "Nowhere at all."

"See? We're on the same page here. And I've seen this go down in movies. There's courting. And romance." Panic seized my breath when I realized I might've revealed too much. I firmed my tone. "Do this right, or we're not doing it at all."

"Okay..." He cleared his throat again. "Miss Shay Morgan, may I have the pleasure of your company tonight?"

I stood up from the cold stone tiles of the entryway, fighting a grin.

Persie sat upright too, bright blue eyes blinking up at me as she waited.

My knight-in-shining-armor fantasy had arrived—over a telephone I hadn't even wanted.

"Well?" His word huffed out in half-laughter. And with it, the untarnished image of my bold and hopeful knight on his white steed shattered to reveal the reality of a dark impatient man, arms crossed, brows raised in challenge.

I ignored his attitude, secretly loving his defiance. "*Seven.*" That would give me most of the day I wanted to myself, then time to get ready before walking there. "What about that Fairmount Park place?" The one from the card he'd given to Joey at the diner a week ago.

"Uh...yeah. I happen to know the owner."

"I know. I remember." Cade and Hannah's restaurant. He probably knew all the restaurant and bar owners in Glenhaven. Small towns made for close neighbors. But if I wanted to walk there—and getting there on my own was the only way I'd agree—the options were limited.

I sighed, growing uneasy. *Can I handle being in the middle of Ben's world?*

Before I chickened out, he agreed. "It's the perfect place. I'll meet you at seven."

The phone disconnected right after his last word. Like he'd sensed my indecision and obliterated that possibility with speed and precision. I stared at the screen as it turned black.

Why *is it the perfect place? Perfect for what?*

Perfect for our first date, for something new. *Don't read anything more into it.*

As I scooped up my backpack, then shouldered my heavier duffel, a thought hit me. "This old place could use some new too." I headed out from the entryway, resolved.

My bright-eyed kitty trotted beside me, an excited spring to her steps.

Caution weighted mine, every methodically placed heel-to-toe guiding me with care through a house I visited the least, even though it affected me the most.

The first room appeared on the left, its double doors thrown wide open.

I paused at the threshold. My feet held fast, rooted to the floor out of instinct, self-preservation...tradition.

But I forged on, determined to break through everything that had held me back before.

A king-sized bed stretched along a wall, a full bathroom opened up straight ahead, but I walked directly toward the low, wide dresser off to my right.

I opened its top center drawer, wondering what I would find. Would it be obvious or hidden? Would they have erased the evidence all these years later? Or would everything remain exactly as I remembered?

What I didn't do is look up into the large mirror. I didn't need to see the rest of the room, didn't want to discover anything new about its inhabitants. I already knew enough.

The old drawer scuffed on its side rails as I pulled. Halfway open, it jarred to a stop. But there in plain view lay my answers. Off to one side, a few baubles gleamed in segmented trays: necklaces, bracelets. But in the center, with nothing else touching it, a single white glove rested on black velvet, flattened fingers stretching toward the back. Ghostly, it appeared as if it could float up, puff out, and slide over a woman's arm. But it would forever remain unfulfilled; its mate had been stolen away.

With me. Where we belonged.

For the first time, a part of me wanted to leave behind the glove I'd taken, rid myself of the past. But a deep-seated defiance kept my stolen glove tucked away, kept it mine.

With a steadying breath, I hiked my backpack higher on my shoulder, shoved the drawer closed, then exited the room, planning never to step foot in there again.

The next room appeared on the right. Over the years, it'd been filled with little-girl dreams. But Barbie dolls no longer occupied the far corner. No Hello Kitty pillow rested on the bed. Teen idol posters that'd been tacked onto the wall had been replaced with vintage travel posters, hung in respectable frames.

The only thing remotely childlike skewed much younger: a white crib stood tall in the near corner where a second twin bed used to be.

Not even one pot of lip gloss sat on the dresser, only a purple wide-toothed comb and a few makeup brushes. On the small desk, one corner held a stack of what appeared to be college textbooks.

LAWBREAKER

My throat cramped. My chest grew heavy. I didn't want to step foot in that room. It felt wrong and foreign. Far different than when I'd first broken in all those years ago.

The last room loomed at the end of the hall. With renewed purpose and a healthy dose of detachment, I walked toward the partially open door that led to a large office. When I slipped through the opening, sameness greeted me everywhere. Floor-to-ceiling oak shelving spanned an entire wall. Yet the space seemed smaller than I remembered, or I felt taller. *Than a year ago?* I wondered if I hadn't been paying much attention last year. Or maybe it had more to do with who I'd become in the three hundred and sixty-four days since. *Or over the last week.*

Every book appeared the same: rare copies and first editions by the likes of Thoreau and Dickens. But with the thick dust that coated their jackets and the shelves between their spines, they didn't seem to be treasured, only collected.

Trinkets and random objects lay in generous spaces, as if cleared specifically to showcase each item. With great satisfaction, I stared at an empty wood surface where a patinaed coin had once lain. In eight years, nothing but dust had replaced it.

Continuing on with my ritual, but venturing into new territory by peering deeper, I crossed to the desk. Using the sides of my fingers, I pulled open the right-hand drawer, somewhere a man who collected prized things might stash a folding knife.

I sucked in a surprised breath.

A folding knife laid there, one a good size-and-a-half

larger than the one I'd stolen. But that wasn't the shocker. Beside it rested a semi-automatic handgun, its black metal gleaming and magazine fully seated, with a loaded spare angled in the back part of the drawer.

In all the times I'd returned, they hadn't changed the front door lock once, hadn't installed an alarm, nor any security cameras. I knew, because I checked every single time.

But the gun? Why would he get a gun?

To defend against intruders?

Without any comfortable answers, I closed the drawer and put the danger out of my mind.

They're not home, Shay. As far as anyone knows, you're not even here. *That's the way it's always been. No tracks. No trace.* How I needed to keep it.

I turned my back on the office. Then I retraced my steps into the center of the empty hallway. The cat had abandoned me somewhere along the way.

My eyes stayed wide open, but my gaze grew unfocused. All around me sat rooms, empty of people, but filled with hints and reminders of who they were.

Their story bled through without me having to stand face-to-face with them. They all seemed cold and indifferent—adult and out of touch with who they'd once been.

But the girl standing in the center of all the emptiness had discovered exactly who she was and no longer needed one stolen thing in her backpack to remind her of it.

"Well, that's new," I murmured, amazed at the revelation.

What have you done to me, Ben?

Somehow the gruff man had burrowed into my head

and my heart...and changed me in fundamental ways. Invincibility charged through my veins. I'd grown up, yet I still felt the most important parts of me snapping wild and alive just under the surface.

My backpack vibrated. "Thinking of the devil..." Ben had probably sent another text.

But I forced *new* out of my mind. I had an annual ritual to finish.

The impersonal guestroom called to me, a haven that sheltered me from the mental chaos of the empty house. I breathed easier the moment I entered the botanical room. Buttercream walls met gauzy window coverings with green silk braids that fastened them back. Colorful flowers had been pressed and framed on the nightstand. A dark purple orchid sat on a small writing desk in front of the window. An ensuite bath held a giant freestanding marble tub, plush ivory guest towels folded over its edge.

I stood tall in my self-designated neutral zone, in enemy territory.

With a satisfied nod that all was well with my annual inspection, I tugged the phone from my backpack and stuffed it into my back jeans pocket. Then I tucked my bags under the large queen bed. Not that anyone would see them. But I left nothing to chance when I stashed my stuff. *No tracks. No trace.*

But when I stepped out through the guestroom doorway and glanced down the hall at an educated man's office, an obedient girl's bedroom, and a grown-up master suite, a fading part of me longed to announce my presence. Kinda like on a street corner not far from there, under a pool of lamplight, when a girl I'd once known who'd fled from her supposed protection visited once in a while to say *See me. I'm here. I'm still alive.*

But the people who belonged to the house I stood in didn't have a right to know, nor did they need to know. The only one who needed to know I still existed—that I still survived in spite of a grave injustice? *Me.*

I walked from the hall toward the front door with a new sense of being. My steps were lighter. My heart beat stronger than ever before.

Because I'd changed. A different person had just trespassed in that house. A grown woman.

My back pocket vibrated. I smiled as I exited the house and locked the door from the outside. And as I stood in the shadows of the entryway, I finally pulled the phone out.

Ben had texted.

Miss me yet?

With a headshake and the remnants of my smile, I repocketed the phone. "How could I miss you? You've been with me the whole time."

Then I vanished into the thick bushes at the back of the house and connected with the woods that edged the upper-class neighborhood.

I had an unofficial appointment to keep back at my real home, deep in the forest that surrounded my park.

LAWBREAKER

"Trin!" I called out into the vast surrounding forest.

The hidden clearing remained the same, as it always had year after year. Access had been granted to only those few who'd been shown which blackberry thickets to navigate through, which mossy boulder to turn left or right at, which overgrown ferns hid a worn pathway under years of pine needles and leaf litter.

A few shafts of sparkling golden sunlight broke through the overhead canopy, shimmering as the wind rippled through branches. A gift had been delivered from the Gods to us mortals, ribboned treasures that begged a child to dart through. And I did. On a deep breath of pure air scented of earth and rain and dreams and possibilities, I raced through ancient sunbeams that'd been strung down from the skies. Warm then cool, sun then shadow, light then dark. Freedom and joy filled my heart as I remembered who I truly was, where I'd come from.

Leaping steps rocketed me fifteen feet up a boulder staircase that'd been etched into the side of a mountain eons ago by water, wind, and probably some massive glacier that had scraped by. When the ball of my foot hit the flattened top, I launched into the air and howled a low *ahhhwwwhhhooo* into my beloved forest, claiming my territory, calling out to those who knew.

"*Ahhhwwwhhhooo...*" replied a faint soprano as I landed onto a giant pile of leaves.

A blur of movement flashed by and raced up the boulders. Melodic laughter tinkled from above before the airspace beside me exploded in a flurry of leaves.

I belly laughed and sat up, propping an arm behind me. "You under there somewhere, Trin?"

"Yes." The pile rustled and she sat up. A lion's mane of dried orange leaves framed round blue eyes that blinked heavily. Plump cheeks had flushed pink. A tiny dimple marked her chin. She grinned.

"You look like king of the jungle."

"*Raaawwwrrr...*" Small hands clawed the air as my favorite cub growled out her best roar.

"Well done, little one. You'll have them shaking in their boots in no time."

"Hey." She rose to her full four-and-a-half-foot height, leaves tumbling everywhere. "I'm not little. I've grown five inches just this morning."

"Uh-huh. How old are you again?"

"I turn eleven next month." She dropped her hands onto her hips.

Same age as me when I'd hit the streets. Strange to think I'd ever been that young. But youth and freedom tended to breed resourcefulness and cunning.

"You keep growing at that rate, you'll be a thousand feet tall by the time you turn eighteen."

"I'm a giant!" She lifted her arms, curled her fists in, and tensed her small biceps in a classic muscleman pose.

"Yeah, ya are." No doubt. The amazing things that kid accomplished put the most notorious pickpockets to shame.

"It's in my blood." She gave a definitive nod, raining crumbled bits of leaves from her hair.

"Royal lineage."

She spun on her heel, threw her arms wide, then timbered backward onto our soft forest pile. "A runaway princess."

I collapsed back down to join her. "Now running with thieves."

"Best place in the world to be."

"Agreed." Especially on a private birthday, my own secret celebration. "Speaking of, were you able to hit Tony's for me last night?"

"Course." She crunched fistfuls of leaves, then tossed them into the air. "Dropped a couple cool by midnight."

"Awesome." She'd been a fast learner. And Rafe and Bear had insisted that if Trin was going to survive on her own, she needed the same skills I'd had.

"Why'd you need me to?"

"Because I'm growing up too." Wouldn't be there forever, needed someone to pass the torch to.

"Five inches a morning?"

I smiled. "Something like that."

"What else like that?"

"I'm going on a date tonight."

"*Ewww...*" She scrunched her face. "With a boy?"

"An older boy." A man. But she'd freak if I used any term that remotely sounded like a grown-up.

The leaves rustled, like she'd moved her hands behind her head. "How older?"

"Older than me."

"Do *I* have to do it?"

"Do what?"

"Date a boy."

"You could date a girl."

She fell silent for a few seconds. "Why do I have to date at all?"

"Don't have to. Just..." I shrugged. "Don't you get lonely sometimes?"

"No way. I've got Lando and Tony and Bear. Plus, a new kid showed up last week."

"At the home front?" Unlike me, Trin came from a foster home. Not the worst of them, but not the best of places either.

"Yup. His name is Michael. He's quiet, though."

"Nothing wrong with that."

"And he likes books."

"*Everything* right there."

"Ya think?"

"I know. Quiet and bookish? That one might be worth it." Worthy of her time, maybe at some later point, someone she could open up to, rely on.

She looked skeptical. "We'll see."

Trust ran thin with that one. I knew the feeling.

But hell, she talked to me. That was something. One day she'd feel comfortable enough to test the waters again. Probably not for a while, though. Trin had never had a dad and her mom died a few years back from a drug overdose. The adults "responsible for her" were strapped, with lots of mouths to feed and a big roof to pay for over all their heads. But at least Trin had a place to go where she could clean up and sleep safe.

Which reminded me, I had a few other favorite places to visit, people to check on, then just enough time to get cleaned up in a giant marble bathtub. "I gotta go." I stood from our leaf pile, then gave her a hand up.

"N'ts cool. The art fair's about warmed up by now. Lunchtime." She waggled her brows. "Tired parents."

"Pockets o' cash beggin' ta be picked." I plucked a few remaining leaf bits from her mass of blond hair. Not that it mattered much. Cute kids were invisible. Made for best kind of stealth.

She flashed a wide grin, then disappeared through the trees to the north.

I headed south, back to where I'd come from.

For the briefest moment, I wondered what Ben would think if he caught a glimpse of my world.

16
FIRST DATES IN MOVIES AND OTHER THINGS THAT SUCK

Ben…

*F**ucking gorgeous…*

Shay emerged from the treed edge of Fairmount Park and stepped into the parking lot. A basic tiny black dress swayed with her every step. Dark hair had been pulled high into a ponytail and long bangs framed her eyes.

And the instant she saw me? A wide smile brightened her face.

A heavy thump reverberated deep in my chest. *Not just gorgeous. Stunning.*

Her pace quickened, like she was excited to see me.

I sucked in a steadying breath, trying to pull my shit together.

It's just a date, Ben. She's just a girl. But she wasn't, was she? One hell of a woman came my way. And based on my overwhelming reaction, Shay Morgan had become something so much more than *just* anything to me. *Why I've been thinking about you all day.*

On and off, I'd wondered what she'd been doing. *Doesn't matter. You're here* with me *now.*

A breeze ruffled her hair and a few strands stuck between her lips. My gaze caught on her luscious mouth while she lifted her fingers to her cheek, then pulled those lucky strands away.

I kicked off the brick planter where I'd been camped to cover the distance between us.

"Hey, you." A blush crept across her cheeks as she stared into my eyes for a second. Then she glanced down at a flower I'd pulled out from behind my back.

"Hey." The only word I could manage.

Delight sparkled in her eyes as she stared at the gift I'd brought. She lifted a hand toward it. When her fingers wrapped around the stem, her pinky brushed against mine.

We both gasped at the electric contact.

She bit the corner of her lip, stared down at the asphalt, then glanced back up at me. "Why the rose?"

Because one rose wasn't over the top. And I'd gotten the sense on the phone that a birthday gift would've made her uncomfortable. I faked a disinterested shrug. "Thought it would score me points. To have that chance."

Mischief danced in her eyes. "Think you deserve one?"

"Yeah, I deserve one." *But if you don't think so by now, I'll work even harder to earn it.*

She slipped her hand into mine, but said nothing. *That*

isn't a no. I'd take that silent step.

As we headed toward the front door, I briefly tightened my hold on her hand a little and leaned down. "By the way, you look..." *fucking gorgeous* or *stunning* seemed too startling to say. "Beautiful." The one elegant word fit her, inside and out.

She blushed and gave me a tiny smile as we entered the restaurant's spacious lobby. We worked our way through a packed crowd of twenty plus, then stepped forward to the hostess stand. A teenage girl hung her head down while she scanned over the reservation list.

I pressed a gentle hand against Shay's lower back. "Two for Bishop."

"Right this way, Mr. Bishop." The directive didn't come from the girl behind the stand. It came from a deep male voice behind us.

Shay turned and blinked. "Cade."

"Told you I knew the owner." I winked at her.

But even though she already knew Cade and Hannah owned the joint, panic flashed across her face. A frown formed, and her breath quickened. Her relaxed grip tightened around my hand. But before I had a chance to react, reinforcements came to the rescue.

"And the decorator." Kiki appeared out of nowhere and looped her arm into the crook of Shay's elbow. "What d'ya think of the place?"

"It's...*wonderful.*" Shay's hand relaxed, then slipped away as Kiki led her into the dining room. Shay darted a glance over her shoulder and a lopsided smile wobbled onto her face.

Yep. You're in good hands. "The pastry chef too," I shouted after them as Kiki wound her through packed tables while Cade and I followed.

"Name dropper," Kiki accused as she turned and stopped before a corner table on the patio.

"Technically, title dropper." Cade glanced at Shay. "My Maestro, Hannah? Oversees all desserts." He nodded at the table. "Will this do?"

With raised brows, I deferred to Shay for direction. It was her night, after all.

"It's perfect." As Shay took the chair Kiki offered her, Shay touched her wrist. "And tonight, you are...?"

The meaningful look exchanged between the two women ran deeper than the question. Gratitude shone in Shay's eyes. Warmth radiated from Kiki's as she smiled. "Helper girl. And kitchen co-conspirator" —Kiki leaned in close to Shay— "if you need to make a quick escape."

Kiki pegged me with a stern look, stabbed two fingers in the air toward her eyes, then swiveled her hand and stabbed them at me, universal code for *I'm watching you.*

Understood. I gave her a respectful nod as Cade handed us our menus.

Then as fast as the Michaelson siblings had descended upon us, they disappeared.

Shay balanced the menu on her lap and gripped the top with folded hands as she tucked it under her chin. "They always like that?"

I opened my menu and scanned over it, pretending not to know what she was talking about. "Like what?"

"Overprotective."

"You mean curious, prying little fuckers?"

"*Awww*...I kinda like it." She drew in a deep breath, then lifted her menu and pressed it flat on the table. "At least they care."

Sensing her mood shift, I glanced up.

The corners of her mouth tugged down into another frown.

I put my menu down and stared hard at her. "I care."

She showed no reaction to my words. Gave no indication she'd heard me at all. Some random spot in the center of her menu appeared to have entranced her.

A heavy ache hit my chest, and I stretched my hand out until our fingertips touched. When that failed to break through, I pushed on and slid my fingers through hers until our hands locked together. "Hey." I waited until she finally blinked then looked up from her menu into my eyes.

Good. I had her full attention. "*I* care. I care about you."

"They act like family to you."

"They are like family to me."

"Seems like friends are a better family to have."

Been my experience. "Sometimes they are."

Her expression grew thoughtful.

Silence followed.

Then her hand eased away from mine and her gaze drifted back down to her menu, which she read like the thing had transformed into a riveting novel. Her attention lingered on the bottom right-hand corner before she finally spoke up. "So, what's good here?"

I played along, ignoring the topic that had shut the conversation down. "Everything. It's all locally sourced. If they can't get it from a nearby farm, delivered by a fisherman, or grown in their half-acre garden, it isn't served."

"The chipotle shrimp tacos?"

"Amazing."

She snapped her menu shut. "I'll have that, then."

An older male server appeared out of nowhere. "Excellent choice, madam." He took her menu. "And you, sir?"

I handed him mine. "Make that two. Plus a heaping platter of nachos."

"Heaping?"

"It's what it's called." And I'd witnessed her shameless appetite.

"With a blue agave margarita, rocks with salt," she added.

"And a Bootleg Black Forest Stout for me."

The server bowed his head, dipping it toward Shay with an apologetic expression. "I'm afraid I'll need to see some ID."

Without skipping a beat, she reached into some hidden pocket of her tiny dress, pulled out a card, and handed it to him. He angled the laminated card toward the nearest light, gave a slight nod, then returned it back to her.

I chuckled the moment the server left. "Oh, so she *does* have an ID."

"Never said I didn't have one."

"He gets to see it on command, and I don't?"

"That's right. It was my ticket to a margarita."

"So you *are* legal."

"Brilliant deduction."

"I'm getting better at it." Still, I stared at her for a long moment. Her defensiveness had returned. And every lie-detector sense I had spiked; she was hiding something. I took a wild guess. "The ID must be flawless."

She lifted her gaze to meet mine, then blinked. "What are you saying?"

That I want to get to know you better. The real you. "That you're not *legally* legal."

"You sure about that?"

"No. But you're not denying it." Our heaping nachos arrived, its platter slid between us.

"I'm legal in one way." She jimmied free a loaded corn chip from the middle of the nacho pile before devouring it whole.

"But not the other."

She munched, swallowed, then gave me a slight headshake. "Nope."

I let out a relieved breath.

Her expression lit up with a mixture of amusement and curiosity. "What?"

"Just glad you're not jailbait." I ate a hefty nacho of my own, to every two she confiscated.

Those deep green eyes stared at me for another couple of beats. "*Annnd*...what else have you deduced?"

"You were legal behind my bar, to serve. That when you told me you were old enough the other day, you were *just* legal: eighteen. Now you're technically another year legal: You turned nineteen today."

She gave a one-shouldered shrug. "No big. But all accurate."

"You told me the truth. You trusted me."

She drew in a deep breath, then exhaled through pursed lips. "I'm getting better at it."

"Trust me again."

"With what?"

"Tell me something I don't know about you." *Something beyond the fragments that I've had to piece together.*

Her gaze held mine. Then her head tilted a fraction. "I've never been on a date before."

"This is your first date...ever?" But then, it made sense. With her wariness, that spiky armor, and her hiding behind half-truths and fake IDs, why would she ever trust anyone enough to sit down with them at any meal, let alone a romantic one?

"Yeah." Her chin dipped in a slight nod.

"Well, I'm honored to take you out on your first." Our drinks arrived, and I took a long pull from my stout.

She tasted the salted rim of her drink, her tongue darting out beside a lime wedge hooked to the wide glass, then sipped the bright blue margarita. "So how does it work?"

"A date?"

"Yeah. All I've ever seen are dates in movies."

"Forget everything you've ever seen in a movie about dating. If it was a thriller, he was a serial killer."

She cocked her head. "What if it was action adventure?"

"Then he was a spy and had ulterior motives."

"Romantic comedy?"

"Blundering idiot."

"And you're not?" Humor sparkled in her eyes.

"Sure as hell trying not to be."

"Then guide me. Tell me how a date's supposed to be."

"Well, if it's a first date, then you should share lots of things I don't know about you."

Our entrées arrived on large plates that each held three grilled tacos propped upright in metal dividers, a trio of salsas in ceramic segmented holders, and a cilantro-cabbage slaw.

She pinched both ends of her first taco, then lifted it from its holder. "What do you want to know?"

I watched her take a healthy bite of taco and thought about it.

Where do I start? A lot remained unsaid between us. I knew she had scar tissue. I had my fair share too. Yet everything seemed to revolve around the same topic, one we'd sidestepped like masters.

Yeah, well, fuck that sidestepping shit. Let's get real. "Family sucks, doesn't it?"

Her eyes widened, then she blinked.

Yeah, I threw it right out there. Something about her *and* me.

Her lips tightened into a firm line, as if she didn't trust any words that might tumble out. She swallowed hard and took a deep breath.

Instinct told me to change the subject. Self-preservation did too. But I wanted to get to know her, breach that mile-thick wall she'd constructed behind her spiky armor.

You're not the only one, Shay. You're not alone. "Here, I'll start. My family sucks ass. Dad's an alcoholic. Mom's codependent. She believes his ridiculous excuses and suffers through horrible emotional abuse, because he's excessively charming and great at apologizing. The millions of dollars a year he rakes in doesn't hurt either, makes her unreasonably forgiving."

The more I talked, the more compassionate Shay's expression became, and the better I felt. Aside from Cade, she was the first person I'd told the truth to. That truth, anyway.

Now for the clincher. "Turns out, he's not just charming my mother. He didn't only pull a fast one on the person he'd promised to cherish and love. Evidently, naïve investors are fair game too. Thing is, the Feds aren't so forgiving. When clients complain, and the numbers don't add up, words like 'indictment' and 'prison' get tossed around the dinner table."

The deep furrow that had formed between her brows began to soften. "*That's* why you're so touchy about breaking the law."

I huffed out a laugh. "Apparently to a fault."

She shook her head. "No. Not with me."

I reached a shaking hand toward my beer. *Fuck.* I hadn't realized I'd been affected so badly. Then again, wasn't every day that I bared my soul. I guzzled down half the bottle before I came up for air. "Your turn."

She coughed out a laugh, then shook her head. "Oh no, I'll pass."

"Don't need details," I offered, willing to accept whatever

leap of faith she'd be brave enough to take.

Dark green eyes stared hard at me, studying, assessing—determining if I was worthy.

A barely perceptible nod was the only warning I got.

17
LONG OVERDUE

Shay…

"**M**y family sucked."

There. I admitted I had one. For the first time in eight years.

Ben did that analyzing-stare thing. "*Sucked.* That's a past tense there."

"Flaunting those awesome observation skills again." I had to tease him; it helped chill the heat on me. And I took his bait, shared something important about me, but only so deep. The idea of exposing painful secrets made my heart race, froze my lungs.

"Are they dead?" He furrowed his brows slightly, voice softening.

I gusted out a lungful of air. "To me they are." My tone flattened. I didn't like where the conversation had headed. I took a deep breath, trying to figure out how to divert it.

"It's why you're on your own, isn't it?"

He'd been beating around that bush for a while. Time for us to end the dance we'd been doing. And there opened up my diversion: talking about me, not...*them*.

"Ask me what you really want to know."

His eyes narrowed a fraction. But I couldn't tell if he'd reacted to my harsh tone or if he was trying to gauge the safety of going there.

Yet all of a sudden, I wanted him to know, needed him to see me...*the real me.*

I tilted my head. "Ask me," I pleaded on a whisper.

"You're a runaway, aren't you?"

Bam. There *it is.*

"I ran away." An action, not a label. The one act of bravery that had set me free didn't cast me in a negative light. It had defined me, but in a different way. The best kind of independent way.

"That bad, huh?"

"Bad enough." My clipped tone signaled that was the end of it—all he'd get from me. But I'd fessed-up. It was a beginning and something I needed him to know in order to go any further.

Ben's image blurred, and I realized my eyes had misted over with tears. I firmed my lips and drew in a steadying breath.

With a sudden headshake, I forced out a laugh. "It's why I like your family." I glanced across the busy dining room at Cade, who stood by the hostess stand near the lobby, then toward the kitchen, where Kiki had disappeared.

He nodded. "For us, the family *we choose* is most important."

"It's why I wanted to work at Loading Zone. Word on the street is that it's one big family."

The corner of his lips twitched. "Is that the word on the street?"

In a flash, his amusement vanished as his mouth fell into a frown. He blinked.

"It's okay, Ben. I'm not ashamed of how I made my way, where I grew up. I'm proud of it. And yeah, that's the word on the street. Which is where I *do not* live, by the way."

Relief washed over his face. "Good. I was worried about that."

"I could tell. I should've dragged it out longer."

He ran his tongue over his teeth. "Right. Because I still deserve to be punished."

"About you firing me? Forever." I meant it. *But only a little.* My slow smile gave me away. But teasing him took the sting out of a painful topic. "So, what were you thinking? A cardboard box? Homeless shelter?"

He leaned back and played with the corner of his napkin. "I didn't know what to think after meeting that hulking guy in the alley. And learning that was the first place you ran to and seeing how he protected you, it seemed like your safe place, your comfort zone."

"It is. One of them, anyway. And Bear is as close to family as I've got. Rafe too." No point in mentioning Trin. *That'd really freak you out.*

Ben swallowed hard. Then he leaned forward and slid

his hand across the table until it covered mine. "But not close enough."

Like real family. To totally let go—believe. I shook my head. "It's hard to let that happen."

"You have to be able to trust."

"Something I'm not big on. *At all.*"

"Yeah, I got that. It's okay. Trust takes time. In small steps. Speaking of, how does getting together tomorrow sound?"

His large hand still covered mine, warmth radiating over my knuckles, the back of my hand. But the intimate contact sizzled through my skin, raced through my body...electric. I swallowed hard. Took a deep breath. "I thought we're getting together now."

"Aha. I knew I had a chance." Mischief glittered in his eyes. He'd loaded innuendo into it.

Okay. I'll go there. "Maybe a chance." Oh, he had *more* than a chance. I'd already decided.

"Tomorrow midday? And into the night?" His tone lightened with hope.

More time, is what he'd meant. And he'd emphasized his last word, asking for far more than time.

The idea of offering him more—sharing all of myself— both excited and frightened me all at once. But then, the best kind of adventures always did. "Yeah, I'd like that."

"And us *getting together* now?"

I blinked. The same low heat from his hand seemed to flare hotter, spiking and snapping through me. I sucked in a gasping breath and glanced up at him.

He arched a brow, challenge and amusement in his expression.

Okay. He wanted to play a little wilder? I could play too. Toss it right out there in the open. "As in sex? Tonight?"

"If you want." He shrugged, like no big. "Probably later tonight. He gripped the edge of the table, then shoved down on it hard enough to make it rattle. "Not sure about here and now. Might break the table."

"Not to mention scandalize all the people around us."

"So, you prefer somewhere private, then. Good to know."

"Says Mr. Straight and Narrow," I muttered.

When I glanced up, we locked gazes. Sensual danger smoldered in his eyes.

I swallowed hard again. Then I decided to come clean. I leaned forward to lower my voice. He leaned forward too. Our lips hovered close enough to touch if we eased in just a little further. I whispered, "I've never done that before."

He angled his head an inch to the left, a slow smile curving his lips. "Sex on a table? Or in public? Should I be taking notes?"

All or nothing, Shay. The real *you.* "Yes. Yes. And if you want to takes notes, up to you. But I've also never done... sex...*at all.*"

All readable expression faded from his face—a total blank, as if every thought, smartass quip, or comeback he'd been formulating had fallen right out of his head.

Then he gave a heavy blink. "You're a virgin."

"There you go again, master of the obvious."

Understanding seemed to dawn on him, like everything I'd revealed so far had fallen into place. "Because you don't easily trust."

The symptom not the cause. But close enough. I gave him a slow nod.

"But you trust me." His tone softened, reverent.

Oddly, I did. Not one part of me doubted my decision. "Again with the obvious. Don't make me change my mind," I teased.

He held up his hands in surrender, breaking our sizzling contact. Which helped me breathe.

I almost laughed, but I got it; he was surprised. Me too...that he'd worked his way into my heart deep enough to convince me to take the plunge.

"Hey, it's not like I don't know how it works. I've watched plenty of porn."

"Porn." He stared at me like I'd spoken some foreign language.

"Sex movies."

"I know what porn is." His warm hand slid forward to cover mine again.

"Why the shock?"

"That's not what we'll be doing."

I blinked. "It's not?"

"Well, the mechanics of it, yeah."

"None of the positions?" I eased my hand back, turned it palm up, then glided it back under his, enjoying the new sensation of his hand across my fingertips.

His cheeks started to pink. But then his lips twisted into a smirk. "Which positions?"

Oh. I'd stumbled right into that one. My skin warmed again until it sizzled into my veins.

Then I took a flying leap, stripping the threat away by tossing it out in the open, in the middle of a busy restaurant.

"Me on top. You on top." *Basic. Not scary.* But then, I didn't want him to think I only wanted safe. "From behind. Against the wall."

He sucked in a slow breath. "Great positions. To start."

His gaze smoldered with that edgy danger again, like he imagined each and every one.

I exhaled a slow breath. "But not tonight."

"Agreed."

Okay, cool. We stayed on the same page about the slow buildup, had lingered there since we'd met. Together, we'd just cranked up the heat.

Kiki appeared out of nowhere, a small plate balanced on one hand, two spoons held in the other. "Happy birthday from us all, but the flourless chocolate cake is compliments of Hannah. She refuses to waddle out here with her stole-a-whole-watermelon belly. And Cade vetoed me running out to buy sombreros for table-singing, even with your Mexican-themed dinner."

I beamed that they'd even thought about it. "Thanks, Kiki. Please tell everyone thanks."

"Ditto," Ben said with a look of gratitude.

We each took an offered spoon and Kiki vanished. The white plate had what appeared to be a cocoa-dusted cylindrical doorstop, with two plump raspberries nestled on a sprig of mint off to the side. Separate drizzles of dark chocolate and raspberry sauce latticed around the edge.

Ben angled his face low, catching my gaze. "Happy birthday, Shay."

I smiled. "Thank you." *For giving me my best birthday ever.*

As we took turns digging spoons into dense chocolate—the best damn moan-worthy chocolate I'd ever tasted—the conversation wandered into lighter non-sex topics. We agreed on a lot of things, like the insanity of current politics, why cream soda beat root beer, and that *no one* can multitask, therefore all distractions should be banned from moving vehicles, like cell phones and screaming kids.

"Ugh." I leaned back, rubbing my full belly.

"Oh, she *does* have a food limit."

"Yup." I groaned. "Tilt."

"Still, I have no idea where you pack all those calories. You're in great shape."

"I don't." I reflected on typical days, the places I hustled, the amount of ground I covered. "I burn them. I walk everywhere, probably a good five to ten miles a day."

His expression turned impressed.

That's nothing. *On my favorite bonus days, I scale rock faces and climb trees.*

The night wound to an end shortly after we finished dessert. But I'd had a great time; Ben gifted me the best first date I could've imagined and a birthday celebration I'd cherish forever.

When we stepped into the parking lot, his hand slipped into mine. "So, I don't get to take you home, do I?"

"No." *Not tonight.*

"But it's customary to kiss at the end of the first date, before she opens her front door."

"You know I've never been customary." I tugged on his hand, leading him toward the park. "Kiss me" —I drew in a deep breath at my words, a hot thrill racing through me— "at the edge of the parking lot. It's practically my front door."

When we reached the edge, where asphalt met grass, he tugged me to a halt, then pulled me toward him. He stared into my eyes. "You know I've been wanting to kiss you since the golf course."

I pressed my hands over his beating heart, remembering how amazing our closeness had felt on the fairway. It felt more incredible now. "I know."

"What you may not know is that I wanted to kiss you at the driving range."

"I knew that too," I murmured.

"And at the bar?"

"The night you fired me?"

"Damnedest thing." His gaze lowered to my mouth. "Those lips spat out such fire. And yet those same full, luscious lips were begging to be kissed."

"You sure about that?"

Challenge fired in his eyes. "Deny it."

"Yours belted out nothing but ego." The only truth I could admit to. Because I wasn't so sure I hadn't wanted to kiss him back then. I'd been trembling with fury. But the scorching heat of that night and the slow burn of everything that had followed had continued—had smoldered ever hotter.

"Ego is all I've known. How I've survived." His eyes searched mine. "But I was wrong. You humble me now."

My heart warmed at his confession.

Time for one more of mine. I let out a shaky breath. "I've never been kissed."

"How old are you again?" His voice lowered, softened, humor edging his tone.

Old enough. But our battle had ended. It had begun in a fierce fight over proving my age, but had become more about the principle, about faith...trust. There was no point in fighting him—or myself—anymore. We had nothing left to prove. We'd already won. We stood in each other's arms in spite of the scars we bore...maybe because of them.

And still, even though he'd already reasoned out my age—the spark of our whole explosion—I spoke it aloud, offered the information again, from my heart to his, freely given.

"Nineteen."

"You're long overdue."

"Seems" —I let out a shaky breath, struggling to think as my pulse began to race— "I've been waiting for you."

His strong arms banded around me. Firm fingertips pressed against my lower back.

But his body remained relaxed, like he safeguarded me but refused to cage me.

And I didn't feel trapped. I wanted to be where I stood. With Ben.

Nothing's ever felt more right.

The next seconds began to slow, like time unfolded one heartbeat at a time—just for us.

His head lowered and his protective hold around me tightened.

My breaths quickened as every nerve ending zinged to life.

Soft lips brushed over my whole mouth, but he placed a tiny gentle kiss to one corner, then feathered a glide across to press a matching small kiss to the other.

Warm breath fanned over my chin.

Aching heat flared everywhere else, from deep inside, spreading outward...*and lower*.

Eyes drifted shut: his, then mine.

All at once, we full-blown connected. Lips pressed together, softly at first, then harder, demanding. Mine opened on a gasp as the building ache flashed hot between my legs.

He groaned low, as if pleased by my reaction, as his tongue dragged across my lower lip, then slid inside my mouth.

My tongue glided along his, testing, tasting. Ben smelled of earth and sunshine. He tasted of wild danger and endless dreams.

Our ragged breaths came in shortened gasps for air.

I gripped his shoulders, hanging on for balance as the earth seemed to tilt under my feet.

He growled as he kissed me harder, demanded more.

Then, as quickly as it had all started, everything slowed once more. Our lips softened again, tasting, sipping. Our breaths began to steady. His fierce hold around me relaxed, infinitesimally.

My tight grip on his shoulders remained, though. With my spinning head and wobbly knees, I didn't trust myself to stand upright should he let me go.

He didn't.

One last incredibly softened kiss, one more taste of dangerous sexy male, and the amazing moment faded away like a fantasy, even as it imprinted on my flesh, seared my very soul.

"Wow," I whispered as we eased apart, blown away. "That's *some* first kiss."

"*Wow*." His whisper gusted out with ten times the ferocity.

And as he held me, he stared at me in wonder, as if he'd never been kissed like that before, had never been affected by another the way I affected him.

I held on to him a moment more, heart still racing, breaths still ragged.

But then, I let go of his shoulders. "Tomorrow." I promised.

"Tomorrow." He gave me a nod, then released his hold. But his expression grew uncertain. Like if he relented and let me vanish into my park, what we'd shared might all poof into nothing but a dream.

I turned and vanished anyway, without even one look back. Maybe he needed assurances, but I needed my control more, my freedom to choose, to do things my way, at my pace.

With Ben's amazing taste on my lips, my body zinging, and my heart soaring, I began to smile. Then I charged off at a full run, straight toward my forest, back to where the trees kept all secrets, night creatures sang with hope, and a crisp wind blew everything clean...whole and new.

LAWBREAKER

Oh, crap. Something new had happened.

I hovered at the edge of the forest, at the perimeter of Miss Princess Persephone's yard, breath held in disbelief.

A room at the back of the house had a light on.

Had they installed light timers? *Doubtful.* In eight years, they hadn't changed a thing: no security system, no light timers, same housesitting agency. I thought about the gun, then forcefully blocked it from my mind. *Not helpful.*

Could I have accidentally left it on?

No.

Every time I entered any house, I methodically swept the premises, light switches included. Nothing had been left on when I'd arrived.

And I sure as hell hadn't switched on anything when I'd been in there.

With leaden footsteps and a heavy heart, I walked toward the front of the house to view the porte cochere. My pulse double-timed and my chest tightened with dread as I rounded the corner. But I gasped when I actually saw it: a black SUV parked between me and the front door.

"*Fuck*," I bit out under my breath. My stuff was in there, my backpack and duffel.

After a few steadying breaths, my spine straightened with determination. In the deep reaches of my heart and mind, I saw the obstacle not as a roadblock but as a test.

Silent as the calm before a storm, I slid my trusty key into the deadbolt lock, opened the front door wide enough to slip inside, then eased it shut behind me. On a slow exhale, I grasped the bronze thumbturn and gradually rotated until I heard the snick of the lock.

When I spun around in the darkness, I sensed a presence there with me.

Then I glanced down.

A creaky half-meow squeaked out.

"*Shoo, Persie!*" I whispered, as if she'd understand my desperate order.

A loud complaining meow followed.

With a sigh, I knelt and rubbed her soft head. *Please be quiet.*

Bright light flashed across the far wall of the entry hall. Heavy footsteps echoed over stone tiles.

Shit. Shit! I stood and pressed myself into the darkest shadow of the front corner.

Persie sat there, her dark silhouette staring up at me. *Traitor.*

But at the last second, as the fronts of two leather shoes stepped into view, she glanced their way while I held my breath.

"Persephone," a low male voice chided. "Come. You'll wake the whole house."

He returned toward the direction from where he'd come. Seconds later, a refrigerator door opened with a sticky release of its seal. The dull sound of a small bag shaking its contents followed. *Cat treats.*

Persie darted away.

So did I, in the opposite direction, toward the guest bedroom.

Chills ran down my spine at the remembered sound of his voice. But I forced the panic from my mind. I had no time to spare. When he returned into the hall, I needed to be gone.

I yanked my bags out from under the bed right as the refrigerator light flicked off. But the illumination along the entryway wall filtered into the hall, and it hadn't changed. His office door remained open.

Where are you? Had he heard something? Did he suspect an intruder?

My thoughts flashed to the gun again.

And Persie, the sentry.

Leaving back out the front door was too risky.

My gaze darted toward the wide window that stretched beyond the small writing desk. A careful prowler would be able to clear that opening and not disturb a thing. *No tracks. No trace.*

I glanced back toward the hall. Very little light made it into the guestroom.

Doable.

With a sharp exhale, I gave a decisive nod. *Done.*

As quietly as possible, I shoved the double-hung window upward. But in the dead silence of the night, the frame scraping against its wood casing sounded like a screech through a megaphone.

"*Go, go, go,*" I mouthed to myself as I heaved the duffel

out onto the dense honeysuckle hedge, tossed my backpack to land beside it, then squeezed my body through the narrow opening.

Once I planted my feet on the ground, I crouched at the lip of the window ledge and peered inside. Dim light from down the hall glowed a faint bluish white, but there were no signs of alarm.

Holding my breath, I stood and stretched up to my full height, exposing my entire body as I gripped solid fingerholds on the window edge, then dragged it back down.

When less than an inch remained, the window resisted against its metal latches. I exhaled and exerted a burst of pressure, seating it firmly home—with a loud click.

I sucked in a breath and waited. Not because I planned to stick around and explain myself if the lights suddenly switched on, but better to have the all-quiet before darting across the huge lawn with my back to a man with a gun.

My breaths had become ragged gulps of air, so I passed the time calming them. *Inhale...exhale.*

My racing heart began to slow, beat by beat.

But as a full minute ticked by, then another, all in the big Tuscan house remained the same, probably the way it always had: loyal wife sleeping soundly, husband up late scheming in his office, obedient daughter waiting in her bedroom.

With a sigh of relief, I turned my back on them all.

The hedge further complicated my escape. Far along both sides of the window, woody branches covered in lush greenery pressed up against the house.

The only way out was over.

LAWBREAKER

With great focus and careful placement, I toed footholds and grasped branches. Halfway over, my foot slipped off a thick branch and my shoulder slammed down into the bush. Greenery smacked my face, filled my mouth.

"Shit," I spat out with a mouthful of waxy leaves. *Nice bush-climbing outfit*: little black dress, flimsy sandals.

One last handhold, legs swung over, a step down, one more, and my feet landed back on solid ground. Since I'd twisted around to clear the hedge, I faced the house. The guest bedroom window remained dark. *All clear.*

However, when I turned and took a small step sideways, my heel caught on an exposed root, and I tumbled backward. My butt struck the wet lawn first, but the momentum thumped my back against the ground and knocked the wind out of me.

Eyes watering, I sucked in a lungful of air and stared up at a dark sky. Must've been thick cloud cover overhead, because nothing sparkled up there.

"Really?" I accused the world at large. "Not even one measly star to make a wish on tonight?"

A gust of wind rustled through elm branches, my only answer.

Something shifted against my scalp. I reached up and wrestled a twig free from my hair. "Happy birthday to me," I grumbled.

But as I stood and grabbed my duffel, then slung my backpack over my shoulder, the greater truth of my words sank in. After eight lonely years, I'd finally had a birthday worth celebrating.

Because of you, Ben.

With a renewed sense of purpose, I walked away from that Tuscan house of anniversaries and birthdays without one glance back. Because I'd finally grown up.

The baggage I carried no longer weighed me down.

And stolen treasure I'd once thought important had lost all meaning.

Time for me to let go. Time to move on.

I entered my woods and yawned wide, suddenly exhausted. *Time to find someplace to crash.*

18
ONE STEP BACK

Ben...

"Uhhh...explain what we're doing here?"

I stared in disbelief at a luxury home as we walked side by side down a mossy stone path.

Shay blinked up at me, humor in her eyes. "Your text said we should hang at my place."

Because I want to know you better, see into your world.

But the multimillion-dollar house we approached stood light-years from what I'd imagined.

"*Your* place." It didn't add up. And I sensed deception in her tone.

I'd also become acutely aware of the physical distance she maintained between us. No hug hello. A good few inches of buffer space at all times.

Maybe you remember our kiss as vividly as I do.

Her sweet fiery taste still lingered on my lips. The heat

from her lithe body had branded my skin. *From one kiss.* My breath caught at the powerful memory. Then I sucked in a deep lungful and understood and fully appreciated her imposed distance. And I vowed to respect that unspoken agreement. *For now.*

"My place for the week, anyway."

Okay. The nuts and bolts of it. "So, we're trespassing, then?"

Once we hit the shade of the outer entry, she turned to face me. "Not *really* trespassing. Technically, the owner gave written authorization for someone to take care of the place."

"Technically, huh? *Sooo...*'someone'...meaning you?"

"Not *officially* me. There's a contract; a homecare company has been hired."

Instead of continuing toward the door, she dropped onto the end of a galvanized steel bench. Maybe she needed to scrutinize me one last time, before she committed to taking me inside.

But based on where the conversation had headed, I wasn't the only one who needed to be vetted. "Not *your* homecare company."

Translation: you break in.

I sat down.

A delicate smile curved the corners of her lips. Her unassuming beauty turned breathtaking in the shadowy light: bare skin radiated health, thick dark hair framed her face, gorgeous green eyes watched me...as if I'd become the center of her universe.

Thank fuck. Because the woman who sat beside me,

wearing her standard black T-shirt and threadbare jeans, had somehow become mine.

She bent her legs up, tucked the heels of her Converse onto the edge of the bench, then clamped her arms around her shins.

"No. It's not my company. But that's okay." With an unfocused gaze, she stared out toward the path we'd walked down, then glanced back at me. "I'm kinda like a friendly unseen ghost. I roam the halls when no one's around. Look after the place. The owners get a twofer: extra security for the house, more one-on-one time for the pets."

"And the *real* homecare company has been hired to..."

"At this house? Feed the fish. Water the plants. The fine print on the back page of every contract has the owners' initials, allowing said caretaker to stay the night and housesit the place, if said homecare company chooses."

Impressive that she'd read the fine print. Exploited it. *Still...* "What if the official homecare company ever chooses to enact that stay-the-night clause for themselves?"

"Not this house. Never this house. It's one girl, Henrietta. And she only stays the night at certain houses. She marks the calendar, so I know in advance which houses are free."

"The calendar." *The more I ask? The deeper it gets.*

She grinned. "The one I hack into."

"Ah, so two kinds of breaking and entering: real space and cyberspace." And yet, the system Shay had devised for great places to stay? Genius.

"Yup. I'm a master at getting past front doors and firewalls."

And burrowing into an unsuspecting bar-owner's heart.

"Where'd you learn that talent?"

"Rafe."

I blinked, surprised at her answer. My head of security had more talents than I'd realized.

Then I nodded at the massive front door ahead of us. "How do you get past this one?"

She popped up from the bench, reached into her back jeans pocket, and pulled out a big silver key. She held it up between her finger and thumb. "My unofficial access, the key to my kingdom."

"You have keys to all the houses?"

"Nope." She tossed the key into the air, then caught it in her fist. "I only made extra keys for a few, the special ones."

"And the rest?"

Her penetrating stare landed on me. She arched a brow. "I'm an excellent lock picker."

I stood from the bench, closing the distance between us. "Lock picker..."

Her gaze rose, staying with mine. "And pocket picker," she reminded.

The accidental bump I'd witnessed in the park. "Thief of all trades."

"The best kinds are." She smirked, then stepped away and slid her big key into the lock of the polished wood door. With a slight push, the large door swung open to reveal a bright interior. She took a few steps in, then glanced over her shoulder.

Oddly, I stopped cold at the threshold. I frowned at the

instinctive hesitation as I reached up and planted my hands on either side of the doorframe. She had stepped inside with ease: Lawbreaking was her world. But it was completely foreign to me.

She must've sensed my reluctance, because she turned right around.

Her eyes softened and she let out a gentle sigh as she tilted her head. "It's your first time."

"Yup. No jaywalking, no gum stealing, I'm going straight to breaking and entering."

"It'll be okay," she assured me with quiet words as she moved forward.

My breathing roughened as her hands smoothed over my abs, around the sides of my ribs, then skimmed up to rest on my shoulder blades.

Her body pressed against mine as she stared up at me with those mesmerizing green eyes. "It's going to be okay because I'm here. We're doing this together."

"Okay." If she could break the law and go inside, so could I. But neither of us moved. *Damn.* She smelled amazing, felt incredible. "But you're gonna have to move first." Because I couldn't, wouldn't if I could. *No way in hell.* "Orrr..."

"Orrr..." Her eyelids lowered, like her standing there intoxicated her like a drug.

Yeah. I'm getting drunk on us too. "Maybe a kiss would make it better."

"Isn't that for little-kid bruises?"

"I'd be willing to go slam my truck into a tree for one."

"Wow." She blinked.

"*Wow*." I repeated. What we'd both felt then.

"It's still *some* kiss for you too."

Yep. Still feelin' it. "I can't remember any other kiss. Yours scrubbed my memory."

"Good." She smiled. "I like that mine's the only one in your mind."

"Your kiss has been on my mind since we broke contact. I'm beginning to get the shakes. Withdrawals count for grown-up kisses, right?"

"Do you *need* to kiss me or *want* to kiss me?"

"Want. Definitely want."

Her eyes searched mine. "Enough to wait?"

"Yeah." I stared hard at her. "Worth the wait."

Surprise registered on her face as my meaning sunk in. *Not just the kiss. Not only physical. All of you.*

"Thank you," she murmured. "I feel the same about you. And I've been waiting a long time."

So, no kiss. Not yet. Still, we remained there, unmoving, soaking it in. I kept a tight grip of the doorframe. Because if I let go, I couldn't guarantee the wait. And it was enough that she held me, while we did nothing more than breathe deeply together.

Until after a tiny smile and brief pressure of her fingertips on my shoulder blades, she eased back and withdrew from our intimate hold.

Then she stepped sideways and swept an arm wide, leading toward the room beyond. "Welcome to my humble abode."

"Your *humble* abode?"

And yet, even though the modern home exuded luxury on the outside, its furnishings were Spartan: two gray microfiber chairs and a matching couch with one yellow decorative pillow paired with artful metal tables, a smaller drink table between the two chairs, and a lower cocktail table in front of the couch. Four slim black picture frames on the walls featured color drawings of plant specimens. A couple of fat beeswax candles on low mercury holders sat on the corner of a sleek fireplace mantel. The room's vibe was simple and inviting.

"This house is special." The door clicked shut behind me, followed by the resounding clank of a heavy lock being thrown.

"Agreed." If the comfortable front room was any indication of the rest, I understood why she'd made a key.

"This is *my* house." She wrapped her arms around her middle as she stepped into the room. "The one that matters. My safe house."

Because it fit her. But I sensed she meant more, like she could depend on it. "A constant."

"Yeah. The closest I've ever had to a home-house."

I scanned ahead over black hardwood flooring that stretched out from the modern living room. "Well, do I get a tour, or what?" I wanted to see all of the place, understand what made her claim it as hers.

"Yep. Shoes off." She'd already removed her Converse and had placed them near the wall by the door.

I toed off my sneakers beside hers, then followed as she led the way.

"Kitchen." She nodded left as we walked past a sprawling kitchen island with a green granite countertop. "Fish." She pointed toward the right at a gigantic saltwater fish tank that spanned from where we stood to the far end of the wall, a good twenty feet.

Her steps quickened across the floor until we entered a large open room which also held only a few pieces of furniture, again covered in modern microfiber, this time in a darker gray. Halfway through, we descended two steps into an additional space surrounded on all three sides by large windows. "This is my favorite spot in the whole house."

"Nice." The basic masculine furnishings were items I would've chosen myself. An ancient metal desk had been tucked under the center window and overlooked an expansive back lawn. Worn black leather club chairs sat off to one side. A chrome table with a glass top held a birding field guide with a small set of binoculars perched on top.

Shay's hand slipped into mine. "Right?" With a slight tug and tightening of her fingers, she led me toward the desk.

A larger set of binoculars rested on the corner. Beside them, a similar device, same length, same black outer casing, but with only a single scope, struck me as familiar. From golf. I nodded at it. "A rangefinder?"

"It's a monocular. He's a birder." She released my hand and picked up the scope, removed both lens caps—first from the eyepiece then from the viewing lens—and handed me the device.

She grabbed the binoculars, uncapped its lenses, then plopped down in a black mesh ergonomic chair that'd been positioned in front of the desk. She propped her elbows onto the desk surface and held the binoculars up to her eyes. "They both have a similar range. But I prefer the binoculars. Pinching an eye shut to stare out of that thing for too long gives me an eye cramp. Same with the one in the corner." She gave a nod to her right but still stared out her binoculars.

Her distancing tactic hadn't been lost on me. The desk chair isolated her. Gave her space.

Fair enough. I'd been invited over and allowed into her inner sanctum. Two steps forward, one step back.

I respected the space she'd cordoned off, but stood as close as possible to the chair without bumping it.

I glanced toward the right where a giant commercial-grade telephoto lens mounted on a tripod aimed its view through a corner window toward the far horizon. Then I raised the monocular up to my right eye and squinted my left shut. "I think it's meant for spotting, not staring into the field for a long period of time. Great for quick focus, though."

After a slight adjustment, I examined the far edge of a pond. Then I pulled the monocular away from my eye to absorb the entire larger space behind the house. On all sides, the lawn was edged by old-growth trees of pine, birch, maple, and many I couldn't identify. Beyond the immediate perimeter, a terrain of endless treetops sloped uphill until a far ridgeline met blue sky.

A low sigh drew my attention back into the room, to the woman seated at my right. She'd settled into the chair, head resting against the high seatback, two hands gripping the binoculars pressed to her eyes. Her lips were slightly parted.

Her chest rose and fell in a medium tempo, too quick to be relaxed, yet her entire bearing had downshifted into happy contentment.

Beautiful. She radiated from the inside out. And I couldn't tear my gaze away. Expensive viewing lenses didn't hold my interest. *You do.*

She must've sensed my focused attention on her, because she pulled her binoculars away and stared back at me a beat. Then her brows furrowed. Disappointment flashed across her face.

And then it hit me like a wrecking ball to the chest; every bit of what we were doing held great importance to her. She wasn't just sharing equipment from some guy's house where she happened to be staying. At her special house, in her favorite spot, she'd chosen to share an intimate piece of herself with me.

Warmth spread through me as I smiled at her.

Her expression instantly brightened, whatever fleeting worry she'd had vanishing.

And my heart stuttered, like she'd zapped me and I'd short-circuited.

I gripped my monocular and held it up to my eye, dedicated to experiencing the moment together, her way. "Ever catch anything good out here?"

I refocused my lens toward the near trees.

A couple of low clunks sounded on the metal desk, her elbows settling. "All the time. Usually I stand guard right before sunrise. Sometimes I sit here for hours. Over the summer, I saw pileated woodpeckers for a few weeks."

"And that's rare?" I had no idea what a pileated woodpecker was. But if she was into it, so was I.

"Not rare, I don't think. But cool. Been hunting an ivory-billed too. *That* would be rare; they're supposedly extinct. Both look like little prehistoric pterodactyls. Pretty sure mine were a mated pair with a nest nearby. Totally cool to watch them peck and investigate their way up a tree trunk. My wakeup call one time? One of 'em jackhammering something metal at the top of the neighbor's chimney."

The neighbors. The house sitter. I pulled down my monocular. "Don't you ever worry about the 'official' homecare person coming by when you're here?" I did. Maybe she'd lived on the edge for years before me, but I saw the risk in how she lived. And I didn't want anything bad to happen to her.

"Nope." She put down her binocs, then leaned back in the chair. "Henrietta sticks to her schedule. Begins at 4:30 a.m. All the dogs come first. Cats are next. Fish and plants are low on the totem pole, only need to be fed or watered every few days. For this one, she only does a daily home-check immediately after her lunch, before her second-round dog visits and afternoon jobs."

She'd had me wait to come over at 4:00 p.m., well after lunch-check. "What about the owner? How often does this guy go out of town?"

"My guy's name is Stephan Bergdorf. He's a National Geographic photographer and filmmaker. Does at least two documentaries a year, sometimes three. For those trips, he's gone six to eight weeks at a time. Plus, he adds different working photography vacations that last ten to twelve days or more."

My adrenaline spiked at her *my guy's* reference. I hated the idea of her having any kind of ownership with some other guy. But I worked on controlling my breaths. No more bursting into clubs, no more reacting without thinking. "Wow. That's a lot of information." *There. Tone neutral.*

She gave an easy shrug. "No big. Comes with the territory. I need a place to stay? I'm gonna know everything I can about where I sleep." She paused and an unsettled expression flashed across her face. "I wouldn't feel comfortable at night unless *I knew for sure* the owner wasn't coming home."

I wondered about her fleeting discomfort. *Had a close call ever happened?* "Henrietta hasn't ever planned to stay the night?"

"Not here. She comes in, does a once-over, waters the plants if it's a Thursday, then leaves within the fifteen-minute time slot she's got scheduled for the place."

"And the fish?" I stared back at the giant saltwater tank in the wall that seemed like it should've been the main event.

"Left to the professionals. The people who installed the tank maintain it, even when Stephan's in town."

"Understood." *And perfect.* She'd done her research. I'd done my due diligence too. The place was ours for the night. No interruptions.

She stared at me with an expression of happiness and relief.

And I realized I'd passed the test. I'd broken the law. I accepted her for who she was. And I'd stuck around, wanting more.

Good. Because I itched to sprint toward the next hurdle.

I took her hand, and eased her up out of the chair. "Where's your backpack? The phone?" Yep. *The* phone. Not giving her a reason for even the smallest argument.

She didn't resist as I kept drawing her toward me. But when she collided into my chest, and I wrapped my arms around her, her eyes widened. She swallowed hard. "Under the bed."

"Well, that was easy."

"It was?" Her hands traveled up my chest until her fingertips landed over my heart. "Wait. What was?"

"I guessed you'd say bedroom. You dove straight for the bed. See how I did that?"

"Tricky."

"Well after last night's porn talk, I figured you'd be the one to bring up the sex again."

"*The* sex."

"*Our* sex. Sound better?"

"Yeah." Her eyes searched mine as she drew in a slow breath.

But her body began to tense.

Two steps forward, one step back. So, I did the only thing that worked with her. I fired out a curveball. "Just like that?"

She blinked. "What do you mean 'just like that'?"

I grabbed her hips, turned her, and hauled her off her feet with a hard yank. She gasped and collapsed onto my lap as we both landed on the corner of the desk.

Off-balance, she threw her arms around my neck. Her soft breath feathered over my lips. Those emerald eyes had darkened, pupils wide with excitement.

I touched my forehead to hers. "No romance? No days and weeks of courting?" My hands slid over her hips until they anchored onto the upper part of her ass. I tightened my fingers possessively.

She didn't laugh at my teasing, at the mock outrage in my voice. Instead she turned to reason, debating my challenge at face value. "Haven't we been courting since we met?"

"*Hmmm...*" I wanted to kiss her so damn bad. But I didn't want to rush her. I needed her to want it as bad as I did. I dragged my lips along the silken skin of her jaw. "Guess we have."

She shivered when I paused at her neck and exhaled below her earlobe. My body reacted with a growing ache as my cock began to harden against the fly of my jeans—under the untried *but far from innocent* woman curled in my lap.

She swallowed hard. "And there's romance," she whispered. "I *did* break into a house for you."

I chuckled low and nipped her earlobe with my teeth. "Trespass. Nothing broken except the law."

At the last word, her body tensed and she held her breath. Then she exhaled and eased back with enough distance between us to stare hard at me. "Is that so bad? Me breaking the law?"

"No." Not for her. Somehow the black and white that I'd lived my life by had blurred into murky gray. "You do what you need to do to survive." In my head, the need justified the means.

All of a sudden, the reasons she'd been so upset when

I'd fired her made more sense. She'd fought to go legit. And without probable cause, I'd burned her to the ground.

Had nothing to do with you. Everything to do with me and my shit.

Good thing I'd had half a brain and a conscience. And enough humility to do an ego-check and chase her down.

The color in the back room shifted into dusk's purple tones. Shadows darkened her features. But after our conversation, with her in my arms and growing braver about opening up to me, I'd never found her more beautiful.

She stared into my eyes as her chest rose and fell.

My head lowered, the urge to kiss her damn near overwhelming.

Her gaze dropped to my lips.

Without warning, her hands jerked wide to grip my shoulders as she leaned back. "Dinner!"

I blinked. "Dinner."

"Pizza." She gave a decisive nod, then lurched away and broke the hold I had on her as she jumped from my lap.

She moved just out of my reach, breathing heavily.

Like you don't trust...

Gut instinct dealt me a solid: Her uncertainty had nothing to do with me.

"Shay," I whispered. "You don't have to be afraid."

19
CONSPIRACY TO COMMIT

Shay...

"What's to be afraid of?"

Ben gave me an intense stare and took a slow breath. He'd gotten all deep on me.

And I'd gone all *no big*.

I dove headlong into a safe zone. "You've seen me eat pizza before."

His eyes narrowed a fraction. "Like an animal."

"Why hold back? It's a greasy, salty mouthful of goodness."

The corners of his mouth twitched. "You're a peculiar and intriguing woman."

Because I'd launched the convo straight from sex to food? *Both basic needs.*

Not that I knew anything about the first. Only studied, analyzed, never experienced. And until last week, I hadn't

261

ever imagined I would. Not one fantasy.

Until you.

But I could only handle so much at once. If we happened at all, we needed to at my speed.

I dialed a nearby pizza place. They didn't question my bizarre directions for delivery.

Thirty-five minutes later, when nightfall had transformed the outdoors into a wonderland of shadow play and insect song, Ben stood behind the neighbor's tall street-side hedge with a large pizza box balanced on his hand.

He shot me a dubious look. "I feel like we just did a drug deal."

"Don't exchange cash for goods much?"

"Not from behind a Japanese boxwood."

"Cape honeysuckle's more your thing?"

"A doorbell is usually involved. And a porch light."

I tugged on a front belt loop of his jeans and led us back across the neighbor's front lawn, careful to keep the trees and an elaborate rose garden between us and view from any windows. "Welcome to my world. Clandestine-R-Us."

When I pulled back a section of overgrown vine and nodded him through, he shook his head, then ducked under a woody branch.

"More like Domino's-N-D-Amazon," he grumbled as he shouldered past a mass of green leaves and lilac-blue flowers. He trudged through to the other side, kept walking a few paces, then stopped.

The last of the branches rustled as I released them.

I caught up with him, then nudged his shoulder as we

walked around the back of the house. "You know, you should try breaking the law more often. Might do you some good."

When he gripped the back door's handle, I put a hand on his forearm and nodded over toward a grassy mound near a tree. Moonglow backlit a light cloud layer, highlighting our shadowy world in a wash of pale silver, and I wasn't ready to leave my outside world just yet.

He diverted toward the patch of grass, settled onto the ground, then flicked open the pizza-box lid. "*Orrr...*you could become a good little law-abiding citizen."

I plonked down beside him, grabbed a pepperoni slice, and took a couple of napkins from the stash he'd pocketed from the delivery guy. "I did. At your bar. We saw how well that went."

"I was wrong. And I promised not to fire you again."

A leaf spiraled down toward our pizza, but I snatched it with my fist. I polished off my first piece, then grabbed one from the side with mushrooms and olives. "You can't fire me. Independent contractor, remember?"

"I could terminate your contract." He grabbed a double slice.

"But you won't. I work my ass off and you know it. Unfireable and irreplaceable."

His left brow arched. "Not far from law-abiding."

"*Ahhh...*but that's only when I'm working for you."

He finished chewing, then wiped his mouth with a crumpled napkin. He stared at me for a couple of seconds. "Would it be so hard to ditch a life of crime?"

I frowned. His instincts had already begun to slide

toward wanting to change me.

I'm fine just the way I am. And I thought he knew that, saw the real me, down deep.

I need you to understand.

We chewed as I thought about what to say. He finished his pizza right as I finished mine.

After tossing my napkin into the box lid, I leaned up on my knees, moving closer to him. "Not hard. Just...different. When you have to find a way to survive, and no one's got your back but yourself, you bend every rule. And maybe you decide someone selfish made the stupid rules in the first place. A neat little black-and-white package to fit their specific life. One size *does not* fit all."

He pegged me with his classic *trying-to-figure-Shay-out* stare.

I pressed my lips together, fighting a smile, and dropped him a *I'm not that easy* silent reply. "Seriously. You should try a little more danger. It'll rough up those perfect straight edges of yours—make your seriousness less fatal."

His expression changed, as if he began to contemplate the possibility.

"You want to. I can see it." For the first time, *I* made a move, twisting in toward him to land on his lap. I slid my hands around his neck, then dragged my fingertips up the back of his scalp before tousling his hair. "Come over to the dark side. It'll be fun."

"Said the spider to the fly."

"Not a spider, a dragonfly. We eat mosquitoes." My blurted statement reminded me of things Trin and I exclaimed, without one care, in the middle of our sacred clubhouse forest.

He glanced at my lips, then stared into my eyes. "You continue to amaze me."

Says the man with me now, in my private forest.

"Birdwatcher *and* insect expert," I added as I tugged at the ends of his hair. He groaned low and put his hands on my hips, adjusting my position on his lap. I began to smile, charged a little with the power I had over him. "Well?"

He grunted softly and touched his forehead to mine. "Well, you keep sitting on my lap," he murmured, "I'm gonna agree to anything."

"To make me stop?" I whispered.

His warm breath feathered over my lips. "Hoping you'll never stop."

I turned my face, brushing my cheek along the soft hairs of his beard. "*Sooo*...you'll do it? Become a lawbreaker with me."

He squeezed his hold on my hips and let out a hard exhale. "You're on." His tone lowered. "But no felonies. I have to draw some kind of line, keep us both out of jail."

My smile widened. "Give me one week. You'll see."

He toppled us backward onto the grass with a growl, dragging us to lay side by side with his arm secured under my neck and around my shoulder. "I already sense I'm gonna regret this."

I settled against him, but frowned at his concern and rested my chin on his chest. "I won't let anything bad happen. I never do."

He tucked his other arm under his head and stared up into the darkness. "Okay, fine. But not a week each. A week total. And no one gets two days in a row; we alternate."

"Works for me. Since today is Sunday, I get Tuesday."

He narrowed his eyes at me. "No way. I get Saturday."

"Why do you need Saturday?"

"Because of the tournament. There will be *no* lawbreaking at the tournament." He gave me a pointed look. Then his brows twitched down for a split second. "Why do you need Tuesday?"

"Because I do. I need every Tuesday. But I'm not gonna tell you why. You'll see."

He glanced back up at a clearing night sky. I relaxed into the crook of his arm and stared up there too, as if the illuminated wispy clouds held the mysteries of our universe. His head moved with a slight nod. "Today doesn't count, then. You get Tuesday, Thursday, and Sunday. I get Monday, Wednesday, and Saturday."

"What about Friday?"

"Let's make Friday open game. Whoever's winning after four days gets to decide."

"Winning?" I fanned my open hand over his broad chest. "It's a competition?"

"You bet your sexy little ass it is." His warm hand slid over mine. "We're each trying to prove a point. Your days, we break the law. My days, we follow it. To the letter. When we're having the most fun, whosever day it happens to be... wins that day."

"And who decides who's having fun?" I stifled a yawn.

Then I blinked, surprised at how easily I'd sidled up next to him. And how right it felt to be there, safe—protected, even. Then I ignored the implications of that, the inherent danger of trusting in it.

It's Ben. *And it's one night. The first in a week of adventure.*

He rubbed my arm with his thumb. "Why don't we aim for a mutual decision..."

A full-blown yawn finally took hold. "Okay..."

My eyes drifted shut. Out of an inherent self-defense habit, I forced them open.

But on my next exhale, the strangest thing happened. I let go, closed them on a sigh, and relaxed every part of me, body and mind. For the first time in eight years, I trusted someone else to be *on* for me.

And as I drifted down into a rare blissful space of safety and peace, my last thought was that we hadn't hammered out the rules of a tiebreaker.

Guess we'll have to leave that up to the Friday.

Earthquake. Shaking. Head vibrating. Shoulders...squeezed.

"...to get up." A deep male voice echoed in my brain.

Ben's voice.

But no alarm bells sounded when I realized he'd invaded my personal space.

"*What* is happening?" I groaned and cracked my eyes open.

Black night filled my vision. Cool air kissed the skin of my arms. Hard hot man lay alongside me, touching me—from my head nestled in the crook of his shoulder to my bare toes pressed against the rough denim of his jeans.

My eyes closed on a contented sigh as I settled back down.

"Time to get going." He squeezed my shoulder and gently shook me again.

"Why? Got somewhere to be?" The dead-sleep wakeup muddled my brain. A spark of curiosity took hold though. I pushed off of the side of his warm body and sat up, even as every part of me ached to curl back up against him.

"Yep. My place. It's midnight, princess. The clock struck twelve. You're on my time now."

I blinked. "Your place."

"My place." He slid his hand into mine and dragged me up off the ground. "Let's get your bags, you're moving in."

My heart began to race. The earth spun faster under my feet. My fuzzy sleep-filled head started to clear. "Moving in."

"For the week."

"Oh." Our week. Our test of which side of the law wins: breaking versus abiding. I firmed my jaw and lifted my chin to stare at him. "I never said I was staying the night."

"It's a given. Mornings. Nights. Middle of the nights..." His last words turned gruff.

"But..." I tried to see his expression, but only his dark shadow stood above me.

"Chicken?" He twitched his fingers around my hand.

"No." *Troublemaker.*

"Wanna renegotiate?" As he lowered his head, his voice softened, teasing. Warm breath fanned over my cheek, tickled my ear.

"No." *No way.* A chance to show the golden boy how I saw the world? Too tempting to ditch.

"Good." Cockiness hardened his tone.

Wow, angel. You sure know how to stoke a hell-raiser.

"No big." I shrugged. I could deal. I'd play nice for twenty-four straight hours: be polite, stroll on sidewalks, wait my turn in lines.

Best part about his first day? Another stroke of midnight would end it. My day would come. *Then we'll break your rusted shackles off.*

But I drew in a deep breath as I stared up at him.

The one shadowy feature I barely made out in the midnight hour was his dark eyes, the spark of light in them—the intensity they held as he stared at me. And behind him, a million sparkling stars dusted over a black velvet sky.

Last night, I didn't have even one to make a wish on.

And still, you came true.

20
GROWN-UP FAIRY TALES

Ben...

"**C**inderella had a sparkling coach. And white horses," Shay grumbled after my truck hit a bump.

"She had a pumpkin. And mice."

"After midnight," she argued.

"It's twelve-oh-seven." I smiled at her complaint-debate.

"And the prince wasn't snippy."

"I'm the prince?"

"None other." She snuggled closer against my side.

We'd driven attached at the hip like that to my condo, all thirteen minutes. She'd murmured random things while half-asleep.

"Ahhh...but the prince wasn't with her after midnight."

"Lucky me," she grumped.

But her actions contradicted her words, because she'd gotten closer than ever to me. As if we'd fallen asleep under that tree where she'd hunted rare birds, and when we'd awoken some kind of curse had been lifted.

"No." I parked outside my building. Then I touched a finger under her chin, lifted gently until her eyes blinked open, and stared down at her. I softened my voice. "*Lucky me.*"

She let me open the stubborn truck door for her but insisted on carrying her own bags. Both hung from her right shoulder; she'd kept her other hand free and silently shoved it into mine.

Got it. She was good with the touching, but still demanded her independence.

However, as soon as I pushed open my heavy front door, I swept her off her feet.

She squealed and clutched the straps of her bags with both hands, but didn't drop either one. "We're not married."

"We're committed for one week. Close enough." More than I ever expected. But exactly where we needed to be.

Humor glittered in her eyes as she stared up at me. Then she glanced around my place. "Where's the bed?"

"Nice. Right down to business." I kicked the door shut behind us.

She thumped a hand on my shoulder. "To tuck my bags under."

"No need to hide your stuff here. Drop 'em anywhere."

She shifted her arm and dropped them right there with a thud onto the floor of the entry.

"Living room. Kitchen." I nodded at each as I carried her through. The rooms were dark. Couldn't see much.

But then, she wasn't paying attention to the scenery.

Neither was I.

Soft lips had begun trailing kisses up my neck. Hard nails scraped up into my scalp.

One of her Converse thumped onto the hallway floor. The second fell with a clunk as we entered the darkness of my bedroom. I lowered her to the ground in the middle of the floor. "Bed." I nodded toward it.

Her lips trailed from my ear, along my jawline, then hovered over my mouth.

I closed the inch of distance and kissed her, slow and soft, one second...two.

Until her hands pressed against my chest.

Indirect moonlight through my huge windows cast a slight glow in the room, enough for me to see the playfulness in her eyes. I kept my hands at my side and sucked in deep breaths as I wondered what she'd do.

She didn't remove her hands from my chest when she glanced at the bed. Instead, she exerted pressure and backed me toward it. A mixture of excitement and fear sparkled in her eyes.

The *fear* part halted my eager thoughts.

I rubbed a thumb over her cheek, slid my fingers into her hair. "We don't have to do this."

"I know."

"We could go at your pace."

"Okay."

I had no idea what that entailed. Had never *not* taken the reins before.

Didn't have long to figure it out, though. She led the way, determination in her gaze.

A sudden push against my chest knocked me back a step. My calves hit the foot of the bed.

She stepped into the space and gave another light shove. I fell backward and hit the mattress. "O-*kay*."

Dark hair fell around her face as she stared at me with the beginnings of a smile.

And I felt like the luckiest guy on earth.

I watched in reverent silence as she shoved down her jeans to reveal bare hips, toned thighs.

She still wore her black T-shirt when she crawled onto the bed, straddled my legs, and climbed on top of me.

Like a patient man, I settled my hands just above her knees. "I'm still dressed."

"I know."

"You're half-dressed."

"*There's* my observant guy."

"All I heard was *my* guy."

"You're talkative."

"I could shut up."

She gave a slight headshake. "No, I like it. So, how does this go?"

"Sex?

"*Our* sex."

Not remotely close to any porn she'd ever seen. And nothing like any sex I'd ever had. Special, because it was us.

"If you're taking the lead, you'd straddle me. Oh, wait. You already are."

She lowered her upper body onto my chest, settled her hands on my shoulders. Her lips hovered a mere inch from mine. "And then?"

I swallowed hard, took a deep breath. "Press your hips down."

"Like" —she curved her hips, angled her pelvis— "this?"

Fuck. "Yeah, like that. How's it feel?"

"Good...I think." Her brow wrinkled.

"There's no 'I think.' You need to know. Find out."

"How?" The softest press of her lips dragged over my mouth.

Tease.

I surged forward, captured her lips, and kissed her so thoroughly, we both gasped for air when we came up for it. "Press harder."

"Show me." She pushed herself back until she sat upright.

"Bossy." I slid my hands up the silken skin of her outer thighs until I gripped her hips, thumbs over hipbones, fingers splayed over her sexy bare ass.

When she curved her hips and angled again, I pulled down and thrust upward.

She gasped.

"Yes?" I eased my tight grip.

"*Oh, yes,*" she whispered, duplicating the move without my assistance.

Her pace increased, matched her gasping breath. "I can't see you."

"Feeling's more important anyway."

"I like the way you feel." Her hands slid under my T-shirt. "Hard. Hot."

And I still have my jeans on. "You have no idea."

A primal urge taunted me to flip her over, strip us both naked, then plunge deep inside her to prove just how hard and hot—and aching for her in every way—she'd gotten me.

But Shay had become the rare bird I'd discovered without realizing I'd been hunting her. Somehow, she'd landed on me, a whole different species from her. And I remained still. I didn't want to startle her, even if holding back meant denying myself.

Her lips parted and a low moan escaped as her pace slowed. "How should I move?"

"Any way that makes you feel good."

"What about you?"

"Trust me, Shay." I let out a rough breath. "I'm right there with you."

"You are?"

"Fuck yeah, I am."

"How do you know where I am?"

"Do you ache between your legs?"

She groaned. "Yes."

"Me too."

Her hip-grinding pace kicked up a notch again. "And you're hard, getting harder."

"And I bet you're dripping wet." I wanted to touch, to drive her wild. But I wanted her to own the moment as hers more.

"I feel" —she gasped— "wet."

"I hear your excitement in your breath, in the gasps that come quicker."

Her hands slid over my chest, slight weight pressed down. "And your heart, how it races."

"Your body is trembling."

"Wound up." She hissed. "So tight."

Fuck. My cock ached to find out just how tight.

"Chase it, then fall into it, trust it..." I watched as her eyes pinched shut, her breaths reduced to shallow panting. "Just let go," I urged.

And she did. On a clipped cry, her entire body shuddered as she collapsed over me.

I wrapped my arms around her, holding her tight through every shiver and quake.

After a dozen or so seconds, she stirred, and rested her chin on my chest. "What about you?"

"What about me?" I pulled in a deep breath as my pulse hammered a painful ache behind the closed fly of my jeans.

"Shouldn't we...*take care of* you too?"

"Do you want to?"

She pushed further up from my chest and gazed into my eyes. "Yes."

My beautiful rare bird wanted to fly again. With me. "Then, *fuck yes*, we should."

Her soft laughter sounded out as she propped higher on her knees. I reached down between them and ripped the buttons of my fly open, freeing all that hot hardness she'd been praising seconds ago.

"What about our clothes?" I wanted her, needed her like air in my lungs, but I could slow down, make her first time however she'd imagined it to be.

I slid a hand up her inner thigh, until my fingers found her slick center.

She sucked in a deep breath.

Spurred on by her reaction, I rubbed...circled...teased low moans and tiny gasps from her.

"*What* clothes?"

"Right." *So* fucking *right.*

I lowered my hand, and she dropped her hips, following my lead, until her *dripping wet* coated the length of my *getting harder.* When I gripped her hips and jerked her forward, she tumbled onto my chest again.

Lips met lips in a fierce kiss. Hips arched in perfect sync. My tip caught.

One forceful thrust and we became one. With her soft whimper, I buried my hands in her hair and deepened our kiss on a low growl.

Slowly we began to move. She angled her hips, chasing her pleasure. I drove upward, plunging deep.

We never broke our kiss. And I didn't hold back. Together we rode a rising wave until we both exploded, her first, me right after.

Our kisses began to soften as we struggled to catch our breath.

Her body relaxed, melting onto mine.

With a heavy exhale, I wrapped my arms around her, holding her tight.

After long minutes, we shared a last tender kiss, then her head settled onto my shoulder. Warm lips kissed my neck. A contented sigh drifted up to my ear.

LAWBREAKER

All felt right in my world. *Our* world, now. She hadn't hesitated, not even a little.

She'd trusted me. One hundred percent.

Yet as we drifted off, somewhere in the back of my mind, I sensed I'd forgotten something.

A grinding noise scoured the inside of my skull.

I rolled over with a groan.

The abrasive sound continued.

I squinted open my eyes. And blinding light assaulted me. I pinched them shut.

What the fuck?

The brief disorientation faded as brain cells kicked in. *Shay.*

My hands slid to the space beside me. All I found was a small indentation where she'd lain. The sheets had gone cold.

A tinny clank sounded, like a metal spoon reverberating off countertop. A hollow bang followed: *a cabinet door slammed shut?*

I grinned at the unusual ruckus. About time someone banged around in that showroom kitchen.

Jeans still on and unbuttoned from last night, I pushed out of bed. On the way out of the room, I noticed her bags had been relocated to the floor just outside the bathroom, clothing items draped over the open duffel. I scrubbed a hand over my eyes as I trudged down the hall. "You trying to wake up the neighborhood?"

"Nope. Just you." Her dark hair had been scraped up into a ponytail. Green eyes shone brilliant in the bright sunlight that streamed through the window from a high angle. She disengaged the bowl of my food processor and dumped its contents, what appeared to be chopped nuts, into a small glass bowl. "It's almost lunchtime."

"Lunchtime." It didn't compute. I never slept that late. And my kitchen air had never smelled so...sweet.

I surveyed a counter that looked like it'd just survived a bomb blast. Flour dusted over the kitchen island's stone surface. Defrosted blueberries filled one glass bowl, toasted coconut another. A large mixing bowl contained dry ingredients. I sat down at a barstool and watched as she added two eggs. Then she measured and poured olive oil and coconut oil, neither of which I had any clue had been hiding in my cabinets.

"And you're making..." *Looks like breakfast to me.*

"Pancakes."

"Sure. Because that's what we eat at lunchtime. And where did you learn how to cook?"

She pointed a green silicone mixing spoon at me. "Pancakes are *anytime* food. And these are no ordinary pancakes." She shrugged. "No big. I've spent time in houses that have expensive kitchens and Food Network."

I cocked my head and examined the ingredients, thoroughly intrigued. "What makes them so extraordinary?" *Besides the beautiful woman making them.*

"Blueberries are normal. But there's no flour in these.

Not the regular kind. Coconut flour, almond flour."

"Coconut oil..." I grabbed the dark glass jar which held the white solidified substance. "Kiki must've gone all out when she stocked my pantry."

"*Kiki* did?" A frown tugged at her lips. She blinked. Then her eyes narrowed.

In jealousy?

"Did you two ever..." She made a corkscrew action with the spoon, and a glob of pancake mix dropped onto the counter.

Appalled, I scowled and coughed out a laugh. "*Hell* no. Kiki's like my sister. She designed the condo, picked it out actually. She furnished it from the chairs and rugs to the dishes and kitchen appliances."

"And coconut oil." She ladled a spoonful of batter onto a sizzling skillet.

"Apparently." I put the jar down.

Silence followed while she attended to our pancakes.

And I'd never been happier sitting at a barstool in my own kitchen.

She seemed comfortable in front of the stove, happy even. And she looked breathtaking standing barefoot in my gourmet kitchen in nothing but faded blue jeans and a gray T-shirt. Then I noticed the ends of her hair dangling from that ponytail were slightly damp.

"You showered." Even I heard my flattened tone of disappointment.

"While you slept like the dead." She flipped four pancakes, one by one.

"I was hoping to shower together." *A long, hot, dirty, soapy shower.* Not that there was any immediate pressure, with her being squeaky clean.

"You were?" A gleam flashed in her eyes. "Don't people shower every day?"

"Those with good personal hygiene do." Wasn't sure where she was heading with her point. But the mischief in her tone piqued my curiosity.

"Then why would we want to take any ol' shower?"

Isn't it obvious? But she was unaware of just how sexy she was. "It wouldn't be 'any ol' shower.' Not with you."

Diverting her attention back to the skillet, she shoved a spatula under each pancake then flipped them one by one into a neat stack onto a platter, all while she tugged her left lower lip in with her teeth. "We shouldn't shower on your day. I'm thinking we should shower on my day."

Because you want to cross some legal line when we do.

A heavy ache kicked up behind the fly of my jeans. Sexy didn't begin to cover the woman standing in my kitchen. Barely innocent, she plastered adventure all over her view of life.

And I wanted to be a part of it.

"You pick the day." Whenever she was ready, wherever she wanted, however she imagined us naked, wet, and all over each other? *Count me in.*

"And these are *extraordinary* pancakes," she continued, as if we hadn't detoured into dirty lawbreaking showers, "not only because of the ingredients, but because of the toppings: I warmed pecans then sautéed them in melted ghee before salting 'em."

She shot me a deadpan look. "And because *I* made them."

End of. Simple as that.

Yet more complicated than I'd ever imagined. Because my heart ached in my chest. Again.

It suddenly hit me just how hard I'd fallen. No one had ever made me feel what the beautiful wild creature in my kitchen had. And I wanted Shay, no matter the danger she willingly braved.

Even with the inherent risks to me.

She hadn't been caught over the last so many years.

What's the harm in chancing a few days?

"*You* are extraordinary."

Her expression went blank, stunned. Which made me briefly angry, then determined. If no one had ever made her feel special, wanted...loved...I vowed to be the one to change that.

I'm going to show you just how special you are.

And I wanted to do so much more than that. Gone were the rotating borrowed houses—once she agreed to the change, of course. She needed a solid place to call home, somewhere to feel safe, someone to protect her.

She'd already trusted me enough to take care of her last night. And she'd committed to a week. I had more than enough time to convince her to take another risk, commit to something more.

Oh, *shit*. My heart sank. "Protection!"

She ladled a spoonful of blueberries over her pecan-covered pancake before glancing back up at me. "I can take care of myself."

"No." I shook my head, stood from the barstool. "I forgot to use a condom." *Fuck. Shit. Damn.* I *knew* my sex-fogged brain had missed something. A *major* something.

She came around the kitchen island, wrapped me in her arms, then kissed me softly. "No. *You* forgot to use a condom. I wanted to feel *all* of you."

I searched her eyes, found only sincere emotion there. "Oh."

And you continue to blow me away.

Her lips twitched into a slight smile. "Was it worth it?"

"Fuck yeah, it was. Best sex of my life." *And more.* The best everything kept happening with her. The week ahead? I couldn't wait.

And yet, something still rattled at the back of my mind. Like I'd forgotten something else.

But then she gave me a sensual kiss again. And every worry fell right out of my head.

21
ICE CREAM WISHES
AND SUPERHERO DREAMS

Shay…

"**W**ell, *shit*. That's what I forgot." Ben stared at the buzzing phone as he polished off a final bite of his pancakes. It vibrated at the corner of his kitchen island, where he'd tossed it from his back pocket as he'd walked by with me in his arms last night.

Before we'd done *amazing* things in his bedroom.

Forgot? His phone? Since that didn't make any sense, because his phone definitely hadn't been needed, I humored up the convo. "To take your clothes off? To take a shower?"

I couldn't stop fantasizing about the fiercely sexy man doing both. One…and then, eventually, after we'd gotten him all sweaty and dirty…the other.

"That the rest of my life sucks."

Okay. Play later. Serious now. His phone buzzed again.

"Not Loading Zone, then."

"No. That's the best thing about my life...besides you."

"Ahhh..." The family he'd grumbled about at dinner. "And I helped you forget the rest of it." Wanting to soothe him, I moved into his space, gave him a hug, then kissed him softly, the way I'd done before—when I'd gotten him to stop thinking and just feel.

He touched his forehead to mine on a sigh. "Yeah, you did."

"But now life's calling?"

"Yep." He stared at the thing when it buzzed a third time.

"Need to answer it?"

"Nope."

"But you could. What if it's an emergency?"

He glanced at me, then snatched the phone up and answered it. "What?" His tone was curt.

I busied myself with cleaning up the mess in the kitchen and loading his dishwasher.

After listening with a blank expression, he huffed out a sigh and scrubbed a hand down his face. "*Just* drinking?"

He gripped the phone harder as he listened. Then he growled low. "Are you hurt?"

A short pause followed.

"Him?" he gritted out.

I closed the dishwasher and began wiping down the counter.

He turned around, facing away from me, and raked a hand through his hair. "Do you *need* me to come over?"

"Then, he'll be fine."

"No." He stalked into his living room. "I won't. Go back to your room. Lock yourself in."

He paced back toward the kitchen. "If he tries to break into the room, or you smell smoke, do what everyone else does. Call 9-1-1."

His thumb punched the phone to end the call before he tossed it back onto the counter.

I stared at him. "That sounded brutal."

"Me or her?"

"The situation. Your mom?"

"None other. Same shit, different day." His expression darkened as he crossed his arms.

"What happened?"

"I don't want to get into it. Not on our day."

"*Your* day." And I wanted to give the strong man I'd come to care about what he needed to enjoy it. "Two minutes. Vent it and forget it." I stepped up to him, pressed myself against his closed arms.

He opened them up and wrapped them around me. "You do have a way of making me forget..."

"So..." I turned slightly and grabbed his wrist, tracked the second hand on his watch, then pointed at him. "go."

He gave me an amused look, then he took a sobering breath. "She said he was shouting, throwing things. Then he yanked down one of his bookcases that had doors. Glass shattered everywhere."

His hands rubbed up my back, as if he tried to comfort who he could in the awful situation. "Shouting meant *at* her. She bears emotional scars from him from years of abuse.

Abuse *she* chose to stay around for. Again and again."

"Are they both okay?"

He tightened his hold on me, rested his chin on my head. "Her voice sounded small, broken. But I've run out of rope with him. He can hang himself with it for all I care. Unfortunately, she cares, whether or not I do."

A long pause followed. I waited, patient.

"He accidently cut himself." His arms tightened for a split second, betraying the pure animosity he felt. "Has a fucking bloody white dress shirt wrapped around his hand. But he won't die of his injuries; asshole doesn't have the common decency to put the rest of the world out of their misery," he muttered.

The force of his tone had begun to fade, so I sensed he didn't really mean that. His loathing toward his father didn't reach the same depth as mine. *Close, but not quite.*

"She asked you to come over?"

"Yeah." He eased back a little and stared down at me. "But she never listens to me when I do. She doesn't have the courage to leave that son of a bitch, but she has no problem dragging my ass across town to play rescuer. Didn't listen to me for two weeks while I stayed there playing mediator."

I understood the whole family-not-listening thing. You're standing there screaming, but nothing you say is heard, because you don't really matter—not to them. "What if it gets worse?"

"There's a fifty-fifty chance it will, and she knows it. But she needs to stand up for herself and live the life she's chosen, so that I can live mine."

"You have to be the one to cut it off." My voice broke along with my heart, aching for all he'd suffered through, everything he'd lost. And it brought back all the messed-up shit I'd endured, had run away from, with my parents.

"Yep." He let out a relieved sigh and glanced at his watch. "Time's up."

Then he dropped his face into the crook of my shoulder and began to kiss a trail up my neck.

I held him tight and shivered at the instant effect his sensual touch had on me. But with a smile, I broke our embrace and pointed down the hallway. "Shower. Ten minutes."

He tugged at a belt loop of my jeans. "You sure no shower today?"

"Solo." I shot him a stern look, turned his shoulders, and gave him a shove. "Nine minutes, fifty seconds."

He glanced over his shoulder with an arched brow. "You gonna snoop while I'm gone?"

"It's not snooping if you know about it."

I passed the time by first using his formal guest bathroom. Then I wandered through his bedroom and living room, riffled through things he'd stowed away in drawers and noticed the stark absence of everything he hadn't. No personal pictures hung on the walls. No mementos sat on any shelves. The expansive floors were bare tinted concrete. Not one of the giant windows had any kind of covering.

He returned as I fastened the second shoelace on my Converse. He tapped his watch. "Seventy-three seconds to spare."

I reclined back onto his stiff black sectional. "Impressive. But I've taken faster. Nothing to it. Soap. Rinse. Dry."

He fought a smile at my sarcasm.

Yep. You might have rocked my world last night, but you still needed to earn the rest of me.

"Well, what do you think?" He swept his gaze around the room, then scraped his keys up from a metal bowl on a skinny table by the door. The bowl wobbled with tinny clank that reverberated off all the hard surfaces around us.

I stood and held my arms out wide, palms up. "It's... echo-y?"

"Yeah." He crossed his arms and shrugged. "Doesn't really fit me."

Good you recognize that.

Last night, we had crossed a cold marble lobby, gone up a bank of gleaming elevators, then walked down a hall paved with fossilized limestone tiles that had continued halfway up the walls where they were capped with matching round trim pieces. After the easygoing warmth of National Geographic's house and the clunky-yet-charming vibe of Ben's ancient truck, Ben's condo and its building felt like a barren arctic landscape.

Not even close to resembling the dryly funny and passionate man I'd begun to know. "Like the Escalade didn't fit?"

"Yeah. Guess I'm going through an identity crisis."

"Hey, we all stumble around in the dark until we find what works for us, somewhere we can relax." God knows I'd been doing it long enough. I still hadn't settled on a place to make mine in every way. But that didn't stop me from searching, from wanting. And even though he'd broken away from his family, maybe he still struggled to define who he was. "Do you own it?"

I walked toward him and passed his kitchen, where white marble with sparkling gray veins capped blond cabinetry. A set of knives clung to a metal bar that stretched in the middle of gleaming white subway tiles. On the other side of a stainless steel cooktop stood a Cuisinart food processor that had been so pristine that morning, my pancakes had to have been its debut task.

Ben moved beside me. "Yes, it's mine." The heat of his presence drew close, but didn't crowd.

And suddenly it didn't matter what kind of place he lived in; home was never about walls or the objects inside them. Home was the people we let into our hearts. And up until a couple of weeks ago, that hadn't existed for me. *Not all the way, not deep.* I turned into his open arms and stared up at him. *Not like now. Not until you.*

"But I've got the place on the market." A defensive tone edged his unnecessary explanation. And he searched my eyes, like it mattered to him, what I thought of his place. As if my judgment of where he stayed flowed through to the man I held in my arms.

"It doesn't matter. Not to me." I kissed him softly. "I know who you are."

You're someone just like me. Searching, wanting.

Minutes later, we stepped out into a gloomy overcast day and began strolling down the sidewalk. A heavy mineral scent tanged the air. But everything seemed bright and fresh to me.

Ben slipped a hand into mine, entwining our fingers together. "Any thoughts on what you want to do today?"

I shook my head. "Today's your day." He made quite clear Monday, Wednesday, and Saturday were his.

"And I'm gifting it to you. No lawbreaking." He gave me a pointed look. "But is there something you'd want to do with a boyfriend?"

My feet planted solid so hard and fast, our arms stretched wide until he jolted to a stop. And I had to take deep breaths to catch up to my thundering heart.

Why the sudden paralysis?

It wasn't like he was trying to trap me or make me do anything I didn't want to. He hadn't slapped on a constricting label of ownership or expectation. At least, it hadn't seemed that way. It sounded like he'd extended an offer.

"Is that what you are? My boyfriend? I've never had one before." *Not even close.*

His expression softened. "If you want me to be," he murmured, tone elevating with hope. He gave no indication that he cared about me being new at the whole trust thing— no judgment at all.

"Yeah." I squeezed his hand. "I'd like that."

What could it hurt? In fact, he'd insisted I try on a coat of legitimacy. Why not give a relationship a go?

Somehow, my feet began moving again. We strolled down the middle of the sidewalk, hand in hand, a first for me. The entire day even promised to hold a record-breaking amount of firsts. And I felt reborn, embracing my *first Monday*, the only one that counted as far as I was concerned.

Thinking back to his activity question, I shrugged. "I dunno. What do normal people do on Monday?"

"You are *not* normal. Don't think of what we have to do. We do what *you* want to do."

The whole *not being normal* thing stung a bit. All I'd ever wanted was to be normal, part of a family. From the very moment that intimate connection had been ripped away, the loss had been devastating and ever-present.

"What do most people do?"

He snorted. "On Monday? Work."

"Oh. Work." With all the goofing off we'd been doing, and when we'd been debating and he'd challenged us to our week, it hadn't dawned on me that we'd be ditching real life 24/7. "You don't have to work? *We* don't?" I knew we had the tournament Saturday—him playing, me bartending—but I hadn't considered the rest of our days.

"No. I texted Gabe last night. Rafe and Cade are both cool to help out one more week."

His expression darkened for a split second, and I wondered if he'd been reminded of his absence in the weeks prior to my starting at Loading Zone...and his earlier family phone call.

But I didn't mention anything.

You don't want him to know your secrets. Don't be digging up his.

The subject got changed the moment he hopped off the curb and tugged me into the street at a break in traffic, within the safe parallel lines of a crosswalk. Once we hit the other side and leapt onto the sidewalk, he cocked his head, narrowed his eyes, and stared down toward the Arts District. We stood at the threshold of the quaint business village where colorful awnings flaunted boutique shops, antique bistros beckoned patio diners, and cobblestone paths led the way.

He glanced back at me. "How 'bout I make it multiple-choice?"

"Great by me. Because I've no idea." Not that it mattered. Because all I wanted to do, the only place I wanted to be, was with him, even if all we did was people-watch. Which is what I typically did during my afternoons: observe all the normal people and imagine who they went home to at the end of their days, once school let out, after the workday ended.

Instead, on my *first Monday*, I'd become one of the normal ones.

He arched his brows and gave a slight shrug. "We can do tourist stuff: museums, historical sites, beer-tasting pub crawl. Or we could be chill and go native: hang at a park, see a movie, grab a bite to eat."

"You could eat?" I rubbed my full belly with my hand, remembering the plate loaded with pancakes. "I'm stuffed."

"Two words I never thought would come out of your mouth."

"Never will again. I overate. I woke up starving after you exhausted me."

Heat sparkled in his gaze. "Prepare to eat those words. With plenty more food. Because I plan to exhaust you again. And often."

I drew in a deep breath as he stared at me. My lips twitched into a smile while I thought about what he'd suggested, what I wanted...

"Maybe dessert," he murmured at the exact moment the same idea hit me.

Only his thought came heavy with innuendo.

Mine went there for only a split second until...

"Like ice cream!" I exclaimed loud enough for couples across the street to hear. Dessert real families ate, one I hadn't splurged on since I'd left mine. But with Ben, I felt brave enough to rewrite the experience. "Maybe in a little while, though. Have to make room."

He stared at me, a mixture of humor and amazement in his gaze as his lips curved into a smile.

Without waiting to hear some witty comeback, I tugged him on down the cobblestone walkway, into the Arts District. "There *is* a movie I've wanted to see, but it's no longer in theaters."

He lifted my hand and pressed a gentle kiss to my knuckles. "Why don't we see whatever's playing at the theater, then we'll go back to my place and rent your movie. We'll do a double feature."

Perfect. I loved the idea of just hanging with him all afternoon.

"So, just go to the movies and randomly pick from what's playing?" I'd walked past theaters many times before and stared at the movie posters. But I had no idea people blindly chose from a poster alone.

"Yep. Even normal people—law-abiding folks and all— can be wild and crazy."

I gave him a light shove, rolling my eyes. "Go ahead, take my breath away, Mr. Tightrope Walker."

He arched a brow at me. "It's called being spontaneous."

"Sounds like my whole life." See an opportunity? Take it.

A few blocks into the Arts District, we ended up at the six-screen neighborhood cinema.

We quietly scanned the handful of movie posters. After a full minute of silence, I crossed my arms and glanced at him. "How do you know the movie will be any good?"

"We don't. Luck of the draw, roll of the dice. We either like it or we don't. It'll be dark, and if we aren't interested in the movie, there are lots of other things we can do that normal people do in movie theaters."

"Oh?" My curiosity sparked with his nonchalant tone. "Like what?" Like he promised we could be illicit, naughty. *But isn't that illegal? Indecent...or...lewd something or other?*

"Pick a horrible movie and find out."

Well, hell. Now I don't know what to pick. He made a horrible movie sound scandalous.

In the end, I chose an iffy Sherlock Holmes movie, skipping an action adventure, a comedy, some sappy romance, and a couple of artsy flicks. I figured with "iffy", I had a fifty-fifty shot at a horrible movie for a chance to find out what his back-up plan entailed.

Sherlock ended up being funny and interesting. But even with my attention riveted to the big screen, I found out what Ben had meant halfway through the movie.

Our clasped hands that relaxed on the armrest, gently broke apart. He lowered his hand until it settled warm and heavy on my inner thigh. When he spread his fingers, curved them downward toward the seat, heat radiated through the thick denim of my jeans. And a deep sizzling ache spread upward.

My breath caught as the aching heat intensified—without him doing any other thing.

He angled his face toward me. And the fingers of that devastating hand curled on my thigh. "You okay?"

I nodded, then whispered, "You're turning me on."

With the shine of a brighter scene on the screen, I caught his smirk before he leaned closer. "I am?" The two words were barely whispered, feathered over my lips.

His hand dragged a little higher, fingers tightening.

And I instantly lost all interest in the movie.

We left the theater amid a throng of moviegoers nearly an hour later. We hadn't done much of anything that a "horrible" movie would warrant, at least I didn't think so. We'd softly kissed. He'd gently stroked, but nothing overtly sexual happened: No clothes came off, no skin-to-skin contact, and his hand had never moved from the middle of my thigh.

Yet my body buzzed, wild and alive. Clearly, there were a whole lot more erogenous zones than I'd realized. His soft lips, rough whiskers, and warm breath traveling across my jaw, down my neck, and over my ear, barely touching my skin, proved to be effective sensual weapons.

Back on the crowded pedestrian street in broad daylight, I took a deep breath to clear my head—with the hope that the extra oxygen would also reset my charged body.

A soft drizzle floated down from a grayish sky like a snow globe. We veered left, heading toward the protective awnings of the shops. Without saying a word, he automatically switched sides so that his broad body blocked the slight wind and mist.

When he slipped his warm hand into my colder one, a thrilling heat spread into all kinds of exciting places. But we kept walking, him oblivious, as I exhaled a slow breath to steady myself.

The end of the awnings marked the outer edge of the Arts District where a handful of quaint neighborhoods began, each unique depending on which direction you turned, a couple with storefronts on the main streets. He glanced down at me. "Where now?"

"You mean, after I blew it picking a horrible movie?"

He tugged me toward him, then enfolded me in his arms. His warm breath feathered over my lips. There it was again, one of his sensual weapons, teasing mercilessly without his doing much more than breathing. His eyes searched mine. "It was a *little* horrible."

"Maybe just a little," I murmured, staring up into darkened eyes that promised so much more pleasure than the small taste he'd given me.

"We're just getting warmed up." His taunting words were as powerful as his teasing breath, because my body pressed closer against his, craving more of his delicious heat.

All of a sudden, my stomach growled between us.

We both laughed at the intrusion. Then I gave him a slow kiss, making a promise of my own, before I broke free and tugged him forward. "How 'bout that ice cream you promised?"

Minutes later, after ducking into an old-fashioned ice cream parlor a couple of blocks down, I slid my hand into his again and led him toward my favorite neighborhood. "Let's walk down Maple Lane." I balanced my double-scoop ice cream cone with my free hand and took a small sugary nip from the very top.

"Sure you're okay in the rain?"

His question was innocent, protective. But he had no idea that I'd lived most of my life out in the rain, exposed to the elements. But we didn't need to go there, he didn't need to know the dirty details about what I'd been through. Not on my *first Monday*.

"I won't melt." *Lighthearted*. Where I wanted to keep the day.

"Your ice cream will." Said the man who'd refused his own ice cream and wouldn't even accept a lick from mine.

In defiance of his suggestion that any harm would come to either me or my cone, I licked an entire surface layer beginning with the bottom of the salted caramel toffee crunch and ending with another slurp off the top of the french vanilla.

He watched with amusement, then shook his head as he began leading me down Maple Lane. "Love these old houses, so full of history."

My heart warmed, happy to my bones that he'd been through one of my favorite haunts before, that we might've even passed each other on the fabled street without realizing it.

"Which one's your favorite?" I hungered to know what he liked, learn more about the man who'd begun to infiltrate my well-guarded heart.

"Hard to pick. I like so many of them. I've been keeping my eye out for one to come on the market. Something with more character than my 'echo-y' condo. But there are only thirty-two houses, and it's rare for any of them to go up for sale. Hannah's house reminds me of these."

After I finished another ice cream lick, I nodded toward one with a fence made of slender tree branches that still wore some of their bark. "I've always liked this one."

Beyond a small rise sat a quaint white cottage with a curving shingled roof. Between the organic fence and the storybook house, a steppingstone path meandered through whimsical free-form flowers, pastels of lilac, cream, and pink, that blurred as they bobbed in the misty rain. Nature's rare snapshot struck me, as if we'd stepped into an impressionist painting brought to life, like one of the priceless works of art I'd spied on while wandering the galleries of public art museums.

"Yeah, it's cool. Look at that chimney."

I tore my gaze from the flower garden. A weathered

yellow-and-pink brick structure rose from the curving light-brown shingles. But the chimney didn't rise in a straight line. From its fat base, it curved left, right, then left again as it narrowed toward the top. A rusty bent piece of metal capped it off.

"Huh. I've never noticed that before." I'd always gotten lost daydreaming in the cozy feel of the flower garden. I stared up at the cottage and smiled. "I half expect Hansel and Gretel to burst out that country kitchen door."

Over the next few minutes, we made our way down the charming lane. He commented one thing or another about some of the houses, a few that he'd taken the time to research in depth, others that he wanted to. All the while, I devoured the rest of my ice cream cone in silence, content to listen and learn about the man more than the houses.

As we neared the end of the street, my heart began to pound a little heavier. The house I wanted to see every single time I walked down Maple Lane appeared right as we turned along a gentle bend.

But before I had a chance to say anything, he paused right at the corner of its property line. "*This one's* my favorite."

I blinked. "*Really?* Mine too."

A ton of emotion hit me at once: relief, amazement, skepticism.

Do you see what I see?

Would he appreciate the sad decrepit house the same way...see her hidden beauty?

The front garden and lawn had died, replaced by clods of dirt melting in the misty rain. Broken bricks had upheaved and fallen over down a long walkway with empty beds on either side. Porch steps sagged. Roof eaves rotted. A paint-chipped wooden railing guarded a derelict two-story with cracked windows and dangling shutters.

He sighed and tightened his hand around mine. "It's been neglected for too long. 'Bout time someone paid attention to it."

Tears began to well in my eyes. *Is this what being normal is like?*

Because I'd been wanting the same thing he'd been after... all along.

One almost-horrible movie, a delicious double-decker ice cream cone, and a stroll down the very lane with a house that I'd felt a kindred spirit with made me think he'd won the day.

But will I be able to live every day like this? Going legit? Abiding by the law?

More importantly, could I trust in that dream again? Or would someone steal it away?

I need to be certain.

Because *my* life wasn't the only one hanging in the balance. Others who'd been neglected far too long still relied on me. They deserved attention too.

He pulled me out of my whirling spiral by tugging me onward, back toward his condo. "Ready for your next movie?"

The movie I'd been wanting to see for a while. About someone who fights for others, risks it all to help those who've suffered, puts her life on the line to save humanity itself. *One soul at a time.*

"Yeah." I gripped his hand tighter and cast a wish up into the cloudy sky that I could have both: the man taking a chance on me and the hearts I fought so hard to protect.

22
A QUIET HEROINE

Ben…

"Thought you already snooped."

Shay opened each drawer of the map table in my office. "That was a breeze-through."

"And this?"

"Is learning about you."

Once we'd stepped back through my front door, she'd taken her time, room by room, her leading, me following. She'd asked a question or two, I'd provided a brief but thorough answer.

The reverent way she took in every little detail of my space surprised me. Slow steps led her around the room while her intent gaze wandered with great care, hovering over each object it encountered, absorbing, learning.

I'd never felt so exposed in my own home. No one I'd brought in had ever shown much interest. *When had I ever wanted anyone to?* I couldn't remember.

Sudden nervousness gripped me, and I realized I'd been holding my breath. My mouth ran dry, and I swallowed hard. Doubts flashed through my head.

What are you thinking? Of my sparse life? Of me?

I sucked in a deep breath. *Shake it off, Ben. She's into you. All you need to know.*

She passed the leather couch parked against the far wall and tipped her beautiful face up to bright daylight, following the expanse of glass to the peak of the office's high arched windows. Then her attention drifted back down toward the black walnut desk, and she bent over it.

As she began to examine the three framed photos on the far back corner, my pulse started to hammer. Because the biggest shocker to accept? The stubborn bartender I'd fired only a week ago had begun to matter to me. On a level I hadn't known I'd been capable of.

Maybe stupid-level. It had tempted me to put everything I'd worked so hard for at risk.

But what had all the hard work and sacrifice been for?

Maybe I've been biding my time, waiting for you.

A soft laugh escaped her lips as her gaze landed on three drunk college guys: Mase, Cade, and me. Each had one arm slung around the neck of another, all with our free hands holding out the saddest three minnows ever to be caught. Proud grins stretched across all three mugs.

"None of your family?" Her fingertips floated an inch above the matte glass of eight-year-old me and my only childhood dog.

"No. I didn't even put them in those polished silver frames. Kiki dug up some ancient photos, *awww'd* over my 'genuine smile', and insisted they were needed to warm the place up."

"She was right." She nodded toward the one with the red Siberian husky. "What was his name?"

"Teddy. Followed me everywhere. Learned to walk with him by holding onto his tail."

She half-turned and stared at me for a moment. "He's family."

"Yeah, I guess he was." The best kind of family, one that only gave unconditional love.

She must've caught the seriousness in my distant expression. Because after a couple of silent beats, she clapped her hands together. "Okay, Mr. Monday. Where's my movie?"

"Where it's most *echo-y*." I nodded toward the living room, where nothing personal existed. "But apparently acoustically solid. Sound dampeners on the walls. A rug on the floor."

"Thanks to designer Kiki." She gave a nod but held no animosity in her voice as we moved into the living room. Then she kicked off her shoes and jumped onto the sectional.

"So, what's this movie you've been dying to see?"

She'd been unusually silent the entire walk home. Contemplative, even.

"*Wonder Woman*."

"Of course." Didn't surprise me one bit.

She settled along the cushions, then grabbed a large pillow in the corner and stuffed it under her head. "This thing's more comfortable than I realized."

Good. Her getting comfortable in my place? Worked for me.

You warm the space up just by being here.

I dropped a nod toward the flat-screen mounted on the wall, tossed her the remote, then headed into the kitchen. "You order it on iTunes. I'll fire up some popcorn."

"Don't suppose you frost up blue ICEEs here?"

I paused midstep, then tilted my head to the side and hit her with a deadpan look. "You had your chance at the snack bar."

After gorging on pancakes, she didn't want a thing at the theater. No popcorn. No blue ICEE. I had to force a bottle of water on her.

But then, I kind of understood. *Nerves.* She'd probably been too excited to eat on her first movie date. And the weird thing? After dozens of dates I'd gone on—and even more one-night stands—I'd been nervous with Shay too. *Fucking butterflies-in-the-stomach nervous.*

When I stopped to examine that as I heated up the skillet, the greater why of it all hit me. *Not one of them mattered as much as Shay does.*

Minutes later, I settled next to the pillow behind her head. Then she shifted, angled enough on the corner space to drape an arm over my leg and nestle the popcorn bowl in the triangle of cushion between us. Then she dramatically aimed the remote at the TV and started her movie.

It rolled out pretty impressively. A wild island with hundreds of striking female warriors. One different among them. Great battle scene. Mystery about her heritage. The risk and sacrifice—from him, needing to fulfill his mission, and her, needing to face her destiny.

She paused the movie and glanced up at me. "Would you say you're a typical example of your sex?"

I did my best to pull off the same humble honesty as Steve Trevor. "I...am...above average." She gave me a coy look, then turned back toward the screen and pointed the remote, rolling the frozen scene back into action.

The movie played on for a few more minutes, both of us quiet until the sailing scene.

She paused it again. "Greek sex texts?"

I snorted. "Ancient porn."

"Twelve volumes full."

"Prehistoric times? No TV, no movies, no gaming or phones. Probably got bored. I would've. Great motivation for experimenting."

"Or mastering." She sat up a little straighter, turning toward me. "*Outliers.*"

"What?"

"A book I read. Ten thousand hours to master something."

I smirked. "You'd like to master sex?"

She glanced at the ceiling for a beat, pretending to consider it. "Maybe."

"With me, I hope." *Damn well better be with me.*

"You wouldn't mind ten thousand hours with me?"

"I think I could tolerate it."

I got a face full of popcorn for my sarcasm. But then she kissed me, and all was forgiven.

Halfway through the movie, she paused it again and pointed the remote at the big screen. "It's her father."

"*Totally* her father."

Shay's emotions ran the gamut from one scene to another. Soft laughter. Tense anger. Quiet observance.

She let out a heartfelt sigh. "They're dancing."

I tangled our fingers together and clasped her hand. "*We're* dancing." How the last few days had been for me, us swaying to some instinctive rhythm as we shared important firsts together.

Then the movie delivered its twist. "Oh." Her brow furrowed, as if she'd been disappointed.

Not long after, she sat upright. "No. No!" Her hand clutched her chest as she sucked in a huge breath. Tears began to stream down her face.

I rubbed a hand over her upper arm, hit hard with her. Choked up. Minus the tears.

Wonder Woman ended, Chinese food got delivered, and we discussed the merits of the film over the next hour, the most I'd ever talked about a movie. But I'd learned more about Shay than I'd ever expected in that short period of time.

Diana Prince had cared about the innocents, about their suffering. But Shay seemed even more affected, talked at length about their plight, empathized about how everything they'd ever known had been ripped away.

And I listened. And agreed. And commiserated with her. Because Shay had meant *more* than those in the movie. And we both knew it.

A comfortable silence fell between us while we finished our dinner, shoulders touching as we sat side by side on the sectional with only dimmed lights on in the living room.

"They never had a date." She pointed a chopstick at me.

"But they did have one night." I tossed my emptied takeout container with the others we'd demolished and scattered over the coffee table.

"I'm glad we have a week."

I nudged her shoulder. "Just a week?"

"Seven whole days."

To start, if I had my way. "And how was your first?"

"Too early to tell." She slid her empty container next to the rest. Then she nestled up against my side, dragged her lips over my cheek, and murmured into my ear, "It's still happening."

A loud buzzing jarred the silence.

My phone lit up the darkness of the kitchen.

Irritated at that damned leash, I sighed. "*Not* getting up to look."

"What if it's important?"

After our breakdown of the movie, after understanding how the quiet pain of those in need affected Shay on a visceral level, I gave her thigh a light squeeze and stood. "Then I'm on it."

But I got confused by the name that flashed up on the screen: someone who hadn't called me in over a year. I furrowed my brow, unsure of how she would take the news. "It's Kiki."

But she popped up from the couch, expression

brightening. "It's for me."

"It is?" I stared at the counter to confirm. "Isn't that *my* phone?"

"Yep." She swiped it up. "I forgot to give her my number."

"Why's she calling you?" *On my phone.* Which meant Kiki knew we'd be together.

She clicked the button, then held it to her ear. "Hey, Kiki! Yep. Hold on..."

I stood there, perplexed.

She held the phone out at arm's length.

"Kiki doesn't only design condos." She arched her brows, wearing a *duh* expression. "She's also creating our naughty golf shirts."

Right. "*Annnd...*I've just lost my date to my designer," I grumbled.

Shay headed toward my bedroom without even a glance back at me. But my lips curved into a slow smile, because she'd settled into using my phone, being in my place, and spending the day with me, *my way.* And there hadn't been any outward sign of discomfort.

In fact, it struck me that something deeper had happened.

Not just with a phone, or my place, or the day. Not with the movie. Or any single thing. With everything.

With *her*...and *me.*

You've found home.

23

PLAYING CHICKEN WITH HIGH VOLTAGE

Shay…

"**S**tay." *Don't leave again.*

Inky blackness surrounded me.

"*I'm not going anywhere.*" *Ben's voice whispered, then echoed.*

"*Oh.*" *An impossible weight crushed my chest. I struggled to pull in the smallest gasp of air.* "*I guess I have to leave, then.*"

With bittersweet pain, I vanished.

Then I began flying…

racing…

soaring…

falling…

plummeting…

"*Shay.*" *Another echo from Ben.*

"Shay!"

I startled awake.

Strong hands gripped my shoulders. Ben's body heat radiated up my side.

Darkness surrounded us.

Gentle lips and the soft roughness of his beard touched my forehead. "You okay?"

I swallowed hard, feeling damp and suddenly chilled. "Where am I? What happened?"

"My bed. You must've fallen asleep talking to Kiki. I found you out cold with the phone in your hand."

"Oh." Well, that was a first. *The passed out...and the phone-hugging.*

"But just now, you tensed up and gasped for breath."

I twisted and slid his phone onto his nightstand, then settled back into his protective arms.

"I dreamt I was flying, soaring high up through big white fluffy clouds. Then I raced over them, zooming from one continent to another, skimming oceans, buzzing mountains... from the empty vastness of sandy deserts to polar icecaps."

"Nice." He rubbed my shoulder.

"It was. I felt free, untouchable. Funny thing: For as fast as I flew, my hair only rippled a little, like a gentle breeze, and my whole body stayed warm and comfortable. The air barely whispered over my skin, crisp and cool.

"But then, all of a sudden, I began to lose altitude... but not speed. I still raced through the sky, only I dropped into the clouds. A dense whiteout misted my face. Then I sank lower. The green tops of pine trees brushed under my fingertips. Squares of farmland zipped by.

"And on the horizon loomed giant metal structures with electrical lines strung between them. Then my speed trailed off. My altitude continued to nosedive until the point where it seemed like I could hit the electrical lines.

"I tried to fly higher, it took enormous effort to even gain a few measly feet of height. But I grew exhausted and fell back into the danger zone again.

"The lines hummed with a constant terrifying buzz. They swayed in the wind, sparking and crackling."

I took a deep breath, exhausted by just reliving the vivid memory. But I'd needed to download the entire thing. And Ben had let me. He'd listened, quiet but attentive.

His hand slid into mine, warm and comforting. "I've had that dream too, playing chicken with power lines. Ever try to touch the wires?"

I gulped. "No way. It's like if I do, I'm gonna die. Ever die in one of your dreams?"

"No, not for real. But I *have* touched my electrical lines. One day I just hovered over them, dared the damn things to hurt me, then clamped on tight with both hands."

"What happened?"

"Nothing." The timbre of his voice lowered.

"*Nothing?*"

"Not one thing."

I let out a soft snort. "Sounds anticlimactic."

We laid there in the dark, holding hands, quiet, breathing, and peaceful for long minutes. Long enough for my racing pulse to calm.

I'd never experienced what had begun to unfold between

313

us—a deep connection with another soul, someone I trusted. Made me want to open up further, keep our growing emotional tie strong and solid.

"What do you think our dreams are about?" I wondered.

"Unable to change altitude? Imminent crash into disaster? Sounds like it's about control."

Control. Like not letting anyone have power over me. "Maybe facing our fears too."

"Don't play with high-voltage?" His thumb rubbed over mine.

I smiled. "Aren't you playing with me?"

"Told you I grabbed on tight."

"Ha!" I gently elbowed his ribs. "With the threat of death. Knew you were a risk-taker."

He rolled over to face me. Warm breath teased across my lips. "Only with you."

"Yeah?"

"Yeah." He kissed me tenderly. "You make me brave. I'm alive when I'm with you."

I eased away a little, unwilling to stop our soul-baring conversation.

"What challenges you the most?"

"My parents." His voice turned gruff. "Hands down."

I let out a slow breath, voice quieting, "And they're the cause of your stressful dreams?"

Because I'd been suffering through mine for years. And a part of me knew the uplifting dreams turning into terrifying nightmares had been about what I'd run from, taunting me and making me question whether or not I'd actually escaped.

"Part of it's *them and me*. Used to be because I thought I couldn't live up to their expectations."

"And the other part of it?"

"Is just me. And the fear that I might *turn into* him."

His father. "But you won't."

"Not if I can help it."

We both fought similar demons. We'd both come out the other side stronger for it.

"You're nothing like him." I had no fact to base my statement on other than gut instinct. But the man who'd welcomed me into his heart, had stolen past my defenses and captured mine, *loved* those lucky enough to be in his world.

"Touch your electrical lines, Shay." His voice softened with compassion. Like he understood my suffering without me having to share the details. "You're braver than you know."

Because of you. With you, I'm courageous enough to catch a lightning bolt.

I settled my cheek onto my pillow, still facing him in the comforting near-darkness. "I wonder if it will ever end. One day...no more nightmares."

"Yep." He lowered his head down too, so our lips almost touched.

"So sure," I whispered.

"Gotta be. Our fears will end the moment we strip their power away."

Dreams transforming reality. "You speak as if you know firsthand."

"Nope. But hoping. And workin' on it." He pulled my hand to his lips and kissed my knuckles softly.

I stared at his dark silhouette, grateful for the quiet time between us. No pressure. Bedmates for the moment. Like a slumber party...one I'd never had.

"Sooo... isn't it after midnight?"

"Probably." His voice relaxed further, sounding sleepy.

"My day."

"True."

I fought a smile. "So, who won Monday?"

"You tell me."

"You did." *No doubt.* "But Tuesday's gonna blow Monday away."

It has to.

Because I needed him to *know* me.

But more than that, I desperately needed Ben to be the one person I trusted to see the world through my eyes and understand why I lived how I did.

Breaking the law? Only scratches the surface.

"No felonies." His tone hardened.

"So you said."

Warm air puffed over my lips, as if he'd snorted. "Yep."

"Define felony..."

"So you hedged." A heavier sigh gusted across my chin. "Why does that scare me?"

And there it was. My biggest fear. Power-line scary. That he wouldn't be able to go the distance with me. That he'd get only get so far into the truth of who I was, and he'd be in over his head, wouldn't be able to stomach the rest.

"So define it." Best way around a power-line fear is to close my eyes and grab hold.

"Pretty sure breaking and entering is a felony."

Great. Already sunk. "Well, I'm at your place now. So that's done."

"I'm surprised you have to ask. Wouldn't the polished criminal like yourself already know?"

"Never planned on getting caught." I shrugged. "Only time it would ever matter."

"A theft felony?" He yawned. "I think it's something like a thousand dollars, maybe fifteen hundred. Probably varies from state to state."

I twisted, reached for his phone, and clicked on the Internet app.

"What're you doing?"

"Looking it up."

He fell quiet while I searched. After a good minute of typing and swiping, I found the info. "In Pennsylvania, a felony with regard to theft is applied to any stolen good or service with a value in excess of two thousand dollars."

I clicked off his phone, casting us again into relative darkness; a new sliver of moonlight had begun to track through his tall windows.

"Theft all we have to worry about?"

Tomorrow? We'll start you off slow and easy. "Yep. And nothing to worry about at all. You'll see. You get to play lookout."

"*Yay me.*"

"You promised."

"I know." Amusement lightened his tone. "Just teasin'."

"How do you steal over two grand in services?"

"No idea. Can't be at a spa, nothing costs that much. Maybe a high-end car detail or repair shop if you liberated your car before you paid for it."

I yawned wide, trying to think of another. "What if someone stowed away on a cruise ship?"

"There ya go."

"Well, you have nothing to worry about. We'll keep things in misdemeanor territory." Under two grand? *No probs.* "But it won't matter anyway."

"Why is that?"

"Because we won't get caught."

His voice dropped to a conspiratorial whisper, "Isn't that what everybody thinks?"

I kissed him, slow and soft. "Most importantly me."

"Me too, then," he sleepily murmured.

I dragged a finger down his chest, then pressed my hand over his heart.

His breathing deepened.

"You haven't tried to have sex with me again."

A low chuckle vibrated my hand. "Doesn't mean I haven't thought about it."

"Why no moves?"

He inched closer, then pressed a gentle kiss to my lips. "Thought I'd leave that up to you."

Control. What I'd needed. And he'd instinctively understood. No pressure. Total control. Which made me feel respected, valued—invincible.

"Even if I take my time?" Because I still wanted our relationship to go slow, let us unfold naturally.

"Worth the wait." His tone firmed.

What he'd sworn before.

"Good." I slid my hand back into his. "Because I wanna wild things up next time."

He tucked our clasped hands over his heart as his breathing slowed.

"Looking forward to it," he murmured, right before we drifted off to sleep.

24
AN ACCESSORY

Ben...

"What am I looking at?"

"Beauty. Chaos." Shay's voice had lowered. The beginnings of a smile curved her lips.

We sat on an old wooden bench on an elevated deck at the center of a U-shaped outdoor shopping area. A bright sun beat down from a blue sky. But the eight-foot-deep covered porch protected us from the heat; its peeling white paint, dry-rotted floorboards, and wraparound railing with many rickety posts made clear that storms from the north battered the place.

Yet not one of the bustling shoppers seemed to mind.

Neither did Shay. She stared at the verdant panorama beyond the buildings.

The great Smoky Mountains had just begun to glimmer with her first fires of autumn color.

Slight weight rested onto my thigh: her hand. She gripped her fingers, tightening down on my jeans. "Complacency and opportunity." She nodded off right.

Got it. Theft. I took a steadying breath. *At least you gave me fair warning.* The basic details, anyway, over another kitchen-destroying breakfast. Apparently, I owned a waffle maker.

I spotted her indicated target-rich environment. "Outdoor coffeehouse." Toward the end of the U on the right, java drinkers hung casually around the half dozen bistro tables lined up along the far railing. Most were a party of one.

"*Ahhh*...not *just* an outdoor coffeehouse. It's indoor-outdoor. Can't save a table outside unless you leave something. Like a jacket, keys, sparkly iPhone..."

"Purse, backpack, laptop." I lifted my newly *purchased* binoculars to my eyes to confirm. She'd insisted the lookout have the right equipment. And no way in hell I'd let us commit another B-and-E felony just to *borrow* Stephan's pair.

She nodded. "And when they come back after ordering, most settle in for a while. They get comfortable with whoever's at the table in front of them, the customers behind them. But watch long enough, and you begin to see a pattern. People take in their surroundings at the beginning, but only for a few seconds. Almost never after eye contact is made."

"Well, sure. Because staring's rude."

"It's the perfect setup. Plus, people don't *only* get up for drinks. They've claimed their space and don't want to leave. But they're drinking. And the majority don't order those tiny espresso cups. They wanna drink big fancy lattes with designs etched into the foam."

"A smoothie." Not that I'd ever tried that fruity sugar bomb.

"Or a large chai tea." She dropped me a *really?* look.

"So sooner or later..."

"They're gonna need to leave the table. While still *saving* their table. Know where the bathrooms are?"

"I'm guessing *not* by their table."

"Nope." She shook her head. "Not inside the coffeehouse either. Only one set of restrooms service all the shops, including all the tourists traveling down the highway who stop here for a break. No idea what the men's room looks like, but the ladies' only has two stalls and one sink."

"So, if someone has to take a leak, it's gonna be a while."

"Usually is." She leaned back, crossing her arms. "Plenty of time."

"For something unfortunate to happen."

"Or opportune." She uncrossed her arms and scooted forward to the edge of the bench. "Watch Miss Louis Vuitton over there."

I pressed the binoculars back to my eyes and adjusted the diopter. "How can you see brand names?"

"That's the beauty of boldfaced vanity. If an observer from a hundred yards away can't spot the narcissistic ego dangling from their arm, it doesn't deserve to be there. Designers cater to women who want to be noticed."

"And we're noticing."

"Everyone's noticing. Especially the wrong kinds of people."

I continued to stare through the binocs. "Nothing's happening."

"*Waaait* for it... It's coming. A few minutes, tops."

I watched the redhead as she repeatedly scrolled a finger up the screen of her phone. A giant coffee mug sat almost out of arm's reach at the far edge of the table. On the opposite side sat the large designer purse; its black leather had a pattern of rainbow-colored symbols I couldn't make out from here. Thick bright-pink straps arched high from the top of each side, above the middle of the bag which gaped open.

"How do you know it's only a few minutes away?"

"Time. The amount of it that's gone by since she began fidgeting. Plus, she downed that drink in less than ten minutes. And with her hundred-and-ten-pound frame, her bladder's gotta be the size of a pea."

"Solid a theory as any."

"Pay close attention." She patted my thigh, then winked at me as she stood. "It happens fast. In the blink of an eye."

"Blink." Bear's nickname for her. *The meaning behind it.*

For an instant, her entire body froze. Panic flashed across her face. As if I'd found her out, discovered the fragility behind her impenetrable armor. But then her expression relaxed as she drew in a slow breath. She gave me a near-imperceptible nod.

Our gazes held for a beat, the gravity of our moment sinking in. I'd drifted into her world. *She'd allowed it.*

And in spite of my serious misgivings, I endeavored to be all-in with her.

Without another word, she spun around and strode

away with purpose, shoulders squared, steps quick.

So as not to attract attention to me or her, I swept the binoculars over the panoramic mountains, then slow-scanned the coffeehouse scene. But I kept a quick-moving Shay in my peripheral sight as I eased back slightly from the binocs.

And just like clockwork, by the time Shay rounded the corner that led to the coffeehouse, Miss Louis Vuitton stood from her table.

I held my breath when the woman reached for her purse. But all she did was cinch the top partially closed before she walked away.

The table right behind hers had already been abandoned. Its laptop, left open at the perfect viewing angle, faced an empty chair with a backpack dangling from one corner.

Of the six café tables lined up along the railing, four were occupied. A threesome of tourists pored over unfolded maps on the far end. A teenaged couple cuddled close together on the nearest one, taking sips of their drinks between tender kisses, oblivious to the world. The next two tables had been commandeered by three young mothers and their squealing youngsters, who thrilled in the sounds of their stomping footfalls as they ran up and down the wooden walkway.

No one along the length of the patio appeared to pay attention to anyone outside their own personal group.

When Shay passed the "target" woman, neither made direct eye contact with one another.

Shay continued on, unaffected.

She strolled past the first two tables and the screen-door

entrance of the coffeehouse. Then she noticeably slowed her pace for several more steps before resuming her previous speed. With flawlessly timed orchestration, she passed Miss Louis Vuitton's table at the exact same moment two of the older kids raced toward her. A wise adult would've stepped out of the way. Shay? Suddenly had her sparkly pink phone in her hand, acting unaware of the impending danger.

Over the next two seconds, the perfect explosion happened...

The kids collided into one another, bounced off Shay, and knocked into the table that held Miss Louis Vuitton's abandoned designer purse.

The coffee cup and its saucer launched into the air, napkins fluttered two feet up, and the purse toppled over. Various items spilled out, some on the table, a couple rolled off its edge.

The drinkware clattered onto the wood decking at the exact moment the mothers lunged forward and started yelling at their offspring.

With an obvious excuse, I swung my binoculars toward the commotion.

Any innocent bystander would've rubbernecked it.

Shay wasted no time. In a blur, she leaned down and swept up several items at once.

Was there a wallet? I zoomed in but couldn't tell. Her hands kept moving, straightening the items on the table. She bent back down and picked up the saucer, the mug.

One mother joined Shay in the cleanup, chasing down what looked like a metal tube of lipstick that'd rolled halfway toward the entrance of a nearby bookstore.

The other mothers returned to their table and barked at the two older kids. Small shoulders slumped before they spun around and began picking up random collateral damage: one napkin at a time, a purse escapee that rested against the leg of the chair, another that had rolled to the railing's edge. Each item got deposited onto the table where Shay stuffed them back into the uprighted purse.

Shay said something to the mother at the table with her. The woman laughed.

Then Shay left the scene. She continued on to the general store and pulled out a bright colored tourist map from a Plexiglas container on the wall. After a bored perusal of all the shops in the center, she trotted down three steps at the far corner and ventured along the edge of the fifteen-space parking lot at the front of the shopping center.

I pulled down the binoculars as everything settled down.

Shay unfolded her confiscated map while she skirted a large grassy area. Then she hooked a left onto a sidewalk that led back to me.

The mothers hovered back around their table, resuming their coveted gossip.

The kids trudged in an obedient line off the patio, down the steps, and onto the grass.

And clueless Miss Louis Vuitton reappeared, walked to her table, picked up her empty cup and saucer, then disappeared into the coffeehouse, unaware that anything had occurred in her absence.

A giant blue map—with sexy toned legs—climbed

the stairs to my right, moved toward me, then crinkled halfway down. Shay peered at me above its edge, amusement sparkling in her eyes.

She looked amazing: dark hair framing her face in loose waves, cheeks flushed pink, wide smile on her beautiful face.

And she'd agreed to be mine.

Damn, I'm a lucky fucker.

She arched her brows. "Well, did you see?"

Back to Petty Theft 101. "Only what you wanted me to. What you wanted everyone to see. That was masterful."

Her earlier *Outliers* comment echoed in my head. Ten thousand hours of practice. *Impressive.*

She gave a disinterested shrug. "No big."

"And the loot?"

"The take?"

I coughed out a laugh. "Right, 'the take.'" Had to get her lingo down.

She crumpled the map and lobbed the wad into a trashcan. Then she plopped onto the bench beside me. Her hand slapped down on my thigh. Crisp green corners peeked between her fingers.

I tugged them loose, then fanned the bills apart to count four twenties. "Eighty bucks. Not bad. And that's a safe amount?"

"Yep." She took the binoculars from me, then scanned the coffeehouse patio with them. "When I leave the wallet, I always leave money behind."

"How much was there?" The whole thing fascinated me—that she gave herself rules, that they held an element of honor.

"Looked like maybe four-fifty. She'd just hit the ATM."

"How do you know that? And if her wallet was loaded, why didn't you take more?" Honor or not, I needed to try to understand her reasoning.

"Because when we first got here, she was standing in front of it, punching buttons." Shay slanted a nod toward the back-left corner of the complex. "ATM's over there. And because I only take what's needed. They have a certain amount to give before suspicion overrides their guilt, and I only like to spread it around in small amounts."

"Spread it around?" An image of hot-dog-stand Tony's tip jar flashed into my mind. But I got the feeling she meant something else.

"You'll see later tonight. Why I needed a Tuesday."

"Understood." *Almost. To give. Spreading it around.* She'd been cryptic about her motives. But I'd agreed last night to be an observer. And with the way she'd been opening up to me on her own, I didn't want to come off as an interrogator.

But maybe I could coax her into sharing a little more. "It's always a Miss Louis Vuitton?"

I threaded my fingers into hers, something I'd come to love in the last couple of days. Because she instantly flexed hers, then curled them, holding on tight.

"Hey, if they're gonna flaunt it."

"Then they're going to be a target?"

She gave a light shrug. "I like to call them givers."

Givers...

Spreading it around...

"Accidental philanthropists?"

Right as I tossed out my clever twist on her definition, all the tiny clues began to crystalize. *You rob from the rich to give to the poor.*

"Even better," she continued, in the dark about my suspected revelation. "And today was a baby hit. Most givers who fly onto my radar aren't even broadcasting brand names. They're oozing *brand* names."

I understood the distinction. "Because there's rich..."

"And then there's the über *rich.*"

"*Stratospheric* wealthy." *Welcome to the world my father had groomed me for.* "Multimillionaires and billionaires."

"They have *whole closets* designed for their collection of luxury handbags: Chanel, Hermès, Fendi, Louis Vuitton."

"Closets you've seen?"

She arched her brows at me. "Do you *want* me to keep talking about felonies?"

"No."

I hadn't even sorted out how I felt about being lookout for the crime that just went down. *Conflicted, at the least. More than a little unsettled. And* for damn sure *worried.*

Even if Shay donated every penny she ever stole, it hadn't been hers to reappropriate. And she'd been good, but no criminal operated in a vacuum: evidence eventually got discovered, even the best thieves got caught.

She shrugged and glanced back toward Miss Louis Vuitton. "They all probably give tens of thousands a year to trendy charities anyway. Those charities have top-heavy management and most of that money never reaches the people who desperately need it...the whole purpose for the charity to exist in the first place."

She valiantly fought to defend those in need, without any concern for her own welfare. From in-depth movie discussions about the plight of the innocents to real-life actions that backed up her convictions, Shay *was* a modern-day superhero. *Humbly, but undisputedly.*

All of a sudden, something more powerful than my concerns chipped away at their foundation.

I put my arm around her shoulder and pulled her toward me.

Big green eyes stared up at me, sparkling with happiness. After searching them for a beat, I lowered my head and brushed my lips over hers.

We connected in a tender kiss, soft, slow, filled with all the burning passion she had ignited.

I'm proud of you, Shay.

And I silently vowed to do everything in my power to protect her.

"Where we headin'?"

The last afternoon hours had been spent touring through Shay's daytime neighborhood stomping grounds. We'd breezed through a local grocery and drugstore she'd frequented for years. We'd weaved through an art park and shared our opinions of the funky abstract structures that twisted through its public gardens.

We'd just come from holding hands as we sat on a weathered park bench, beside a giant rock outcropping. That's when she'd gone unusually quiet. She had glanced up at the ragged boulders several times, then stared off at a dense forest at the edge of the park when we'd finally stood to leave. I'd gotten the sense that everywhere she'd brought me to held great significance for her. But the park bench, the outcropping, that forest? More than the rest.

And when her stomach had growled an hour past dinnertime, I'd insisted on a hearty meal at a steakhouse at the end of the block. She'd scrunched her face with a headshake and took us to a nearby greasy spoon instead. Then she'd downed a burger and classic fries, a chili dog with spicy curly fries, and a large Coke. I'd done my best to keep up with her, but had only managed to eat two-thirds of what she'd packed away. She had insisted on paying from her stolen eighty bucks.

"We gotta hit Mickey D's." She released my hand and darted out into the busy street.

By the time my brain caught up with her abrupt action, she'd raced across the first couple of lanes and stood in a narrow median. My breath caught as three cars sped by, two in the far lane, one mere inches from her. Then she jogged across the third lane, heading toward the fourth.

When a red light stopped traffic to my left, I felt halfway-comfortable enough to step off the curb.

After she reached the sidewalk, she spun around. Then her face lit up with excitement. "Look at you. Jaywalking!"

No shit. "Step by step," I ground out with a toothy smile

as I crossed the final two lanes, nervously glancing left and right. To check for cars. And cops.

I stepped onto the sidewalk and into her waiting embrace. She lifted up on tiptoe, slid her hands up my back, and pressed a soft kiss to my lips. "I'm winning you over, crime by crime."

"We'll see," I grumbled. But then I deepened the kiss, got lost in the sweet scent of her hair, the warm goodness of her heart, and all my grumpiness faded away.

When we broke free, then angled into a shopping center's parking lot, famous golden arches greeted us. And her while-bolting-into-traffic answer finally registered.

"McDonald's?"

"None other."

"But you just ate a mountain of food. You're still hungry?"

"Not for me. For my friends." She gave me a pointed look as I held the door open for her. "Every Tuesday."

Ahhh... Now we get to the mystery behind why Tuesday.

And instead of learning about her through places, I'd get to meet her people.

"Bear?" The only one I knew, besides Rafe.

"For one." Our turn came at the counter. She ordered five Quarter Pounder with Cheese meals then changed out her last twenty to fives. While we waited, we grabbed stacks of napkins and an assortment of condiment packets: ketchup, mayo, salt.

After we collected our food and drinks, Shay lined the bags up on a stretch of counter. She opened each bag and dropped in napkins, condiments, and a five rolled lengthwise.

Food for now, snack money for later?

Now I understood the greasy spoon. Only place we'd pig out on a dime. Altogether, she'd spent all of the eighty down to the last nickel.

"And the others?" I held the door with one hand, balanced a tray of Cokes on the other.

"Lando, Charlene, Decker...and Trin." Her voice softened when she spoke the last.

"Who's Trin?" I hadn't dug much all day. Not about the bench, the boulders, the forest. But the way her heart melted when thinking about someone else? I had to ask.

"My protégé."

Before long, we rounded a corner at the beginning of a lower-income residential street. Laundry hung from clotheslines. A chained dog barked. Beater cars rusted along the curbs.

A young kid with shaggy blond hair and big blue eyes hesitantly approached us from the nearest side alley.

Shay smiled wide, held up her hands full of McDonald's bags, and nodded the kid over.

"How old is he?"

"*She* is about the same age as I was."

"*Nooo...*" I gusted out on a harsh exhale.

"Yeah. But no big. Street kids are tougher than you think." Shay held out one of the bags.

The girl snatched it while eyeing me warily. She skirted around to stand beside Shay. "What's with the old man in the beard," she whispered without removing her watchful gaze.

Shay angled her face toward her. "He's *my* old man with the beard."

"*Ohhh...*" The girl's brows raised for a brief second, then pinched together. She scowled and shook her head. Vigorously.

I'd been considered. Then rejected.

I cleared my throat and held out one of the Cokes. "Old man standing right here."

The girl stared at the drink. Then she flicked an offended glance at Shay.

On a sigh, Shay took the drink from me and handed it to her. "Trin, this is Ben. It's okay. He's one of the cool ones."

"*No* grown-up is cool," she scoffed.

"Well," —Shay gave me an amused look— "he's cooler than most."

I hadn't missed the subtle distinction that Trin hadn't been introduced to me, I'd been introduced to her. Because what Trin thought, how she felt about me, mattered to Shay.

Trin blasted out a clear don't-talk-to-strangers vibe, so I tossed out a neutral icebreaker. "What's Trin short for?"

Trin's eyes narrowed. "Nuttin' ta you."

"Maybe it's short for Katrina." Only a guess. If wrong, then a taunt. And either worked.

Her nose scrunched in disapproval. She took a long slurp of Coke, then raised her brows slightly. She pointed the top of her straw at me. "Or maybe Trinity, like from *The Matrix*."

I arched my brows. "Is it?"

"Not sayin'."

The more defiance she spat out, the more I saw the girl in her. A lot like Shay.

"Ben is short for Benjamin."

"No one's askin'."

My lips twitched as I fought a smile. "You always act so tough?"

"Only ta grown-ups tryin' ta get all up in my business."

"Fair enough." No winning her over. Not on an introduction.

"We gotta go." Shay held up the remaining four bags and crinkled their tops.

Trin sighed heavily and frowned.

"Hey." Shay nudged her shoulder. "You wanna hit Tony's on Friday for me?"

All trace of pouting vanished as Trin's bright blue eyes lit up with hope. "Can I?"

The pickpocketing. The cash drop at the hot dog stand.

The heavy reality of their discussion struck me. I remembered the guy in the suit that Shay had "bumped" to get flush with cash. And I cringed at the thought of scrappy young Trin getting close enough to a guy like that.

She was too cute, too young, too...innocent. *Way* too at-risk.

And then the real shocker slammed into my head and heart.

Beautiful, strong, courageous Shay. You'd been all of that too.

As we left the neighborhood, Shay glanced at me. "Kiki made plans with me over the phone last night, for tomorrow morning. I just remembered."

"For the golf-shirt thing?"

"Yeah. Should take just an hour or two. That okay?"

"Of course, it's okay." More than okay. Hanging around Kiki? I couldn't think of a better influence for Shay. Or a better match of personalities.

"Wanna come?"

"Where you going?"

"Pro shops at three different country clubs."

I choked out a laugh.

"What's so funny?"

"It's just..."

"I come from the streets." She rattled her fast-food bags as we turned down a dark alley. "It's okay, you can say it. No big." She shrugged, unapologetic. "No denyin' the truth."

"It's *truth* when it comes from you. Sounds like judgment when it comes from me. And I don't, by the way. Judge you. *Respect.* That's what I feel for you." Without doubt.

When the alley spilled us out on an intersecting street, she stopped then stared up at me a couple of beats. "Is that *all* you feel for me."

I ran a hand up her arm and stared into her expressive searching eyes. Ten nights ago, we'd stood in a different dark alley, on opposite sides of everything. So much had changed in an instant. "No." *Not even close.*

She gave me a slow nod. Then the corners of her lips twitched, she stepped back, and crossed her arms, bags crinkling. "I come from the streets *annnd...*"

You're gonna make me say it. "And go straight to the opposite."

"Where money lives?"

I snorted. "That too. I mean you went from gritty real to

sparkling shallow, from scrounging and surviving among the poorest...to negotiating business in a sport played to alleviate boredom among the richest."

"And if I told you all the money made will go straight from the rich into the pockets of the poor? Legally?"

My heart thudded hard with pride in her for what she wanted, who she needed to help. The very streets we stood on had made her into the beautiful person she'd become. Immense relief followed...*you might not have to steal anymore.*

I pressed against those bags she held between us. Paper crinkled and crunched. But the mundane noise sounded perfect to my ears. Because we stood at the brink of our two worlds melding.

With slow tenderness, I kissed her. "I'd say you're a genius."

25

THE BUSINESS END OF A SWING

Shay…

"*Mm…morning.*" Ben growl-purred the baritone greeting.

I sighed, then sleepily smiled. "Morning."

"*Shaaay…*" His lips twitched at the corners. "What are you doing?"

"I'm layin' on you." *How 'bout that?* No hesitation. No reservations. It felt natural—safe. I shimmied my hips, basking in the incredible warmth he radiated. "What's it feel like I'm doin'?"

"But what are you *really* doing?' Strong hands skimmed up my back, under my T-shirt.

I rested my chin on his chest, staring up at him, well aware he'd slept stark-naked all night, even though I hadn't. "Does it seem like I'm doing something else?"

"I don't know." He gripped my hips, then pulled down as

he thrusted up. "You tell me."

"Oh, *wow*." No mistaking that iron hardness, even through my cotton boy-short underwear.

"Yep. 'Oh, wow.'"

"All from just me...on you?"

His fingers traced lazy circles on my back. "Apparently."

"Not morning wood?"

"Not even close." He blew out a measured breath.

"Harder?" I gave my hips another tiny shimmy.

He groaned low. "Like rock beats paper."

"I thought paper beats rock."

"Not from where I'm layin'."

That hardness gave a tantalizing kick up against my sensitized nerves. I gasped as a sensual ache fired through me. My whole body shivered.

He groaned again. "You have some kind of power over me."

I wiggled my hips faster, more than thrilled by the action and his reaction. "A superpower."

He hooked his thumbs into my waistband and tugged my underwear halfway down my hips. "Why aren't you naked?"

"*Uhhh*, because you tried to strike up hour-long conversations with my cagey homeless friends on each Mickey D's delivery? You dragged my ass back here late, and I was tired."

"That question was rhetorical." He bent his leg, hooked his foot into the fabric over my butt, then dragged my underwear down my legs. "It means *get* naked."

"What did you think of everyone? You never said."

"I was too busy being impressed with you last night. And they were...interesting?"

My underwear got caught on my second ankle. I shook it free. "*Good* interesting?"

"Yes. Good." He yanked my shirt to my shoulders, then pulled it over my head and arms. "No more talking about anyone else. I'm busy being impressed with you now. And it's *my* day. *My* rules."

I pressed my lips together, hiding a smile, unwilling to go down without a fight. Even though my skin tingled awake and my breath quickened as flashes of pleasure spiked between my legs. "We never decided who won yesterday."

"You did," he clipped out.

Before another syllable made it out of my mouth, he arched up and kissed me...hard at first, then softer and a *hell* of a lot sexier.

A guttural moan vibrated in my throat as a constant deeper ache unfurled between my legs, throbbing and undeniable.

All of a sudden, he gripped my hips and the world spun.

I squealed out midair, but then my back hit the bed, and the rest of the air knocked out of me. "Thought *I* was gonna make the next move."

He shifted, sitting up before leaning back. "You did."

As he adjusted, the soft white sheet slid down his muscular chest, drifted over taut abs, then got caught at his lean hips.

My gaze traveled back up from the dusting of black hair below his navel, along the primal black markings tattooed around his chiseled biceps, to a face I'd come to love, from the scruff of his beard to the fierceness in his charcoal eyes.

Mischief glittered in his gaze before he grabbed my hips again, flipped me over, and dragged me down a good foot. My forearms braced against my pillow, my cheek pressed against cold sheet.

There you are. The real Ben. Filled with ferociousness and passion. Only instead of a devastating storm barreling down to destroy me, he'd become the vibrant lightning bolt I wanted to catch.

"But *I* wanted to wild things up." Face my fears, rewrite more of my memories about touch. *My way. With control.*

"You had your fun. Now I get to play."

With a resigned exhale, I relaxed onto the sheet.

Maybe his way was better. *Surrender control.* Trust him, completely.

The warm pressure of his hand slid up the inside of my knee, my thigh, until his fingers slicked through my center.

I gasped as an electric jolt of pleasure sparked hot, then sizzled outward, deeper.

His expert fingers teased, massaging in light slides then firmer presses, fast flicks then slower circles.

My breaths grew ragged. Low whimpers sounded from my throat. A heavy ache coiled tight inside, and I began to shake with the need for release.

All the while, his strong protective body curved over me. The thrilling mixed sensation of rough beard then soft kisses branded a fiery trail over my hip, toward the center of my back, and meandered up to my shoulders.

Skin to skin, heart and soul, every move he made, each soft caress, made me feel cherished...loved.

"*Sooo* wet." His growled words vibrated against my shoulder as his weight shifted. His circling fingers vanished, but a firm blunt pressure stroked across my sparking nerves, once...twice.

Then the pressure dragged backward. His blunt tip caught at my entrance.

But he didn't move.

His heavy breaths fanned across my shoulder blades, then fogged forward up my neck, across the shell of my ear.

I panted, breathless, consumed with aching need and undeniable want.

When I turned my face, he kissed me, soft and slow.

"*Please*," I begged, arching my hips back.

"Please...*what*?" He pressed the slightest bit inside, then pulled back.

My pulse raced through my veins, throbbed mercilessly between my legs.

"*Please*," I rasped out. "I need..."

"Need? Or want..." Another slow press forward, a little more inside. And then a slower drag backward.

I swallowed hard, overwhelmed with sensation. "Want. Definitely want."

"Enough" —he pushed forward, inch by inch— "to wait?"

But instead of pulling back, he eased forward, stretching me wide, filling me up...further, deeper, claiming everything, all the way.

His muscular body covered me. His hands skimmed up my arms before his fingers curled into mine. But inside? Where hot hardness owned every aching nerve ending? He didn't move.

Our banter finally penetrated the haze in my brain. What we'd said before, about a kiss.

"No." I smiled, then bucked under his solid weight. "No waiting."

A warm half-laugh feathered over my ear. He eased back a couple of inches, then pressed forward again. "Not even if I make it worth the wait?"

I shook my head, arched my back as best I could, then gyrated my hips. Which resulted in a delicious twitch from him inside me. I moaned low. "Not unless you want me to die of ache."

"Maybe only near-death *pleasure*..." His hips jerked forward, burying himself deeper and igniting a new round of sizzling sparks.

But the next time he moved back—gave me enough wiggle room beneath him—I took advantage of the opportunity. I drove my left hip into the mattress, twisted my upper body, and lodged a shoulder against his chest.

Somehow, he shifted with me, anticipated where I'd be. As I twisted around, he grabbed one of my calves, bent my leg, then angled it up against his chest. The other leg followed, until both of my ankles were at his shoulders. And before I could pull in a solid breath, he surged forward, claiming all of me with every generous inch of him as he pinned me back down to the mattress.

I gasped at the intensity as I gazed up at the beautiful man who'd stolen my heart.

Dark eyes stared down at me, penetrating, as if willing me to feel every emotion he did.

I do. I feel you. "Right there with you," I whispered.

One corner of his mouth twitched up. His fingers touched right above where we connected, first with firm steady pressure, then leisurely tormenting slides back and forth.

Between one beat and the next, he eased back, then drove forward. His fingers grazed across my clit before circling over it harder...faster.

White-hot pleasure sparked through me, and I threw my head back into the pillows with a low moan. But the pressure only built further...breath held, pulse racing.

In a slow-motion collapse, he lowered down onto me. My legs fell along his sides until they cradled his hips. Hot damp skin covered me from belly to chest. Tender hands caressed my face.

And his soft lips captured mine as he began to thrust deep inside me with fierce hard strokes.

I held on, lost in our passionate kiss, as we rode the cresting wave of pleasure together.

Low moans mixed with small whimpers, his, mine. I couldn't tell. Didn't care.

As I hung right at the edge, every last nerve ending taut, sparking hot and ready to explode, he froze. His whole body tightened. He drew back a little and blinked hard, brows drawn low, tension etched into the severe lines on his face.

I surged forward and kissed him. My hips curved up, drawing him deeper. I arched, then curved, chasing my orgasm, plunging over the edge. He thrusted hard once, twice, a third time...then he sucked in a tortured breath and groaned, letting go, falling with me.

Long seconds dragged by as we held on to each other.

Gasping breaths started to lengthen.

Racing hearts began to slow.

A glittering shaft of sunlight rested on his skin, and mine, warm and brilliant.

After a lazy minute or two, he eased back a little and stared down at me, surprise and wonder in his gaze.

I smiled, so incredibly happy to have caused him such intense emotion.

His brows twitched down infinitesimally. "Why does this feel *so*...."

"More?" More than I'd ever hoped for, so much deeper and righter than I'd ever imagined.

"Yeah." He brushed strands of hair out of my eyes. "*More.*"

"No idea." Something rare had happened between us. We'd forged a connection that breached our differing worlds, strengthened by the sameness we'd endured.

I wrapped my arms around him, holding on tight to his strong body and fierce heart, uncertain if we'd be able to weather whatever difficult challenges we'd face.

And I knew challenges would come. Adversity always tested the happy.

Pinching my eyes shut, I forced out the fear that had

edged its way into our blissful moment.

A firm kiss pressed to my forehead. Then he let out a long exhale. "Me either."

His heavy sigh spoke volumes.

And the way he curved his body around me, held me close against him, said he feared too.

But he held on all the tighter. As if his actions proved he'd refuse to budge one inch when the going got rough.

Me too. I clamped my hands over his arms, holding on, unwilling to let him go.

"Me too," I whispered.

I'm going to fight for you too.

Kiki and I walked into the last pro shop right as my phone vibrated. I pulled the sparkly pink thing out of my back jeans pocket and smiled. It gave me a serious happy every time its brightness hit me. Because Ben had given it to me. And he was the one vibrating my ass.

Running late. Ten minutes, tops.

Kiki gave me a quick nod while I typed a reply to Ben. Then I heard her ask someone to let the general manager know we were there for our appointment.

No worries. Our spiel is quick and boring.

Business stuff.

I scrunched my nose.

Before I had a chance to stuff the phone back into my pocket, it vibrated again.

You just made a face, didn't you?

I laughed. Three women examining golf shoes all jerked judgmental stares at me. "Geez. What is this, a library?" I muttered.

But I didn't budge. I stood five feet away from them in an open carpeted area between ridiculous women's accessories, designer men's golf shirts, and the front counter with its display of enameled ball markers and club-branded coffee mugs.

There a hidden camera in here?

I scanned up and around the ceiling and spotted all three obvious security cameras.

Nope. Just imagined you sayin that.

"Kiki Michaelson. It's a pleasure to see you." A portly man with salt-and-pepper hair and wire-rimmed glasses strolled in through the open french doors, from the country club's main lobby. "What brings you here today?"

I pocketed my phone and stood beside her while she

draped the samples of our shirts over the counter. He stepped around to the employee side, sweeping his gaze across an expanse of windows that revealed a row of shining golf carts, eager attendants, and members walking up with their bags before he landed his attention back on us.

"Mr. Jensen, this is my business partner, Shay Morgan. We have an exciting opportunity for you."

The man gave me a cursory look from above those wiry glasses, but extended no hand to shake.

No surprise. We'd gotten the same icy reception from each of the managers at all three pretentious clubs.

I'd gone ahead and worn the dark gray collared golf shirt Ben had picked out for me. But the jeans stayed. My way of being defiant in an established world full of suffocating rules. I compromised on the shoes: ditched the beat-up Converse for my cute black sandals.

But Mr. Jensen wasn't looking at my feet. Not my jeans, either. He'd no doubt already looked down his nose at them the moment he'd walked through the doors.

"Exciting," he droned out with the enthusiasm of a weary basset hound.

Yeah, this'll go well. The guy wouldn't know exciting if it bit him in the ass.

Kiki rattled out the spiel: to inject freshness into golf fashion, modern lines with an edgy vibe, appealing to a younger generation.

"...and the *young at heart*," I finished with my strong belief. Because I planned to never grow up. But there had to be grown-ups out there that still wanted to embrace their playful side. Mr. Jensen *wasn't* one of them.

He gave a pointed glance at the judgy threesome. Those women weren't either.

Kiki gave me a knowing look, then rolled her eyes toward Mr. Jensen.

We'd lost him at "exciting." She knew it. I knew it.

But a wicked smile curved her lips. *Yeah. She's gonna go the distance anyway.*

"You haven't heard the best part." She lifted the top shirt, a solid black. "Besides having the softest Pima cotton, the most comfortable cut in the arms, and the requisite collar, each has a witty golf saying."

"Witty." His tone deadened further.

And naughty. I bit back a smile. Miss Politically Correct Kiki had begun to toy with him.

Kiki held up a collar corner. "I dream of a" —she pointed toward the other corner— "*slow, long* stroke."

I lifted the next shirt, joining the fun. "Give me your... *hard steel* shaft."

Mr. Jensen's pudgy face began to turn beet red.

Kiki plucked at the herringbone's collar. "*Drive* straight into...my sweet spot."

He began to shake. "Well, I...never," he whispered.

First time for everything. "I like to play...with a *firm* grip."

"Never!" he barked, a vein bulging in the center of his forehead.

Kiki scooped up our samples before Mr. Elitist's scorching glare burst them into flames. "You're making a mistake, Mr. Jensen. Because Victoria Michaelson wouldn't have her grip any other way. No self-respecting golfer would. And I'm certain she'll be proud to wear one of our quality shirts. And so will all of her friends."

"I won't *allow it* on my course," he ground out through gritted teeth.

"You're just a manager here. It's not your course. It's *our* course, the members."

"It's breaking the rules."

"Which rule? It has a collar." Kiki fingered the corner of one, right below its embroidered saying.

"It's profane."

"Do you see the word 'fuck' on here, Shay? Because *hell*, I don't see it."

"Well, *damn*. I don't. Don't see 'shit' either."

Mr. Jensen frosted us with a glacial glare. "Ladies, this is a *reputable* establishment. It's not what the words actually say, it's what people who read them will be thinking."

"And you have the authority to censor their minds?" No way in hell I'd let that slide.

Kiki gave me an approving nod. "We know *you* have a dirty mind, Mr. Jensen. Shouldn't we leave it up to members who choose to wear our shirts and those who read them to find out if *they* appreciate them?"

His face reddened again. "Go ahead and try it. I'll have you thrown off the course."

"Us?" I arched my brows. He couldn't hear clearly through the haze of his criticizing anger.

Kiki crossed her arms. "You mean my mom? Her friends? You go ahead and try it. I think every member of this club would pay a thousand dollars a pop for tickets to see that happen."

"*I'd* pay ten times that." A deep voice boomed from behind us.

Ben.

Kiki shot a smug look at Mr. Jensen, whose expression had morphed from disgusted outrage to aghast mortification.

But in a cool split second, he schooled his expression and gave a cursory nod toward Ben. "Mr. Bishop." Then he shook his head, as if to clear it from all things disreputable. "Good day, Miss Michaelson, Miss Morgan." He gave a polite nod toward each of us, then hightailed it over to the shoe threesome. "Ladies, may I help you with something?"

Yeaaah...whatever.

Without giving a damn about propriety, I breezed by the asinine group discussing the merits of various golf shoes and threw myself into Ben's waiting arms.

"*Ooomph*," he grunted as my body slammed into him. But then he wrapped his arms around me and kissed me soundly.

"Hey, bro." Kiki knuckle-bumped him as I eased back from his embrace. "How long you been here?"

"Long enough. They all been that brutal?" He glanced from her to me.

I gave a halfhearted shrug. "Nothin' we didn't expect. Can't change eons of staunch tradition in a few minutes of shop talk."

"Never fear." Kiki gave me a determined look. "My mom and her connected friends? *Totally* gonna love and wear these shirts."

"Speaking of who's wearing what..." Because I kept forgetting to ask. "What exactly is the dress code for the gala Saturday night?" I glanced at Ben, then Kiki.

"Ball gown, cocktail dress," Kiki replied, tone matter-of-fact.

"Yeah, I got neither."

"Ben gave a nod toward Kiki. "I bet our designer could help us out."

Kiki's face brightened. "And by *designer*, you both mean *fairy godmother*, right?"

I shot Ben an amused look. "She had a pumpkin." I mimicked the grouchy tone he'd used.

"And mice." His lips twitched at the corners.

Kiki stared at Ben, then me, then shook her head. "Not even gonna ask. And I'm outta here. Gotta meet my mom, AKA our future biggest golf-shirt supporter, for lunch." Kiki pointed at me. "Friday." Then she held a thumb-and-pinky-hand-phone gesture near her ear. "Call me with a time. We'll raid my closet."

"Done." I nodded with a grin.

Ben put his solid arms around me again, in full view of Mr. Jenson and his judgy ladies.

I didn't care who saw or what they thought, about me, Ben, or our edgy shirts. Inventors and adventurers didn't waste brain cells on stupid customs and outdated rules. They made their own and forged ahead.

"This is turning into an awesome day. And it's *your* day." Especially with its sexy beginning, and *in spite* of all the stuffy business in between then and him holding me now.

He huffed out a sigh with a resigned expression. "Well, brace yourself. It's about to get a little tricky."

"It is?" I cocked my head, curious.

"How do you feel about dinner with my parents?"

My heart leapt into my throat. My lungs seized.

But I stared up into beautiful charcoal eyes filled with compassion and saw a humble plea in their depths.

I gusted out a long breath and decided he deserved an honest answer.

"Terrified."

26
DUST UNDER THE RUG

Ben…

"**I** think I need to go." I led her outside toward the covered patio.

Once we sat together on a stone bench, she gripped my hand, solid, unwavering.

But her confession weighed heavy on my mind. I knew she'd experienced trauma somewhere there, with family, with her parents. She hadn't wanted to share her story with me yet. And I didn't want to push her.

What had idiot me done instead? Asked her to brave my demons with me.

I let out a sigh. Maybe explaining why would help. *Both of us.* "Normally it's my mom who calls, like on Monday. She guilts me with a thousand reasons why I should take up the yoke as a good supportive son when she can't make one decision to save herself."

My gaze fell toward the ground. Disappointment and an unfamiliar sense of being lost fogged my brain.

She placed a gentle hand on my thigh. "And this time?"

I glanced into beautiful emerald eyes that glittered with compassion. "My dad called. His voice was small, faltering. For my whole life, whenever that man spoke, words boomed out, charged with confidence. But earlier...I've...*never* heard him like that: hesitant, uncertain—defeated. He asked if I could make it to dinner tonight with him and my mom. He said he knew I wouldn't want to and that he deserved my anger and resentment. But if I could find it in my heart to give him one more chance, it would mean the world to him... to Mom. My dad's voice broke at the end. And I heard her crying in the background."

That call shook me like nothing ever had.

She gave my hand a firm squeeze. "Then we'll go. I've never been to dinner with parents before. But how bad could it be? Yours are dysfunctional. So were mine."

With her last words, her tone quieted. A frown tugged at the corners of her lips.

That *were* hadn't gone unnoticed. The trigger affected her. But she didn't elaborate.

And I felt like an ass for dragging her into my difficult situation. "You sure? We don't have to do this."

Her brows lowered as her expression hardened with resolve. "I want to. It'll be good therapy for me. For both of us."

Gratitude filled my chest. I had no idea what I'd done to deserve the resilient woman beside me. But I planned to do everything in my power to shield her from becoming collateral damage from my family's shit. "Thanks. Sorry to have it ruin one of our good days."

"No." She snuggled up against me and kissed me softly. "Nothing's ruined. No one says it has to be a downer for us. Does it suck for them? Yup. But they made their choices and they're *still* making them. All we're doing is going to dinner. We'll make some rules to be sure we're having a better time than they are."

I let out a dry half-laugh. "That shouldn't be too hard."

But anger simmered in my gut that our own flesh and blood affected us like this. Family should be about love and protection...not emotional torture.

"We *will* have fun tonight." After a beat, her brow wrinkled. "That sounds morbid, doesn't it?"

"Maybe. But we've had to do whatever we could in order to survive. Why should tonight be any different?"

"It shouldn't." She tugged me up from the bench and led us across the side lawn, leading toward my truck. "So, let's spend the afternoon making rules and having our own kind of fun."

Almost eight hours later, we rang the front bell at my parents' house. I didn't have a key (on purpose) and wasn't about to let myself in.

Shay looked glorious: skin flushed a pretty pink, loose

tendrils of dark hair framing her face, emerald eyes glistening with contentment.

She'd also planted herself on the opposite wall, seven feet away.

Then her luscious lips began to curve into a smile as she stared at me.

My heart stuttered. "Damn, you're stunning when you're happy."

She let out a soft laugh. "I'm sex-drugged."

We'd spent all afternoon playing in bed. And on the kitchen counter. The couch got officially broken in. So did my truck. But we'd missed one thing. "We never got around to making rules."

"I blame you."

I smirked, thinking about the wildness of the afternoon. "I blame me too."

"Not that it matters." She moved from her camped spot on the wall, stepping closer.

I stood still. I wanted her to find her own comfort zone on the precipice of meeting my parents. Even though the night had everything to do with seeing my dad one last time before the indictment came down, "meeting the family" still carried heavy relationship meaning. For normal people, it meant acceptance-pressure. For us, decades of baggage was about to break open and spill out.

She skimmed her hands up my chest as she searched my eyes. Then she lifted a hand to smooth her fingers over my tense brow before she cupped my cheek. "I'm flying high enough not to care what happens. And I'm *with* you, no matter what."

I kissed her softly, grateful to have someone on my side for a change. "Remember that feeling in about fifteen minutes."

The door opened. "I thought I heard someone." My mother, poised as ever, stood in a blue evening gown. Her gaze landed on my black T-shirt and jeans, then traveled to Shay's short black dress. But her icy stare froze on the spot where Shay's hand covered my heart.

I tightened a protective arm around Shay's waist and shot my mother a deadpan look. "You heard just fine."

My father appeared behind her. "Laura, are you inviting them in or interrogating them?"

"I'm not sure *who* I'm letting in."

I clenched my jaw, biting back a retort. "Mom, Dad, this is Shay. My girlfriend." As if the possessive touching hadn't been her first clue.

Finally, my territorial mother stepped back and allowed us to pass.

"It's very nice to meet you Shay," my father said as we walked through the entry into the dining room. "You'll have to excuse my wife. You're the first girl Ben's ever brought here."

With good reason.

But Shay wasn't any *girl* at all. She was the first woman who got me *and* understood what I'd been through. Because she'd been there too. Maybe not in the same situation, but in all the ways that mattered—where trust and betrayal had shaped who we'd become.

Turned out, we had to excuse his wife all night.

I hadn't given them a heads-up I'd be bringing someone.

And my sweet mother thanked me for it at every opportunity.

By taking it out on Shay.

But Shay took every venomous barb and backhanded compliment in stride. She never once lashed out.

Me? Not so civilized. I fired off one-liners, tit for tat.

But by dessert, Shay's nerves had worn thin. It came across in the rigid set of her shoulders, the strained smiles, more frequent deep breaths.

My mother balanced a fluff of crème brûlée on her spoon. "What college did you say you graduated from, dear?"

"She didn't," I ground out.

Shay put a gentle hand on my forearm. Her *it's okay* glance at me? My only warning.

"Didn't say...or didn't go?" Kindhearted Mom cast a critical stare at Shay.

With a loud clink, Shay dropped her spoon into her half-empty ceramic ramekin. "We didn't say. And I didn't go to college." She folded her white cloth napkin with slow precision, then placed it beside her abandoned dessert. "I didn't attend one day of high school, either."

Mom's hardened expression began to falter as the color drained from her face.

But Shay leaned closer to her, picking up momentum. "I didn't grow up in a loving home. I *raised myself* loitering on park benches and climbing trees. In the mornings, I ran wild in shadowy forests. Most afternoons, I kicked back on dead leaf piles where I daydreamed of rich houses filled with spoiled kids and entitled parents."

My mom blinked, speechless. A first.

"Well, I like her." Dad clapped me on the shoulder.

Mom's gaze drifted from Shay, to me, then landed on Dad. "Who *are* you?"

"A man who's making amends. You might try it sometime."

I stared at him in disbelief.

Yeah, who the hell *are you?*

My whole life, I'd fought for him to stop emotionally abusing her, us. Then at the eleventh hour, when his whole life was about to be stripped away, he'd miraculously become a good guy?

I shook my head, not buying his load of bullshit for even one second.

"Son, might we have a few minutes alone?"

My gaze shot to Shay.

She cast me an amused glance, then gave my hand a light squeeze as we stood. "Go. I'm good. I'm made of tougher stuff than she's ever imagined."

When I scanned the room, Mom had abandoned her chair and stood by the window. The maid had already begun to clear the table. I had no idea where the two of them would go or what they'd talk about.

But Shay kissed me soundly, then gave me a light shove. "*Go.* I'll be fine. Go make me proud."

Five minutes later, my father and I stood in his private study. He'd lit up a cigar and poured himself half a glass of thirty-year-old single malt scotch. He'd offered me both. I'd declined the first, accepted the second. Didn't mean I had to drink much. But with him putting forth all the effort, the least I could do was drink with the man.

And he *had* been acting different all night—as sober as a functioning alcoholic could.

Then he tossed something small onto his desk; it clicked on the polished surface and slid toward me. Weary of the games he'd played over the years, I stared at it for a brief moment. Then I pegged him with a hard stare, disinclined to play ball. I didn't make a move to pick it up. Not a damn thing that man owned had ever been of interest to me.

And greater tension suddenly poured off him, like he'd tossed out a live grenade.

A bad feeling churned in my gut.

I glanced back down at the object. It looked like a memory stick. "What's that?"

He let out a gust of air. "It's a copy of the list."

The list. The pit in my stomach soured further. "List of what?" I didn't want to ask. And yet, I had to know. Because no matter the circumstances, the man was facing his demons. The least I could do was face mine with him.

"Not 'what.' *Who.* All the people who invested in the fund. And all their account information."

The fraudulent fund. Victims of embezzled money.

I sucked in a deep breath and took a healthy swallow of scotch. Then I scrubbed a hand down my face. "*Fuck*, Dad. Pretty sure the FBI didn't say 'hand over everything you've got *but* your extra copy.'"

"I forgot I had it."

I sank down onto one of his club chairs. "*Sure* you did."

He downed the rest of his scotch. Then his shoulders slumped and his vacant gaze stared at some random spot on his desk. "When they burst in here, my whole world turned upside down. They ransacked everything. They bulldozed it all and left a pile of rubble. Collectible books tossed onto the floor, pictures scattered loose over the desk. They plucked the stuffing out of every cushion, unframed every painting."

Crickets playing tiny violins.

Hard to have sympathy for a criminal. *Karma's a bitch.* "What did you think would happen when you got caught? Oh, *that's* right. Didn't think you'd get caught, did you?" Concern for Shay flashed into my head, because their crimes were too similar to ignore.

"The first time? I didn't have a choice."

"*Bullshit.* You always have a choice."

"Not then. Not the way I saw it. We were almost broke. I never told your mother."

My mother with the ten-million-dollar trust fund.

Dad eyed the scotch decanter. But then he glanced back at me, forging ahead. "When no one noticed, the next time seemed easier. By the third and fourth and fifth time, I didn't think at all. Investments came in, money flowed out. After a while, I stopped thinking about where it came from. They were dollar figures in accounts, nothing more."

"Until it *became* something more, something personal. For you."

"I thought about all the people I'd hurt. All the lives I'd destroyed."

Never once thinking about the two lives you'd wrecked at home, the ones who'd come first, the ones who could've saved you long before you'd ever been in peril.

Making amends, my ass.

But no sense in pointing that shit out. Nothing I'd ever said before had gotten through.

He'd have to find his way there on his own, if true remorse for him was even possible. "I'm not a priest. And this isn't a confessional. If you're searching for some sort of redemption, fine. But you won't get absolution from me."

A clock ticked its second hand into the silence.

I glared at the "forgotten" evidence.

Then I wondered which had come first: the alcohol or the crimes. Had addiction dulled his judgment? Or had he broken the law, then used alcohol as a crutch to mask any guilt he felt.

Not that it'd mattered. We'd all become the carnage in the wake of his recklessness.

"What kind of investors? Corporate investors?" I suddenly had to know. People like him?

"No." His voice shrunk. "Personal investors."

"*Fuck.*" Hardworking people that scrape together money to invest with the dream of sending kids to college, maybe retiring one day. Real people like Gabe and Rafe and...hot-dog-cart Tony.

He said nothing further. He just stared at his empty scotch glass, a broken man.

I clinked down my half-empty glass on his desk as I stood, then scooped up the flash drive. My father clearly wasn't in his right mind. If he couldn't do the honest thing and turn the hidden evidence over, or the marginal thing and destroy it, I'd take care of it for him.

When I turned to go, he stood and opened his arms. "Thanks for coming over, Ben. It meant a lot to me."

I gave him a hard hug. "Sure thing, Dad."

After a deep breath, he pulled back.

I pegged him with an unforgiving stare. "Hope you find what you're looking for."

Then every cell in my body pinged with urgency to find the one person I cared about most.

27
STEALING TIME

Shay…

"**W**ell, *that* was painless." Ben let out an exasperated sigh. "Now what?"

We stood outside his parents' enormous house in the wealthy rural outskirts of Glenhaven. He'd probably stood on that exact sidewalk square a million times growing up, yet he looked so hopelessly lost.

I grabbed his hands, then tugged hard to get him to look at me. "Now, we go have fun."

"You said *that* was going to be fun."

"And you believed me?" I'd planned to inject some kind of dry humor into the situation. But the vibe in there? *Way* too heavy.

He flexed his hands, then tightened his hold on me as he searched my eyes. "Are *you* okay?"

"Yeah." His mom had been a royal bitch. I'd expected

things to be tough, but we'd walked into a hornet's nest of old wounds and scathing insecurity.

And the level of loyalty between his dysfunctional parents? Astounding. But no different than other fucked-up parents I'd been shocked by...and had forcefully chosen to forget. All through dinner, I'd battled hard to keep all that trauma locked down tight.

I glanced toward the glow of the city. "But a horrible movie and ice cream might make it better."

The tiniest quiver lifted the corner of his mouth upward. The beginnings of a smile.

There you are. I grinned, my heart warming already. "Let's go have some *real* fun."

"Thought this was supposed to be my day."

I nodded and looped my arm around his, tugging him back toward his truck. The night was crisp and clear, and I drew in a refreshing breath. "It is. We can make it legal. Just like Monday was your day, but you gifted the choice to me. And you gave me multiple-choice options."

He yanked open his stubborn truck door, cocked his head and stared at me, mulling the idea over.

I dropped my hands on my hips. "Did you have any other plans?"

"Not a single one."

"Then why are you looking at me like that?"

"I'm trying to decide how long you've known how to have fun while not breaking the law."

"*Ha ha.* Not every bit of fun involves stealing and trespassing."

His broad smile finally came. Like a giant *gotcha!*

I didn't know if that'd been his plan all along, to get me to admit that. But he seemed proud of me.

"*Sooo*...what are my choices?" His brows raised slightly.

I blasted out the first quirky assortment that popped into my brain. "Quaker village, chocolate factory tour, self-guided independence walk."

He blinked, then glanced at his watch. "Those can all happen after 8:30 p.m.?"

Dammit. I scowled. "No." Which meant we couldn't do any of those. Not on his day.

"Oh, I know! We'll go train jumping."

He leveled a suspicious look at me. "Please tell me that has *nothing* to do with jumping off a moving train."

"It does not." I got in the truck. "You'll see."

He rested a forearm on the bottom edge of my open window, leaning in. "Trains run this late?"

I pushed up out of the window and kissed him, not caring what we did as long as we found our happy balance again. My body sizzled with a low ache on contact, as if programmed to remember all the delicious things that his sexy kisses led too.

When we parted, we'd both gone breathless. *Good.*

Distraction? A must.

"Maybe." It'd been a few years since I'd been on a train. "Gotta check their schedules." I nodded toward the driver's seat, itching to start our spontaneous adventure.

LAWBREAKER

We had just enough time to catch the last westbound train. "I've never been on a *paid* train ride before."

Ben waved the tickets in front of my face. "Well, I'm glad I'm here, then. We still have a chance to reform you."

That last sentence dropped, tone heavy.

Like his father had already become a lost cause. But it wasn't too late for me.

Only I didn't want to be changed. I celebrated who I was. *I need you to see that...see me.*

We still had a few more days. Plenty of time to convince him.

After the train left the station and we handed over our tickets, I took him by the hand, determined to distract his sexy law-abiding ass into the here-and-now.

"What are we doing again?" The coach door closed behind him.

We'd searched the entire train, front to back, scoping it out for empty coaches. In past years, there'd always been one or two, especially late at night. But apparently, tourists and commuters were ghost-town light on a Wednesday. We found three.

"We're picking the best racetrack. And this one's perfect."

He spread his arms wide and planted his hands on the gray fake-leather headrests on either side of the aisle. He peered over my shoulder toward the far end of our empty car before he glanced back over his shoulder toward the one we'd just left. His inquisitive gaze landed back on me. "Why this one?"

"It's the most invisible. Empty car behind, empty car in front, empty car for us."

"To *dooo...*"

"Watch and learn." I gestured a sweeping arm at the first row of seats and nodded him over.

With a cocked head and half-smile, he stepped aside.

Then I kicked my sandals off, bunched the excess material of my short dress into my fist, and plastered my body against the cold surface of the metal door.

After two deep breaths, I leaned forward, then launched off the door at a sprint. With every step, I leapt higher and higher, racing faster and faster across the aisle's newer blue carpet as the train bulleted over a hundred miles an hour beneath me. My feet touched down with only inches to spare before I slammed into the back door, barely missing its latch.

Ben stared at me, then shook his head. He cupped his hands around his mouth. "It's official! You're insane!"

"*We're* insane!" I pointed at him. "Your turn! And be sure to jump as high and straight up as you can!"

He stared at me for another handful of long seconds, shook his head again, then plastered his body against the door, exactly as I had. Then he leaned forward, expression fierce. "*Ready... Set...*"

"Go!" I jumped into the air on the rubber doormat and shot my hands straight up in the air.

Ben sprinted faster and jumped higher, covering the

distance in record time with his longer legs. I had to lunge out of the way to avoid his collision with the door.

His face lit up with pure exhilaration. Then he dipped his head down, eyes glittering with mischief. His lips came within kissing distance. "Let's do it again," he whispered.

"Okay." I spun around—without giving in to the kiss—and marched back the other direction. "But we can only run toward the back of the train. The secret's in jumping against."

Ben drifted a seductive glance down toward my bare legs. "The secret's in watching you run in that sexy dress."

"Go." I leveled a stern look at him while pointing toward the front of the coach. "Innocent fun now. Scandalous fun later."

We each ran the course three more times before we collapsed into a couple of cushioned seats while gasping for air.

He couldn't stop grinning.

Mission accomplished.

I slid my fingers around his neck and finally kissed him soundly. Then I glanced at the window. Only dark glass and reflections of the interior stared back at me. "We're only in the air for a split second, but it's like the train speeds by without us." I clutched a fist to my belly. "I can feel the difference in my stomach."

"How fast does the train go?" He squinted at the reflective window, then glanced down at the carpeted aisle, as if he could decipher our speed through X-ray vision.

"In this high-speed rail section? Up to a hundred and twenty-five miles an hour."

"You looked it up?"

"I did." I shrugged. "No big." *So what if I like to back up my kid thrills with adult factoids?* They'd made something super-efficient? I'd taken it *supersonic*.

"Well, there ya go." He shot a hand out and braked it midair with a jerk. "We're running in the opposite direction." His tone held finality.

I gave him a nod. *You get it.* "Only way it works."

He slow-nodded back. "And every time we're in the air, we're creating drag, even if it's infinitesimal."

"It's like we're stealing back time."

He stared wide-eyed at me, then blinked. "Einstein would love to be sitting with us right now."

"He would?"

"His famous formula, *E* equals *m c* squared, came from him wrestling with the idea of time, the speed of light, and two simultaneous lightning strikes hitting a train at opposite ends."

I asked a dozen more questions about Einstein.

And the train zipped along.

I yawned, then rested my head on his shoulder.

He draped his arm around me. "Where are we going, anyway?"

"All the way to Harrisburg, if you want. Then we've got at least four hours to kill. Trains don't start back eastbound until 5:00 a.m."

He gave a nod.

For the next few minutes, a natural silence fell between us.

But with every second that ticked by, his mood tanked. His breaths shallowed. Tension rolled off his shoulders.

My heart ached, that someone so strong, could be so tortured.

He shifted away from me, dug something out from his jeans pocket, then held it up. With a fuming gaze, he bored a hole into the small rectangular object. "If only we could *really* steal back time."

I stared at the tiny thing pinched between his finger and thumb. "Looks like a flash drive."

"It's fucking *evidence*. Complete account information on all the people my father screwed."

Holy shit. "What're you gonna do with it?"

"I'm thinkin' 'bout chucking it off the train."

"Who are 'all the people'?"

He gusted out a heavy breath. "Folks who worked hard, saved their money" —his expression hardened and fingers turned white as he pinched the drive— "then invested in my father's higher-risk fund for the chance of a better return."

My mind flashed to the dozens of people I knew, then the hundreds I'd encountered on the streets over the last eight years. Not all homeless suffered from mental illness. Many had been hardworking Americans with well-paying white-collar jobs. Misfortune happened in a flash. And too many never recovered from it.

Most had been helpless to stop whatever chain of events had caused their downfall.

A crazy idea crystalized in my head as I stared at the priceless treasure he held in his hand. My eyes narrowed as my thoughts raced. "What time is it?"

"After midnight, I think. Why?"

Perfect. "Because you won your day." *No doubt.* "But now it's *my* day. We might not be able to steal back time. But what would you say if we could steal back their money?"

His gaze slowly scanned toward me. His expression? Dead serious. "I'd say...I'm listening."

Not I'm interested.

Not I'm in.

That's okay, Ben. You're almost there with me. One worthy crime at a time.

28

PAVED WITH GOOD INTENTIONS

Ben...

"**W**ait. What. Is. Happening?" Shay shoved against me with surprising upper body strength.

Dark hair tumbled every which way in loose wild waves.

Long black lashes brushed her cheeks, eyes pinched shut to block out offending sunlight.

Brows scrunched down.

Lips tugged into a tiny frown.

Unaware. Cranky. And absolutely *adorable.*

And I was the *luckiest* fucker on earth; she'd chosen to share her secret world with me. Watching her sleep for the last hour had also helped take my mind off of my dilemma. And had given me time to process her unconventional, disturbing, *and highly illegal* solution to it.

I blocked out my concerns and kissed the top of her head. "You crashed. Hard."

She squinted a wary eye open. "Where are we?" she grumbled.

"On your train."

A slow smile curved her lips. "*Our* train, now."

"*Our* train," I agreed. But not the same one we'd stolen time on. And not the 5:00 a.m. return either.

When we'd first hit Harrisburg, we'd inhaled the largest breakfast known to man at another of her favorite greasy spoons. Then we went birdwatching along the Susquehanna River. After that, we wandered around Fort Hunter Park before exploring its mansion—on our own, while expertly evading the official tour guides and hosts.

We'd eventually caught the packed noon train to head back. Once we'd claimed two side-by-side seats, she'd settled heavily against my shoulder.

And she'd fallen fast asleep minutes after we'd pulled away from the station.

I nudged her. "You clenched my hand so tight a moment ago, I thought you'd break bones."

Her hand eased its death grip. "Sorry. Had another bad dream."

"About?" *Hell, we'd had plenty of stress-ammunition last night at dinner.* "Low-flying power-line diving again?"

I offered her the half-full coffee I'd been holding since before we boarded.

She gave a disinterested headshake, to the coffee and my attempt at humor. "No. This one was different." She sat up straighter and flicked glances at the nearest passengers, forward, across, and behind us.

Apparently satisfied about any potential eavesdroppers, she continued in a lowered voice, "I walked into a community library. Not a big one like my main downtown one. The space was small, geared toward family and kids. There were brightly colored play areas that had tables covered with pop-up books, puzzles, brainteaser games, and wooden trains."

She gazed up at me with a gentle smile. "You were there."

"Dreaming about me already?" I lowered my voice, "Are we naked?"

She arched a brow. "You are *fully clothed* and up in a tree house that'd been built into an entire corner of the building. I know you're up there, and you know where I am, even though I'm down away from you. We can't hear each other, don't talk to each other, but everything felt good—safe.

"As I wandered around the place, I realized a river ran into the library from under the corner of the tree house, toward the center of the main room. Right after it came out, it forked and flowed in two different directions."

She swallowed hard. "I crept toward the river, and as I got closer, knowledge came into my mind, little bits at a time, about an alarming creature that lurked in the water."

"A crocodile?"

Her brow furrowed and she gave a quick headshake. "A giant child-eating snake."

"An anaconda?"

She let out a heavy breath, clearly disturbed by the image. "Yeah, I think so."

"You've been watching too many adventure movies."

"I saw the snake." She shot me a pointed *shut-up-and-listen* glare. "Then I glanced around. Little kids were running back and forth, laughing and squealing, hopping on steppingstones to cross the river. Parents watched and cheered them on. No one seemed to know."

Her brow furrowed. "I panicked and ran to the help desk to warn the librarian."

"Good. Person of authority."

"Right? Except she seemed to know. And didn't care. Then I realized that parents knew too. *Not one person* was alarmed or even bothered that their kid might be devoured." Between words, her breaths reduced to choppy gulps. "I didn't understand it."

"What did you do?" I rubbed a soothing thumb over the back of her hand.

"I called 9-1-1 with the librarian's phone. I waited with the damn thing held to my ear, but nothing happened. It just rang and rang; no one picked up on the other end. In my gut, I got the sense no one would save us, no one had our back."

Something told me the dream paralleled her past: No one had protected her.

"While I was on the phone, the snake slithered up to the ladder of the tree house, then morphed into a man. You blocked his way at the top of the ladder, staring down at him. Then you and Anaconda Man talked, you above, him below, but I couldn't hear what either of you said."

She paused and took a deep breath, gaze unfocused as if she searched her thoughts.

"In the dream, I somehow understood that he'd revealed his true nature, and you'd told him he wasn't welcome. But if he tried anything—if he went up against any innocent in that library—you would destroy him."

Definitely about her present. *Going up against her past.* I tightened my hand around hers. "Damn straight, I would."

Lost in reliving her dream, if she'd heard me, felt me, she gave no indication. "With no one down where I was to help, I wandered back to the river to make sure I hadn't been imagining things. And there was the massive snake, head up and scanning side to side, hunting as it undulated through the water.

"All of a sudden, I straddled the fork in the river, one foot on either side. The snake's head snapped around. Its eyes focused on me. I couldn't move.

"But then I looked up and saw you.

"You appeared at the edge of the tree house, told me to reach up, then you grabbed my arms and yanked me up into the air. When I landed, you'd lifted me even higher than where you were, my feet on the railing, your arms locked around my legs."

She paused. Took a deep breath, then blew it out. "That's it."

"That's enough, though, isn't it?"

Her gaze locked on to mine, those expressive green eyes searching. And just like the dream, she understood without us having to say a word. Her chin dipped with a brief nod. "Yeah."

"They didn't have your back." I gave her hand a solid

squeeze, then lifted it up and kissed her knuckles. "I do. And I will. Always."

I offered up the lukewarm coffee again. She accepted it and gulped down a few healthy swallows.

An overhead announcement blared something, the doors closed, and our train accelerated eastward once again. The temperature remained balmy. A constant metallic tang permeated the air. Muted conversations chattered in a low hum all around us. Bodies jostled with the occasional rock of the coach.

After she handed me back the cup, she slumped in her seat. "Do all parents suck?"

About the dream. Because she knew I knew. The gist of it, anyway. Something bad that she still struggled with to such a degree, she could only process through it small steps at a time.

I shrugged, then did my best to answer the generic question at face value. "From every kid's perspective? Probably."

"*Nooo...*I'm serious. Specifically. Do you know anyone whose parents are amazing?"

"I guess we're all human, flawed. None are perfect, but Cade and Kiki's parents come pretty damn close, I suppose. Even then, I think their parents hit a rough patch when Cade was in high school."

"But their parents still *loved* them through it all, right?" Her voice broke halfway through.

My heart broke with it. That she'd had to endure horrific pain so young. Alone.

I put a comforting arm around her and pulled her close, gently rubbing her shoulder. If she needed to go down the path, face her massive anaconda, I'd destroy it for her any way I could. And so, I told her the truth. "Yeah, they did. If I had to pick a set of parents, if any of us really had a choice between our own and someone else's, we'd probably all pick the Michaelsons'. For all their understandable faults, they have a pretty cool family."

"Who has the worst?"

"Don't know. I'm an only child of an alcoholic mentally abusive father and a codependent mother."

Her fingers drummed once on my jeans. "The child of a *criminal* alcoholic about-to-be-incarcerated father and his soon to be prison-widow mother."

I coughed out a laugh. "Thanks for that distinction."

She dropped a single nod with a smirk. "No probs."

"But really, none of us besides Cade's family had it all that great. Mase's dad is an uncaring career politician and his mom's a snobbish socialite. They only had kids because their social circles expected it and any family outings gave great media optics: boosted approval ratings and garnered votes. Kids served as useful career props for them."

"Rough."

"Yeah. It's why Mase surfs. At first, surfing for him and his brother was just to escape an unloving family life. Now it's his passion. The only place he feels free."

"Kind of like Loading Zone for you. That nightclub is your passion."

"More like an obsession."

"But Loading Zone is so much more than just your business. It's not just a place where you escape, or become free. They've become your family."

"Not just my family. Now your family too."

"So Mase and you hung out a lot at the Michaelsons' house?"

"All the time. Why we're so close. But we're not the only ones the Michaelsons opened their home to. Hannah got tucked into the fold; she had an absentee mother and a sperm-donor father, was raised by her grandparents until they died. Similar story with Kiki's boyfriend, Darren. Darren and his sister never knew their dad, and after their mom struggled for years with depression, they...well...they *lost* her."

Didn't need to dredge up those details. Wasn't my story to tell. And not the point anyway.

Shay went quiet.

She didn't need to say aloud how bad hers had been. The story lay hidden in her questions, her sadness and hesitation. Whatever her family past, it'd been bad enough for her to run away from. And I got the feeling she hadn't ever wanted to go back.

Trust doesn't come easy for you. Why I didn't push her for something she wasn't yet ready to share. If and when she felt safe enough to do it with me, I'd be there for her.

When the silence dragged on, I tucked her tighter against me. "We're all your family too now."

Her tense muscles relaxed as she exhaled. "Even Cade and Kiki's parents?"

"Yup. Even Victoria and Garrett. They've taken in strays

ever since I've known them."

"Hey!" She shoved herself away from me. "I'm not a stray."

"Aren't you?" I thought about my unstable childhood. How alone I'd felt. And how many times I'd escaped to anywhere that wasn't my house. "Aren't we all?"

All of a sudden, she startled, her brows lowered, then she leaned away from me and pulled out her pink phone from her back pocket.

"Rafe," she murmured as she swiped the screen to retrieve the text.

I saw the message when she angled the screen toward me. Two words.

All set.

Great. Am I? My head spun with the enormity of what she'd suggested, how to right my father's wrong.

Shay pocketed the phone then stared hard at me. "We can do this. We have to."

"You say that as if we have no choice."

"We always have a choice."

Depended on perspective though, didn't it?

I'd been fighting while paying my dues, treating people with dignity, and earning every penny and ounce of respect along the way.

She'd battled her way by beating the system, taking without asking, and justifying by judging her entitled victims.

"You're asking me to ignore everything I've ever believed in."

Those intense green eyes held me accountable. "I am."

Because in one rare brief moment, for the very first time, we had the power to make a life-changing difference to more lives than either of us had been able to impact before.

Save countless lives. Even at the risk of our own.

The flash drive burned a hole in my pocket, branded the decision in my mind.

There'd never been any real choice. I realized that now. But I took ownership of our dangerous next step and vowed to have it make all the difference in the world.

I gave her a soft kiss, then whispered, "I'm in."

No matter the consequences.

"You've got to be kidding."

Later that afternoon, I stared at an old corrugated steel building that had been emblazoned with a large skull and crossbones and a glowing red **VIRTUAL PIRATES** sign.

The three of us stood in a potholed parking lot inside a rougher industrial area on the outskirts of Philly. A group of five preteen kids skateboarded up, scraped to a halt, then tucked their boards under their arms and entered the business through its solid metal door.

Shay tore her gaze from the entrance, stared up at me with a frown, then glanced at Rafe. "You're sure it's safe?"

Rafe gave a hard nod. "You'll see."

I stepped forward, determined to carry out our felonious

plan. Shay had come up with the idea and Rafe had connected us to the talent, but the responsibility for the events we were about to set into motion fell on my shoulders alone.

I yanked open the door and was blasted with deafening sound that vibrated my chest cavity. Bass thumped under technofunk that spooled so fast, it jumpstarted my heart like a defibrillator shock.

The rest of the assault to the senses?

We'd stepped into a virtual warzone.

Of kids.

Playing games.

Intermittent bright lights flashed from every corner of cavernous darkness. Invisible speakers blared a cacophony of electronic noise. Bomb detonations exploded. Gunfire erupted. A group of kids that'd been huddled around a giant screen shouted in triumph and jumped from various seating surfaces. Their screen flashed blinding white before it fizzled in a rain shower of pixels that transformed from gray into black.

Shay seemed impervious to all the blinding lights and deafening sounds. Instead, she walked through the room, inspecting the place. She toured gaming suites that lined the perimeter of the expansive room. Each space had its own giant monitor, a half dozen black microfiber club chairs, and twice as many kids, aged from kindergarten to some looking ready to graduate high school.

When we reached a narrow hallway, she peered through tall windows beside doors on her left, then her right. Rafe and I silently followed. But after she remained frozen for several seconds, attention glued to whatever existed on the other side of that glass, I eased in beside her.

Nine little ones, six boys and three girls who couldn't be much past kindergarten, sat behind tables custom-made for their height. They each stared at their own open laptop that had black screens with lines of green characters glowing brightly. The walls beyond them had been painted in foot-wide vertical color stripes. Movie posters featuring Wolverine, Deadpool, and Batman—from *The Dark Knight*, of course—had been tacked on. *Sure. Rainbows and antiheroes.*

Shay's shoulder bumped against mine, weight behind it as if she'd swayed. With a sudden jerk, her hand clasped mine. She wove our fingers together then tightened with a solid grip, as if she needed an anchor.

I gave her a firm squeeze back. *Whatever you need.*

As we watched, an adult stepped into our line of sight. The children's instructor appeared to be a young woman with a slight build, long straight brown hair, and a full tattoo sleeve on her right arm that ran down from under the short sleeve of her faded T-shirt. She turned as one of the children asked her a question, then she glanced up at us. She smiled and held a finger up, a signal for us to wait.

"C'mon." Rafe walked behind us and held a hand up toward the instructor beyond the window. "We can wait back in her office."

Shay sucked in a deep breath, like she'd forgotten to breathe. "Why have I never heard of this place?"

"You did." He stopped halfway down the hall, then

pegged her with a hard look for a beat before his eyes softened. "I tried to get you to come here from the start. You weren't interested."

"You should have tried harder."

He coughed out a dry laugh, then we continued down the hall. "Yeah, right. You know what you were like back then."

"Skittish."

"And hardheaded."

Sounds familiar. "And I bet you trusted no one."

He gave a nod as he held the door open for us, then we entered a large office area. He cast me a knowing look. "Our girl's come a long way."

"She sure has." *Even in the last couple of weeks.*

An elbow jabbed my ribs. "Ow." I glared at her and rubbed the spot. "What was that for?"

"What's with this 'our girl'? I don't *belong* to either of you." She tugged her hand free from mine to emphasize the point. "And I *still* don't trust anyone."

Rafe arched a critical brow and pointed at me, then himself. No words required. The evidence spoke for itself. We wouldn't be here with her if she hadn't begun to trust.

She crossed her arms, defiant as ever. "*Much.*" She mumbled the correction under her breath, bristling at his point but willing to accept the truth of it.

"And you are *most definitely* my girl." I put my arm around her, pulled her close enough to whisper in her ear. "It doesn't take anything away from who you are. It also means that I'm your guy. That I have part of me to give, *only* to you."

The hard set of her shoulders softened, and she glanced up at me with a slight smile.

Seconds later, before we'd had a chance to take in our surroundings, the kindergartner instructor burst in. She clapped hard once, then rubbed her palms together. A wicked kind of excitement sparked in her eyes. "Well, kids, what nefarious act have you brought for me today?"

Relief and anxiety warred within me.

She wasn't much older than Shay. Definitely not older than me.

But the young woman oozed unmistakable confidence. Like whatever criminal tasks we asked of her would be no big deal because she'd done thousands before us, and we'd be nothing more than a blip on her radar before she went on to do a million more after we'd gone.

When I glanced at Shay, our ringleader and the one with the deets on her plan, she held my gaze for a moment.

Trust me she seemed to say with a steady look. "Break the FBI seal on frozen investment and bank accounts. Then steal the stolen money back from the thief."

The woman stared at Shay with a dumbfounded look. Then she whistled low. "FBI, SEC, *and* FDIC. One multi-leg transfer?"

Shay gave a slight headshake. She pulled out the flash drive I'd given her on the train, then placed it on a narrow worktable that jutted from the wall. "Hundreds, I think. Maybe more."

The woman kept her assessing gaze locked on to Shay. "That's a massive risk. We break that invisible crime-scene tape by breaking that freeze, we're talkin' federal crime. You prepared for the consequences if you're caught?"

Shay and I had discussed it. Briefly. The woman meant one felony count for each hacked transfer. Two, if the law counted the federal-level breach itself. "Have you ever been caught?" *Has it gotten warm in here?* Sweat beaded across my brow.

Rafe chuckled.

The woman shot me an incredulous look.

"*I'm* a ghost. Let's see if you can be too." Challenge lurked under the woman's words.

Shay eased out of my hold and stared hard at me, then her lips twitched. "Danger. Intrigue. Big-ass payoff for a lot of hardworking people. Think you can handle it?"

Risk federal prison? A six-by-eight jail cell right next to good ol' Dad?

No one got a guarantee when they stuck their neck out. But someone had to do the right thing. And if not us, then who?

I blew out a harsh breath, decision made. *All in.* "What the fuck...let's do this."

I had no idea how our actions now would settle with me later. But my welfare didn't matter. We were the only ones who had both the means and the motivation.

But the inevitable fallout?

I hugged Shay tight to my side again and squeezed her shoulder. Some to comfort her, more for me.

Maybe with the talent we'd enlisted, we'd leave no trail. Remain invisible. Protect everyone.

Still, my stomach churned. I'd rocketed so far out of my atmosphere, I struggled to breathe the thin foreign air.

Stop with all the fucking *worry. You committed. It's done.*

I pulled Shay closer, into a fierce half-hug.

My girl was a phenomenal ghost herself.

Hopefully she'd teach newbie criminal me how to be one too.

29
THE HARDER THEY FALL

Shay…

"**Y**ou're *crushing* me," I muttered as I wriggled out of Ben's death-hold.

But when I glanced up, my heart ached for him. The poor guy looked ready to crack.

A deep wrinkle creased between his brows. That dark bearded jaw clenched. Without me under his arm as a human stress-ball, his hands fisted, then relaxed, then fisted again.

He'd obviously stepped out of his comfort zone the moment we walked into the gaming center.

Try again. He'd stepped out of the safety of his world the moment he met me.

Still, he'd learned of the danger, then the increased risks, and kept walking by my side anyway.

I took his hand and gave it a solid squeeze.

He squeezed back, then exhaled, muscles relaxing a

degree. He needed to be grounded, remember why we'd come. Not to break the law. To help those in need. *By giving them back their own damn money.*

A teenaged boy burst into the room with a tray of four to-go coffee cups. He pulled out each cup, lining them up in front of chairs that were tucked under a long, narrow worktable. "Here you go, Heart."

"Heart?" I glanced at our hacker.

"Harriet." She grabbed the coffee nearest the wall and swept a pointed finger at the three of us, then toward the remaining cups. "After my grandmother. But everybody calls me Heart."

Ben hooked a thumb toward his chest. "I'm—"

"*No,*" Heart interrupted. "No names. Better that way."

"Got it." Ben lifted one of the cups, took a sip, then nodded toward the far wall. "What are all those?"

I lifted my coffee and turned toward the wall. Rafe grabbed the last cup, cocked a chair out and took a seat, then leaned back, watching the rest of us.

Large wire cubbies stretched from corner to corner, floor to ceiling, on that wall. In each cubby of the top seven rows, various-sized laptops leaned at an angle against one another. The bottom few rows had a crate in each cubby, each crate filled with like-kind items: electronics, cords, smaller memory sticks, external hard drives. A library ladder hooked onto a rail three-quarters of the way up.

"Burner supplies." She scanned across her impressive hardware collection, searching, focusing either on some actual cataloging system or a mental list she'd committed to memory. With a nod, she planted her coffee on the worktable. She then glided the library ladder over to the far right, climbed up to the top row, and grabbed one of the laptops. With a waggle of the laptop, she glanced down at Ben. "I've preprogrammed each one for specific tasks. This one's got a worm that'll break down their walls."

Ben and I took seats in the padded folding chairs while she returned, took her own chair, then plugged in his dad's drive. Fingers flew over keys with muted clicks. The screen flashed from one data set to the next.

"This is gonna be a while." Heart didn't glance up...or stop typing.

But an enormous flat screen on the wall suddenly illuminated to life, mirroring what Heart's laptop showed. Numbers began to scroll up the screen in columns and rows faster and faster, each growing indistinguishable as it morphed into a pulsing dance of bright green pixels.

After another few minutes of tense silence, Rafe stood. "Yeah, I'm out." He downed the rest of his coffee, crumpled the cup, then tossed it into the trashcan by the door. He planted one hand on the door and the other half-turned the knob before he paused. He glanced over his shoulder at me, then shifted his gaze to Ben. "Gotta open the club. We good?"

Ben stood and crossed the room. The two clasped and embraced in a half-hug with a clap on each other's backs.

When they parted, they stared hard at each other for a long moment. Ben gave a single nod. "*More* than good."

Then Rafe slipped out the door.

Ben turned and stared at the giant screen of dancing

numbers. Arms crossed, shoulders set, feet planted shoulder width apart, he dropped his head a fraction.

Tension vibrated into the air as Heart clicked away, oblivious to all the heavy emotion behind her.

But I wasn't oblivious. His discomfort hit me hard, dead center in the chest.

"You okay?" Dumb question. He wasn't. But stupid-obvious seemed the best place to start.

"Yeah."

Liar.

He gusted out a sigh. "No."

Better. I'd almost called him on it. But he knew the harsh truth. What we were doing wasn't easy. And it was hard as hell for someone like him, a guy who'd been battered by those who hadn't given enough of a damn about him, one who had a lot to lose—for himself and many others who depended on him—if he ever got caught.

I got up and walked over to where he still stood near the door. He didn't register my presence, just stared blankly up at that big screen with a doom-and-gloom expression, as if hell itself had entranced him.

"Hey." I slid my hand into his and gripped hard until he finally stared at me. "C'mere." With a gentle tug, I dragged him away from the visual evidence, distanced ourselves from the flash drive, our accomplice, and the felony taking place—little keystrokes, big money.

I led him to the far back of the room, where a low black sectional commanded the corner, then pulled him down onto the soft cushions. He didn't resist, willingly toppled down with me. We lay in a heap for a few moments, my arms wrapped around him, a heavy leg draped over mine, his left cheek resting on my chest, right above my heart. His back rose and fell in quick tempo with every shallow breath. But as the seconds ticked by, his breaths grew deeper, slower.

Not one word left my lips as I held him. Wasn't my struggle. And nothing could be said to lessen the pain.

After a couple of calming minutes, he drew in a deep breath, gave me a light squeeze, then leaned back and claimed his own separate cushion. He glanced up at the screen, at the digital maze that led to our stolen pot of gold.

"It's *killing* me that I have to get my hands dirty to make this right."

I know. Nothing I could do. He'd already decided to fight, my way.

But maybe he needed to talk it out.

I could play therapist. "Two wrongs don't make a right?"

"Something like that." He heaved out another sigh. "Wish there was another way."

"Me too." For him, anyway. To spare him the grief and turmoil.

"How do you do it so easily?"

"Simple. For me, there was never one way or another way. There was *the only way*. Not hard to take the only option you've got."

"You have options now."

"I know. Why I ended up at Loading Zone in the first place. I wanted to give a go at being normal, earning money the old-fashioned way, hard work for a paycheck."

He let out a dry laugh. "Till I went and fucked that up royally."

"No you didn't. I'm here, aren't I?"

"Not without a valiant fight."

"Nah." I shrugged. "That's just attitudinal me. We're always where we're supposed to be."

"You must believe in destiny."

Huh. "Maybe I do."

One thing eventually led to another. We chose a simple path, then jerked a hard left to an easier route whenever a roadblock appeared. The question was, after all the twists and turns, did we end up in the same place we'd always been headed toward? Or did we find ourselves in a new and unexpected place, then decide to stay there?

"Actually, being here at Heart's place makes me want to do more than steal for others."

"It does?" Ben's expression had suddenly gone blank, flat—and unworried.

Good. Anything to distract him from the emotional hole he'd plummeted down. Not a damn thing useful in that bottomless pit of regret.

"Yeah." I thought of everything younger stubborn-ass me had missed out on. "She's helping so many kids. Giving them a family, a home, a sense of belonging and purpose."

"You'd want to do that?" His voice had gone soft with wonder, like he'd discovered some new facet about me.

If he'd looked harder, or if I'd let him get closer than I had, he would've seen the real me there all along. But instead of being offended that he hadn't rooted out what really made me tick—even though I'd expertly hidden it—I shrugged. Then I lied. "No big."

And then all of a sudden, because I'd never had anyone to share my darkest secrets with, and front-and-center sat a captive audience and someone who seemed to care, I decided to lay it all out on the table.

When I looked up though, he stared at me intently. Like he wanted to know me. As if he cared on a level deeper than I'd ever expected.

The words got locked up in my throat. I swallowed hard. Took a deep breath. Tried again.

"That's all I've *ever* wanted. A real family. A real *home*... one filled with people who belong to you and you belong to them."

He'd already said I had family in him, his friends, but he needed to know how much it'd meant to me, that it'd been my everything. For years.

Compassion filled his eyes. "Not an empty house for a week, left with only a dog or cat."

"Or fish."

His hand went to my knee and gave a gentle squeeze. Only a few minutes ago, I had pulled him over to the private corner to comfort him. And yet, I'd been the one that needed consoling.

We made a hell of a pair. A law-abiding bar owner, who had trouble swallowing down his felony, and his sidekick criminal, who struggled to find her way of going legit.

"Do you think it's possible for someone like me?" My voice sounded quiet to my ears. I cleared my throat and spoke with more force. "To quit a life of crime completely? Will I be able to give up what's come so easily?"

"I dunno. You get a rush off it?"

I had to think about it. There'd always been a thrill, excitement from breaking the rules. And even though I'd broken the law thousands of times, every time I did, my heart raced at the point of greatest risk. "Yeah, I do. Think I'm addicted?"

He cocked his head. "Maybe. Doesn't mean you can't sweat it out, quit cold turkey."

Wouldn't be too hard. I'd done eight years of crime, alone. By the time I'd gone to his bar, I'd already had enough. Things had gotten lonely. Dogs and cats and fish only went so far. People needed people.

"You have family now," he repeated. "And a home."

"I do?" I found it hard to believe in, even though he'd said it a couple of times. But he really hadn't known me. *You're still barely scratching the surface of learning who I am now.*

"Yeah, you do." His hand and arm looped through the crook of my elbow, and he tugged me onto his lap. "You've got me. I'm your family *and* your home."

Settling against the warmth of his body, I pressed my ear to his chest, found comfort in the steady beat of his heart. And still, my mind couldn't fully accept it. I let out a shaky breath, wondering when the rug would be pulled out from under my feet again.

But for how long are you mine? Nothing lasted forever. Life had taught me that.

With a shaky exhale, I gave him a nod anyway. I'd heard

him, even if I couldn't completely believe what he'd said—hardened my heart a little because the survivor in me refused to trust it.

Better to have more than one family, just in case. I had Bear, in a way. And Rafe had always had my back. And maybe Kiki, someone new. But she belonged to Ben first, would remain loyal to him if that rug got pulled out again.

"What did you have in mind?" He rubbed his fingers over my back in lazy circles, pulling me out of my own emotional hole. "What *more* would you want to do for kids like Heart's?"

I relaxed a little and opened my mind. "I'm not sure. The naughty-shirt idea with Kiki is my first attempt at a business. Maybe we can hire some at-risk kids. Donate profits."

"Those are great ideas."

"They're a start. I want to go bigger. Give kids a place to stay, something for them to learn, like Heart has."

"You know a lot about housesitting."

"Don't you mean house-*trespassing*?" I teased. Then a sudden brilliant thought hit me, and I pushed off from his chest and sat upright, staring down at him with widened eyes. "Wait. What if it's not one thing? What if it's a lot of things? Like how to be an entrepreneur? For each kid to figure out their strengths, or develop the skill sets, to be able to start their own business."

"You could teach them, lead them, maybe have a support network where everyone helped each other out."

"Like a business family."

"Doesn't have to be *all* business. Friends made along the

way. But yeah, a business family, like Loading Zo—"

"Ka-ching!" Heart shouted and pumped a fist in the air.

We startled at her sudden excitement, nearly tumbling off the sectional together. I grabbed his hand as our feet hit the floor, then we jogged across the room.

The big monitor on the wall had gone dark. No idea what we'd expected to see on her tinier screen, but we hovered near where the action was.

Ben stared at her laptop, then glanced at her. "Are we in?"

"To your dad's accounts? Yeah. I'm under the freeze layer. Not sure how long it's gonna last, don't know if the Feds have any kind of additional background alarms on this, but we're here for the moment."

"Now what?" Ben looked at me.

Easy. "Rob from the rich. Give to the poor."

"Robin Hood." Heart grinned wide at me, then Ben. "I like it."

I gripped Ben's hand a little tighter. He gave a light squeeze back. Then he glanced at me with a slight nod.

Got it. The whole thing had been my idea. And he wanted me share in its execution. "We want it all to go from the frozen accounts to the smaller accounts, where each transfer originally came from. All the information to be able to do that's on the drive, right?"

"Yeah." Heart frowned as she clicked into another area of her computer, opened another file from the flash drive. "Problem, though. Not enough money. Looks like ninety-seven million swam upstream. We'll be lucky if we can get half that to flow back down."

"So, what do we do?" I knew nothing about finances, not a damn thing about bank accounts and hedge fund investments. The money I touched was the physical kind, green and stuck to my fingers easily. "Some to everyone?"

"No." Ben gave a stern headshake. "Not all are the same. Some of those accounts could be rich friends of my dad's, the country-club crowd."

"Others might be retirees, mom-and-pop businesses." *Like Tony.*

Ben stared hard at me, eyes glittering, jaw clenched. He sucked in a slow breath. It hit him like a sledgehammer, imagining the actual people his dad had callously sucked dry. The kind of people I rubbed elbows with every day, victims of the system.

But the ones on that drive were people Ben could help— with one word from him and a few keystrokes from Heart.

"Could you find those kinds of accounts?" His arms folded over his chest as he stared at the flash drive stuck into the side of the laptop, an electronic nut we still needed to crack.

"Depends. What am I looking for?"

"Smaller monthly amounts, I think. Like the same dollars from every paycheck."

"Okay." Heart's fingers flew over the keyboard. The screen flashed white and black as she danced in and out of various files. Inside five minutes, she shook her head. "No dice. I've isolated fifty accounts so far, no standard monthly amounts. This wasn't set up like a typical 401(k)."

He glared at the laptop, as if willing it to give up his father's secrets. "What *did* you see?"

"Couple of them had transfers in the tens of thousands. One, over a hundred thousand."

"And the rest?" His brows hiked a fraction, a first glimmer of hope.

Because she didn't have to say it. Ben thought it. I thought it. The remaining accounts *had* to be what we were looking for.

Heart tilted her head as she scanned through the section again. "A thousand here, a few thousand there. A handful of fives, one for ten thousand."

"And you sampled fifty accounts." She'd only scrolled down a page and a half. "How many accounts are there?"

Heart pointed a finger at the bottom of the window she'd pulled up. "Five thousand four hundred and seventy-two."

"*Jesus.*" Ben gave a heavy blink. "Can we do that?"

That many files, so many transfers.

"Wait a minute, guys." Heart glanced at me, then Ben. "What if a mom-and-pop investor did a one-time transfer with their entire life savings? Unless you know *exactly* who the rich entitled guys are, we might be screwing over the mom-and-pops." She stared at her laptop screen for a few silent moments. "I can calculate what everyone put in percentage-wise and reverse it. Everyone will get their original share of what's left over."

Ben gave a hard nod. "That's fair. Do it."

"Better buckle up, kids" —she laced her fingers together, inverted her locked hands, then extended her arms out,

401

stretching them away from her— "it's gonna be a wild-and-hairy nail-biter afternoon."

Heart clicked away, then paused and closed her eyes. "Okay, Heart. Here's your shot," she murmured to herself. "Be the ghost *and* make a political statement." She stared up at the ceiling a few seconds, then glanced at us with a smirk. "I'll use the bank president's authorization code to turn off the frozen account's alarm system and disable the federally mandated transfer limits. Then I'll customize an auto-exec program that will activate when the bank prez logs into their system. A microsecond later, all the smaller accounts will have their money back, as much as we can give 'em."

"Impressive. How do you get paid for this?" Ben asked.

"For this job? Not in dollars. Robin Hood wouldn't pocket a single coin off this, and I won't either. Besides, good Karma points go a long way."

"So does brain food: giant espressos and loaded pizzas." Ben clapped his hands then rubbed them together. "What'll it be, ladies? I'm buying."

Ben's guilty conscience? That struggle with getting his hands dirty, even to right the wrong his father hadn't thought twice about? Gone.

Oh, how easily the mighty fall.

And yet, he'd gotten to where he needed to be with it all. No regrets. No looking back.

But a heavy question nagged at the back of my brain as I stepped into his arms and gave him a much-needed hug... for him, for me.

How will you feel when it's all over?

30
FLY ON THE WALL

Ben...

"Well, that went faster than I thought it would."
But not quite like ripping off a Band-Aid. *Not as painless either.*

Shay nudged a shoulder into mine. "Blink of an eye."

Well, okay. I sighed and gave her a soft kiss. *You make everything feel better.*

It wasn't even 6:00 p.m., but Heart had stood from her worktable seconds ago and had shot her hands up with a *Done!* proclamation.

Heart picked up the laptop, pulled out the flash drive, and shrugged, like the whole thing had been a walk in the park. "Light-speed results only happen because of preexisting programming. I've spent years surfing the data slipstream, dedicated months perfecting bulletproof software. Getting a custom order like yours is the fun part: How do we inject

403

creativity into it without leaving any fingerprints? The only challenge is any new security. But new is relative. Days, weeks. Every time hackers create a unique data breach, security levels rise. If I'm lucky and have the time, I'm right there with them, in lockstep. A fly on the wall, watching their every move. Hard to keep me out when I'm already in."

Our hacker knew her shit. "No detection? We're clean?"

"Squeaky." She gave a nod, expression confident. Then she held up the flash drive in one hand and the closed laptop in the other. "Store or burn?"

The laptop too? She hadn't been kidding when she'd called everything 'burner supplies.' "Why would we want to store them? And where in the hell would that be secure?"

"Some people do. To access later, I guess. I own a fortified air-conditioned storage unit: access-code driven gate, security guards, cameras. No one comes and goes unless they expect to be seen. But once in the unit, they're in a protective bubble."

Shay cocked her head. "You own the *unit* or the *facility*?"

"The whole enchilada. Turns out people pay a lot of money to store their useless shit along with their priceless art."

"And their secrets." Skeletons in fortified closets.

"That too."

I stared at the flash drive, at the incriminating evidence against my father, the tool we'd used to kick things back in favor of the victims. I made no move to take it, wanted to never touch or see the damn thing again.

"Burn." Shay and I spat out our wish simultaneously, the

only option I could stomach.

"How will you burn it? We need the evidence obliterated. No loose ends."

"I know a guy who works at a crematorium. It'll cost you twenty for his pizza dinner. I'll drop it off on my way home." Heart grabbed a large USPS Flat Rate box from a shelf and began assembling its corners. When I gave a puzzled look at the packaging, she chuckled. "Our tax dollars at work. Free boxes for anyone. Great under-the-radar packaging."

I gladly dug a twenty out of my wallet and handed it to her. "Thanks, Heart. You're a lifesaver."

Shay slid her hand across my back, put a flat palm to my ribs, then squeezed as she rested her head against the side of my chest. "Thousands of times over."

By the time we hit the parking lot outside, the sun had dipped below Philly's cityscape horizon off in the distance and a silvery afterglow painted the sky.

Shay glanced up at me. "Now what?" Her tone softened and compassion shone in her eyes.

Damn, you're amazing. That she'd thrown herself into our vigilante justice *and* crutched me along the way. "You tell me. Today's your day. I'm in your capable hands." Because she'd already worked a miracle. Tuesday and Thursday had been hers to guide us into whatever lawbreaking fun she had in mind. Yet Tuesday's dark side had been about helping others. And our Thursday so far hadn't been petty theft and misdemeanors. We'd gone as far into felony as you could get, without hurting someone.

She tapped a finger to her chin, thinking. "High-energy or low-chill?"

My shoulders drooped and I exhaled a weary sigh. "Low-chill. *Please.*"

With a firm nod, she took my hand and led down an alleyway that headed us in the direction of downtown Philly.

Three blocks down and another to the left, we started to jog to catch up to a dwindling line at the back door of a city bus. We grabbed a couple of nearby seats right as the bus sputtered smoky diesel exhaust with the driver's engine rev before trundling down a four-lane traffic artery.

The sight of the pollution stuck in my mind. "I read in the news last month they plan to switch the city buses over to all electric."

She nodded absently, saying nothing to my random factoid. Instead, her gaze wandered across our city as it rolled by. The faraway look hinted that even though she sat beside me, her thoughts had already traveled miles away—maybe to our mystery destination.

My anxiety from the last few hours began to ebb as six stops came and went while twilight dimmed to near-darkness. We disembarked at the seventh stop, right in front of a popular Chinese restaurant.

When the bus motored off again, we crossed the street to enter the downtown area. A ten-acre park sprawled to our left, its sidewalk lampposts flickering to life. The courthouse, with its stately columnar façade, towered above us at the peak of a mountain of steps. To our right, where we veered toward, stood the city's magnificent renovated public library.

We crossed at a cobblestone crosswalk, but when we hopped up onto the high curb at the corner, her grip on my hand tightened, and we paused.

"There," she murmured and gave a nod toward the edge of the park. "Like clockwork."

Sadness weighed her tone and unshed tears glittered in her eyes. My chest suddenly ached for her, for whatever pain she'd voluntarily suffered to bring me there. I wanted to pull her into my arms, rescue her away from the cause of it all.

Yet I didn't...couldn't. Whatever spur-of-the-moment plan she had for us had obviously become important. Vital enough for her to endure clear heartache.

Instead, I let her be my guide. The day had been designated to her, after all. A day to break the law, to show me the appeal. But all day long, she hadn't tried to convince me of anything. From the official marker of midnight on, every single thing she'd done had been for the benefit of others—not herself, and not me.

An urgency to see the world through her eyes rippled through my gut, and I tore my gaze away from the brave and generous woman by my side.

Edging the park, intermittent pools of light from streetlamps fought to defeat the growing darkness between them. But anyone would've had to have been blind to miss the true war that waged, silent but powerful, piercing the heart of our vibrant city.

Homeless milled about. Some in small groups of three or four, others standing alone. Park benches were filled. Down the street we'd just crossed from, covered stoops of each of the closed shop doorways had their darkened corners filled: young kids huddling together, a lone woman wrapped in a tattered jacket, a tall man with watchful eyes that peered out from behind a rainbow-striped scarf.

Shay nudged me. "These are the same kinds of people you helped today. Where they would've ended up, maybe tomorrow or next month."

I frowned with a heavy sigh. "I had no idea there were so many."

"There weren't. When I first hit the streets, there were still empty benches. The forgotten had choices back then, when the shelters still had room to spare."

My gaze continued, tracking back through the park, scanning over the packed sidewalk at our right and beyond. "Wow. What's going on at the library?"

"That's our new favorite place. A last refuge."

"'Our'?" Confusion clouded my brain. After discovering how many we'd saved with our hacking stunt—and the reminder of how close any of us truly were to living on the streets—the distinction between "them" and "us" had blurred.

"All of ours. City park's a public space, but so is the library. Clean restrooms, filtered water, chairs and tables to sit at."

Of course. "Warm and dry, out of the elements."

"Yup. Same city that's electrifying our buses just did a ninety-million-dollar renovation of their beloved place of knowledge."

I nodded, remembering the news I'd read last year. "Benefactors funded a chunk of it, but the library charter required tax dollars to cover at least half of it."

"Sure." She tugged my hand, leading me toward the library's grand entrance. "It's what keeps it public, more of our tax dollars at work. So that a single mother raising two young kids can bring them somewhere to get excited about reading."

We walked through the echo-y main entrance hall, with its floors, pillars, and walls made of elaborate marble, then entered the main part of the library to join a packed house. Not one chair sat empty. No couch cushion remained vacant. Even floor space in many areas had been commandeered. Up through the center atrium, at every table and gathering space on each floor within view, the same pattern appeared: overcrowded.

No silence existed. *Impossible with this packed arena.* But at least the respectful sound hovered at the low range of murmured conversations.

"This is where I first learned to hack," she whispered. "Rafe taught me the basics. Enough for what I'd needed."

"Is that what Heart was teaching those kindergarteners? How to hack?"

She shrugged. "Maybe." We climbed wide marble steps toward the second level. "They were coding, for sure. Learning how to create programs."

The image of how deeply she'd been affected by those little ones back at Heart's place had burned into my brain. "Is that what you would've wanted to do? Code? Or hack?"

"No." She gave a quick headshake as we rounded the corner. We followed an ornate wooden railing halfway along its length, then leaned our forearms on it. "I'm a people person."

LAWBREAKER

We stared down at the dozens of obvious homeless people in various nooks and crannies visible from our vantage point. I glanced up through the open center at the four floors above us, imagined the multitude of rooms that spanned in every direction on each floor. There had to be hundreds of homeless we couldn't see.

"And these are your people." My mind spun about the overwhelming need right in front of our eyes that had no clear solution.

"They're *our* people."

"Yeah, they are." Every single one of them.

She'd made it her life's mission to help save the victims of the indifference in our cruel world. A real-life hero.

You saved me too.

I had no idea what would happen to us from what we'd done today. If we'd get caught. If we'd pay the price the law demanded.

But I couldn't think in what-ifs. The enormity of how many people were in need short-circuited my brain.

I turned to her, wrapped my arms around her, and dropped my head. On a deep inhale, I turned my face into the soft skin of her neck.

"You're my person. It's been a long day, and you're the only one I can handle being around right now. I need to knock our low-chill down a notch."

All I wanted was to be grateful for what I had.

And hold on to it, any way I can.

31

ILLEGAL REPRESENTATION

Shay…

"Hey, sleepyhead. Good morning," I murmured against Ben's temple when he stirred. After a deep inhale, I stretched, catching the bed covers with my arms and tugging them down.

He groaned before muttering something unintelligible. Then he snuggled closer and dragged me downward, yanking the covers back up over our heads. "Pretty sure it's midafternoon."

I hummed, content. "No big." Nothing out there demanded either of us. Everything we needed? Existed in his bed.

We'd come straight from the library, ordered enough Chinese to survive on for days, then stayed up till dawn binge-watching *Suits* while cuddling on his sectional.

We hadn't gotten naughty since our Wednesday

afternoon sex-a-thon, but every moment we'd spent together since his parents' dinner had been big for him...and for me. All we'd seemed to want was low-key touching, holding hands, or laying in each other's arms.

But forty-eight hours later, my body hummed to life, thrilling at the delicious slow-burn of his touch, beginning to ache for the pleasure he expertly delivered. I exhaled a calming breath, determined to wait to be sure he'd gotten there too.

Then my brain kicked on, tamping things down even further. And my usual worry settled in. "Don't you have a golf tournament tomorrow?" The inevitable end of our amazing week loomed ahead.

What happens to us then? After the tournament's gala, the first pseudo-date-thing he'd finally gotten me to agree to.

"Yeah." The soft scruff of his beard trailed from the base of my throat up the side my neck. A gentle kiss pressed below my ear. "So?"

"*Sooo*...don't you have to practice or something?"

He snorted, fogging warm breath over my skin. "Hell, if I don't know how to golf now, one day won't make a difference. Besides, I've played that course a thousand times."

"Okay, good." I relaxed into his hold. "Let's just stay here, then."

"Great by me. It's Friday," he ran a hand up under the back of my T-shirt. "Who won Thursday?"

I let out a sleepy sigh. My eyes drifted shut as I snuggled against him, drawing in his earthy masculine scent.

"You did." Okay, so the fun parameter had gotten

redefined. Having a great time wasn't always about the thrilling excitement of jumping trains and movie dates...or spending whole afternoons in bed. Yesterday had been more important, finding common ground as we selflessly tested what we were made of.

And he'd done an impressive job of sacrificing his morals for the good of others.

But he still struggled with it. Why we'd stayed up all night and into the morning. But even though he'd gotten some sleep, the little he'd managed had been fitful, restless.

He'd jostled me awake almost every hour. My heart had ached for him every time as I wrapped my arms around him and lulled him back to sleep.

"It's a tie, then. So, Friday's yours." His fingers tucked under the back waistband of my underwear.

"It's *ours*." Since midnight, we'd already been glued to his TV, having an awesome time together rooting for the lovable lawbreaking attorneys Harvey Specter and Mike Ross.

Friday. Something about Friday. "*Oh, damn. We forgot.*" I launched out of bed to grab my turned-off phone from my backpack that laid on the floor near his bathroom. We'd unplugged the moment our takeout had arrived. "I've gotta head to Kiki's. Borrow a dress to change into after my shift."

"Shift?" He propped up on an elbow and squinted at me through bright sunlight that streamed in through his huge windows.

"Bartending. Working the tournament?" I dug past my stolen artifacts and found the phone at the bottom. I switched it on. With a flash of light, it began to power up. But my gaze drifted to the corner of a white satin glove that had wrapped around a tactical folding knife.

"Not tomorrow. Invitation Only doesn't host the event. The club does. Tomorrow, you're a guest."

What he'd said took a minute to register as my mind drifted to the other items in my backpack: the empty tin of lip gloss, the ancient coin. Four talismans that I'd religiously laid out every single night for eight long years had been completely forgotten...five nights in a row.

Something unexpected had happened when I'd invited Ben into my world.

Or maybe it'd been when he'd swept me into his.

Obsessions from my past had lost their power over me.

And I'd immersed myself into my brand-new present.

I glanced up at him. *All because of you.*

But since the last forty-eight hours had been incredibly difficult for him, I wondered what the next forty-eight would bring.

I *definitely* didn't like the neutral label he'd slapped on me. "A guest."

"*My* guest."

Better.

The phone *bleedled*. Two texts appeared. The latest text was from Kiki about picking me up at 4:00 p.m., which gave me an hour.

I typed back:

OK

An unknown number had sent the earlier one, right after we'd turned the phones off. I clicked into the text:

It's Heart. Didn't burn drive. Extra locked file at end of list bugged me. Cracked it wide open. Found more.

I glanced up at Ben. He stared at me, eyes narrowing. But I was pretty sure his talent with those assessing looks didn't include mind reading.

I fired back a quick reply to Heart:

More?

Ben moved, curving forward onto his hands and knees.

The white sheet drifted off his side, exposing his magnificent naked body. Rippling muscles, primal tattoo, dark beard and rumpled hair, my fierce wolf stalked forward, devouring me with a hungry gaze.

"Beautiful," Ben growled out as he crawled closer. Heat glittered in his eyes, like he saw everything under my T-shirt and underwear.

And I saw every incredible inch of him, straight through to his heart.

The phone chirped. I glanced down:

MORE

Sounded dire. But dealing with it the right way would have to wait.

I texted back:

Keep it. Talk later.

I tossed my phone onto my backpack then stalked toward the bed, directing my full attention at the extraordinary man in front of me. "Sexy as sin."

The second I stepped within reach, he hooked a hand over my left butt cheek and pulled forward. His nose and lips dragged along the strip of skin above the waistband of my boy-short underwear. "How much time do we have?"

"How much can we do in thirty minutes?"

He tugged my shirt over my head, then began trailing tender kisses down my neck, between my breasts. His fingers tucked into the sides of my underwear and drew them down my thighs. "I can do amazing things inside thirty minutes."

"Show me," I murmured against his ear as I ran my fingers through his hair.

I mentioned nothing about Heart's message, had no intention to. He'd had a hard enough time dealing with the lines we'd already crossed.

Instead, I stuffed the problem into the back of my mind and got very into the most important thing...the man right in front of me.

I leaned down and captured his lips, kissing him with all the tenderness I felt.

You don't need to handle more. Not when I can do it for you.

"Fairy godmother at your service." Kiki swept her hand wide in front of her "closet" on the lower level of her place.

From the moment we'd gotten out of her car, I'd walked beside her wide-eyed, mouth agape. We'd passed by junkyard sculptures arranged in a maze through a sunny botanical garden, then entered a warehouse building more massive than Loading Zone, complete with a living room, gourmet kitchen, an entire back half dedicated to creating her metal artwork, and a cantilevered loft that jutted out above us. Finally, we'd arrived to stand in front of the unconventional wide-open closet that had half a dozen garment racks fashioned from galvanized pipes.

"Well, what d'ya think?" She scanned over her fashion collection before her gaze landed on me.

I stared at the overwhelming amount of silk, satin, and sequins. "I think Cinderella had birds. With ribbons."

"Yeah, well unless they're animated, birds in warehouses crap on dresses."

Birds crap randomly in secret forests. A world away from here.

"Besides, her first dress was torn to shreds. Her fairy godmother saved the day."

"I'm not sure about this." I hovered fingers over various fabrics, separated out one here, another there, to see more than glimpses from the side. "Everything you've got is so..."

Fancy, elaborate, way out of my element.

"Appropriate for the occasion." She moved beside me, then pulled out the last one I'd touched. "Simple. Elegant. We'll try this one and a few others. You're gravitating toward darker colors."

One by one, I tried on dresses while she broke the news of two pro shops wanting to sell our shirts and I shared my interest in having at-risk kids make them and my wish for donating profits to charities.

After the third floor-length dress, I shook my head. "None of these seem to be working." One was too bright. Another way scratchy. Two had choking collars. And I didn't like how the last clingy dress bunched at my hips.

She scrunched her face, scanned down my body, then glanced at our outcasts.

All of a sudden, her face brightened and she snapped her fingers. "I've got it."

She unhooked a black garment bag from the far end of a rack. "I forgot about this one."

"Yeah? I'd almost forgotten about coming here." Because I'd been luxuriating in bed. My thoughts flashed back to Ben, about his struggle and the mysterious text from Heart.

Kiki gave me a pointed look as she unzipped the bag. "Your fairy godmother would've hunted you down." She handed me a basic black satin sheath that had spaghetti straps.

The soft material slid down my body, whispering over every curve. My lips parted as I took in my image in the full-length mirror, then lifted into a tentative smile. I glanced at

Kiki through the reflection.

She wore a wide grin and clapped her hands together. "It's perfect."

"You know, I've never had a best friend." Never had a girlfriend. Nor a real friend. Hadn't ever trusted anyone enough to come close.

Instead of her asking why, she gave me a warm hug. "You do now. One that would do anything for you."

Just like that. On instinct. She'd given me loyalty based on knowing me for only a handful of hours pieced together over the last week.

But they'd been intense hours. And we'd bonded.

She didn't belong to Ben first. I knew in my heart, she belonged to me too, no matter what happened.

A sudden thought struck me, and my breath caught. I turned and grabbed her hands.

"Kiki, I have to ask you something."

Her brows twitched down a fraction, but she gave a solid nod. "Anything."

"If something should happen to me, please promise me you'll still do our business the way we talked about. The at-risk kids, the donations...everything."

She frowned. "What's gonna happen to you?"

I shook my head. "Doesn't matter. Could be anything." With Ben teetering on the edge, with me needing to fix his something *MORE*, with our week ending and me not knowing what the next would bring, I hadn't a clue.

When she hesitated, lips parting as if to finally ask the questions she'd been holding back, I gave her an unyielding look. "Promise me. Promise me you'll have my back if I can't be here."

Her eyes narrowed. "You *will* be here. Nothing's gonna happen to you. But *if* some crazy thing happens, yeah" — she gave another solid nod— "of course, I've got your back. Anything you need." She dropped her chin a little, gaze boring into mine. "Anything."

"Good. Thank you." I breathed out a sigh of relief.

Because I have a sinking feeling some crazy thing might happen.

32
WHAT BRAVE GIRLS DO

Ben…

"Y ou don't need to." I frowned.

Shay didn't need to prove a damn thing to me.

Her adventurous spirit? Selfless actions? Bright soul and generous heart?

All I need to know.

What I remained clueless about was why she'd insisted on bringing me to Glenhaven's prestigious Hidden Manor subdivision.

We stood on a shorn patch of grass near their automatic entry gate. Twilight had begun to gray the sky, but with our elevated view and the remaining light, we could still make out the features of nearly every house. Each expressed a different architectural style: colonial, tutor, French provincial.

"Yeah, I do." She drew in a full breath, then exhaled slowly. She'd been rooting around in her small backpack, had finally pulled out a thin credit card holder, pinched a laminated card between her fingers, and tugged it free. She held that card in front of her at eye level, stared at the information on it, then lifted her gaze to stare at the houses below us.

After a beat, she reached her hand out, brushing over my forearm, and offered the card to me. It was her driver's license: the one thing I'd asked for at the very beginning, evidence I no longer needed.

But ever since she'd returned from Kiki's, she'd been dead serious and vitally focused on a private mission. And based on her grave demeanor, the motivator had to be about more than her age. A deeper truth needed to be set free.

And she'd chosen to share it with me.

I won't let you down.

"I believe in you." Not merely my trust. Unwavering support. No matter what she needed to unload.

Her gaze tore away from the neighborhood below and met mine. Gratitude and warmth glittered in those beautiful emerald depths. The intensity of her look alone said she believed in me too, without having to utter a word.

"It's the Tuscan house." She stared down at the neighborhood again, dipped a nod toward a two-story that had a tan stucco façade with iron railings on its window balconies.

"What is?" I didn't follow.

"The address. The one I put on my driver's license. It's the Tuscan house."

I held the card, because she'd given it to me. But I didn't

glance down at it. The incredibly important thing she needed to reveal had nothing to do with the plastic in my hand.

"And that means something." I felt her apprehension and the gravity of the moment heavy in the air between us, in the weighted tone of her voice. She'd never done anything by half measures, not without good reason. And she hadn't kept her driver's license from me just because of an address.

Since we'd arrived almost ten minutes ago, she'd stood beside me, but at arm's length, feet planted shoulder width apart, arms crossed, confident—unbreakable. But in the last seconds, her crossed arms had shifted, hands sliding to her ribs into a consoling self-hug. Her head had lowered a few inches, gaze unfocused.

I gave her the small amount of space she needed, the independence to be able to battle whatever demons she faced herself, on her own terms.

"Yeah." Her voice broke. She cleared her throat and squared her shoulders, but tightened her arms around herself. "It's where I ran from. A place I used to call home." She swayed a little.

No. Fuck independence. *You brought me here for a reason.*

I closed the distance and wrapped my arms around her. "It's okay, Shay. I've got your back. Tell me everything. If you want to, if you need to. We can handle it together."

She sucked in a deep breath, then stared out toward that Tuscan house.

"Every night, he'd tuck us in and read a bedtime story. For as long as I could remember, he'd sit on Brennan's bed. She was three years older, and the two of us were inseparable.

We always had grand adventures, played out all the fairy tales read to us in our bedtime stories; we became the princesses." Her voice trailed off.

Then she glanced up at me. "Look at my ID."

I loosened my hold only enough to pull the card up. I did as she asked, scanned over the identity information: her picture, address on Hidden Manor Lane, birthday last Saturday. *Yep. Nineteen. Just like you said.* Her *real* ID, not the fake birthday-margarita one.

Her finger tapped the top edge. "At my name."

Shannon Morgan.

She didn't say it aloud, which also meant something. *Distance. Disassociation.* Keeping her ID from me from the very beginning had been about burying who she'd been. She demanded to be defined by who she was, how she lived: out loud and vibrant.

I touched a finger under her chin and lifted gently until her watery gaze met mine. "You'll always be Shay to me."

After a shaky breath, she gave a barely perceptible nod. "Thank you. For accepting me as I am."

I stared down at her, chest aching with emotion. And then it hit me. What she meant to me. How deep it went. And not one part of me wanted to hide it. "I accept every part of you...because I love you."

Her lower lip began to quiver until she bit down on it. Then her eyes searched mine. "Sure you want to know what happened?"

"Only if you want me to. Only if it helps you for me to know." I had a feeling it'd been bad. But I didn't need to know the details, not for me.

She gave a firm nod. Then her expression hardened, and she glared toward the house. "It was a month before my eleventh birthday. Instead of sitting on Brennan's bed, he moved to mine. She seemed relieved, curled onto her side to face the wall and fell asleep long before he finished the story. Then he put the book down, and he began to straighten my nightgown, but he kept smoothing it down from my shoulders to hips. Gradually, it changed to be from my belly button down. Over and over."

Her entire body began to tremble. She held her breath and went rigid in my arms.

I drew in a tense breath and kissed the top of her head, gently rubbed her back. "Breathe."

Fisted hands clutched at the back of my shirt as she sucked in a lungful of air.

She swallowed hard. "His heavy hand stopped at the top of my legs, then pressed down, hard, between them. He said I had a grown-up birthday coming, and he wanted to give me a special gift. If I was a good girl, he'd even give it to me early."

Sick twisted fucking bastard.

My protective hold tightened around her.

"I panicked, kicked off against the wall, and stumbled out of bed over his legs. He tumbled to the ground with a loud thump. I backed out into the hall and kept repeating '*no...no...no*' again and again, my voice growing louder and louder, until I was shouting in the middle of the hallway."

She exhaled, long and slow. "*But no one* heard *me*. My sister came out from our room, eyes wide with panic. My mother opened her bedroom door with a deep scowl, but didn't come any closer. I pointed at the man still sitting on my bedroom floor—the one I'd trusted, the one that had kept me safe all those years—and told them he'd touched me in a bad way. 'Tell someone.' That's what they'd taught us in school, how to protect us from predators."

"Good." I had no idea whether she'd ever shared her story before, but I got the strong feeling she hadn't. I wanted her to know she hadn't screwed up. "You did the right thing." I'd have beaten the shit out of him. *Want to now.* But she'd only been a little girl.

"You would think." She shook her head. "Both my sister and mother told me it was all okay. Like I'd misunderstood or something. That it was a good kind of touching. Brennan stared at my mom for a couple of seconds before glancing in at him. Then Brennan looked at me with these pleading puppy-dog eyes and told me that it was a good birthday present, that it would only hurt a little but feel good a lot. My whole family was in on it. My mom had been letting him touch Brennan for years."

I gusted out a breath. "*Jesus.* No wonder you ran away. They all betrayed you."

"That night I refused to sleep in my bed, in the room I shared with Brennan. I flipped out at the thought of even sleeping under the same roof as them. And they gave in to my demands. I put shorts and a shirt on, laced up my tennis shoes, and stormed out of the house to sleep in a giant kid-sized dollhouse they'd built out back. When all went quiet and the house had been dark for a while, I literally ran into the woods and kept running until my legs ached, my lungs burned, and I collapsed on the bench I brought you to on Tuesday."

Thought that bench had been significant. It'd been her first safe haven. "And you've been on your own ever since," I murmured.

Firm hands pressed to my chest as she eased out of my hold. She stared up at me with moisture glittering in her eyes. "Safer that way."

An unexpected undertone in her words rattled me. It sounded like she was breaking the news to me about *how it is*, not *how it was*. Uncertain, I volunteered some clarification. "Until now."

The corners of her lips twitched a little until they curved into a wobbly smile. "Until you," she whispered.

Good.

I fully wrapped my arms around her again, holding her tight. And just as desperately, she clung to me.

But even though I'd been there for her through her deepest confession, it still seemed like she held a vital part of herself back.

It's okay, Shay. I can handle whatever you need to do. Whatever makes you safe.

I let out a resigned sigh.

Sure as hell hope that includes me.

33
PHYSICAL EDUCATION

Shay…

"**W**ell, how'd we do?" Ben tipped back the remainder of his second beer. But just like he'd done with the first bottle, he eyed a small amount of remaining liquid at the bottom before he slipped it into its cardboard six-pack slot, right next to his first.

"With what?" I finally got past the European-craft aroma wafting out of my bottle and took a small sip of my first beer ever. *Uck.* Definitely an acquired taste.

He twisted the cap off a third with his forearm, then gave me a pointed look. "With our agreement. It's Friday" —he glanced at his watch— "hour and a half till midnight."

"Well, since you're contributing to my underage drinking" —I clicked bottle necks with him when he held his beer up— "I'd say were do*ing* spectacularly."

He angled an affirmative nod toward me, then took a drink.

I arched a brow at him. "And it's not a done deal yet. Still got two days and one night."

But he'd been quiet since I'd shown him my childhood home, confessed why I'd run from it. No negative judgy or rejection vibes rolled off him, just...sad, maybe. Which sucked. Because the last thing I wanted was for him to feel sorry for me. A part of me also wondered if it was just mental exhaustion. Maybe our hacking-crime weighed on his mind to such a degree, he didn't have the capacity to process any heavy new thing...not right away, anyway.

He hadn't pulled back physically, though. In fact, it seemed like he touched me more than ever: hand firmly on my back even when he'd opened the convenience store's door, arm pressed alongside mine when he paid the cashier, fingers entwined as we drove to the country club, walked along its pathways—trespassed across two fairways.

And as we sat on a high knoll that overlooked an empty high school football field, his casually extended leg had been resting against mine for a while, the warmth of his thigh radiating through both layers of denim.

He took another long pull of his beer, then raised the side of the bottle up to his right eye, squinted his left, and peered through the remaining three inches of liquid out toward the abandoned field still lit up by its massive overhead lights.

I took another experimental sip of mine, scrunched my face at its weird wheat-y taste, then slid it into the carton beside his nearly emptied two.

"Why do you do that?" I stared at his discarded bottles. "Leave an inch in each one?"

He swung his bottle-spyglass toward me and examined me through the amber liquid with a huge eyeball. After a hard blink...or maybe a wink...he withdrew the bottle from his eye, drank it down to his obligatory inch, then nestled his almost-empty in a line following his other two. He stared at them, but made no move to grab a fourth.

"My dad's a functioning alcoholic, has been ever since I can remember." His gaze swung toward the stadium lights when they went dark. "He emotionally abused my mom. But sometimes things got physical."

He fell silent for a few seconds...then a handful of seconds more.

I put a gentle hand on his forearm, anchoring him. "Bad?" *Obviously.* But he'd gotten stuck somewhere inside a powerful memory.

After a slight start, he glanced at me. "Yeah. Bad enough. And right before I met you at the bar—"

"—when you fired me..."

He blinked heavily. Then his lips twitched a little. "Yeah. *The night I'd been a total ass.* I'd just bailed after two weeks of the worst it's ever been. She had begged me to stay there, try and help him. Stupid me agreed. Turned out, he didn't want help, of any kind. And all attempts I made to get *her* to see reason, leave the bastard to save herself—like I'd done my entire life—fell on her chronically deaf ears."

The entitled woman who'd raked me over the coals at our meet-the-parents dinner had ironically been victimized herself, struggled for control too.

"Alcoholism is supposed to be hereditary. But I swore never to be like him. Never be addicted." He shot an unforgiving glare at the beer bottles. "The liquid left at the bottom, quarter-inch for liquor, inch or so for beer, is there to remind me. Make me respect. Make me think hard before drinking another. Keep control."

What we all seem to be fighting for.

He lifted a discarded bottle out, examining its last inch. Then he released it back into its slot and glanced at me. "Think it's fucked up?"

"Hell, I break into my parents' house once a year on my birthday. Who am I to judge?"

"Saturday?" He hiked a thumb back between our shoulders, as if to indicate the past.

"Yep." No need to tell him the frightening details—about how I'd almost gotten caught in my own childhood home.

Instead, I nodded at his alcohol-control test. "Tastes like crap anyway."

He shrugged, said nothing.

Something didn't compute. "Why did you open a bar, then?"

"Wasn't just me, Cade and I came up with the business plan. There's a shitload of money to be made with a well-run bar. The idea started out as a joke...the reality turned out to be family."

Silence followed between us, the comfortable kind. I tapped my sandaled foot against his shin. He absently scratched his fingernails over the fabric of my jeans.

After a few minutes, he opened a fourth beer and took a long pull from it, expression faraway as he stared over the football field. "Pretty sure my father got perp-walked today."

Good. The image rang true for the crime. "*Damn* sure my father should be."

"Well, we're a pair."

Two peas in a survival-pod. "In spite of our sucky ancestors."

"Let's go do it, then." He clinked his half-empty fourth into a slot, grabbed the whole six-pack, then stood, offering me his other hand.

"Do what?" I slid my palm over his, wrapped my fingers around his large thumb, and heaved myself up from the ground with a grunt.

"Go be who we are. Go do something we've never done before and have a blast at it."

He stated our mission with conviction, but with almost too much force, like he tried to convince himself blast-worthy fun was possible against the overwhelming melancholy odds.

No big. Don't read into it. After all, he was brand-new to the whole lawbreaking thing.

I scuffed a hand back and forth over the seat of my jeans. "Great. Now I'm all wet and grassy."

He leaned closer as he guided me down the hill toward one end of the football field. Warm breath fogged up the side of my neck until soft lips pressed a kiss to the top of my ear. "*Perfect.* Then we need to get you out of those clothes."

A heated shiver danced through my body at the sensation, and his suggestion.

I tangled my hand together with his and glanced at the low-slung block building we approached. Then I shifted my gaze to him, eyes widening. "Why, Benjamin Bishop, are you suggesting we get naughty while breaking and entering?"

Maybe you're accepting your criminal side better than I realized.

At the corner of the building, he gave me a brisk kiss, pointed two fingers at his eyes, then swept those fingers wide across the space behind us.

Got it. Lookout. I dropped him a single nod.

He gave my hand a firm squeeze before breaking away. As he walked off, he leaned over a wide gray trashcan at the corner, discarded his six-pack, then approached double metal doors.

I scanned down the long block wall, over branching sidewalks, and across the football field.

All clear.

But all it took was a simple thumb press, a solid grip, and a heavy pull for the door to open.

He shrugged. "Sorry, babe. Only trespass tonight."

I jogged the short distance between us, slow-crashed into his chest, then carefully pulled the door shut behind us until only a metallic click sounded. "And lewd and lascivious, I hope."

"Damn," he murmured as he brushed his lips over mine. "*Fucking* love the way you think."

We kissed for a breathtaking few seconds before a clunk echoed out and snapped our attention down the hall.

Overhead lights had been dimmed in a tiled corridor

that appeared to stretch the entire width of the building. Along a blue-painted interior wall, two alcoves darkened its length, one fifteen feet away, the second farther down. Another muted clunk sounded. From the nearer alcove.

Hand in hand, we snuck toward the sound. Another set of metal doors appeared in the shadowed cutout, one propped open with a janitor's cart.

Even though I paused, uncomfortable with the danger of an unknown so close, he tugged me on through the door, as if he felt he belonged there.

But we still peered around every corner, crept past every locker-filled aisle.

"Ugh!" I whispered fiercely, scrunching my nose. "What's that rank smell?"

"High school boys' locker room," he murmured. "Half those guys haven't learned what laundry is yet. Sweaty gym clothes that ferment in a locker for a week or more will do that."

"Doesn't their teacher have a nose? That burning tang hangs in the air. It's making my eyes water."

"Coach does. Mine made us clear our lockers every Friday. Doesn't matter. Teen-boy stink permeates everything, sinks into walls, becomes one with paint."

"What about teen girls'?"

"You mean the girls' locker room?"

I nodded.

"No clue what that's like. Teenage boys only get to dream about it."

"Wanna find out?"

He dropped his chin an inch, gaze locked with mine. "*Fuck yeah*, I do."

Another clunk sounded. We'd been talking low-register, but we still fled the smelly room. And out of the corner of my eye, I caught a sopping-wet mop head lift out of a bucket at the other end of a locker aisle.

Hands tightly clasped, we ran toward the other alcove. After we slipped inside, we both eased the door shut.

We glanced at each other...and burst out laughing.

A partner in crime was more fun than I'd expected.

With the space all to ourselves, I slowly spun around, then began to investigate.

The overheads had been turned off, but dimmed light from an office area cast enough glow to guide our way.

The block walls were royal blue with a fat ribbon of gold trim running along the room a couple of feet below the ceiling. Shining white brick-shaped tiles spanned the walls in an open shower area. Chrome showerhead nozzles sparkled. Square porcelain sinks glistened.

"I've never been to high school." I jostled combination locks with my finger as I walked down a row of lockers.

I wondered what it would've been like...if I'd been normal. If I'd had decent parents that would've allowed that alternate reality. If I'd had friends and teachers and homework.

"Didn't miss much." He walked along with me, but on the other side of a row of benches.

I glanced at him, brow raised.

He shrugged. "Awkward kids: jocks and geeks alike. Drugs and alcohol and sex."

"Not learning?"

"That too. But you found a way without all this. And look how you turned out."

I cast him a dubious look.

He shot me an unforgiving one. "You're a beautiful, sexy, intelligent, and brave woman with one of the biggest hearts I've ever encountered."

Well, okay then. And yet... "You just described how I see you."

His gaze held mine for a beat, serious as he exhaled a slow breath.

Then he gave a nod down toward the row of lockers and tapped a finger twice to his nose. "And?"

"Better." The janitor had to have already cleaned the girls' side. Laundry bins sat empty with a slight lemony scent of disinfectant. White towels were neatly folded on metal shelving units.

I walked ahead, hooked a finger around a chrome lever, then lifted a quarter turn.

Water sputtered then sprayed from one of those sparkling nozzles.

"Oh, look." I glanced at him with an arched brow. "There's a shower."

"All about it." He reached back, grabbed a fistful of T-shirt from between his shoulder blades, then yanked the material over his head.

I watched, mouth gradually falling open, as he kicked his shoes off, shucked his jeans, then strolled casually and completely naked onto the white tiles toward the water.

And he stared at me with heated intensity the entire time.

Until he turned to step under the spray. Water rivulets danced their way over taut shifting muscles, as if delighting in such a glorious surface to play on.

And I thrilled in the raw masculine sight.

He dipped his face out of the stream and shook his head, causing water droplets to fly everywhere. Then he pressed fisted hands against the tile wall, tilted his head, and glanced at me.

Gaze fierce, features dark, muscles tensed, he stood proud and magnificent.

I blew out a measured breath and committed the spectacular sight of him to memory, every hard line, all that strength, the soul-searing possessive way he stared at me, as if I was the only thing on earth he wanted.

The moment would remain ours forever. *Mine to cherish.* Even if the *MORE* turned out to be too much for him to handle. *A memory all to myself, just in case. Tucked safely into my heart.* A hundred times better than anything stuffed into a backpack.

His chest expanded on a slow breath. "You coming?" Teasing lips twisted into a smirk as he reached down and wrapped a hand around the base of his hard length, then stroked upward. "Or watching?"

"Coming." I raced to remove my clothes: kicked off shoes while I scraped my shirt and sports bra over my head, hooked thumbs into underwear and jeans as I shimmied out of them.

"Not yet, but soon." His hungry gaze raked over my naked body. He straightened from the wall and reached a hand toward me. "We need to get you wet first."

The moment I slipped my hand into his, he yanked me forward to collide against his chest. And the warm strength of his arms wrapped around me while he claimed my mouth. Soothing hot water rained down over us. The bite of cold tiles met my back as his fingers slid down between my legs.

And the world hazed into a cascade of sensation.

Firm touches...

Soft kisses...

Urgent strokes...

I shivered and gasped when a spark of pleasure sizzled through me.

My hands tangled into his wet hair as I lost myself in each wonderful kiss, some sweet and tender, others rough and demanding. A decadent ache built from deep inside, unfurled with gradual heat until it charged every nerve ending.

Without warning, the strokes of his fingers quickened. My body tensed and my breath caught as ache coiled... *tighter...deeper.*

Low whimpers escaped my throat as I held on to the only man I'd ever trusted, the one person who'd earned all of me.

And under his expert and demanding touch, the pleasurable ache snapped taut...then exploded into a million sizzling sparks.

My unexpected scream got swallowed by his growling kiss.

In a sex-drugged haze, I dimly felt the world shift: body slid up wet tiles, hips gripped by strong hands, legs parted as lean hips slid forward up my thighs.

Soft bluntness pressed at my entrance.

In a snap of sensation, everything crystallized as he plunged fully inside.

I moaned low, gliding my lips over the soft scruff along his jaw.

He growled, the sound guttural, primal, as his breath fogged over my ear.

Hard. Hot.

Delicious stretch.

Aching need.

Then we began to move.

He drew back, then drove deep.

I arched my back, then curved my hips. "Not much... traction."

Another thrust. A slow grind. "Plenty of friction," he murmured.

A single acute spark of pleasure flashed through me, and I gasped. "Agreed."

On the next slow drawback, his darkened gaze fell to our point of connection, scanned up every inch of my body, then locked on to mine. He arched a brow. "You *said* against the wall."

I bit my lip and curved my hips toward him, craving more of his hard length. "And?"

He exhaled a heavy breath and dipped his head a fraction as his gaze intensified. "*Fucking* spectacular."

LAWBREAKER

I only caught the carnal glitter in his eye for a split second before he lunged closer, thrust harder, and captured my mouth in a breathtaking kiss.

Up...up...up... my pleasure spiraled, exquisite ache building from every incredible stroke he delivered.

With each hard pound against me, deep within me, I slid up the wet tiles. But his strong hands curved over my shoulders to pull me back down.

"Hold on." He groaned against my neck, panted ragged breaths over the shell of my ear. "Don't let go."

As if I'd ever want to.

Everything felt *greater* than ever before, him, me, us together...in a locker room of a school I never got to attend.

With a fierce love I never thought possible, I clung to a man who'd shown me there was another way.

Water-spatter echoed off tiles.

My heartbeat thundered in my ears.

Shortened breaths turned into ragged gasps.

The gentle bite of teeth clamped onto the crook of my neck.

I let out a low groan as delicious ache became burning need.

Our bodies strained, both of us hanging on the edge.

A loud clank reverberated a split second before bright lights flickered on.

Ben shot an arm out and cut off the water.

We froze, clinging tightly to one another, breaths held.

"Anyone there?" a gravelly male voice called out.

Somehow, the incredible searing ache flashed hotter the instant we both went still.

In desperation, I gripped Ben's wet hair. "I'm gonna come," I murmured over his ear.

He thrust once more, body going rigid. "Me too," he growled on a low whisper.

The lights went dark.

The door clanged shut.

And we let go, exploding into a powerful simultaneous orgasm in one another's arms.

We stood there for a long time, holding each other tight, connected in so many ways beyond something physical: dreams and fears, triumphs and demons.

Eventually we came down from our high, breaths calming, pulses slowing, muscles relaxing. He eased me down from the wall, but held on to my shoulders. Then he turned the shower back on, and we rinsed in silence in the near-darkness.

We locked gazes often, hearts filled with emotion.

But every now and then, instead of compassionate softness, I detected the tiniest flash of something else in those dark charcoal eyes...conflict, uncertainty. Not long enough to mention. Which was good. For both of us. Helped to keep the treasured experience as pure as possible.

He turned the water off, then grabbed us towels from a nearby stack.

As he wrapped a thin white towel around lean hips, he pegged me with a hard stare. "*Now* you've done high school."

I fought a smile as I tucked an end in over my breasts. "You've given me the *very* best part."

"Ditto." He scooped up our clothes and rolled them into

a ball. "*This* is what high school kids fantasize about."

My gaze stuck on the bundle of our clothes tucked under his arm. Then I glanced at his near-nakedness, at mine, at our "borrowed" towels—the only thing about to save us from streaking across a high school football field.

"Why, Benjamin Bishop, are you stealing high school property?"

"These threadbare pieces of shit? I'm doing them a favor."

He strode into the office, grabbed a fat blue marker from an overflowing cup of pens, then scrawled a message diagonally across several weeks of the giant paper calendar covering the center of the metal desk: **BUY NEW TOWELS!** He jammed the tip down on the dot of the exclamation point. About to cap the marker, his fingers hesitated, an inch apart. Then he scrawled a quick addition, his signature: **CONCERNED TAXPAYER**.

My heart melted. "Look at you. Taking up the cause." A baby step. But a step, nonetheless.

"You trained me well."

Did I?

My thoughts raced over all the things we'd done, and over the turmoil he quietly suffered because of those acts, whether they'd been relatively harmless or not. Then my mind settled on the one last thing I knew I had to do alone.

I'm holding on, Ben. Even if I have no choice but to let you go.

34
IMPOSTER AT THE BALL

Ben...

"**D**amn, I've missed you." I slid my putter into my bag for the final time after a long tournament, then pulled Shay fully into my arms.

"You've been busy," she murmured against my neck. "Conquering eighteen holes takes concentration."

I turned my face into the softness of her hair and drew in a deep breath. I savored the faint scent of her floral fragrance, had been looking forward to it. "Thought about you all the way. On the greens, when I spotted you in the gallery, your outrage at foxes stealing balls popped into my mind. Down fairways, I remembered how you stood in my arms while you'd convinced me to enter this tournament. And at tee boxes, I had your ridiculous swing-mantra in my head."

She pulled back and those beautiful green eyes sparkled with amusement. "'Yeah...whatever'?"

The very one. "When I was trying to get *you* to take the whole thing seriously."

"*Well...*" Soft lips pressed to mine in a tender kiss. "Looks like it worked for you. You won the tournament."

I exhaled my first relieved breath in hours, grateful to have her in my arms. "The only thing I'm serious about right now is you."

Her body went rigid for half a beat, then relaxed. Not long, but enough to notice.

And every time I'd caught her in the gallery along the fairways or on the greens, she'd given me a warm smile the instant we'd locked gazes, but then seconds later, her expression had turned wistful, sad almost.

The worrisome change had distracted me from my own shit—my childhood-golf trauma—made me focus on my concern for her.

"You okay?" Maybe her tolerance had worn thin for the country-club crowd, too many entitled people in close proximity for too long.

She tilted her head, gave me a warm smile. "Yeah. I'm good."

I gave her a stern look. We'd been around each other almost 24/7. I didn't need my lie-detector senses to know something was up.

"Smooth moves, Bishop." Kiki sidled in beside her.

I shrugged. "Shay asked me to step up. I had to kick ass for my girl."

Shay leaned in toward me and pressed her hands to my chest. Her fingers drummed a double-pat as she stared into my eyes. "For the charity."

"That too."

Kiki looped an arm around the crook of Shay's elbow and began to tug her away from me. "Ready? Only so much fairy-godmother magic I can accomplish in two hours."

Two hours? Shay took five-minute showers and wore no makeup.

I grabbed Shay's hand, not ready to let her go.

She glanced back as her fingers slipped away and pierced me with the same intense expression she'd had in the locker room the night before. As if she couldn't believe that I stood there with her...because of her, who she was.

But some part of me clanged out in warning that she needed me to know something else, understand some unspoken thing about her.

I'm here because of you.

And I already know and understand.

Still standing here. Not going anywhere.

Ever since our shower fantasy last night, she'd been a little distant.

Then again, so had I.

We'd both been through a lot of shit in the last few days, good and bad.

We just needed more time to settle into it all.

Yet her reminder last night of our timeclock boomeranged into my brain: two days and one night. And almost twenty-four hours had ticked by since then.

We still have tonight, then all of tomorrow.

Plenty of time to convince her that we needed more of it, more of us.

"They've let riffraff into the country club." Cool judgment frosted out from a polished alto female voice.

"*Hell*o, mother." I didn't turn and hug her; she hadn't been about the warm fuzzies. And all the family touchy-feely *damn sure* wasn't for me. I followed her gaze. It was locked on to the back end of a sexy little ass in a black golf skirt.

"*That girl* had the audacity to attend *your* event?"

"*That girl* is *my girl*, her name is Shay, and she's the only reason *I'm* at the event."

Her heavy sigh filled the space between us. Then the slight weight of her grip on my forearm made me glance at her.

A sudden happiness glittered in her eyes and she wore a rare smile. "Well done today. Your father would be proud."

The same father who'd pressured a young son to excel on the course for all the wrong reasons. One who'd put the almighty dollar and prestige above everything, before family, before showing any kind of real love. One who'd nearly beaten his own son with a golf iron—on our very own country club course—in a drunken rage, who'd stopped short halfway through the brutal downswing before throwing the club... and any remaining respect the son might've had for him... away.

But I took her compliment for what it was, heartfelt in the only way my mother knew how to express it. "Thanks, Mom."

Her expression pinched, brows lowering, mouth tightening. She smoothed a hand over the yellow fabric over what was likely a thousand-dollar sundress.

"How you holding up?" We hadn't spoken since Wednesday night. I'd avoided calling, for so many reasons.

"It's horrible," she wailed in as low a tone as possible while still getting the full impact of her martyrdom across.

I struggled to keep my eyes from rolling. "It hasn't even been a full day."

"Longest day of my life."

"You're being overly dramatic. And you're forgetting you just watched your son win his first ever one-day tournament."

Her shoulders slumped, voice neutralizing, "What am I supposed to do? I've never been on my own before. I don't even know where to begin."

"You'll manage."

"Where do I start?"

"You should start by being nicer to Shay." Yeah, I swung that full circle.

Her voiced steeled. "Why would I want to do that?"

"Because I care about her. A lot." I shot her a nonnegotiable glare. "If you care about me, if you want me to care about you enough to improve our relationship, then you will care about her."

No idea where that ultimatum had come from, but the moment it shot out of my mouth, it worked for me. If my mother was willing to put in a genuine effort for Shay, then I would do the same for my mother.

"Now, if you'll excuse me." I dipped a respectful nod toward her. "I have to drink, eat, shower, and change. There's a gala tonight."

At which, since I'd become the unofficial guest of honor, all eyes would be on me.

Me? I planned to be all about Shay.

"Hey, Ben."

I glanced toward a soft and unfamiliar lilting voice, almost two hours after I'd last seen Shay and Kiki.

A pretty young girl stood ten feet away in the wide hallway, beside a potted palm. She wore a conservative pale-blue party dress with a white sash tied at the waist in a perfect bow. Shining blond hair had been sleeked down into a single sparkling barrette that dangled three fat spirals.

Do I know you? My brows twitched down in confusion.

Vibrant blue eyes hardened a split second before she shot me an incredibly familiar *duh* expression. But before, it hadn't come from a four-foot-something girl.

Then it hit me. And I blinked, amazed. "Trin?"

"Gotcha." She grinned with pride.

"Yeah, ya did."

Her expression grew serious in an instant as her chin dipped down in a satisfied nod. Then with an inspecting gaze of herself that swept downward, she plucked both sides of her dress toward the bottom and pulled it wide. "This is the work of Kiki and Shay. Well, mostly Kiki."

As if the dress itself was the magic and not the transformed girl wearing it.

Kiki took her fairy godmothering seriously.

"You look very beautiful, Trin."

She stared at me a long moment and tilted her head, as if she evaluated the compliment. "Thanks." Then her eyes narrowed, and her critical gaze scanned me from head to toe. "You look cool. Kinda James Bond-ish."

I gave a slight tug to the lapels of my tuxedo jacket. "Thank you." After a beat, I leaned down a little. "Only for the most important ladies in my life."

Her brows raised slightly, her head turned a little, and she adopted a coy expression while she pointed at herself and mouthed *me?*

"Definitely and especially you."

I folded my arms and leaned down a little further. "Someone else, too. Maybe you know where I can find her? About yay tall" —I cut a bent hand into the air at my shoulder height— "dark hair, green eyes...smart mouth."

She leaned closer toward me and whispered, "She'll find you."

Of course. *Control.*

Music from a live band began to stream out through open double doors that led into the ballroom. I tilted my head toward the festivities and held out my hand. "Would you do me the honor of my first celebration dance?"

Without hesitation, her small hand slapped onto mine. "You bet I would." Then she shot me a sideways glare. "But we are *not* grown-up dancing."

I coughed out a laugh and shook my head. "Wouldn't dream of it. How 'bout we let you lead?"

That small hand had an amazing grip as it led me to the exact center of the dance floor, then broke away to stab a finger against my sternum. She took a giant step backward. "Ready?"

It was early; dinner had yet to be served. The music had just begun playing, rhythm upbeat. And we stood in the middle of an empty dance floor in a large ballroom...alone.

And I didn't give one flying fuck who saw me. Reveled in it, actually.

I gave her a solid nod. "Ready."

Trin began some random jerky movements: shoulders bounced, knees knocked, elbows flared. The entire time, her head was thrown back, eyes closed, easy smile on her face.

Shameless, wild...free.

Her eyes cracked open, her entire body froze, and she shot me an even heavier *Duh!* expression.

I grinned and tapped into the crazy, reckless part of me Shay had helped me discover.

Then as if on their own puppeted strings, one of my hands jerked wide, then the other. My left hip shoved sideways. My right foot kicked out.

"Yes!" Trin jumped straight up in the air, landed with her shiny white shoes spread shoulder width apart, then immediately mimicked my wilder spastic dance moves.

A crowd soon gathered, half of them watching in amazement at our choreographed epileptic fits to music, the other half making their best attempt to join in the fun.

The band played another fast-tempo song to pander to their crowd before they wound the rhythm down into something much slower.

Trin propped her hands on her hips and eyed me warily. "No grown-up dancing."

"Understood." And so I did the only thing one should, given the once-in-a-lifetime circumstances. I downshifted into a slo-mo version. Each one-tenth paced hand-jerk, hip-shove, and foot-kick was executed with smooth precision, like some remedial Tai Chi student.

Trin busted out laughing.

The thick crowd around her began to part, and flowing black material appeared behind her pale-blue dress.

I froze, bent arm stuck out at a ninety-degree angle, as my gaze traveled up over sexy curves, glowing skin, upswept dark hair, and emerald eyes that glittered with amusement as they captured mine. *Whoa.* "Beautiful." All I could manage.

She cast an affectionate gaze toward Trin. "May I cut in?"

"About time," Trin huffed as she smoothed her palms down the surface of her blue dress, as if she'd been inconvenienced. "Dudes in tuxes are walkin' around here with silver trays of crackers with tasty-lookin' toppings on 'em. I need to lighten their load."

Shay fought a smile. "They've brought those hors d'oeuvres out for you to take. You don't have to steal them."

"Says you." Trin scanned the room and dipped a nod at one possible target, then a second. "I'm feeling like playing a game I've just invented called Dash-N-Dine."

Without further explanation, Trin aimed toward the nearest waiter and vanished into the crowd of people.

Shay's attention finally landed back on me. She stepped forward and cocked her head, eyeing my chicken-wing arm. "You want me to work with that?"

I lowered my protruding elbow to my side, then held

out my hands in the more traditional male dance position. "Better?"

She slid her hands into mine, but tightened our stance as she pressed her incredible body flush against mine. "You tell me."

"Yeah. *Way* better." *All I want. You and me, dancing. The rest of the room can take a hike.*

Except Trin...

And her waiters...

I exhaled a resigned breath, remembering why Shay had convinced me into playing in the first place. And then my chest burned with gratitude for the incredible week we'd had together because of it.

"Why the big sigh?" She nipped my earlobe with her teeth.

"Happy."

"Sure?" A low hum vibrated against my neck. "Sounds a bit like frustration."

"Wish things were a little different tonight."

"Why?" She pulled back, brow furrowed.

"Wish I had you alone. All to myself."

Her eyes narrowed, then her gaze searched mine. "Is that the only thing you wish was different?"

A concerned expression flashed across her face. It only lasted half a heartbeat.

But my slow brain finally connected the dots with all the strange vibes I'd been picking up from her, the wistfulness.

Something big weighed on her mind. About me. About us. About what we'd done.

"I wouldn't do anything different."

Her dark brows furrowed deeper. "You sure?"

"You know I wished there was another way." I shrugged. "But there wasn't. Now it's over."

"But what if it isn't...over? You just legally won a ton of money to help people. What if what we did comes back to bite you? Risks Loading Zone? Puts the charity in jeopardy?"

"You having regrets?"

She gave a firm headshake. "Nope." She kissed me softly. Then she closed the gap between us by pressing her body against mine once again.

"Good." Because believing in what we did, without question, was the only thing holding me together about it.

"I just need to *make sure* you don't," she murmured against my neck.

My heartrate skyrocketed at the conviction in her measured tone.

I tightened my hold on her. *Why did that sound like something you're about to do?*

35

THE THING ABOUT WOLVES IN SHEEP'S CLOTHING

Shay…

A s we danced, I pretended the night was as Ben had wished, ours alone.

He kept a tight hold on me the entire time, through one slow song, then another, and a third romantic ballad after that; the band appeared to be catering to the man of the hour with the large gathering slow-dancing around us proving it a wise choice.

As the last notes faded away, he kissed me, slow and tender, filled with deep emotion.

And I melted into the intimate touch, savored our private moment in a very public place, as his lips brushed over mine in unspoken promise—that there would be more to come… later. My body hummed in response, warm and alive.

We spoke the same language on a physical level.

If only we were able to bridge the gap with everything else.

His inability to fully move on from what we'd done—the crime I'd encouraged him to commit—made me worry our worlds were too different.

If he didn't see the other side, the bigger picture, then it meant he didn't get me, didn't understand the place I'd come from and the people I belonged to.

And if we had all that stacked against us... *What hope can there be for us?*

The split second our bodies pulled apart, he was whisked away by the adoring Golf Membership.

He shot me a quick apologetic glance over his shoulder.

I smiled and blew him a kiss. No reason to make him worry. He'd find out soon enough.

"Just once, couldn't what we wish for ourselves matter?" I muttered as I found a quiet spot where I could observe the room from its outer edge.

Can two people from totally opposite worlds even survive together? As I swept my gaze across a crowd glittering with custom jewels and shining with designer clothes, I struggled to find any evidence we could.

Of course, the purpose of tonight's event wove together our commonality, even if connected by the barest thread: Ben's prize money would help the less fortunate, all those who'd been forgotten, the ones my heart ached for—who I would sacrifice anything for, even tonight.

Even for you, Ben.

As minutes ticked by, the number of people flowing into

the room multiplied. The band continued to orchestrate the festivities, playing livelier celebratory tunes.

Trin had taken an empty chair in a far corner. She balanced a silver tray filled with hors d'oeuvres on her lap and had acquired an audience of three boys and a girl, all about her age. They sat on the floor around her, listening with rapt attention, probably to one of her wild adventures.

I spotted Ben again and stared at his profile as he spoke to a handful of men, one being Cade, another Whoosh.

Ben laughed at something Cade said.

But seconds later, a moving group of people blocked my view.

It struck me that Trin blended right in, Ben appeared right at home, of course, but I remained the one who felt like an outsider. Maybe it would've been different if I'd been younger like Trin or Ben when first exposed to the entitled. *Maybe if I hadn't spent years hardening my heart, surviving under the radar of the very people I now stood among.*

For me to take on generations of status and privilege would be... "Ridiculous," I muttered. *Impossible.* Hundreds of people filled the room, laughing, comfortable, every one of them set in their ways. Buying and wearing naughty T-shirts was one thing. Understanding the needs of the underprivileged and honestly caring enough to make a difference beyond a mere tax write-off? *Totally different beast.*

In the next seconds, the crowd on the expansive wooden dance floor thinned just enough for me to catch sight of Ben again.

And his gaze—hard and uncompromising—landed on me.

In that split second, my knees went weak, my breath caught, my pulse quickened.

What have you done to me?

That he had that kind of instant power over my body... *my heart*...frightened me.

But then he sucked in a deep breath, as if he needed steadying himself, as if I rocked his world in the same way.

Which makes what I have to do so much harder.

All of a sudden, a slender arm looped through mine. "What're you doing standing here all by yourself?" Kiki's bright blue eyes sparkled with mirth. "Should we be plotting chaos?"

"I wish." She would've been such a great girlfriend to have while growing up, a best friend to share secrets with, someone to trust.

But I had her support now, in a way. Better late than never worked for me—the rapidly developing theme for the night.

I scanned across the room to pinpoint the rest of my crew. But Trin had vanished. Ben had also gone MIA.

Watchful gaze on the open doors that led out into the corridor, I leaned closer to Kiki. "How 'bout a place to go pee?"

"Kiki!" A grinning threesome of glamorous older women who'd just entered the room waved her over.

Kiki waved back at them, held up her index finger, then gave me a pointed look. "Well, if all-out pandemonium is

457

your goal" —her gaze shifted to pan the room from corner to corner— "we could hike up our skirts and fertilize the potted plants."

Oh, damn, Kiki. I bit my lip to keep from laughing. *We're gonna be great lifelong friends.* "And if I wanted just a tiny scandal?"

Her dark brow arched. Then she glanced at the doors with a short nod toward them. "Ladies' room is to the left, down the hall. But be sure flash someone for me, will ya? And then tell me all about it. Now, if you'll excuse me, I have some unsuspecting potential naughty-shirt customers to corrupt."

I let out a low chuckle. "Good luck," I muttered as I walked past her. With the pretentious crowd around us, our slick fairy godmother had her work cut out for her.

As promised, halfway down the wide outer hallway, appeared the ladies' room.

Beyond its door stretched a large sitting area, filled with sprawling furniture covered in sumptuous fabrics. The setup tempted those passing through the impressive anteroom to stay awhile.

And many bedecked women had done just that: a conspiratorial pair whispering as they leaned close together on a low-slung ottoman, an older woman on a stately wing chair in the corner, a chatting young trio occupying a wide couch. And still, more than half the furniture remained unoccupied.

My four-inch glittering heels didn't break stride across the plush carpet as I glided through the lion's den. Confident? Sure.

Because not one of them intimidated me.

I'd become alpha of an entirely different order.

A wolf in a borrowed ball gown stalked through their privileged lair. An invited imposter.

Had any of the women sensed it?

When I cleared the room, I glanced back to check. But no one looked my way. Each remained occupied or self-absorbed. Not surprising. Their world required a level of nonstop indifference that rendered someone like me—unintroduced, therefore unimportant—practically invisible.

My attention swung forward the moment my foot clicked on hard tile. And I realized I'd entered a cream marble fantasy. The floor gleamed a pale ivory kissed with misty swirls of the faintest gold. Three wide curving sinks in a similar hue balanced on pedestals that rested below oval gilded mirrors. Six wooden doors stained in a rich mahogany, none of which were closed, led to generous stalls; each was encased by plastered walls that stretched from floor to ceiling.

Beyond the sinks, a pair of tufted silvery green fainting couches flanked a manicured Ficus whose glossy green leaves nearly brushed the ceiling.

"Wow," I breathed. No point in hiding my amazement. The digs were impressive, far beyond anything I could've imagined.

Wolf. Remember who you are. Not an innocent lamb. Definitely not an opportunistic lion.

Brushing off the momentary awestruck paralysis, I went into an open stall, carefully gathered the silken material of my dress, then made quick work of relieving myself. Muffled conversation hummed low through the thick door as I drew a length of velvety-soft toilet tissue from a ridiculously ornate gold holder. The curlicue lever that flushed the toilet matched, of course.

While washing my hands at one of the sinks, I did my best to look disinterested in anything but myself, examined my neutral frosted lipstick, paid particularly close attention to an imaginary hair that I smoothed behind my ear.

But in the background, my radar had fully fixed on the drama unfolding in front of a mirror, one sink over.

"...would think Franklin would know me by now. *Can you believe* this gaudy thing?"

Two midthirties women, a redhead and a brunette, examined some glittering monstrosity encircling the redhead's wrist.

"Margaret," the brunette chastised on a fierce whisper. "Look at the size of those stones. And they're flawless *pink* diamonds? The bracelet had to have cost him a chunk of his trust fund."

Margaret's wrist got lifted by her friend to angle it closer to the brighter overhead lighting.

Hundreds of rainbows burst onto the walls and ceiling as the innocent offending diamonds caught the light.

"Great," Margaret huffed. "So, he spent a fortune on my least favorite color, and I'm stuck with it? I *hate* it. I'd wear long sleeves all the time to hide it" —she dropped her arm to her side— "but look how stupid. My sleeve catches on the settings."

"Maybe you could...*lose* it," her friend suggested.

Oh, how I would love to help you with that. "Or hock it." I plucked a white rolled washcloth from a pyramid stacked on a shelf, then began to dry my hands. "Word on the street is you could get twenty-five cents on the dollar."

Two sets of widened eyes stared at me, unblinking, like I'd magically poofed beside them from thin air.

Perfect. Shocking the entitled never failed to amuse me. I took advantage of their stunned imbalance and went for the kill.

"Or..." I flicked a glance toward the oblivious women in the sitting area, then at all the unoccupied bathroom stalls. I leaned in closer to my aghast audience. "Say it was *stolen*," I whispered, then shrugged. "It'd be believable. A jealous friend? Some new member masquerading as a manipulative opportunist?"

Or a talented opportunistic eavesdropper in the bathroom. Thank you, *universe.*

As I tossed the fluffy washcloth into a linen-lined basket, I glanced at Margaret with a final piece of Karmic advice. "I'd go for the insurance claim. Then donate the entire amount to charity. Franklin'll be so impressed with your selfless act" —I made a point of staring at the aging socialite's barren left hand— "he might spend another fortune on *one* stone and put a ring on it."

Margaret's friend blinked, then glanced at her. "And *this* time, tell him what color diamond you like."

Annnd...my work here is done.

I exited the bathroom ecstatic with how the fortuitous events had unfolded.

Minutes ago, when I'd left Kiki and Ben in the ballroom, I'd intended to go deep-sea fishing.

But I had no idea a great white shark would jump right into my lap.

Fifteen minutes later, Trin and I stood near the end of the wide hallway, waiting for the inevitable main event.

Ben still mingled in the ballroom, surrounded by his adoring fans.

Then with a startling crash of wood slamming into wall, the french doors at the other end of the corridor had burst open, and a piercing female screech silenced everyone within earshot.

An animated Margaret strode down the carpeted pathway, naked wrist held high, flaming hair flowing in her wake, fury in a wild-eyed gaze.

"Someone stole my bracelet!" Her screamed accusation echoed from the rafters.

Well, damn. *Look who's the wolf in sheep's clothing now.*

A large portion of the crowd from the ballroom began to spill into the hall to investigate the commotion.

Margaret's gaze swept over the gathering witnesses to her outrage. Then she zeroed in on me for a split second before her eyes narrowed as she stared at Trin.

Out of protective instinct, I stepped into her line of sight, lowered my chin, and shot a dangerous glare back at her. *Oh, no, bitch. Not a chance in hell you're going after my cub.*

She huffed out a breath, then moved on, scanning across the hushed gathering of her flock.

"*Who*ever you are, you *will* pay for this." She examined each face, acting as if one of them would have a big red GUILTY stamped on their forehead. "That bracelet was one-of-a-kind. And it was a gift from my Franklin."

Big fat tears began to roll down her cheeks.

Whispers broke out amongst the flock.

Then suddenly, the crowd parted and Ben strode through, gaze stern and locked on its target—me.

I'd seen that focused intensity once before. Two weeks ago. From behind his bar.

Wasn't afraid then. Not cowering now.

Here we go...

I straightened my shoulders and stood my ground.

Trin wisely bolted.

No one else stood nearby.

He stopped a good three feet from me.

Distance.

His breaths quickened, like he struggled to breathe.

Anger.

I cocked my head at him, surprised at how well everything had played out. Had he caught Margaret's brief suspicious glance at me...or was that quick distrust all him?

I arched my brows.

His eyes narrowed, and he did that analyzing-stare thing again, something I hadn't been subject to in days.

Hardening my jaw, I folded my arms. *Stubborn irritation.*

All you'll get from me tonight.

"Did you do it?" he finally whispered, tone riddled with uncertainty. "Did you take the bracelet?"

And we'd arrived back to square one: Ben jumping to conclusions, not giving me the benefit of the doubt.

But his encore worked out in everyone's favor. How things needed to be.

Playing my part, I let out a heavy sigh. "Does it really matter?"

Pain and confusion glittered in his eyes as they searched mine. And he widened his stance, like he adjusted for steady footing in the middle of an earthquake.

But we'd both been trying to find our solid ground, a place where we felt safe, hadn't we? And all the while, we'd been struggling to figure out ourselves, let alone each other.

After a few contemplative seconds, he gave a firm nod. "It's Saturday. My day. So yeah." He gusted out a labored breath. "It does."

No, it doesn't. Because all that mattered in our chaotic, immoral, unfair world—in spite of what anyone tried to convince themselves of—was the substance of a person's heart.

And after the last solid week together, if he hadn't discovered what made mine beat, he never would.

But how it all went down in those few minutes was exactly how it needed to, for me, for Ben. But the reality of him ringing true to his elemental nature, quick to judge, against me on instinct—after I'd shared all of me with him— still cut...deeply.

I clenched my jaw and shot him an unforgiving look, hardening my tender heart all the while. "Believe what you want." He wouldn't get a clear-cut answer and definitely not from me. "Life's easier that way." No second-guessing. Cut and dried. His gut instinct influenced by his perspective.

Our twisted, broken society tried to force us to live by black-and-white rules. Yet nothing ever played out that simple. Most of us, the ones who suffered and scrounged and did more of the dying before they ever got a chance of fully living, existed in the shadowed expanse of the gray in between.

The world belonged to the downtrodden, the misfortunate...the forgotten ones.

And I belonged to them.

His expression shifted from confusion to full-on hurt. Probably something to do with my tone, cold and final... decided.

Exactly the way it needs to sound.

The glaring heavy silence stretched into a death sentence for us. But I knew I had to end it. And him angry and hurt seemed for the best.

"Well, been nice knowin' ya." I punched plenty of attitude into the statement. Even though I meant none of its subtext. Ben had changed me on a fundamental level, showed me for the first time what it felt like to be truly cherished, loved. That brief glimpse would have to be enough to get me through the time yet to come.

But all that would have to wait until later.

In that moment, I focused on his shocked expression

over my obvious dismissal. Then I imprinted that evidence into my brain as I turned and walked away. And no matter how tortured my lungs felt with every breath of sucked-in air, I held on to that image along with the one of his distrust.

Because it was safer to swim in that shallow end. Those destined to be heroes, the ones who risked everything to save others, didn't get to allow themselves to be loved. Not for long. Because the inevitable pain it caused to the one who did the loving would never be worth it.

"It's better this way," I muttered to myself. I drew in a shaky breath, doing my damnedest to believe my own words. My chest burned at the instant loss, a deep and gaping wound I suspected would never heal.

But when I stepped into the crisp night air, I didn't turn an expected left toward Glenhaven, toward my park, my people, all I'd ever known.

Instead, I hooked an unfamiliar right, prepared to fall on my sword.

36

ALWAYS SOMETHING THERE TO REMIND ME

Ben...

Stormy emerald eyes raged at me one last time.
Dark lashes lowered in a heavy blink.
A flash of black silk disappeared out a closing door.

Feeling began to return. Agonizing pain followed. Sweet scathing medicine burned down my throat.

My head blessedly spun again. The world tilted with it.

Round and round, the whirlpool sucked me back down into numb oblivion...

Off in the distance, an announcer blared. "...year's tournament is none other than our very own Benjamin Bishop."

A bizarre distorted Kiki stepped into my hazed line of sight. "What did you say to her?"

The broken record of events played again: voices muted yet echoed, images colored but faded.

The gut-wrenching emotions? Sliced deeper, became more painful with every uncontrollable rerun of what had gone down.

I stared over Fun-house Kiki's shoulder—at the closed door. "It's what I didn't say. Or what I should've said."

The door loomed closer as I pushed past Kiki.

Her superhero iron grip clamped onto my arm. "Where are you going?"

"After her." My voice sounded tinny, otherworldly.

"No, you're not. She wanted you to win for her, for the charity. You need to get up on stage and announce that. I'll go."

War raged within me as I stood there. I didn't give a fuck about the event.

And it didn't *matter to me whether Shay had stolen the bracelet or not.*

I knew that in my heart. She needed to know that too.

Emerald eyes raged.

Dark lashes lowered.

Black silk flashed.

The door closed.

Searing pain torched my heart, agonizing...devastating.

Too much. Overwhelming.

Medicine downed. Throat burned.

Blackness returned...

"Why so glum?" Whoosh asked, face strange and twisty. "You just won the tournament."

"Yeah, but I lost the girl." My otherworldly voice had weakened, had grown thready.

Emerald eyes glistened with tears.

Dark lashes lowered to mask her emotion.

Black silk flashed to hide a disappearing act.

The door slammed shut.

Consciousness returned in slow drips of awareness. The wrenching pain followed, merciless and absolute. But somehow the fucked-up dreamscape torture felt better than my empty reality. I deserved it. I'd sure as hell earned it.

And so, I drank. Down, down, down into oblivion...

A trippy-looking Trin stood in the hall, stared down at a pink sparkly phone.

"Is that Shay's?"

Bulging eyes narrowed to slits. She clutched the phone to her chest. "Mine now."

"Where is she?" I rasped, voice barely registering.

Trin shrugged with one shoulder. The action cartoonishly bounced her joint sky-high then snapped it back into the socket. "Gone."

Emerald eyes filled with emotion.

Black silk caught in the door.

A slice of light glimmered from in between.

Loud coughing jarred me awake. I cleared my parched

throat. My head throbbed. *Which wake-up is this? The tenth? The hundredth?*

But I didn't want the drunken dreams to end. They'd begun to evolve. Like my subconscious had discovered the end of an unraveling thread and decided to pull on it.

I lifted my thousand-pound head, squinted at the bottle in my hand, and stared at the last inch of amber liquor. "Inch is for beer," I groused. "I still got three-quarters left." I tightened my hold on the neck of the bottle and began gulping.

A hard jerk yanked the bottle from my grip. Narrowed blue eyes glared at me from a pissed-off face. *Kiki.* The real one.

"Hey! I was drinking that."

"Already *drunk*. What do you think you're doing?"

"Hey, if it worked for my father."

"It didn't. He's in prison."

"Yeah, well, so is she." *News delivered courtesy of front-page headlines.* I yanked the bottle back from her and took another healthy swallow. Then I laid my cheek on the cool cement and closed my eyes.

Seconds later, I heard Kiki from over in the kitchen. "Code red."

Nails drummed on the counter in rhythmic clicks. "I dunno. Whatever color the highest level of alert is for your best friend hugging a bottle and kissing the floor."

A loud gasp sounded, followed by a heavy sigh. "No. He is *not* pushing *your baby* out of his vagina."

Keys clattered onto the marble. Her phone got tossed

beside them. "Apparently, someone is. Any minute now. Out of *her* vagina. *Ewww*...now I just thought about Hannah's *vagina*. Brain bleach! STAT!"

"I don't have a vagina," I grumbled.

"Suck it up and prove it, Bishop." Something hard nailed my ribs.

"Ow. Did you just literally kick a man when he's down?"

"Get up. You got five minutes." Her voice trailed down the hall.

"To do what?" I pushed myself up off the floor, ignoring my throbbing head, the spinning world. "And where you going?"

"Grabbing Shay's stuff."

Tapping a hand down the wall with every step for balance, I followed her into my bedroom just in time to catch her shoulder one of Shay's bags, then the other.

"What're you gonna do with it?" I wanted to yank them away from her. Shay belonged here. So did her stuff.

"She asked me to give the duffel to Trin. She wants the backpack thrown into the trash. And then we're heading to the hospital. The first Michaelson of the next generation is about to be born."

My brain got stuck on the *she asked* part. "You talked to her," I whispered. Then I blinked, shocked, trying to absorb that.

Kiki scrunched her nose and pushed a hand between us as she stepped back. "Keep your distance. You stink." She strode into my closet, yanked a shirt off a hanger, then threw it at me. "Change into that."

I attempted to catch it but missed. I left it on the floor and just stared at her.

Kiki folded her arms and stared back at me a beat, then she sighed heavily and walked out of the room. "She left me a note," she called out from down the hall.

I did as she asked, scraped the sweaty shirt off my back, tossed it onto the bathroom floor, then scooped up the clean one and shrugged into it as I followed her down the hall.

"I didn't get a note."

Back in the kitchen, Kiki handed me a glass of water. "I know."

I gulped down the entire glass as I glared at the Sunday newspaper on the counter between us. Then I clunked the glass down and pinched my eyes shut to block the headline above the fold: **ROBIN HOOD TURNS HERSELF IN FOR HACKING SCHEME**. She'd also confessed to a handful of other petty theft crimes, like Mr. Financial District and Miss Louis Vuitton. The spotlight piece covered where the stolen Robin Hood dollars had gone, the unsuspecting victims of financial crimes, and the growing plight of the city's homeless.

No way you could've fed a reporter that info in a few hours Saturday night.

The paper had to have known for days.

Why the hell hadn't she told me?

Why didn't I see the signs?

But I had spotted them: her growing hesitance, the wistfulness. Only I'd brushed the symptoms off, believed we had time to fix it all. And her questions directed at me? Had been tests from her. *That I'd failed, spectacularly.* Fuck, *I wish*

I could steal back time, our secret wish on the train.

I let out a heavy sigh and scrubbed a hand down my face.

"She won't talk to me." I'd tried. The prison had explicit instructions from Shay: Deny all contact from Benjamin Bishop.

"I know," Kiki repeated. "She did it to save you. To try and save them all."

My heart damn near exploded right there in my chest.

My superhero.

Right then and there, I vowed she wouldn't be the only one. Her sacrifice wouldn't go to waste.

"What day is it?"

"Tuesday."

"*Fuck me.*" Three whole days wasted with me sunk at the bottom of bottles. I blinked out the window and stared at the setting sun.

I grabbed my phone and keys, but pocketed both. "Drop me off somewhere?"

She frowned. "You're not coming to the hospital?"

"I will. Got an important errand to run first."

To begin with, I gorged myself. I couldn't remember the last time I'd eaten. Had to have been Saturday.

Then I walked down a lower-income residential street. Laundry still hung from clotheslines. The same chained dog barked. Beater cars along the curbs continued to rust.

The same young kid with blond hair and blue eyes popped out from the alley, hair shaggy and wild again, clothing back to threadbare jeans and a faded tee.

"No blue dress?" I teased.

Trin narrowed her eyes at me. "One-time thing. Party's over."

I held out the tray of Cokes, then gave a nod to the five Mickey D's bags cradled in my arm.

She leaned in, reached out, and swiped one of each without getting too close, then stepped back a good ten feet, eyeing me warily.

"Not on your good side?" Not that I'd expected much. I got the drill. I remained a foreigner in their world. *For now.*

She slurped a couple of swallows of Coke through the straw as she watched me. Then she gave a headshake. "You dance cool, but you're a grown-up. And my loyalty's ta Shay."

"Fair enough."

We kept up the staring contest for another dozen seconds or so.

She remained motionless, unblinking, expression blanked.

One more thing. "You got Friday covered?"

I got her classic *Duh!* expression. "As promised ta *Shay.*"

Right. Obviously, Shay'd talked to Trin. And Kiki. *I'd* been the one kept in the dark.

None of that mattered. Shay had been brutally betrayed in her life. The people she'd trusted back then, the family that should've had her back, had let her down.

I never should have questioned her. *I'd* betrayed her. *I'd* let her down too.

Control. What she'd needed. So, she'd taken the uncertainty of us recovering from my fuck-up right out of the equation.

I tipped a nod at Trin, then headed toward the rest of my new weekly Tuesday stops.

"You're wrong, Shay. We can recover. I won't ever doubt you again."

Still standing here. Not going anywhere.

My unspoken thought from Saturday night echoed in my mind.

And I planned to wait however long it took to prove my loyalty...and tell her in person.

After three more dinner deliveries, to Charlene, Lando, and Decker, I began to walk down the alley from that very first night. I shuffled my feet in a coded fast-fast-slow rhythm, exactly as Shay had instructed me on last Tuesday's food run. The scuffing noise announced the approach of a friendly, she'd explained.

And as I neared the vicinity of the dumpster, a giant shadow appeared in the dim moonlight, right on cue. "Who you?" Bear growled.

"Ben. Shay's friend. Yours too."

I held up the last Coke in one hand, the last food bag in the other. *When squared off with a grizzly, hand them your food.*

To my relieved surprise, the dark giant waved me closer with a tilting sweep of his head, fuzzy dreadlocks swaying. "Come close, Ben." The same slow and soft words vibrated out, the same hooded eyes stared me down, but thanks to last Tuesday's feed-and-greet with Shay, I knew Bear tended to be more bark than bite—once he'd had the time to sniff someone like me out.

With eyes that darted beyond my shoulder often, he eventually reached for my offering of food and drink. "No Shay." More a statement than a question.

"No." Unfortunately for all of us. "Looks like you're stuck with me awhile."

"Shay can't lose you like I lost...Shay can't...she can't... lose you...lose you..." Bear clutched his food bag while he stared vacantly over my shoulder, rocking his massive frame forward and backward. The repetitive speech was a thing for him. The rocking too. Shay had warned me to be patient, to listen. Because even though Bear had social issues, difficulty dealing with emotions, and a patent refusal to assimilate into society, he had a ferocious protective instinct and a genius-level IQ. *Asperger's syndrome.*

I sighed, nodding. "I can't lose Shay either."

"Love hurts." He put his Coke on the closed lid of the dumpster, then opened his food bag.

"Yeah, it does."

"Love hurts." He grabbed a fistful of fries, then shoved that giant paw in front of me, ends sticking through grimy fingers in every direction. "Blink hurts."

Not wanting to offend the guy—the one Shay had instinctively run to, the guardian who'd looked after her as she'd grown up—I did my best to choose a fry that wasn't touching his hand.

I twisted it around and popped the free-air end into my mouth.

"Love hurts," he repeated.

Yeah, it does. Shay had explained to me that his riddled phrases and repetitions told a story.

"Blink hurts." Bear rocked forward, then back again. "Love hurts...Blink hurts."

Shay's advice flowed into my head: *There's a story to everything from his mind. Be patient. Listen. You'll puzzle it out.*

"Love hurts." He shoved half the burger into his mouth. Once he swallowed, he repeated once again. "Blink hurts."

The sequence was important. He was trying to tell me something.

"Love hurts," I repeated as the meaning dawned on me. "Blink hurts." My drunken fog cleared enough for it to crystallize. "Shay's hurting because of love. She...*loves me.*"

Bear gave a hard nod. "Love hurts."

37
LOVE-ABIDING

Shay…

Warm sunshine kissed my face, the *free* kind above grass and trees, connected to parks and forests, as far as my running legs and wild imagination could take me.

Eighteen months, to the day.

How long I'd bargained for.

The deal I'd struck.

The sacrifice I'd been willing to make for them all—for Ben.

And I would've done so much more.

Blinding glare off a chrome bumper made me shield my eyes as I searched for Kiki's Prius.

But instead of a silent electronic car, there at the edge of the parking lot rumbled a fern-green classic truck.

478

And a gorgeous dangerous man leaned against its back fender.

Ben.

My heart leapt at the sight of him.

Dammit. I thought I'd locked my emotions for him down tight.

With a deep scowl, at him and me, I strode right on past him.

But by my next full breath, he appeared beside me.

I slowed my pace.

He matched me, step for step.

"Shay, *please.*"

I ignored him and kept walking. I figured it'd take me a few hours at a solid clip, but my own two feet would bring me back home to Glenhaven by nightfall.

"Shay," he kept at it.

Clenching my jaw to prevent my mouth from blurting out any number of things, I focused on a pair of blue-and-white tree swallows that swept through the sky.

"I never should've questioned you. Not whether or not you stole the bracelet—whether or not it mattered." He cleared his throat. "It *didn't* matter. And idiot me should've said that, right then, without hesitation."

My chest began to burn at his words. But I kept walking, lasered my attention straight ahead, at the treetops in the near distance.

A heavy sigh sounded out beside me. "I fucked up. Big time. But I got the sense, still feel it now" —he pulled ahead and stared hard at me— "that you *wanted* me to fuck up."

Tears misted my eyes at the truth of it. That he got me after all.

"I *know* you." He weighted the words with conviction.

I stopped dead in my tracks.

He moved right in front of me, locked gazes with mine. "Still standing here. Not going anywhere."

My breaths grew ragged. He looked incredible: black hair windblown over his forehead, dark scruff of beard edging his jawline, charcoal eyes doing that penetrating-stare thing.

"Why?" I didn't get it. Anyone with sense would've written me off, run far *far* away.

"You know why."

I couldn't reply, didn't find the words because I couldn't think straight, had to suck in great lungfuls of air because I found it hard to breathe. I hadn't expected him to be there. Didn't want to face the *why* of it. Wasn't ready to admit to what I'd been ignoring. Denial had served me well while I'd done my time. Dealing with him in my first seconds of freedom? *Overwhelming.*

Prison itself had had a nice set of rules. So had the female inmates who ran the joint. Those who survived in that environment understood them: *You have no control. Trust no one.*

But I'd already learned those rules years ago.

And yet, Ben had taught me something in one short week. It was okay to count on someone else, sometimes. That I didn't have to be strong all the time.

Maybe I don't have to be alone, fighting for everything.

He took a step closer, leaving an inch or so between us

as he searched my eyes. "It's also *one* of the reasons why I did Mickey D's every Tuesday with your crew, my crew now too."

You did? You took care of my family? Your family *now too?*

My lower lip began to quiver; I bit it into submission.

He slowly raised his hand, brushed gentle fingers over my cheek, into my hair. "Because I love you."

In the middle of my next shaky breath, he leaned forward that last inch and kissed me, soft and tender, filled with warmth and passion.

And I shut down my protesting brain and kissed him back, wrapped my arms around his neck, and held on to a man I never saw coming and couldn't believe still stood there.

As the kiss wound down, when the salt of my tears mingled into our mouths, I pulled back. "I love you too," I whispered without doubt...uncertain only about admitting it.

His eyes glistened with moisture.

I narrowed mine, stepped back, then dropped my hands onto my hips.

Ben was the man who held the carefully knotted corners of my rug...who'd yanked it out from under me—twice.

Take control. "But that doesn't mean anything. I'm not snapping right back into *us* again."

He blinked in surprise.

My heart sank at my own gut-instinct words too. Because as much as the idea of trusting Ben again scared me, it kinda gave me something to work toward, something to hold on to.

Besides, he'd made an accurate point. I *had* wanted him to fuck up. I'd needed *him* to throw believable distance between us for him to buy my inevitable exit—in order to save him.

What I'd been trying to convince my doubting self of for eighteen months.

That I'd made the right move by cutting him out of the decision-making process.

But standing in front of him after all those months, seventy-eight long weeks...five hundred forty-eight lonely nights...I wasn't so sure.

Still... "I'm not goin' down that easy."

He gusted out a held breath, chuckled low, then swept an open arm back toward his truck. "Wouldn't have it any other way."

The next moments all unfolded in a surreal blur, him opening his sticking passenger door, me getting inside, him running around the front hood with a hopeful grin like an eager high school kid on his first date—like we'd done a year and a half ago, but as if it was yesterday.

He gripped the steering wheel, then glanced my way. "Where to?"

"Everywhere." My brain jammed with a billion thoughts at once.

He gave me a stellar *Duh!* look. One I'd seen on Trin a thousand times. "Where to *first*?"

My mind blanked again. Everything I'd missed for so long fought for dominance.

But the most important one? I already had, whether or

not I let my stubborn-ass self admit it: *Ben. By my side.* A good foot of safe distance spanned between his body and mine on the truck's bench seat. But his nearness after all that time apart still charged the air between us. And some elemental part of me ached to move closer, hover exploring fingers over his tribal tattoo, inhale the earthy scent of him, taste the saltiness of his...

His face lit up. "I've got an idea." He put the truck in gear and we rumbled off.

I almost laughed at my near-naughtiness to his oblivious innocence. Instead, I just let go, and let him take control, for a while anyway. I emptied my mind of every ounce of worry and basked in sensations: the crisp wind through my open window as it danced across my face, the brilliant colors of nature and textures of architecture, the metallic scents of the city mixing with the sweetness of her parks, horns honking, birds singing.

After twenty minutes of driving and one pit stop, where we ended up was on a favorite park bench that sat beside a beloved rock outcropping. The white rolled-down bags of three quarter-pounder-with-cheese meals sat between us—one for him, two for me.

After we polished off our food and drink, I made him scrabble up the boulder outcropping with me. I pointed toward the far tree line. "That's my forest, the place I grew up."

A place I'd missed terribly. *My home. Where I got grounded. Where I became charged.*

"Wanna show me?" He arched a brow.

Yeah. Somehow my fears of trusting him began to melt away, little by little. And I wanted him to get to know me again, know more of me than I'd been willing to share before. The most vulnerable part of me sensed it was safe with Ben. *Always had been.*

"Race ya!" I scrabbled down without waiting for his reply.

Another beautiful chuckle reverberated somewhere above me.

And we ran, together, me taking the lead, him chasing me down, laughing as we both darted around trees, lungs burning, skin tingling.

Through blackberry thickets, hidden by overgrown ferns, past one mossy boulder, then another, I brought him into my secret sunbeam-filled clearing. Eyes falling closed, I drew in a ritual breath of the pure air of my forest that was scented of earth and rain and dreams and possibilities.

Then I glanced at Ben, who instinctively did the same while he wore an expression of childlike wonder.

You get it.

Maybe he'd been one of us, like me and Trin—the dreamers, the adventurers, the heroes willing to risk everything for what we believed in—*all along.*

"Watch!" I called out as I bounded up my boulder staircase. At the top, I launched into the air and howled my low *ahhhwwwhhhooo.*

When I landed onto the spongy leaf pile, crumbled bits went flying. I marveled at that; it was spring. Which meant Trin had to have stocked our leaf pile just for her...or for me too—for a freshly sprung jailbird.

I lifted my head.

Ben just stood there, arms folded, watching me exactly like I'd asked.

"Aren't you gonna take a turn?"

"No." His dark gaze glittered with fierce emotion. "Be free. I'll be right here, waiting for you."

In a wonderful cloud of leaf bits, I jumped up, kissed him, then ran and climbed my staircase and leapt, three more times.

A good hour later, and after a thorough dusting of my hair, T-shirt, and jeans, we were back in his truck again. "Where we goin'?" He'd made some mysterious phone call before we'd gotten back into the truck, where he'd told whoever was on the other end, "Thirty minutes."

"It's a surprise. Consider it a belated birthday present. And maybe a little bit more."

MORE.

That triggering word echoed in my brain to become an important thing I wanted him to know. "There's something I kept from you that I have to explain."

He arched a brow at me, amusement sparkling in his eyes. "Just *one* something?"

I narrowed my eyes. "Listening?"

His expression humbled and he gave a firm nod. "Intently."

"Before Heart burned the drive, she unlocked hidden evidence that proved your father had committed *more* crimes: insider trading, conspiracy, fraud. On a much larger scale. And that evidence gave me an opportunity to help you, to help so many others." *Made me* have *to want you to fuck up.* "I hope you understand what I did and why I did it."

He glanced at me, made a left turn at the light, then nodded. "I do understand. Something to do with that spotlight article, right?"

"Yeah. Some young girl reporter hassled Lando months prior. I lured her away, showed her that the real story wasn't one homeless guy who guarded a record store, got her to see that an entire parallel city of homeless struggled right in the middle of one of the most celebrated places in our nation. But the reporter felt like that story wasn't enough for her editors, that they would want more."

"And in your lap, fell my criminal father."

"Yep. Everything I'd done, all that I'd stolen and given away to help others was only part of the story. Hardworking folks, most barely making ends meet, were only one step away from suffering an unfortunate incident or becoming victim to a criminal act. They're the next in line. And your father's greed could've sent any number of them there."

"Good story."

"Almost. Providing evidence of the greater crimes was the clincher. With that, the Feds took down an entire ring, some of the Who's Who of Wall Street. And providing them that info gave me what I needed to cut a deal."

"But why cut a deal at all? That's what I still don't understand. Why did you turn yourself in?"

I nudged his shoulder. "For you, silly. I didn't want the crime you'd committed to hang over you, risk Loading Zone.

With me, they got the only perpetrator they know about. To protect you, I told them I stole it from your father's study. No point in going after anyone else if I'm all there was. I turned myself in, because I needed to give you a clean slate. It gave me one too."

"You gave *us* one."

My muscles tensed at the *us* part. Even though we'd eaten on a bench and run wild through my forest, played in my hidden clearing, I hadn't let myself get too much in my head about it. For the last year and a half, I hadn't planned on seeing him again. And with all the visitation-meetings Kiki and I had had to run our thriving naughty-shirt business, if she had known that he'd planned to pick me up, she'd kept it from me.

"We'll see. For sure *you*. And *me*."

"Sounds like there's an *us* in there somewhere."

"Don't know, Bishop. 'Us' sounds complicated."

He gave a hard nod. "Takes a lot of trust to make an *us*."

"It's like you're making my *non*-us argument for me."

"Just sayin', we could work on it. Commit to work toward the *us*."

My brain still couldn't process the idea. I began to believe my past had programed me to distrust the future with someone, no matter how tempting. But oh, how my heart *wanted* to say yes. A familiar compromise hit me. "Maybe, we could give it a week. And see." A week seemed small, safe.

He arched another amused brow at me.

"That one week we shared got me through the last eighteen months," I mumbled, more to myself than him.

LAWBREAKER

Whenever things got rough, every time my spirits dragged, I relived every heart-stopping moment of our golf-scrambling, movie-watching, and train-jumping. And when my heart ached, I replayed every amazing sensual moment: our clock-struck-midnight first time, the rock-beats-paper wakeup call...our sizzling locker-room shower.

Something else important had gotten me through those endless nights, though: another wrong I'd made sure to right. "One other part of the deal I'd struck? That the authorities investigate my father and mother. Interrogate my sister. Charge them to the fullest extent of the law." *Make sure the infant who slept in that new crib didn't suffer,* remained *innocent.*

"Wow." He glanced at me with wide eyes, pride in his expression. "Good for you. That's huge."

I nodded. "Yeah, it was. I made it clear that I had to remain out of it, though. They had to make that case all on their own, and I didn't need to know the outcome." I wanted no part of that mess. I'd already moved on. Why I'd had Kiki toss the backpack. *Only way to live in the present is to let go of the past.*

All of a sudden, my attention got drawn outside of the cab. He'd turned down Maple Lane.

We slowed to a coast and all of my beautiful houses paraded by us. I leaned out, whispering hello to the white storybook cottage with its whimsical flowers and curvy metal-capped chimney.

Toward the end, he eased around the lane's gentle bend, pulled up to the curb, then cut the engine—right in front of our favorite house.

Only...the property no longer looked sad and decrepit.

Vibrant flowers and fresh sod gleamed under the warmth of the sun. A new brick pathway stretched forth like a red carpet, even and straight. Porch steps and roof eaves had been replaced and painted. It had a bright white railing, unblemished windows, and righted shutters.

The house looked glorious, shining there in a happy shade of yellow and trimmed in green.

His words from when we'd first walked by together echoed in my mind. *It's been neglected for too long. 'Bout time someone paid attention to it.*

After he opened my truck door, then led me to the yard's front walkway, I finally stared up at him. "Someone sold it to you?"

"Not exactly."

He nodded toward the opening front door and waved for someone to come outside.

A little old woman took a few tentative steps but stopped at the threshold of the porch, remained in the shade.

Ben slipped his hand into mine and led me up the freshly bricked path until we stood at its end, right below the new porch steps.

He gave my hand a light squeeze. "This is Helen."

A brightness sparkled in the elderly woman's silvery blue eyes. Her slender white eyebrows raised, her expression growing hopeful. "I'm a decent cook. And I keep a tidy house." She glanced back through the open front door, voice beginning to tremble. "Too many years it's been just tired ol' me breathin' between those walls. Be nice to have youth and excitement in there again."

"The place inside isn't half bad either. Helen's been letting me sneak upstairs, strengthen the floorboards a bit to handle the traffic of a couple of '*young'uns*' trudging around up there. Well, we're a couple, anyway."

"A couple?"

He turned toward me, searched my eyes deeper than ever before, as if for some new answer he hadn't yet found. "What if it isn't *just that one week* for us. What if we had more?"

My brow furrowed, total confusion jumbling my brain with that last word. "More?"

"What if you didn't have to be alone? Didn't need one single week of memories to get you through the dark nights? What if we make new memories for all the nights?"

"More...traffic." My brain tried to connect the floorboard-strengthening to the *more*.

Helen's head dipped down a fraction, and her expression hardened into stone-cold serious. "More excitement too."

I blinked, finally understanding their meaning—that tempting *us* he'd been talking about. An *us* with Ben was something I wanted, and could have, if I was brave enough to take the leap with my heart. My mind flashed to a young runaway in the woods, to a girl over the years who'd provided for others, to Wonder Woman who leapt first, offering her heart to countless others, without fear or concern for herself.

Then I straightened my shoulders. And got honest with myself. No more denial.

I love Ben.

And I wanted to make him happy. Which meant I needed to face my fear of betrayal.

So, I did what he'd suggested one night long ago...

Touch your electrical lines, Shay. You're braver than you know.

I leapt.

Mind made up, I gave a brave heartfelt smile toward Ben, then glanced at our new friend. "Are you okay with that, Helen? Him *shacking up* with me...in your house?"

"Yeah, about that." He tugged something out from inside of his T-shirt collar. *A necklace?* He reached behind his neck, unfastened it, then bent down on one knee. "What if we made this thing real? Made it legal?"

I stared down at a sparkling diamond ring held in his hand, a platinum chain hanging from it. "You want to marry me?"

"I do. No more running away to protect you, or me. Only holding on."

I just stared at him in disbelief.

"Wear it around your neck for a week, if you want. I've been wearing it around mine for eighteen months." He drew in a deep breath. "You and me, Shay. Your way, my way, there's no difference to me anymore. It's *our way* and the only life I can imagine living."

Ben...for more than a week. Him being my family, my home...forever. *All I've ever wanted.*

Tears blurred my vision, then dripped down my cheeks as I nodded. "Yes," I whispered as I tugged on his other hand, completely honest with both of us as I invited him into my arms, "I want all of that too."

"Well, thank the sweet Lord for that!" Helen clapped her hands once. "I didn't have to fake a livin'-in-sin conniption." Helen walked up to us, put a gentle hand on each of our forearms, and focused her bright blue gaze on me. "And it's *our* house now. Your man here bought half ownership, and with no heirs, I'm giving the rest to you as a wedding present" —she winked— "after I'm dead and gone, of course."

"Well, it's about time, James Bond!"

I turned to see Trin standing at the curb behind us, hands megaphoning her mouth.

Kiki hooked an arm around her neck. "I *knew* my fairy godmothering would land you the prince."

Ben gazed down at me, then gave me a tender kiss. "And we'll live happily ever after."

I arched a brow, easing back a bit. "Even if the prince is bright, boring, a total rule-follower and she's dark, edgy, will probably break *at least* one law a day?"

"Even if. Because a wise and generous-hearted woman once told the prince he needed a little more danger to rough up his edges—make his seriousness less fatal."

"A very wise woman. *Life is meant to be lived*," I repeated, remembering.

"And your prince is looking forward to spending every wild, crazy, and *sometimes* lawbreaking moment of it...with you."

EPILOGUE

EXTENDED CREW

Six months later...
Shay...

From the shade of a maple tree at the far edge of the lawn, I took a breather from my dream world to soak it all in.

Balloons in rainbow colors bobbed from ribbons tied to the wraparound railing.

Spiraled crepe paper, draped from post to post, rippled in a slight breeze.

Presents hidden under boisterous wrapping with shiny bows sat in a pile on a side table.

Absolutely no clowns or balloon animals were in attendance: orders from Cade.

All the decorations were for little Oliver's second birthday, the first party at our house.

A warm presence edged into my awareness.

Ben.

His hands slid over my hips from behind. A gentle kiss pressed to my temple before the soft scruff of his beard trailed down my cheek. Warm breath feathered over the shell of my ear.

"What're you doing all the way out here, alone?"

I let out a contented sigh and smiled. "Just stealing a moment for myself."

And as I slid my hands over his, my fingers brushed over both of our wedding rings: his basic gold band, my original platinum-mounted diamond, all we needed.

We'd gotten married on the seventh day of our very first entire week together, in our secret forest clearing. Only three other people had been there with us. The pastor of our local church, and fierce supporter of the homeless, had expressed heartfelt honor to make us legal in the eyes of God. Trin had scoffed when I asked if she'd be a witness, had insisted on being both flower girl *and* maid of honor. Kiki had taken her role as fairy godmother to heart, adorning me in a gauzy white dress "perfect for a forest bride marrying her prince." Trin had worn a similar lilac dress with green ribbons hanging from dazzling crystals. We'd both worn botanical woodland crowns in our hair, mine simple baby's breath, Trin's made of sprigs of lavender and tiny white roses.

Everyone else understood that we'd eloped, had gone to our own private world to make things official, our way.

Weeks later, Ben had sold the condo, and we'd moved into the upper floor of Helen's house. But together with Helen, we'd dusted every corner of our dream home with laughter and love.

And an entire half year later, each day was filled with both adventure and generosity. Every night, I pinched myself, unable to believe I got to fall asleep safe and protected in Ben's arms.

Surrounding us both? A bigger close-knit family than I'd ever imagined.

I'm no longer the girl standing on the fringes, only the observer.

I've finally become a part of it all.

"Come on. Let's dive back into the fray." I took Ben's hand and led him across the lawn.

Helen stood beside her latest friends, Chloe and Daniel. When my adoptive grandma had discovered there were bakers in our midst, she'd insisted on weekly visits to Sweet Dreams, the bakery Hannah had founded and Chloe and Daniel now owned. Unfazed by Daniel's Mohawk, piercings, and dry commentary, she'd become best buds with rockabilly Chloe, and Helen even wore one of her own original dresses from the 50s to the party.

Mase's girlfriend, Leilani, was able to fly out with him from Hawaii. Darren and his sister, Logan, came with Kiki.

Trin chased around Oliver while Oliver chased Ava, and he squealed with joy every time he captured the German shepherd's tail. Ava patiently held it still, but kept walking forward, dragging him along.

"It's how he learned to walk." Cade folded his arms, overseeing his firstborn from a bench on the porch. "Our ingenious son just grabbed onto her tail and let her do most of the work."

Ben shot up a raised fist, then pointed at our boy latched on to the dog's tail. "Uncle Ben taught 'em that. Go Ava 'n Ollie!"

Beside Cade, Hannah rolled her eyes. "His baby sister will be able to take bold steps all on her own."

Cade startled straight up. "Baby sister?" He dropped a wide-eyed gaze at her very flat stomach.

She shrugged. "Someday."

He shot her a warning glare, lips pursed. She kissed him soundly.

Victoria and Garrett watched over all of the activity from a shady corner of the porch, proud grandparents. I'd been over to their house dozens of times in the last six months, and they were everything Ben had described and more. They brought me into their fold as true family, becoming the loving parents I had always wanted.

Kristen's husband Jason leaned back against the happy yellow house, his wife nestled within his arms as they watched the kids play.

I'd invited Rafe to come, but he'd declined. I didn't ask why, but understood. It was hard for people from my world to handle too much goodness from the other side.

Kendall rushed out the door, jogged down the steps, then waved at everyone. "Gotta go. Meeting a new client."

Just then, a tan vintage FJ40 Land Cruiser with a white roof nudged up to the curb, nose in.

Mase stood from his lawn chair, whistling low. "Cherry ride!" he called out to the driver who was obscured by shadow and the reflection of the flat windshield.

The only response was a subtle hand wave out the driver's window.

"Client?" Kiki narrowed her eyes at the rumbling engine. "Can't he get out of the vehicle?"

Kendall shrugged. "Jax 'doesn't do social.'"

Then she stopped in front of Ben and me and gave us both one huge hug. "Awesome party. Love the house." She eased back and gave me a warm look that glittered with affection. "Welcome to the family."

"Get you guys drinks?" Mase crossed to the nearby cooler as Kendall disappeared and the FJ drove off.

I nodded. "Cream soda."

Ben held up a couple of fingers. "Two."

Mase furrowed his brows. "No beer?"

"No alcohol. Two years sober, and counting."

I gave Ben's hand a gentle squeeze. Being sober by choice was something he was proud of, we both were. He'd admitted to me that he had drowned in several bottles of scotch in the days after I'd left him.

But then he saw the truth, realized what was most important in his world, and went after it. Part of that involved never touching alcohol again...except for responsibly serving at his bar, of course.

Something that had kept him going was the hope that he and I weren't done yet. That we hadn't broken up; we'd simply taken a pause.

Another mission he'd undertaken? Helping my crew, my people...*our people*.

"Here ya go, felon." Mase extended a cream soda bottle

toward me.

I arched a brow at him.

"What?" His expression went all innocent. "Too soon?"

I shook my head with a smile and swiped the chilled bottle from him.

Then I casually scoped out his personal-security situation.

Ben gave me a pointed look after he accepted his soda, then chuckled. "Better watch yourself, Mase. Mess with my wife, something's bound to go missing."

"I'm not worried. I've got my pockets locked down."

Trin brushed by him. "You sure about that?" She turned and proudly held up a turquoise-and-green wallet like she'd stolen the Olympic torch.

Cade popped up from his bench and jogged down the steps. "Is that *Velcro*?"

"His crazy vintage surfer wallet," Leilani explained while shaking her head.

Ben blinked. "*Old-man* surfer wallet? You stuck in the 80s?"

I shot Trin a chin-up. "What kind of greenbacks does he have to donate? Anything good?"

Mase let out a defeated sigh. "Two Benjamins and a Jefferson. Go on" —he waved *whatever* hands through the air— "empty me out. It's yours for the cause. Just gimme back my wallet."

Trin grinned, plucked the money out as instructed, then tossed him back his Velcro time capsule.

Our girl slapped the money onto Ben's open palm.

"How are things going, by the way?" Ben asked as he glanced at me.

He meant the new foundation. In the weeks immediately following the spotlight article, one hundred and sixty-five people, all victims of Ben's father, had called or emailed the reporter, expressing their appreciation to her and their Robin Hood heroine. When the reporter had done a follow-up article to share that those victims wanted to help others, eighteen hundred more stepped up with their support.

The reporter had contacted me in prison, I'd asked Kiki for help, and together with the guidance of Victoria Michaelson, and under the umbrella of The Unity Foundation, we'd formed a separate foundation with my dream in mind, the one I'd shared with Ben on Heart's couch.

Once I'd gotten out, and after a few months of getting everything legally set up, I'd approached Heart yesterday to see if she wanted to partner up with me. "Awesome. Heart enthusiastically agreed."

That's where all the newest donations were being funneled: The Robin Hood Initiative.

Ben folded the confiscated bills with precision, then slipped them under the collar of my T-shirt, down into my bra.

I glanced at the slight bulge, then shot him a deadpan expression. "I'm not a stripper."

"Couldn't you be? Just for me?" he murmured into my ear. "Make my dream come true."

"Yeah," I whispered, then gave him a soft kiss. "Just for you."

Because of you.

Because you believed in us—even when I wasn't brave enough to trust...

All of our dreams are coming true.

THANK YOU!

Thank you for experiencing Ben and Shay's romantic adventure with us in *Lawbreaker*.

If you enjoyed the book, please express your love for *Lawbreaker* by recommending it to friends in person, by email, on Goodreads, and through book clubs and reader groups.

And if you value reviews to help guide you into your next book, as we do, please help other readers by sharing your review of *Lawbreaker* on your favorite retailer and book community sites.

Incredible thanks to everyone for extending your love of *Lawbreaker*.

Reviews are cherished love notes to authors
and tantalizing invitations to readers.
Appreciated by all. ♥

Want to read more of your favorite characters from *Lawbreaker*?

In the **Unbreakable** series...

Kiki & Darren's romance ignites in…
Heartbreaker

Mase & Leilani's passion flares in…
Rule Breaker

Cade and Hannah fall in love in the **No Weddings** series...
No Weddings
One Funeral
Two Bar Mitzvahs
Three Christmases
For Valentine's
(a steamy nightcap novella)

Coming soon in the Highland Legends series…
Born of Mist and Legend

Want a pre-order alert for upcoming books?

Keep informed of new releases by joining their Email Subscription list:
www.katbastion.com/email-subscription/

One lucky subscriber will win an eBook of their choice from the backlist AND a $10 gift card each time a pre-order or new-release announcement is sent.

We promise to email only a handful of times a year to announce pre-orders and new releases.

ABOUT THE AUTHORS

Kat Bastion won several awards for her bestselling debut novel *Forged in Dreams and Magick*.

Kat and Stone Bastion's bestselling first novel *No Weddings* and the No Weddings series were named Best of 2014 by multiple romance review blogs.

When not defining love and redemption through scribed words, they enjoy hiking in vivid wildflower deserts and ancient tropical forests.

Stay in touch with them on their social media pages:

Twitter: @KatBastion

Twitter: @StoneBastion

Facebook: Kat & Stone Bastion

www.talktotheshoe.com

www.katbastion.com

Keep informed of new releases by joining their Email Subscription list:

www.katbastion.com/email-subscription/

One lucky subscriber will win an eBook of their choice from the backlist AND a $10 gift card each time a pre-order or new-release announcement is sent.

We promise to email only a handful of times a year to announce pre-orders and new releases.

CHARITY SUPPORT AND AWARENESS

Your purchase of *Lawbreaker* helps the victims of human trafficking because a portion of the net proceeds of all Kat and Stone Bastion's books are donated to charities who support them. These charities are creating legislation and prosecuting criminals, rescuing and restoring victims, and raising awareness in the effort to eradicate the tragedy of human trafficking.

Please visit the Charity Support and Awareness page on their website www.katbastion.com and blog www.talktotheshoe.com to learn about some of the organizations they donate to and to find out how you can further support them.

"A single act of kindness is the foundation of many miracles."
~ Kat Bastion, *Utterly Loved*.